SURVIVAL IN ANOTHER WORLD WITH MY MISTRESS

NOVEL 1

WRITTEN BY **Ryuto**

ILLUSTRATED BY **Yappen**

Airship

Seven Seas Entertainment

Goshuzinsama to yuku isekai survival Vol. 1
©Ryuto (Story) ©Yappen (Illustration)
This edition originally published in Japan in 2019 by
MICRO MAGAZINE, INC., Tokyo.
English translation rights arranged with
MICRO MAGAZINE, INC., Tokyo.

Seven Seas press and purchase enquiries can be sent to
Marketing Manager Lianne Sentar at press@gomanga.com.
Information regarding the distribution and purchase of
digital editions is available from Digital Manager CK Russell
at digital@gomanga.com.

Follow Seven Seas Entertainment online at
sevenseasentertainment.com.

TRANSLATION: Julie Goniwich
ADAPTATION: Will Holcomb
COVER DESIGN: H. Qi
INTERIOR LAYOUT & DESIGN: Clay Gardner
COPY EDITOR: Jade Gardner
PROOFREADER: Mercedez Clewis
LIGHT NOVEL EDITOR: T. Anne
PREPRESS TECHNICIAN: Melanie Ujimori
PRINT MANAGER: Rhiannon Rasmussen-Silverstein
PRODUCTION MANAGER: Lissa Pattillo
EDITOR-IN-CHIEF: Julie Davis
ASSOCIATE PUBLISHER: Adam Arnold
PUBLISHER: Jason DeAngelis

ISBN: 978-1-64827-892-1
Printed in Canada
First Printing: April 2022
10 9 8 7 6 5 4 3 2 1

CONTENTS

PROLOGUE
The Sudden Beginning of My Survival Life

9

SURVIVAL IN ANOTHER WORLD WITH MY MISTRESS

YOU'VE HEARD of survival games, yeah?

I'm not talking about getting your cardio in by chasing your buds in the woods somewhere with airsoft weaponry. I mean the kinds of games where you gotta collect materials to make a home base while managing your hunger and thirst. Y'know, like that one famous foreign-made game where the world's made of blocks and you gotta dig up the ground and cut down trees to build a house and go adventuring.

There aren't too many console survival titles, but my PC gamers in the crowd know what I'm talking about. I happen to be a bit of survival sim nut.

"Survival game" is the general descriptor, but they actually run a pretty wide gamut. You've got games set after the fall of civilization where you have to cut out a niche for yourself in the post-apocalypse. Others are cut from sci-fi cloth and set you up making a crash landing on some unexplored planet in an escape pod after your spaceship wrecks, and you've got to wrangle the local flora and fauna. You've got the occasional game that strands you up some snowbound mountain and wave after wave of games that drop you into a world overrun by zombies. And then there are the ones that aren't so dire, where you build your own town and go adventuring in a civilized world.

Sorry for rambling; I figured you might need a preamble to explain the kind of situation I found myself in now.

To make a long story short, what I'm trying to explain is quite simple: I love those kinds of games.

Yeah. I love games. Emphasis on *games*.

"How the heck did I wind up here?"

My name's Kousuke Shibata. I was a twenty-year-old bachelor. I had a white-collar job. I liked playing PC games, and every night, I went for a run around town.

And now I found myself standing at the edge of a vast waste-land with a dense forest behind me. I saw no sign of man-made buildings, let alone any kind of road. I was wearing my underwear, shirt, sweatshirt and sweatpants, socks, and my favorite walking shoes. The only possessions I had on my person were my smart-phone, the key to my house, and my wallet.

I should have been fine since I had my wallet, right? I had a couple 10,000-yen notes in there, so I could flag down a taxi and find my way home no problem once they drove me downtown. And that would be true if this were Japan. Or even Earth.

"Where the heck am I?"

Up in the sky, I could see ocean, land, and clouds—like a whole other world made to Earth's specifications, so to speak.

You read right. In other words, I could see a terrestrial planet hanging in the sky plain as the sun and moon back home. It shared the sky with a crater-scarred moon. Both of them were huge. The planet took up about 30 percent of the sky, and the moon was the size of my fist when I held it up for comparison.

There's absolutely no way I'm still on Earth.

It was a miracle that I hadn't choked on the atmosphere, or roasted alive, or frozen solid.

Wait, I thought, *could it just be a dream?* I pinched and slapped my cheeks like you'd normally do in this sort of situation, but I still didn't wake up. *Damn it.*

"I'd be cool with this if it were a game. If this were a *game.* That doesn't mean I'd like to give it a spin in person!" I fell to my hands and knees, orz-ing like someone acknowledging their superior in the comments section.

Be that as it may, I couldn't stay on my knees forever. I'd get hungry and thirsty and have to take a crap, and eventually the sun would set. I didn't see any wildlife around, but that didn't mean nightfall wouldn't bring any out.

Only a fool goes out after dark unprotected, said my encyclopedic survival sim skills, and the handful of things I knew about actual life in the wild feebly chimed in. Surely there'd be zombies, skeletons, or some other warlike creatures—anything could be out there, no matter how grotesque or mind-bending to imagine.

This was no joke—I'd be easy prey for some nocturnal carnivore, stumbling blind in the dark. I needed to find a place where I could safely spend the night.

"But what do I do?"

In survival games, the player can always make basic tools so long as they have the raw materials. Sometimes they even use their bare hands to cut down trees or break rocks...but I couldn't do that.

Should I give it a try? Nah, there's absolutely no way.

I picked out a decently sized stone from the ones that were scattered across the wastelands as an alternative. It was about the size of two of those stones you'd place on top of jars for pickling foods, which were a bit bigger than my hand. If I struck it against a rock, I was sure that I could effectively chip away at it until it took on a sharp point.

Having a pointed tool like this would make exploration easier. It would be much more efficient for cutting vines and woodworking than my bare hands could ever be. It was a Stone Age solution, but I was better off with crude tools than no tools.

"Mmph!" I hit the stone against a biggish rock over and over. After a dozen or so tries, I finally got a point that looked good enough. I was worried that all the noise I was making might draw the attention of some creature higher up the food chain, but I was safe for the time being.

I called the stone with the pointed tip and easy handle Stone Knife #1. I tucked it into my sweatpants pocket since I'd spotted some other rocks that looked good for throwing.

Humankind's great advantages are the stamina for long-distance running and our talent at throwing things. Sure, dexterous fingers for making tools and higher reasoning faculties should be on that list, but I wasn't so confident in those. And I wasn't completely confident in my stamina for long-distance running either. After all, the most exercise I did every day was that nightly lap around the neighborhood.

"First, I've got to find shelter." That was one of the basic necessities for surviving.

Most people assume the most important thing is water. I did too at one point. But after playing so many survival games, I came to see the light. The absolute highest priority was finding a place to hunker down through the night.

In that game with the world made of blocks, I had gotten too absorbed in walking around collecting materials and been attacked by the zombies and skeletons that came out at night. In games where mankind's been destroyed and zombies run amok, I wound up being devoured by the zombies that started running around. In the snowy mountain survival game, I froze to death come sunset. Based on all of these experiences, I knew it to be true.

I'd die eventually without food or water. That much was a fact. But without safe ground of some kind, I wouldn't even make it through the first night.

"If this were a game world, then I'd be busy making a shelter that was raised off the ground right about now." In other words, a very simple shelter with the floor rested on top of pillars. In most games, hostile characters couldn't climb pillars without steps, so you'd generally be safe so long as you took refuge in a place that was too high for them to hop up and reach you. If it had walls and a roof, even better.

However, that didn't work all the time; some games had enemies that would aggressively strike down the pillars.

In any case, making walls and a roof seemed way out of my league for now, from both a material and a technical position. I turned my back on the windswept wasteland and headed towards the dense woods.

The wasteland had rocks and stones scattered all over, but none of them were big enough for me to hide behind. I figured I'd go climb a tree in the forest instead. Trees were a consistent asset. You could climb up one and hide yourself among the foliage so you couldn't be seen from the ground.

However, I still had to be careful of things like bugs, snakes, and lizards. As a kid, I'd promised my older brother that I'd look out for scratches and other signs on tree trunks before I climbed them. The last thing anybody wants is to fight with some iguana-looking critter for real estate, you know?

And so I set out into the forest.

CHAPTER 1
The Sudden Beginning of My Survival Life

DAYS 1+2

17

THERE I WAS, making my way through the forest. We lump all forests together as one category, but there are actually all kinds, and everyone envisions different things. The forest I found myself in had an old-growth feel to it. To put it simply:

Thickets! Trees! Bugs! Hrrrrngh!

Yeah. That about summed it up. My discomfort index was skyrocketing. It was gonna be kinda sorta really hard to push my way through the thicket without proper equipment. Not to mention, my only clothes—my sweatshirt and sweatpants—were bound to get all tattered before I knew it. Still, with no means of surviving in the wasteland, I didn't really have much choice. Off I went, all by my lonesome.

It would be dangerous to venture aimlessly into the deep woods, so I wandered around near the edge. After about an hour of searching, I turned up a tree that I thought I'd be able to climb. There was a bit of a clearing around it too, so it seemed like a good place to make my base.

"Now, let's take a look." I carefully checked the perimeter and the state of the tree.

From what I could tell, there weren't any animal tracks or unnatural marks on the tree. There were no signs of dangerous-looking insects like bees or ants.

You might think it's strange that I was worried about ants, and I get it; your average domestic ant in Japan's no threat, but you have to remember they're cousins to the hornet—any unfortunate soul who's stepped on a fire ant hill can tell you that.

Speaking of bugs, I had yet to find any strange varieties of insects, however much you might expect to find them on faraway planets or alternate Earths. Not to say that I actually wanted to run into any.

Anyway, the tree looked safe, so I slowly eased my way up it. I'll admit, I was scared. I made it about two meters before I screwed up and looked down. I would have to find some way to anchor myself or I wouldn't be able to sleep.

I slowly climbed down and took a breather. What did I need next? Probably fire and water. So long as I had water, I could survive for a time without food. Seeing as a fire would drastically improve my *immediate* chances of survival, I figured that was the higher priority—which was a shame, because while I knew how to start one in theory, I'd never actually done it before. I figured I ought to get to it while I still had some daylight to work by.

First, I needed the straightest branches I could rustle up. I gathered large wood chips, supple branches, flat stones, and assorted small bits of kindling.

I was afraid I'd wind up barbecue if I couldn't contain the flame, so I cleaned up the fallen leaves near my base tree, dug a small hole with Stone Knife #1, and placed a big wood chip inside. I used Stone Knife #1 to hollow it out in several places.

Next, I would snap a straight branch in two and whittle the points on the ends. Then, I would pack the wood chips into the hollow, hold the branch between my hands, and rotate it—except I wouldn't because it was clear that this would only end in blisters and wasted effort with my limited stamina and willpower.

And this was where my sweatpants would come in handy.

"Lalala, c'mere, string."

I pulled the drawstring from my waistband and tied it around the supple branch, turning it into a bow. I wrapped the "bowstring" up in the straight rod I had made, planning to make frictional heat by moving the bow back and forth to rotate the rod. Basically, I would recreate the tried-and-true bow drill method.

I pressed the rod down using the flat stone and stuffed the wood chips into the hollow where the rod would do its work. Now all I had to do was move the bow back and forth.

It was hard and painful. The bow broke, and I couldn't get it to catch fire... After much trouble, I somehow wrung a couple of sparks out of it, but I still couldn't actually get anything to catch.

"Damn it! But don't think I've been defeated yet!"

This time I prepared even more wood chips and shavings for my starter. That was when I realized that crushing dry leaves would probably be best. I was stupid, so stupid. I wouldn't be surprised if my soul gem had turned completely black, if I might shamelessly steal an idiom.

And at last, I had my fire. I already had kindling prepared, so I turned it into an open-air fire right away.

"Ahhh, so warm."

The sun was about to set, so I stopped staring at the fire and went to gather more kindling from nearby.

"I'm starving."

As I stared into the fire, I started wondering how I wound up here. I couldn't come up with any rational explanation. Was this my punishment for some sin I didn't know I'd committed? I looked up at the sky and took in the planet and moon hanging overhead.

There's no world where this is normal. Absolutely not. Did I die? Is this the world we go to after?

What even were my final memories on Earth? I cast my mind back.

I was messing with my phone, watching TV in the living room. I didn't have any family. My parents were divorced, and my mother, who had taken custody of me, suddenly passed away two years ago due to cerebral apoplexy. My dad, being who he was, already had a new family, so I was living on my own now; it felt too awkward to move in with them.

I had that day off, and... Oh yeah, I'd left my apartment to stop by the bank after lunch. And that was the last thing I remembered. Those "stepped out the front door and got whisked to another world" plots were infectious enough *without* infecting my own life.

Another world. That was what this place had to be. At the

very least, I knew this wasn't Earth. Was I now yet another fantasy protagonist? The prospect didn't particularly fill me with excitement. There was somethin' depressin' an' lonely 'bout havin' ta survive all 'lone in the woods, to the point that it was driving me to affected folksiness.

I didn't mind the genre. Getting immersed in the world of a story was an opiate for a heart aggrieved by the world's hardships. It was pretty clear before I changed realities that I wasn't the only one feeling desperate to retreat someplace where the rules make sense and work in your favor.

But this harsh survival game, where all I had was the clothes on my back, wasn't what I wished for at all. Not at all. Nuh-uh. If I had to wind up in another world, then why couldn't they have given me some kind of well-known power to cheat with? I was a modern-day kid who grew up cozily in Japan with all the necessities of life—electricity, gas, running water. I was born in the 90s, damn it! How the hell was I expected to survive plunked into a situation like this?

"I'm so hungry," I said again, feeling the point bore repeating. I was pretty thirsty too. Damn it all. It wouldn't do to starve. I could feel my willpower chipping away. "Tomorrow I need to find food. Or water, at the very least."

The kindling I had collected was smoky, perhaps because it was moist or still alive. I didn't mind; it seemed like the sort of thing that would keep bugs and larger pests away.

As I gazed at the flames hugging my knees, tears welled up in my eyes. The smoke's fault, obviously. Damn it all.

If only this were a survival game, I could just press the F key or E key right now to bring up the fire's crafting menu right about now... Hmm? Wait a minute.

Cooked Meat—Materials: Raw Meat ×1 *Not enough materials!
Pure Water—Materials: Water ×1 *Not enough materials!
Torch—Materials: Wood ×1 *Not enough materials!

"Hmmm?!"

Suddenly this pop-up menu-looking thing appeared over the fire. I gaped at it. *It looks like a crafting menu. Why? Is this really actually a dream? If it is, then I'd like to wake up already!* I tried pinching my cheeks again—even lightly whacking myself with the stones I'd picked up earlier, but I still didn't wake up. Naturally, it really hurt.

"I just need to accept that this is reality."

For whatever reason, there was a crafting menu here. As you'd expect from a simple fire, I couldn't make anything too fancy, but nevertheless, this was a huge discovery. I wasn't sure if it had appeared because I was thinking about crafting menus or because I had imagined pressing the right key to bring it up, but this would be useful to me. I could survive out here so long as I had this.

For the time being, I started experimenting with closing the menu.

After some inspection, I discovered that I could do all kinds of things by picturing keyboard shortcuts.

I could access the object in front of me with the F key. By imagining I was pressing the WASD keys, I could move in all directions regardless of my posture, movement speed, and inertia, and accelerate by holding the SHIFT key at the same time. Doing so made me incredibly tired, though. Lastly, by imagining hitting the space bar, I could jump about head-high. This also worked after I jumped of my own volition, meaning I had kind of a jury-rigged double jump.

I also discovered that I could make myself crouch with the C key and even lie flat if I held it down. I could move in some really weird ways by moving my body on its own and imagining pressing the keys at the same time.

"I bet the way I'm moving would freak someone out if they saw me right now," I murmured as I did a running jump of my own accord, slammed the space bar, and slid diagonally midair. I could jump stupid high, so I could easily climb to the top of a tree too. Moving like this wasn't that big of a deal, though. It was a huge asset toward my survival, sure, but I'd turned up something much more important.

"Tab brings up the inventory!" You heard me right. Just like in many survival games, I could bring up the inventory by pressing Tab in this world.

From the inventory menu, there was a lot of stuff I could access, such as my stat screen and a basic crafting screen for all the stuff I could assemble without more specialized tools.

"I've found the crafting menu!" I was super excited. My chances of survival increased exponentially. I now had the power to create modern conveniences by picking up whatever random stones and branches I found lying on the ground. There was nothing to fear now!

So long as I can use the crafting menu, there's nothing for a survival sim completionist like me to fear!

How naive I was.

"Even if I had the tools to make them, it's not like I'm any good at throwing axes or javelins. I've never used a bow and arrow either."

I had lined up all kinds of tools I crafted using materials on hand in front of the fire.

First, I made a stone axe. It felt wrong not to; it was the foundational tool of so many games. It was amazing. I took an ordinary stone and a gnarled piece of wood and turned it into the perfect stone axe with a straight handle and sharpened stone edge. Now I could spend time chopping down trees and splitting skulls, should anything hostile show its face.

Shame I'd never cut down a tree or faced off against a wild animal in my entire life and had no idea what I was doing. Ha ha ha!

Next, I made a stone spear. I used a stone and piece of wood for the materials. I know, I know, that went without saying. Sorry for stating the obvious. This one had a spearhead that looked like it was made of chipped stone instead of a blade like the axe. The tip was sharp enough to easily pierce an animal's hide and potentially mess up its vitals with a clean hit. The balance wasn't bad either, so it seemed like it'd work for stabbing or throwing.

I gave throwing it a shot, and it flew reasonably far before sticking into the ground. I didn't know why the tip didn't break, but it was all good to me! If I was going to actually use it as a weapon, I figured it'd probably be best to prepare a bunch of spears and throw them in succession. I bet I'd cause a lot of damage on a hit.

Then I made my favorite: a bow and stone-tipped arrows. I crafted the bow using a very supple branch and a nearby creeping vine-looking plant that looked like it'd make a good bowstring. When I nocked and let loose an arrow, it flew pretty far. There were two problems, though: it didn't fly straight, and I couldn't hit my target. I'd need practice.

Finally came the star performer: a stone knife. It was a very sharp blade with a wooden handle, and it did a phenomenal job. Scraping off pieces of trees and cutting plants with it was practically effortless. To my dismay, it broke after I got too carried away hacking off tree branches. I had to be careful with how I handled it, especially since I didn't want to cause myself any undue lacerations.

"Well, now I can breathe a little easier." I felt a bit safer now that I had weapons, crude as they were. Then I noticed something interesting. "Huh. Now that I've got a stone knife, I can craft more kinds of stuff."

Knives were also tools for making things, after all. I was able to craft crude stone implements just by putting stones and pieces of wood together, but by using those tools, I could make even more things out of wood and plants.

For example, my crafting menu now included things like wooden plates and a basket made of woven fibers from plants or wood. There were two things in particular that looked quite useful.

"A wooden canteen and a pump drill fire starter kit sound like good things to have."

It went without saying why a canteen would be good, but it was incredible I could make that fire starter kit. It was an evolved version of the bow drill I had made. The main part of it was an axle like a long spinning top. You fitted it into a hole in a bar, which acted as a handle. There was a string wrapped around the axle that was tied to both edges of the bar, and pulling the handle up and down caused the axle to rapidly rotate left and right, creating enough friction to throw sparks.

Huh? You don't really understand what I mean? That's the best I can do to explain it; go look it up on the internet. The important thing here was that I had obtained a tool for easily starting fires. I had managed to make a fire from wood and grass, so I decided I'd collect more to keep on me.

"Having an inventory sure is handy."

I could even store the tools I'd made in my inventory. Normally, it would've been near impossible to go around carrying all these heavy stone spears, axes, and whatnot. On my actual person, I had two pockets in my sweatshirt and two pants pockets that I could use for storing stuff. I would've been really weighed down if I only had those and my arms to carry things in.

In the end, I had three stone spears, one stone axe, one bow, twenty arrows, a wooden canteen, a fire starter kit, some chopped wood and bark to use as kindling, a stone knife, and a woven-fiber basket I could sling over my shoulder for carrying throwing stones. It had taken some trial and error to figure out the menu, but in just three hours, I'd kitted myself out with a small Stone Age armory. In your average light novel, this would definitely be considered a special ability that let me cheat at life here...

"What a lame-ass ability."

Sure, it was beyond regular human intellect. However, the only thing I could do with it was effortlessly make crude tools. And since I was still clumsy at using those tools, I didn't feel overpowered at all.

"This is the kind of thing you'd expect a minor character to have."

Given the choice, I'd prefer the ability to make whatever tool I wanted appear or something like that. Being able to half-ass emulate a survival game like this was stupid beyond belief. Why? Games like this usually had a god mode (where you could be invincible, fly, and go through objects) or a creative mode (where you could get an infinite number of materials). Console commands were apparently *also* off the table. I couldn't use actual cheats here at all. It was such a stupid power, yet it was currently my only lifeline.

"Time to get some sleep. Going hunting at night on the very first day always results in death."

Using the crafting menu and another feature I discovered, I managed to figure out a safe way to sleep in the tree: I made a hammock using plant and wood fibers. However, I had never used a hammock before; could I actually hang it and use it? Once again, my newfound superpower came to the rescue.

"Huh, this is pretty handy."

I switched to place mode by calling up the UI and pressing "Use" on the hammock. A three-dimensional, semi-transparent hammock appeared to me. I moved my eyes' center of focus to an appropriate position and thought about placing it there. The hammock popped up precisely where I wanted it.

I used my double jump to climb the tree and then lay down in the hammock, which was hidden among the branches. Thankfully, it didn't get all that cold overnight. If it had reached freezing, I would've been up a creek without a paddle.

"Ugh, I'm so hungry..."

Tomorrow I'd go foraging. I had been worried about not being able to sleep from hunger and thirst, but I zonked out then and there, probably from fatigue and anxiety. I hoped tomorrow would bring better things.

Heyo, Kousuke here. Today I'm going to be playing day two of Survival in Another World.

If only this were a game! But no, this was still my actual life! I was reminded of all of the people who used speech synthesizer apps to play the main characters of games where they had been thrown into horrible situations and then forced to find means of survival.

I would be a bit kinder to everyone if I got to go home to my world. Maybe dial back the impulse to laugh at other people's misfortune so much.

Anyway, it was morning. I was incredibly thirsty. Water was clearly my first priority. A forest needed a steady and abundant water source. The question was, where could I find it?

Hmm. I can't come up with any good ideas. The only thing I can do is wander around and hope I find some. I have everything I need in my inventory, so I don't need to stick to the border between the wasteland and the forest now. I'll spend the day exploring the forest for water and things that look edible.

"Time to register these shortcuts." I assigned numbers to the items in my inventory so that I could take an item out at a moment's notice. Just by thinking it, I could switch between holding the spear, axe, knife, and bow in an instant. "It's like a magic trick."

Then it suddenly hit me. If I could double jump regardless of what I was doing, then maybe I could do something similar with my weapons and tools.

After some trial and error, I discovered that by imagining left-clicking the mouse, I could do a basic action with a weapon—or rather, I could do an ideal action with it. It felt really weird surrendering direct control of my body, but now I could use the spear and the bow. Using the bow actually displayed the sight for the bow in my vision. Now even an amateur like me could shoot like a marksman!

By combining my own actions with a command input, I could even fire one arrow after another at the speed of light! Although the second shot would inevitably be a vastly inferior one. In other words, I would have to train if I wanted to get better at it. I'd have to really work hard to make that happen. Ha ha ha.

But then...

"Crap. Oh, crap. There's somethin' over there."

I was glad to have found a source of water, but there was something dangerous-looking there already: a lizard. Wait, was it a lizard? Maybe it was a wolf? But maybe it was more like a lizard? At any rate, it was equally scaly and furry and as big as a large dog, and sure as hell didn't look herbivorous. I was glad for the small mercy that first contact hadn't been with anything in the vein of a certain monster-hunting game's earth-shakingly huge walking death machines.

Maybe this was its territory or something because it was snoozing away in a sunny spot. Would it be possible for me to sneak over and fill my canteen? But if it stirred and gobbled me up, that'd be game over for yours truly. At the very least, I was sure I'd be seriously injured, contract some infectious disease, and die sweaty, delusional, and soiling myself.

Time to retreat. If I wanted to challenge it, I'd need to set traps or something to even stand a chance. I calmly imagined the C key and entered stealth mode. Then I imagined the S key and smoothly started moving backward. Heh heh heh. This way, I wouldn't make some careless mistake like stepping on a twig and making a big ruck—

Rustle rustle rustle!

Because I wasn't watching where I was going, I wound up

plunging into a bush. I quietly looked toward the lizard-wolf. *Please! Don't notice me! I beg you!*

Our eyes met. Unfortunately, we didn't fall in love. Which meant...

"GISHAAAAAAAA!"

"I suspected as much!"

It tried as hard as it could to intimidate me.

Oh yeah? You wanna try? Come at me, bro! I leveled the tip of my stone spear at it. *If this was inevitable, then I would've been better off getting a blow in while it was asleep! Damn it all!*

The lizard-wolf didn't suddenly lunge at me; it held back, cautiously measuring the distance between us. I didn't know what its movement capabilities were, but in this kind of case, victory went to the one who made the first move.

"Take that!"

Kousuke threw the stone spear! The lizard-wolf nimbly dodged it!

"SHAAAAAAA!"

"Oh yeaaaaaah?!"

The lizard-wolf used body slam! Kousuke took out a stone spear and immediately struck it! The lizard-wolf took damage, but Kousuke was knocked back! *Ugh, this isn't the time to be pretending I'm reading game text!*

"Ahhhhhhh! Huuuuuh?!" I panicked. The stone spear I used to counter its attack broke, but I was lucky enough to stick it into its mouth, so now the lizard-wolf was on its side on the ground flailing.

Stone axe in hand, I ran over to the writhing creature and swung down with all my might. And continued hacking at it. The next thing I knew, the blade of the axe was gone and I was whacking at the lizard-wolf's messed-up head with the handle.

"Urgh?! Blaaaaaaargh!" It was so grotesque that I puked. I was but a commoner who had only ever killed bugs. The only time I had ever touched something dead was when my mom died. I couldn't really handle watching slasher films either. Even fairly corny, low-grade gore in games had left me queasy in the past.

"Phew. Hah..." The only thing that came out was bile, but I felt a bit better after. I had to contend with reality.

First things first: I need to deal with the carcass. Can I put it in my inventory? As I thought that, I realized I could access the carcass of the lizard-wolf. I gave it a try and opened its inventory.

"Nice, I don't have to carve it. This is a godly feature."

Its carcass contained a reasonable amount of raw meat, bones, fangs, tendons, and pelts. I moved all of these into my inventory, and then the lizard-wolf disappeared; all that remained was a puddle of blood.

This was incredible, although the blood was a bit of a nuisance. It was quite possible that it might draw other dangerous creatures.

So, in my crafting menu, I spent some time mass-crafting wooden canteens, filling them up with water from the spring, and then putting them into my inventory. Each canteen could hold approximately a liter of water, so I filled fifty of them.

That should be enough water to last me for now. Now I need to find a safe place to make a fire and make this water drinkable.

I was thirsty, but I wasn't about to start chugging canteens. Who knew what kind of germs, poisons, or parasites were lurking within? If I got diarrhea here in the wilderness, then I was obviously going to wind up dying of dehydration. That's not even touching on the question of what horrible business might be native to this world, ready to do me in with illnesses never before conceived by a human mind.

I checked to make sure I wasn't injured and left the spring after thoroughly washing the blood out of my clothes. Along the way, I picked up more stones and wood. I remade my lost stone spear and stone axe while looking for a place to rest, like I did yesterday. I found a tree and clearing in a spot that seemed a good enough distance away and started a fire. Using the fire starter kit was faster and took much less effort than the bow drill had.

"Water, water..." From the fire's crafting screen, I picked drinking water and cooked meat and started crafting. It only took about ten seconds to craft the first item, but those ten seconds felt like forever.

Then I took the crafted "Drinking Water" out from the completed column, took off the cap, and gulped it down. It tasted good. It felt like the water was spreading to every part of my dehydrated body.

"Ahhh, water is so good."

I took a breath and then checked out what I had in my hand. *It's water. Yup, water. Water inside of a water bottle. The wooden canteen disappeared and turned into a water bottle? Well, whatever.*

Or maybe this isn't something I should just brush off? I mean, this water bottle is 1.5 liters. I actually made more *water.*

Isn't a net gain good, though? Well, uh, best not to think about the details. It's probably something like whatever was in the impure water changed into pure water and increased the volume by half. Yeah, that's gotta be it. Best not to dwell on what might have actually been in the water for that theory to work.

I looked closely at the meat in my inventory to find it was labeled as "Raw Meat (Lizaf)." So I guessed that lizard-wolf was called a lizaf. The fact that it had a name must have meant that creatures existed to give it a name, right? I couldn't be the only person in this world.

I had my next goal: find wherever these people lived. I felt a little wary; I had no idea what kind of language barrier I'd have to deal with, let alone what kind of reception I could expect. It'd suck if they caught me and made me their slave, but that'd be better than them catching sight of me and clamoring, "Food! Eat!"

Still, humans can't live on their own. If I got sick or badly injured, that'd be checkmate for me. I didn't have much choice but to go looking for the natives.

In the meantime, I cooked the meat. I wasn't strictly *okay* eating some unfamiliar animal's meat, but a guy's gotta eat.

"Omph! Nom omph! Nom!" The lizaf meat tasted kinda like chicken. Definitely didn't have the flavor of pork or beef. It was pretty mild and fibrous—more like chicken than anything. But it tasted pretty good. All I did was get it cooked through over the fire. The fat had a sweetness to it. I found that a little concerning, but the meat was tender and tasty. I was sure it'd taste even better salted, but I had no idea how I'd possibly get salt. Maybe if I were close to the ocean.

Does the crafting menu have anything? I thought. *Hmm, wait a minute. My crafting recipe list didn't increase until I put the applicable materials into my inventory first. If I put whatever the materials for salt would be into my inventory, would salt be added? It's essentially dirt.* I had seen a show on TV one time about how kangaroos would lick dirt that had sodium in it. It was a reddish-brown kind of dirt. Was there anything like that around here? I had no idea, so it might be worth it to just dig up some dirt and stick it in my inventory.

Crafting bricks and concrete by combining stuff like clay, dirt, stones, and gravel was a staple in survival games and sandbox games. Things like limestone, clay, and gravel actually required processing and stuff to be made, but most games didn't bother being accurate about manufacturing processes.

"Maybe I could even consider making a base?" Having a safe shelter made of concrete or brick was appealing. If I made a base, it'd be best to be near a source of water—a lake or river if possible, or a spring at the very least. It might also have been possible to dig a well, but I didn't have the technology for that.

I might have been able to finagle it if I used my ability, but I didn't think it was necessary to go to the effort at the moment. I'd give it a try if I found there was no civilization around and decided to finally settle down somewhere.

"At any rate, I need something to dig up dirt with."

Luckily, my search for food and water had only taken the morning; I still had lots of time left in the day for other things. It was also important that I continue testing my ability to be sure I had an accurate grasp of it.

I opened the crafting menu and looked to see if I could find something like a shovel. I found a shovel with a stone edge further down the list, so I tried crafting it.

"Hmm, it's not very easy to use." It didn't work as well as a shovel with a steel end. However, it was dozens of times better than trying to dig with my bare hands. I exuberantly dug using the heavy stone shovel. As I dug, combining command inputs in time with my own digging, the dirt went into my inventory.

"Am I digging twice as fast as usual doing this?" The "Dig" command was usually one action comprised of thrusting your shovel into the dirt, raising your shovel, and then discarding it. However, it was also possible to store the dirt in my inventory immediately after picking it up. I didn't need to discard the heavy dirt first, so it wasn't really tiring work. By combining that with the command, I was able to do something like double shoveling, so I was able to dig up dirt at incredible speed. I hummed as I dug along relentlessly. Despite my situation, I was keeping pretty calm. Sure, I was constantly on edge, but there was a part of me that was enjoying this.

"This should be about enough." I dug up all around the area where I was planning to spend the night. Most of it felt like mulch, but some seemed clay-like, so I was a bit hopeful about my efforts.

I opened my inventory expectantly to find a reasonable amount of "Fertile Forest Soil" and "Clay." However, there was far more "Fertile Forest Soil" than "Clay." Maybe a 7:3 ratio.

"Let's see, do I have more things I can craft now?"

A composite bow had been added to weapons, which was a bow made of wood and reinforced by animal tendons, bones, or metal plates. It required the bones and other materials from the lizaf; I didn't know any other use for them, so I went ahead and got one made.

Next, I checked recipes I could craft using the dirt, which was what I really wanted to know. There was a long list of farmland blocks and other building blocks—adobe, for one thing—I could make now. If I combined stones and clay, then I could even make cobblestone walls. However, I didn't have that many stones, so I probably couldn't make a great number of them at the moment.

However, the farmland blocks... At the very least, I now knew that my ability had assumed I would be producing food via agriculture. The fact that I could make building blocks meant that they had considered the possibility of me building a base for myself. But who *was* the entity who'd given me this power? I had no idea if such a being even existed, but if they did, they had some pretty particular ideas about how I was supposed to get by.

Well, let's just put those thoughts aside for now. Back to the matter at hand; is there anything else I can make? Like salt. That'd be nice. I desire salt.

"Of course things can't be that easy." Salt was nowhere to be found in the crafting menu, much to my chagrin. However, I did find something interesting. "I can craft a furnace, huh?"

The recipe required clay, stone, animal pelt, and wood. This definitely meant that I could potentially craft things with iron. Metal tools... I felt excited at the prospect. But where was I going to find iron ore? And what did I use for fuel? Maybe charcoal would work? As for iron, I'd probably have to mine or collect it from somewhere.

In a certain block game, you'd find it eventually if you just dug deep enough. Would that work in this world too? I'd have to try to find out, but I doubted it would yield any results. I didn't know if it was the case for this world, but back on Earth, ores with lots of iron in them were usually found at the bottom of ponds and springs. I had heard that sand and stones in rivers contained iron as well. Also, reddish-colored rocks were actually colored that way because they contained oxidized iron, so presumably you could get iron from those too. At least, I was pretty sure I had heard something like that before.

Should I head back to the spring? Looking at the sky, I had a feeling that the sun would start to set soon. The clock on my smartphone said it was 3:47 p.m. I didn't know if this was the actual time or not, since I didn't have a clock to compare it to, but I had woken up just past six according to my phone, so I didn't think it was too off.

I looked up once more at the giant planet and moon-looking thing. Every time I saw them, it reminded me all over again how I was in a foreign land. What was I going to do from here on out? I could feel the panic starting to creep in; I doubted that someone who could send me back to my world would actually aid me. After all, I had never heard of other worlds outside of novels and games that were meant for entertainment.

Maybe I'd have a chance if there was a secret rescue task force that the government put together to protect the civil liberties of the Japanese people from the secret epidemic of otherworldly kidnappings? Yeah, right. Like something like that actually existed. I had to face the facts.

"Guess I'll call it a day." It was important to get proper rest so that I didn't burn myself out both physically and mentally. Surely. Probably. Maybe. I had to also control how much food and water I consumed.

Searching for food is going to be my main goal for tomorrow; searching for iron and salt can be side goals. At the same time, I also need to run a bunch of tests to see what stuff I can put in my inventory to increase my crafting repertoire. I've got to master my ability if I'm gonna keep on living. The more things I can craft, the more things I can do. I'll do my best.

Today, I gathered lumber and grass—or rather, I cut the grass and then collected it—to use for kindling and crafting materials, and then I placed my hammock up in a tree. I made a fire, ate lizaf meat, and then went to sleep. I'd tossed some green wood on the fire, so it'd thrown up a bit of smoke; it was uncomfortable, but maybe someone from civilization would spot it and come looking—or so I hoped. In the short term, it made good insect repellent. Damn all of those bugs.

CHARACTERS

コースケ
Kousuke

CHAPTER 2
The Sudden Beginning of My Survival Life

DAY 3

43

I SUDDENLY FELT LIKE I was floating—no, like I was falling. I braced myself for impact as I snapped awake.

"Grargh!" I didn't know what I hit, but my body hurt and it knocked the wind out of me. I rolled over instinctively and put my hand down to try to stand up.

"Oof?!" I immediately felt a sharp pain in my hand.

Ow! That hurt! That really hurt?! What the—what's going on?! I looked up, but there wasn't much light. All I saw was the rapidly approaching outline of a foot.

"Gwuf?!" I felt faint from the shock of the kick as it connected, barely present for the pain. I had never been attacked like this before. I'd only ever gotten into scuffles that led to an exchange of blows as a kid, like a normal person.

I'll die if I don't fight back. And I do not *want to die.*

The moment those words popped into my head, a voice came that sent chills down my spine.

"Resist and I'll kill you." Something heavy pressed down on my head. The owner of the voice was probably stepping on me. "What's a human doing in a place like this?" From what I could tell, it was a woman's voice.

I didn't know how to answer her. Maybe I could just tell her I had gotten lost?

"Why are you silent? Answer me."

"I don't know. I just got lost." It was hard to speak with the copious nosebleed I just developed.

"Tch. O Life Spirit."

A pale green light lit up the gloom, and my body didn't hurt so much anymore. Even the stab wound in my hand stopped bleeding. I could still feel some bumps and bruises, but I certainly felt better than before. Was this some kind of magic?

"Now you should be well enough to talk. Speak." Her voice was cold as she kept her foot firmly planted on me.

Wait, her voice? We could communicate?

"I don't really know what happened myself. All I know is that I was suddenly standing at the edge of the wasteland and the forest, and the only things I had with me were my clothes. I have no idea where I am! I pushed my way through the forest to survive and then I looked for water and food; that's it. I burned green wood since I was hoping someone might find me. In other words, I'm lost and in distress." I ignored my doubt that she'd be able to understand me and just spit it all out. As I spoke, I frantically tried to come up with a way out of my current situation. If could take her by surprise for just a second... But maybe that was beyond all hope.

She seemed like the type who was used to scuffles—*battles*, probably. She could use something like magic, and she had that sharp weapon she'd stabbed my hand with. If she wanted to kill me, I had no doubt that she would have in the first place. I didn't need to prepare myself for the worst quite yet.

"Do you really think I'd believe something so ludicrous?" the woman demanded.

"It's the truth. Look, don't believe me if you don't want to. You're free to just go on believing what you want to believe, averting your gaze from the truth, plugging your ears, and attacking me nonsensically."

"I don't like the smooth way your tongue waggles."

"Look at that, we're just two peas in a pod here. I don't much care for how barbaric and violent you—grph!"

With a creaking sound, she increased the pressure on my head.

She's gonna break my skull. She's gonna break my skull. She's gonna break my skull. My brains are gonna come spilling out! But I'll put on a brave front. I really don't like this woman. Even if she overpowers me physically, she'll never break me mentally! Oh, is this one of those situations where you shout, "I'd rather you just kill me now, then!"? She's planning to assault me, isn't she?! Like in those doujinshi I used to read?! I'm not even into dubcon, *let alone non-con!*

"Did a human—a *human* of all things—just call me violent and barbaric?" the woman said.

"I-I have no idea what you even are! But you must be pretty narrow-minded if you think all of us humans are the same. Then again, I don't know how violent and barbaric the humans of this world are, but you shouldn't just assume I have anything to do with them. I only just came here the day before yesterday!"

I'd hardly call humans gentle, intellectual creatures, but how am I supposed to know what this woman's relationship with humans from this world has been like? That aside, it sounds like the woman currently stepping on my head isn't human. Especially from the way she says "human" like she found a bug in her mouth. Is she an elf, or some kind of beastfolk, or what? Are the humans of this world so bad that they've earned that impression? If so, they must not have made many technological and cultural advancements yet.

After a moment of silence, her foot squarely affixed to my head, the woman said, "Who the hell are you?"

I considered her intentions again for a moment before answering. "My name is Shibata Kousuke. Family name Shibata, given name Kousuke. I'm twenty-four years old, though my age might be calculated differently; I don't know how many days make up a year in your calendar. Anyway, back in my world, I've been considered an adult for four years. I think the world I came from is far away from here. It doesn't have a huge planet in the sky. Also, the moon is much smaller."

"Have you ever heard the word Adol?"

"Adol? What's that? Someone's name?" The only Adol I knew of was a redheaded adventurer from a famous action RPG.

"What if I told you that a being called Adol was the one who put you in this situation?"

"Did he seriously? The hell, Adol? You suck. By the by, how long do you plan to keep your foot there?"

"Heh heh. I wonder, can you cash the checks your mouth is writing, talking about the architect of your fate so?" The woman chuckled for a moment in amusement before removing her noble foot from my head.

I shook my head and brushed the dirt from my cheeks and hair before looking up at my assailant.

"Wow! You're actually a beautiful dark elf! Bpht!" She kicked me right in the face for that comment. *Why?!*

"This is what you get when you call me a 'dark elf' just because of the color of my skin. And don't you forget it."

"I'd prefer the lecture to getting kicked, you barbarian."

She must have been holding back or something because my nose wasn't bleeding, but that kick was strong enough that I could see stars when I closed my eyes. *If I get a brain hemorrhage, I'm gonna come haunt you as a ghost, you son of a bitch! Not that she's anyone's son.*

I rubbed my nose as I stood up and gave the woman another look. She was pretty, all right. Like, the level of beautiful that you'd only ever see on TV. She had flawless dark brown skin with light-colored hair. It wasn't white—maybe closer to silver. It shone even in the dim light. She was wearing a skintight leather body suit of sorts, and her chest looked like it was ready to burst out. She was incredibly blessed. I'm talking about the sort of proportions that prompt table-banging, wolf-howling, and open-mouth drooling.

"Where do you think you're looking?" she asked.

"Your rack. What about it?"

"Not one to mince words, are you? I like it." She smirked.

She was pretty, all right, but I didn't like the way she was grinning and looking at me. Those were the eyes of a gal with a body count, and there was no mirth behind that smile, however much I might have wished there was.

"So, there's something I'd like to say," I ventured.

"Oh? Go on, then."

"I'm in a lot of pain right now, and I have no medical supplies; if I get hurt, I'm probably just gonna keel over, so I want you to heal me with that spell thing you did before. You're the one who attacked me out of the blue or whatever, so I can ask at least that much from you, right?"

"Hmm. The thought has some merit to it, but I still don't believe that you're not a minion of the Holy Kingdom yet."

"Oh, is that how it is? We should keep getting to know each other, then."

I tamped down my pain and collected my hammock that was hanging in the tree. The rope had been cruelly cut off on one side, but after I put it into my inventory, it looked like I could fix it using some of my materials. I started the mending process and looked back at the woman to find her watching me curiously. *Crap. I probably shouldn't have shown my cards like this.*

"That was an interesting trick you just did. How did you make it disappear?" she asked me.

"Do I have to tell you?"

"If you desire to prove your innocence."

"Like I'd be completely honest with you. Let's face it, we don't trust each other."

There was no doubt about it: this woman was dangerous. She was probably only talking to me like this because she knew she could kill me at a moment's notice. She had some gigantic knifelike thing hanging on her waist, and I still didn't know what other magic nonsense she might have tucked away. I wouldn't have been surprised if she had been trained for battle. Never mind that her armor, however impractically formfitting it may have been, looked like it offered a whole lot more defense than my sweatshirt and sweatpants.

"Owww. So are we gonna make with the carefully censored disclosure of personal details or nah?" I asked as I sat cross-legged on the ground.

"Very well." She leaned against a nearby tree and eyed me curiously.

At least she's willing to talk. Maybe she's more understanding than I thought.

The conversation leaped from topic to topic, including the names of our worlds, geography, world affairs, religion, myths, the planet we could see, culture, food, clothes, military affairs, politics. I learned that the name of this world—or land or the planet itself—was Leece. The huge planet in the sky was called Omicle. The moon was Lanicle, and the sun was called Sycle. We were currently on the edge of the woodlands known as the Black Forest, which was located on the southern tip of a continent called Pence.

It turned out that outside the forest was a vast wilderness known as the Great Omitt Badlands, which took about ten days to cross on foot. If I had gone out to the badlands instead of the forest, I'd have died like a dog for sure! Moreover, there were all kinds of insectile monsters lurking underground out there, and it was difficult even for seasoned travelers to traverse alone.

As for the situation in the world at large... The people of this continent were currently at war. The human supremacist Holy Kingdom and the Empire, which was comprised of many different nations filled with different races, were fighting for sovereignty over the fertile lands of central Pence. Therefore, oppression toward non-humans had escalated in the Holy Kingdom, resulting in frequent uprisings and revolts all over. The Empire had retaliated by alienating the provinces close to the Holy Kingdom's borders, prompting a large-scale slave uprising. Both countries had their own domestic troubles that went unattended as the effort continued. Troubled times had come to the world.

This Black Forest here in southern Pence stood between the Great Omitt Badlands and the Holy Kingdom's domain.

Elves had always lived in this forest, and refugees from other races unable to withstand the Holy Kingdom's oppression had been crossing the Great Omitt Badlands and gradually gathering here. The Holy Kingdom had noticed the refugees' movements, so the locals and dispossessed alike were concerned that the Holy Kingdom would be sending soldiers their way before long.

"Would they really bother doing that? There isn't much value in passing through those badlands just to attack this forest," I said.

"We elves are valuable merchandise among humans. Beautiful slaves who don't age are quite desirable to humans all on their own, but then you have to consider the asset of an elven womb."

Unions between a human and an elf always produced a child with deep magical powers. Deep by human standards, at least. Human nobles would mate with other races so that they could maintain bloodlines that possessed stronger magic than the peasantry.

That reason sounds suspect to me, but I can very well understand why humans would desire elves for slaves. Uh-huh.

"For now, I believe that you actually aren't a human from this world," the woman said.

"Great, thanks. Now heal me."

The woman went ahead and healed my wound. My whole body felt nice and warm, like I had just gotten into a hot spring. *Mmm, this feels great.*

"Hmm. The life spirit seems to like you a lot," she mused.

"It does? I can't really tell one way or the other."

There was a green sphere of light flying around me. *Is this what she means by the life spirit? Maybe I'm going to awaken my own innate magical powers too?! Oh man, maybe I could be a wizard or something. One who uses spirit magic?*

"But I don't sense any magic within you at all. You've got no talent for it," the woman told me.

"So much for that idea!"

Damn it, don't get my hopes up like that!

"Well, let's get going," she said.

"Go where?"

"To my village. If you'd prefer to be put down by another elf or a beastfolk, you're more than welcome to stay here."

"Please allow me to accompany you, ma'am," I said immediately. I wasn't a fan of the idea of being murdered in my sleep.

"Kill him!"

"Kill him!"

"Kill him!"

"Burn him! Let him burn!"

"Death to humans!"

"Kill him! Death!"

Everyone's favorite idol Kousuke here. Having arrived at the woman's destination, I found myself basking in the supportive cheers of my fans.

In other words, I was terrified. This was my first time being faced with such blatant malice. They were all calling for my head with a bloodthirsty glint in their eyes. My legs trembled in fear. I wouldn't be surprised if I wet myself. In fact, it was probably just a matter of time before I really did.

I spotted a man with animal ears in the crowd, his body covered in scars. Elsewhere, a woman with wings where her hands should be. A person whose gender I couldn't tell with a lizard's face. A woman with the lower half of a serpent. They were all humanlike, yet not human at all. No one had escalated from verbal abuse to throwing stones yet, but I had a feeling that was also merely a matter of time.

My heart pounded. My field of vision narrowed. My throat was dry. What the hell did I do to deserve all of this?

I'd followed the woman to the village just as she had invited me to. She had exchanged a few words with the male elf standing guard at the entrance and then left me with him while she went on ahead. The man immediately dragged me into the village and kicked me down in the center of the village square.

The way the guard had looked at me in that moment flashed in my mind. That was not the look of someone who saw me as a human being—though that went without saying, really. He was an elf, after all.

My thoughts were all ajumble. *Am I going to be beaten to death by this mob? What did I do to deserve this? Damn it, I shouldn't have followed her.*

People with wooden sticks and stones had finally started showing up. *If I'm going to die,* I thought, *I don't want to suffer. Just let it be over in an instant.* It seemed far more likely that the crowd wouldn't be so considerate—these folks would want to drag things out. If death was all that awaited me, then maybe I was obliged to fight back.

I had made a reasonable number of clay brick blocks for building with. Maybe I could place them all over to confuse the mob, and maybe they wouldn't be able to get through it if I fenced myself off.

But now I was pissed. *Why is this happening to me? I'm being blamed for something I had nothing to do with, and I refuse to be beaten to death. Bring it on!*

"What do you think you're doing?!"

There came a roaring wind, less a gust and more of a shock wave. It was enough to blow me and the people surrounding me back.

I rolled until something stepped on my back. I recognized

the impression of that noble foot. I heard the voice of the woman who had led me here.

"I found this in the woods. Who gave any of you permission to hurt it?"

"Owwww ow ow ow!" I groaned as she dug her sturdy leather boot into my back. I wanted to tell her to be a bit gentler with me, but I was having a hard time forming coherent syllables.

"This is my possession, and I'm the only one allowed to torment it. Got it?"

The mob was silent at the woman's declaration; she left no room for discussion. I felt like I caught a sympathetic glance or two from some people. *Wait a minute, weren't you all about to kill me? Why are you all looking at me that way now? Is being with her worse than death? Hey, answer me!*

"Tch. Nate's such a limp-dick. I can't believe he used such an underhanded trick." She was probably talking about the guard who'd dragged me off. There seemed to be some beef between the two. "Well, whatever. I showed up before anything bad happened to you. Now get up. We're leaving."

She kicked me again. *Ow! That really hurt!*

"Hell, I don't deserve this kind of treatment," I groaned.

"Oh, and put this on." She held out a leather collar.

I beg your pardon? You want me to wear this? Is this what I think it's supposed to be? Like, a slave collar or something?

"If you don't put it on, you'll wind up in the same situation I just saved you from. Or do you want to see if I show up on cue next time?"

After a moment, I cussed. "Damn you."

You can't make an omelet without breaking some eggs, or so the saying goes. I could just shove the stupid thing into my inventory. It's not so bad, right? I should just put the dumb thing on. It's just a collar. I prayed it wasn't cursed.

But I was a bit excited about the prospect of becoming such a hot elf's slave. *Or maybe I'm not? It's not like I'm a masochist or anything. I swear. It's the truth, I tell you!*

"Heh heh. It suits you," she said.

"Don't be so happy about it. Hey, you're not going to chain me up or anything, are you?"

"Pet dogs require a collar and leash, don't they? I need to make sure you stay by my side when we go on walks."

"I'll get you back for this..."

And so, the elf woman put a leash on me, and we walked from one side of the village to the other. On the bright side, I now knew the village's whole layout! It was divided into roughly five sections. The farthest out was an area where they were building some kind of sturdy-looking edifice, and inside that was the area where the non-elvish population had set up. Beyond that was a square that acted like a neutral zone of sorts. Past that were these strange magical gardens tended to by the elves. After that field was a protective wall woven from living trees, and on the inside of that was where the elves had their workshops and residential area.

The woman had mentioned that the non-elves were refugees who had come here to escape the war. I could tell. The architectural style of their homes wasn't uniform at all; frankly speaking, all of the buildings looked pretty shabby.

What surprised me most during my tour were the magical gardens. They had layers, like a multistory parking garage; they felt like a hydroponics facility but filled with magical light. I had never seen or heard of a hydroponics operation on this scale before. In a sense, the elves here might have put Japan to shame agriculturally.

I couldn't see inside the workshops, so I had no idea what those were like. Same for the homes of the elves. I had no idea what was supposed to be coming together in the new development at the far edge of the village, but the buildings looked solid enough.

"Behold, my home," the woman announced.

"Ooh."

It was a splendid elven-style home. After seeing the rest of the village, I felt I could assertively say that her home was much nicer than the others. It was a log house that felt alive, so to speak. Like living trees had been coaxed to twine and bind together, similar to the village's inner wall. And by splendid, I meant the place was huge.

She showed me in, and a smell hit me the second I stepped inside. It was gentle and refreshing in some senses. I felt inclined to call it the aroma of the forest. I took a deep breath and felt life seep back into my body.

"Is that your thing, taking a deep breath the second you enter a woman's home?" she asked.

"Get your mind out of the gutter. There's a nice smell in here, okay? Like some kind of incense or something."

"I haven't used anything like that, though."

The chain jingled as she pulled me in. The woman brought me into what seemed like a living room. She had a lot of rattan-looking furniture. She released the chain and walked toward the back, so I sat down on the couch. I had to wonder how long I'd have to wear this collar and chain.

"That doesn't come off. Oh, but you can take the chain off when we're at home," she told me.

"Thank you, Mistress. Satisfied?"

"I do wish you'd be a bit cuter."

I took off the chain and put it into my inventory. I wondered if my crafting recipes had increased by adding it in, so I was messing with the crafting menu when the woman came back. She was holding two steaming wooden cups.

"Don't ask a man to be cute," I retorted.

"But obviously it'd be better to be cute than not. It would please your mistress."

"Like I care about that... But I'll give it some thought."

"Heh heh. Good. Still, you're less perturbed than I thought you'd be."

"Any idiot can tell when you make it that obvious."

It was obvious what her intentions were by putting a collar on me and then dragging me around the village by a chain leash: she was showing everyone that I was her possession, and if they laid a finger on me, she'd crush them.

It was impossible for me to live in this village as an ordinary citizen since the elves and refugees all saw humans as their enemy. If I tried living here without a guardian of some kind, I'd probably go missing by the next morning. They'd kill me and bury my body in the middle of the night or leave me for the monsters. And no one would care that I was gone. It wouldn't even cause a commotion. If anyone noticed I was missing, they'd probably be like, "Oh yeah, that guy used to live here. He must have left, since he didn't like living here." And that would be that.

Then what if I just went and lived by myself elsewhere? That would never work. I would probably run into one of the villagers in the forest eventually, and it was highly likely that they would just try to kill me on sight.

If I won, then the village would go searching for them. Once the body was found, I doubted a very bright future awaited me; survival on my own was hard enough as it was. I would surely die a dog's death before long.

Then would it be better to leave the forest? The answer was quite obvious: no. It would be impossible for me to survive alone out there in the badlands. I didn't have nearly enough food, water, equipment, technology, or information to do it. I'd wind up either collapsing and dying or being eaten by monsters.

From that perspective, my current situation was actually a stroke of incredible luck, if not divine favor. If she weren't so interested in me, it was very likely that this woman would have ended me by now. It was a miracle that she found me. It was a miracle that she decided to hear me out. It was a miracle that she was influential in this village. It was a miracle that she came running to my rescue before I was killed. That all of this coincided was a miracle of its own.

"Something on your mind?" the woman asked me.

"Yeah, I guess. It feels like a miracle that I met you, and I'm grateful for it."

"Oh? So you can say cute things. But you might not feel that way for long, you know."

"That's future me's problem."

That was the truth. I had no idea what this woman's aim was, but I was still alive even though she'd had plenty of chances to kill me. She must have wanted me for some reason or another. It was still possible that she'd eventually decide to abandon me, so I needed to prepare myself as best as I could so that I could keep on living no matter what the future held.

"I'd appreciate if you'd stop insinuating things already. Let's just keep things simple," I told her.

"True, especially since we'll be living together from now on. Hmm, where do we start?"

"How about with your name? I still don't know it yet."

Upon hearing that, the woman shot me a look of amazement before she seized up with laughter. *Huh. So she can do more than glare.* She'd been wearing such a menacing look on her face this whole time that it took me by surprise.

"Wow! You're totally right! I'm sorry about that. Pretty much everyone around here knows my name; I completely forgot that introducing yourself was a thing." She'd laughed so hard that she had tears in her eyes. She looked so pretty that it actually left me at a loss for words. "I'm Sylphyel, and I'm one of the protectors of the Black Forest. The humans apparently like to call me the 'Witch of the Black Forest.'"

"Sylphyel... That's a pretty name." I wasn't just sweet-talking. The name had a "pure and fragile maiden" ring to it. Admittedly, a far cry from "killer elf with a bangin' bod."

"What's with that look on your face?" she asked.

"To tell the truth, that name's got such a wholesome, virginal ring to it."

"Hmph. Well, that would have described me once. While I am still a maiden, I wouldn't necessarily call myself *wholesome* anymore. What's that look for? You want to find out whether it's true?"

"I'd say that I'd love to, but I'm afraid of what would happen if I did, so I won't." I had a feeling she'd snap my neck if I pushed my luck.

"Aw, how boring. So, what should I call you?"

"Please call me Kousuke. Is it okay if I call you Sylphy? Or should I address you as 'Mistress'?"

"You can call me Sylphy when we're alone, but it'd be better if you call me Mistress when we're out in public."

"Makes sense. I'll make sure to call you Mistress in general, then."

Sylphy made a strange face at how easily I agreed to it. "What's with you? Do you not have any pride or something?"

"Of course I have pride. It really sucked how we met, but I knew I was going to die sooner or later, and you saved me from that fate. I may not know your real intentions, but that doesn't change the fact that you rescued me. I'm just carefully considering where you rank here, being my protector and all."

Sylphy paused for a moment before she smiled and said, "I see. That's admirable."

Hey, stop that. You're just trying to get me off my guard with that kinda look, aren't you? I haven't had a woman in my life recently, and on top of that, I've been through quite a lot with all this "trying to survive out there on my own" business. Give me some consideration here.

"Uh, sooo, are you going to tell me why you're protecting me?" I asked.

"No reason, really. If I had to say, it's because I find you curious."

"Yeah, right."

"I know it's wholly unexpected, but it's the truth. I'm just interested in who you really are, the situation you're in, your ability, and your knowledge. I just had this feeling like I couldn't leave you alone."

"I see. So, does this kinda thing just happen on occasion here? People showing up from another world, like me?"

"Oh? Why would you think that?" Sylphy smirked as she cocked an eyebrow.

Yup, that's more the Sylphy I'm used to.

"Because we tell tales like that for entertainment in my world. They're all just fantasy, though. Oh, but there are some legends with similar premises."

In a way, the story of Urashima Taro was the story of someone traveling to another world. Based on how you looked it, the stories of Momotaro and Kintaro were stories of people who had been reborn in Japan from another world. And then there were stories of people who had been "spirited away" to another world.

"Hmm, I see. As it turns out, I have heard similar tales myself. In the Holy Kingdom, they say that Adol, the king of the gods, has sent disciples from the World of Gods; they have similar tales in the Empire as well. We elves have legends of the rare people who wound up lost here after traveling through the Spirit World. Such people are said to appear at the border of the forest."

"Oh, is that so?" I happened to be standing at the border of the forest when I came to this world. "What do they say about these lost people?"

"That they appear during a time when the people of the forest are in danger, and that they will bring those people to victory. Well, I can't be so sure that you actually possess that kind of power."

"Yeah... Please don't put your hopes in me." I was just a regular guy who liked games. I was no soldier, scholar, or politician.

"But you do have some kind of strange power, do you not? I'd be very happy if you told me about it."

"Well, it is my lifeline, y'know." I put on airs as I frantically thought this over. *Do I tell her everything or just the bare minimum? I don't have the option to tell her nothing. Now's the time to show her my worth. Plus, I might lose her protection if I don't cooperate here. Then I'd have no means of survival.*

I glanced over at her. Sylphy was grinning ear to ear. Damn this woman and her teasing.

"Give me some time to think about it a bit more before I tell you everything," I said.

"Hmm? You can't do as I say? Or are you returning a favor with spite?"

"No, I'm grateful to you, and I do feel like I owe you. But I still don't know much about you, or how you think, or your intentions. My power and what I know might be very dangerous depending on how it's used. Besides, I don't know how much I should meddle with this world, considering I come from elsewhere. With all of this in mind, I couldn't possibly just trust you completely."

"Again with that smooth tongue-wagging. It's too bad I can't just shut you up."

"I wouldn't mind at all if you wanted to shut me up with your lips."

"That's a good idea. We should experiment later." Sylphy grinned bewitchingly; I swallowed involuntarily.

I couldn't help it. She was totally my type.

"There is some truth to your words. It's good that you're basically sensible. But surely you can tell me *something* about it," Sylphy insisted.

"Yeah, sure. Let me show you what my ability is." I took the chain, the stone spear, the stone axe, the hammock, and some spare bits and bobs from my inventory and showed them to her. "I have something called an inventory. It's like I've got my own private storehouse. I can put weapons, materials, food, water, and even bulky and heavy stuff in there too. I still haven't tested its size and weight limitations, though. At any rate, it's a power I gained when I arrived in this world. I've only been using it for about three days now."

"Huh, that does sound handy." There was a dangerous glint in Sylphy's eyes.

Stop looking at me like that or you'll spoil your beauty, I thought as Sylphy took the stone spear from me.

"Hmm. This spear is crude, but it's plenty sharp enough to kill an animal. Did you make this?" Sylphy asked me.

I hesitated. "Uh, yeah, I did." *Uh-oh.*

"Oh? Did you make this stone axe too, then? This all must have been pretty hard to make."

I hesitated again. "Uh, yeah."

When we were first talking about life in the world I came from, I'd talked a bit about the useful tools we had easy access to and how I'd lived in a safe and tranquil environment. Could a man who had lived that kind of life made such a fine stone spear in three days without any tools, using only the lumber and stones he scavenged? I didn't even have to think about it. The answer was no.

"Heh heh. I'll stop my investigating there. You should be a bit more cautious," Sylphy said.

"Thank you," I said stiffly.

How careless! She saw right through me. I should've shown her the stones and grass instead! I'm such an idiot! I don't know how much she's figured out, but she must have pegged that I've got some kind of ability to make these things effortlessly.

"I can tell that you're going to be a great beast of burden. That alone makes you plenty useful to me. It's quite troublesome having to carry home large prey when I go hunting, you see."

"Oh, wild game? Hmm, I'm not sure how much help I can be there."

"What's that supposed to mean?"

"Well, I killed one of those things that are part wolf, part lizard... A lizaf? I didn't put it as is into my inventory, so I don't know if I can put animal carcasses in there yet or not. My inventory ability has this feature where I'm able to harvest parts of the monster. I got meat, bones, and pelts from the lizaf, and once I stored those in my inventory, it disappeared. The only thing left was a puddle of blood."

"So that's what that was."

Sylphy had seen the mess I had left behind. Maybe that was what led her to me? It wasn't too surprising. I was just an amateur trying to cover my tracks. There was no fooling a professional like her.

"How much did you harvest from it? Show me," she demanded.

"I don't mind, but I can't just drop meat everywhere. And they'll go bad if I just hold them all in my bare hands."

"That makes sense. Hold on a moment."

I watched Sylphy go get a plate or something to put the meat on. As it turned out, I had a big wooden plate I'd made in my inventory, but I wasn't about to show her too much of my hand, even if it kinda felt too late for that.

"Put them on this."

"Will do." I started putting the lizaf meat on the big wooden plate she'd brought out. I estimated it was about four kilograms worth of meat.

"Is this all of it?"

"I ate some of it already, but this is all that's left. And here's all of the bones and the pelts I got." I didn't tell her that I had used a bone, a pelt, and its tendons to make a composite bow. That was my trump card, after all.

"Hmm, so you didn't get any of its organs? I suppose the amount of meat kind of makes up for it... What part of the body was this from?"

"No clue. All I know is that it's lizaf meat."

In fact, I had ignored that part. When harvesting its body parts, I grabbed the meat and put it into my inventory as 500-gram lumps of meat. I had eaten two of those, so I had gotten about five kilograms worth of meat from the lizaf. However, each piece of meat looked practically the same. Had it been automatically restructured? The way it looked kinda reminded me of sirloin.

"Well, these certainly look easy to eat, so there's that. Shall we try some today?" Sylphy asked.

"Sure, why not? How many should we use?"

"Two should be more than enough. By the by, were these all of the bones and pelts you got?" Clearly she knew this was too little for one lizaf. She was a sharp one.

"I used some of them. I admit it. But I want to keep what I used them for a secret."

"Very well, then. Just so you know, we're going hunting tomorrow."

"Aye aye, ma'am. By the way, are you hungry? I sure am." We had walked here without any breakfast. I didn't know what time it was, and it wasn't like I could take my smartphone out in front of her to check, but I estimated it was around noon. The tea had quenched my thirst, but it didn't do anything for my empty stomach.

"Then let's have something to eat. Have at it, then," Sylphy said casually as she sat down on what looked like a rattan couch.

I saw that coming. I was her pitiful slave, after all. Obviously, no mistress would ever cook for her slave.

"Mistress, would you deign to instruct your pitiful slave in the way to use your cookware and seasonings?"

"If I must. I won't tell you again, though." Despite her sigh, my kind and noble mistress stood up from the couch.

Thank you.

We stood in the kitchen as she taught me about this world's seasonings. I recognized salt, but I didn't really know about the others. She was pretty flush with the stuff, so she let me taste some of them. I recognized the ones that tasted like pepper, paprika, mustard, cinnamon, garlic, and ginger. I didn't know what the others might be.

She didn't have sugar, but she had something like honey. It was sweet and syrupy but it didn't taste quite like anything a bee made. Nectar, possibly?

Also, she didn't have condiments like soy sauce and miso. I wasn't too surprised about that.

"What do you folks eat as your staple food?" I asked.

"What we make by kneading and baking that," Sylphy said as she pointed at something like a big tote bag.

She told me to open it up and look inside. There was some kind of powder in there, probably something like flour.

"Hmm, well, I'll see what I can whip up." I set about slicing up the lizaf meat, sprinkling salt on it, and mixing it with the honey. Since it was like chicken meat, I had a feeling it would do well with a salty-sweet kind of seasoning. I minced a single garlic clove and rubbed that into the meat as well.

I left the meat to marinate for a bit and surveyed what we had for vegetables. Sylphy had all kinds, but I didn't know how to eat a lot of them. There were root vegetables, leafy greens, something that looked like cabbage, and ones that looked like fruit—I felt a little spoiled for choice.

"Which are the crunchy ones that you can eat raw?" I asked.

"That would be that round one—that's a cabbaj—and the thick black one—that's dicon." Sylphy pointed at the bright-red cabbage-looking vegetables and the black radish-looking ones respectively.

Okay then, I'll just assume this is a red-colored cabbage. I used a knife I found in the kitchen to slice the so-called cabbaj in two. I took out the core, sliced off a tiny bit, and tasted it. *Yup, this is definitely cabbage, but red.*

She had purple onions, so I gave those a taste as well. *Yup, it's a regular red onion. But maybe a bit on the salty side? And purple all the way through. Hmm, guess I'll use this too.* I went ahead and shredded the onion and the cabbaj.

I would try the dicon another day.

"Now for the million-dollar question: What's this stuff? It's definitely some kind of flour." I didn't know if it was wheat flour or cornmeal, but whatever it was, it probably solidified when kneaded with water and cooked.

I tried kneading it with a bit of water from a water jug. *Hmm, it's not very sticky. Well, whatever.*

I glanced over at Sylphy to find she was watching me with a smirk on her face for some reason. She was drinking something straight from a porcelain bottle. *Don't tell me she's got some kind of alcohol. Oh, to be in my mistress's place.*

"I'm warning you; I've never worked with any of these ingredients before. Don't get angry if I make something that tastes terrible."

"That's a problem for future us." She kept grinning.

With the variety of vegetables and seasonings she had, I was sure she knew how to cook, but she showed no sign of helping. *Fine. Fine then! I don't care how this turns out!*

Sylphy lit the fire for the cooking stove for me, but it was really hard to adjust the heat on this thing. I had a feeling that I'd get a roaring blaze if I threw too much firewood in, so I tried to be very careful. First, I tried dropping a bit of the flour I had thinned out in the water on a heated frying pan. *Yeah, this seems like wheat flour? That's probably what it is.* I dropped a bit more in, and the thin batter cooked about how I guessed it would.

"Don't you think you've been sneaking a few too many bites?"

"I told you, I have no idea what any of these taste like!" I cooked the marinated meat as I responded to her heckling.

I had diced the meat and cooked it through. I tasted it and threw in a bit more salt. It was pretty underwhelming, flavor-wise, but it was probably pretty good for my first time. I added a little bit of water and some seasonings to the pan to make something like a sauce and then plated up the food.

Next, I cooked the batter made of that flour and made a sort of rudimentary flatbread. I made them over and over. I wound up with six of them and piled them onto a big plate. I put the plates with the chopped vegetables, thin bread, and meat on the table.

"Hmm, and how do you eat this?" Sylphy asked.

"Like this." I put some of the vegetables, meat, and a little bit of the so-called sauce onto the thin flatbread, rolled it up, and held it out to her. Ladies and gentlemen, a lizaf taco—er, burrito. "Just bite into it."

"Hmm..." Sylphy did as I instructed and took a big bite out of the burrito. She chewed on it for a bit and then swallowed. "Not bad."

"Great. Can I have some too?"

"Yes."

Having gotten my mistress's permission, I helped myself to my own burrito. The crunchy cabbaj and purple onion had a good texture. The marinaded lizaf meat wasn't bad either. It probably could have used a little extra seasoning. I brought some paprika and mustard from the kitchen. She took the paprika and added it to hers too; she must have felt the flavor was a bit lacking as well.

"Well, I think I did okay. I'd say it's pretty good for a first attempt," I said.

"Yeah, it's not bad. Maybe we could wrap this in leaves and bring it along to eat later when we're out."

"It might still be okay if I make it in the morning and then we have it for lunch. I'd be afraid of food poisoning if we ate it any later than that."

"True. What if we put it into this inventory of yours?"

"I'm not sure. I guess I could test to see whether food goes bad in my inventory. I probably should've left a piece of the raw meat to try it with."

"Yeah. Well, the rest of it should keep for several days if we salt it."

As we chatted about my inventory, I wrapped Sylphy's burritos. I was her slave, after all. This was the least I could do for her, since she was letting me live here.

"Well, that wasn't a bad meal. I'm going to go out for a bit, so you stay here in the house. I don't have to tell you any rules since you're not a child, right?"

"Yeah, don't worry about me. I'll stay put."

She pointed out the bathroom to me, so I had no worries there. I had no idea what errand Sylphy was going to run, but she'd told me that we would be going hunting together tomorrow, so I doubted she was going to be busy arranging my execution.

I planned to spend my time alone testing stuff with my inventory and the crafting menu. I was grateful for the little reprieve.

"Be a good boy now." And with that, Sylphy left.

I took a break to digest for a bit before I got to work.

"This'll be best for measuring how time passes in my inventory."

I lit tinder using the remaining embers in the stove and put that in my inventory. "Burning Tinder" appeared in it. I waited a bit and checked again. The "Burning Tinder" hadn't changed at all.

I waited a bit longer and then took the tinder out over the stove ashes. It looked just as it did when I had first lit it. However, it immediately burned out.

"Hmm, I can't make any conclusions off of that."

There was a strong possibility that time stopped for things that were put in my inventory. I had cursed this place as a crappy video game when I first got dumped here with only the clothes on my back, but now I was relieved to see that the properties of my inventory had put me on easy mode.

I lit several pieces of tinder and put those in my inventory. Now I wouldn't have to worry about going through the effort of lighting more fires. Farewell, pump drill fire starter. Still, I left it in there; you never knew. Better to have it and not need it than need it and not have it.

I was done experimenting with the inventory, so I started monkeying around with the crafting menu. Unfortunately, there wasn't really anything new I could make. Well, there were some new items I could make using the lizaf bones, pelts, and fangs, but I had a feeling that they had the same properties as things made with stone, so I just ignored them. I did decide to make some arrows using the lizaf fangs, though. Could never have too much ammunition. However, if I could make iron, then I could make iron arrowheads instead... But I might want these during tomorrow's hunting trip, so I figured I might as well make them.

The composite bow's my trump card for the time being, so I'll make a regular bow that's safe to show Sylphy. I wish I could practice, though. I can't practice in here; Sylphy would probably kill me if I made holes in the wall—I suspect literally.

I've got nothing else to do now... I guess I'll see if there's anywhere for me to sleep. If there's not, I'll make a bed. She'd at least let me hang a hammock, right?

I set to exploring Sylphy's house. I didn't want to intrude on her privacy, so I just peeked a little into the rooms besides the living room and bathroom. I wasn't some weirdo who liked snooping around in a woman's room and rummaging through her clothes and underwear.

Sylphy had a big house, but it wasn't too hard to grasp the layout. At the back of the living room was Sylphy's bedroom. Next to that was a storeroom, which was where she put all of her daily necessities. The living room also connected to a hallway that led to the bathroom, and behind that was a decent-sized garden. The soil was packed down tight, so it was more like a sports ground than a garden. There was also something like a storage shed, but that was locked.

"Hmm. Where am I going to sleep, then?" I could probably hang a hammock in the living space that comprised the living room and the dirt floor kitchen. The other option was that locked shed in the garden.

In any case, I'd probably be hanging my hammock indoors somewhere. I'd need a stand for it. "I'm pretty sure I saw one in the crafting menu."

I used some of my leftover wood to make one and put it together with the hammock.

"Huh, not bad." I placed it in the garden and tried lying down in it. It was pretty comfortable. Unlike when I hung it in the trees, I'd constructed this hammock to spread to both ends by the wooden poles, so my body lay flat and it was easier to sleep in. Not to knock the setup I had out in the wilderness; the smaller profile had probably kept me out of the local predators' sights. I decided to make another regular hammock.

The hammock took a little while to craft. Once it was done, I walked to every corner of the garden. The stones and grass could be used as materials, so I collected them one after the other. Even the tiny pebbles could be used to craft arrows if I had enough of them. The grass could be used to make ropes and hammocks, so those weren't pointless to have either.

Once I was pretty much done with that, I opened the crafting menu and started making intermediary materials. What I meant by that—take hammocks, for example—was I would use the grass to craft fibers and then turn those fibers into rope. After making multiple ropes, I used those to make the hammock. In that example, the fibers and ropes would be intermediary materials.

I sat down on the hammock I had put in the garden and started pumping out intermediary materials one after the other in the crafting menu. This would save me a fair bit of time later.

Plus, there was a chance that more recipes would be added if I increased my stock of intermediary materials. I sat in silence as

I made gravel and stone blades from stones, sand from the gravel, and more.

"Hmm, not much has been added," I grumbled to myself as I made a cushion using a sack and cotton I had crafted from fibers.

I seemed to be missing some kind of key tool, or maybe I needed some other material, but I just wasn't getting any new recipes.

"Ugh, that's disappointing," I griped some more as I fiddled with a weapon called a bola I had made. It was made of three ropes and stones. There were stones bound to the ends of each of the ropes. You were supposed to whirl it around and then throw it at someone to catch them. It went without saying that just hitting anyone with this sort of thing would be pretty painful.

I had never actually used one of these before, so I didn't know how effective it would be, but it was probably more useful than just throwing stones. Better to have it than not.

I took out each of my hunting weapons, and Sylphy came back while I was checking them over. She appraised the standing hammock and all of the crude weapons I had lined up on the ground and smirked. "What a nice assortment you've got here. Can you actually use these?"

"If you're asking whether I could use these to kill something, then yes. I definitely got in a solid hit on that lizaf with a stone spear, and the stone axe was enough to lop off its head. I haven't tested the bow yet, but I know that the arrows are strong enough to stick into trees. As for whether I can actually make good use of them, I'm not so sure, to be honest. I'm just a regular person who's never even gotten into a fist fight with anyone before, let alone trained in how to use a weapon."

"I see. You've got some unusual weapons here too."

"Yeah, that one's called a bola." I gave her an explanation of how it worked since she seemed interested. She must have liked the idea of it because she asked me for one. I still had materials left over and could just queue another one to craft when she wasn't looking, so I offered her the one I had already made. I had a feeling she'd be much more adept with it than I ever would be.

"I'm guessing you can make all kinds of things, then?" she asked with her trademark smirk.

Whatever her intentions, it was probably best to be honest. At present, I was still scared to tell her everything. I didn't know what she intended to do with me. However, if I revealed everything to her and she knew that I had utility, then I probably wouldn't have to fear for my life. It was a hard call to make.

"Yeah. But I can't make something from nothing. I need materials," I told her.

"Oh? I see here that all you have are weapons made out of stone. Do you think you could make weapons out of metals too?"

"I don't know. Like I said, I've only been here a few days. I still haven't grasped the full extent of my abilities yet," I said vaguely as thoughts whirled in my head. *She definitely already knows that my abilities extend well beyond my inventory. Based on her questions, there's no doubt about it. Trying to hide it now will probably just make me more suspicious.*

Plus, it was pretty much guaranteed I would be in Sylphy's care for the time being. Since she was so interested in me, it would be best to sustain that interest for as long as I could. She probably liked unusual things, or maybe it was more like she was starved for amusement. In that case, I should continue to satisfy that craving.

"However..." I trailed off.

"However?"

"I do want to find out if I can make things made of metal. However, I don't have the materials to test it out. More specifically, what I need is iron ore and fuel."

"Hmm, materials, you say?" She pondered this a moment with a finger to her chin. I had piqued her interest for the time being. "I know where iron ore might be found, but I don't know about fuel. You can't use regular firewood to refine iron, right?"

"I don't know. It'd be impossible based on common knowledge, but it might work with my power. But generally speaking, I'd need coke made of processed coal or, at the very least, charcoal. In either case, I won't find out for sure until I try it."

"Hmm. So, you can't try it now?"

"I could if I had iron ore. Or maybe even scrap iron."

"Then I might have something that could work." Sylphy grinned. Not the joyful kind of grin either. That smile scared me!

Sylphy walked right over to the locked shed. She unlocked it and opened the doors.

I grimaced reflexively at the smell. "Blech. What the hell is that smell?"

"My spoils of war." Sylphy stepped away from the door to the shed with a smirk, so I peered inside.

Inside I saw rusty swords, armor, and shields. None of them looked useful at a glance. So that must mean the smell was...?

"Hey, was that armor smeared in blood or something at one point? That sword and that helmet too."

"Ha ha ha. It's really annoying to clean them, okay?"

The armor and helmets didn't look like they'd fit Sylphy. I didn't have to think too hard to figure out what exactly she had meant by "spoils of war."

"Are you telling me to use these? They look like they might be cursed or something," I said.

"Ooh, so you've recognized their good points! It *is* said that armor of the dead does have that kind of power in them."

"Really? That's terrifying."

"But you can melt them down without any problems. Any trifling curse should completely vanish when they lose their original form and are purified by flames."

"Are you sure about that?" I didn't trust that grin on Sylphy's face at all. However, I didn't have any magic skills or fantastical power—like the ability to see curses like junior high school kids like to pretend they have—so I had no other alternative. "I guess I can give it a try, but I really don't wanna touch these."

"They should be fine so long as you don't put them on. Just be careful with the weapons."

"So what are you suggesting I do?"

"Just use that power of yours to put them away. You won't have to touch them that way, right?"

"You must be a genius."

I did as she suggested and put all of the rusty weapons and armor scattered around the shed into my inventory. It was amazing that all I had to do was get close enough to put things away.

I opened my inventory to see what I had.

Rusted Sword × 4
Rusted Spear × 3
Rusted Dagger × 6
Rusted Hatchet × 2
Rusted Shield × 2
Rusted Helmet × 2
Rusted Armor × 2
Rusted Leggings × 5
Rusted Gauntlets × 5
Cursed Rusted Sword × 1
Cursed Rusted Spear × 2
Cursed Rusted Helmet × 3
Cursed Rusted Armor × 3

"Holy shiiiiit?! Some of this stuff actually was cuuuursed?!" I freaked out.

"Hmm. I probably should clean up in here occasionally."

"Why are you acting like I've found dirt in the house or something? This is serious!"

"It's not all that different. Anyway, go ahead and try making metal weapons already."

"Huh? Well, fine, I'll give it a try."

I found a spot in a corner of the backyard that seemed appropriately bare of anything flammable and placed the small furnace I had in my inventory. Sylphy's eyebrows twitched, probably out of surprise at suddenly seeing the furnace appear.

"What did you just do?"

"It'd be too much of a pain to expla—fine, fine! I'll tell you. It's a bit different from weapons that we hold in our hands, like the stone spears, but I have a way to easily place things like this furnace straight from my inventory. You remember how I had a hammock up in a tree? I did the same with that and that hammock with a stand I put over there. I'm thinking of calling them 'placeable objects.'"

The things like the stone spears and stone axes that could be held were simply "items." That meant things like the furnace, hammocks, and the clay brick blocks I had yet to place anywhere belonged to a different order. I suspected I might eventually come across something that doesn't fit into either of these two categories, though.

"Hmm, I see. Keep going, then," Sylphy prompted.

"Right-o."

I opened the crafting menu for the furnace and looked over what I could make. First, I needed fuel in order to get it to work. Plenty of what I had in my inventory would do the trick: the pieces of wood I had picked up, or the fibers, ropes, or hammocks that I made from wood. However, there seemed to be a timer for how long the fire would last, and since it depended on the item, wood seemed like it would be the most efficient at the moment.

However, the furnace couldn't refine iron with pieces of wood as its fuel. I could make charcoal by throwing pieces of wood into the furnace to craft, though, and using *that*, I would be able to refine iron.

"At least, that's what it looks like to me." I told Sylphy what I had figured out as I looked at the flames in the furnace lapping at the wood. I figured it'd be okay to tell her what I could do since I was the only one who could actually see the crafting menu. That way, I was still the only one who knew what I could craft and how long it would take.

In other words, I was vague about what I could make, how many materials it took, and how long it took since I was planning to pocket some of the materials for myself right under her nose. Still, I had to be careful about how much; I didn't want her to think I was useless.

"Hmm, so fuel really is our biggest obstacle here. Well, if that's what we need, we can just get some from the forest," Sylphy said.

"I guess we could collect some while we're out hunting tomorrow? I'd like to collect some iron ores too, if possible."

"I hear that those can be found in the streams in the depths of the forest. I suppose we could make our way that far in, especially since we'll be able to bring a lot back with us thanks to that power of yours."

"Just leave the hauling to me." The charcoal finished as we were chatting. I had started crafting it before we started talking. "I've finished making charcoal, so I'll see if I can refine iron using this."

"Yeah, go ahead."

I took the wood out of the furnace and added the charcoal. The light and heat coming from the furnace grew stronger.

"Looks like those flames are pretty hot," Sylphy commented.

"Now I'll check which of these I can use."

I was afraid to start by using one of the cursed things, and the weapons might still be barely usable, so I prioritized melting down the regular rusted armor.

"I have to say, this seems so easy. I thought refining iron required lots of training?"

"I'm probably special." Actually, I was most definitely special. Refining iron was actually arduous work.

To start with, there was no way you could make something satisfactory with such a shoddy furnace. It required a furnace that could withstand high temperatures, which meant you needed fireproof bricks that could tolerate that kind of heat. Furthermore, charcoal couldn't burn hot enough to melt lumps of iron that weren't even made of iron sand. You might have to get rid of impurities such as sulfur first too. There were just all kinds of things normally involved in the process.

My crafting menu disregarded such troublesome matters altogether. It helped me steadily craft items with just fuel, materials, and time.

"And thanks to that, ta-da! I've made an iron ingot."

"I don't know what you're referring to, but very nice...I think?"

"I think turning worthless scrap iron into usable fresh iron ingots is very good work indeed." If I remembered correctly, you needed a high-grade electric furnace back in the world I came from to retrieve good-quality iron from scrap. It was pretty incredible for someone to wring that out of such a shoddy furnace.

"Hmm, that's true. Turning trash into something usable is a pretty remarkable feat. But you're not done yet, right?"

"Of course I'm not." I took the iron ingot back from Sylphy and refined more of them.

"Ta-da! I made an anvil and hammer!"

"Right, a blacksmith's iconic tools."

"Yep. I should be able to make all kinds of things with these and the furnace now."

I placed the anvil near the furnace, held the hammer, and opened the crafting menu for the anvil. With these, I could make steel equipment using the iron ingots as materials.

"So, you're not going to hammer the iron?" Sylphy asked.

"Nope. I doubt I could even if I tried."

"Lame."

"Don't jump to conclusions now, my lady. You're sure to change your tune after you see this." I took out the steel knife I had just finished crafting.

Her bored look immediately changed into a smile. And what a smile it was; if only it graced her face more often. Why did she always have to wear that mischievous smirk when *this* was the alternative?

"Mmm, not bad," Sylphy murmured as she gazed closely at the blade, filed her fingernail with it, and tested it. Since I was a complete amateur, I had no idea what she was doing.

*But see? I'm useful, right? So please feed me, woof! I am but a
dog; you are my mistress, and I will show you what a talented dog I
am in order to please you. Pride? Give that to the dogs. Oh wait, I'm
a dog now. Ha ha ha.*

"Right? See? I can make all sorts of things. I think."

"Ha ha ha. You're so desperate."

"Because I don't want to die!"

To put it simply, this village was enemy territory. If I took a
single step outside of this house, it wouldn't be all that surprising
if I got pummeled and buried. Although Sylphy *did* show me
off to a bunch of people as her possession. So, I might actually
be okay if I tried? Maybe. But it was game over for me if I lost
Sylphy's protection.

"I'll be taking this. I'm going to use it to persuade those thick-
headed, senile old fools."

"Okay."

She could have it no problem, since I was sure I could make
another one before I ran out of fuel. However, I was completely
out of wood, even though I had thought I had collected a lot. I
would have to gather as much firewood as I could tomorrow.

I continued crafting until I ran out of charcoal. I made more
iron ingots, which I then used to make tools. However, I could
only craft a few more things. I decided on a steel knife and a
hatchet for gathering firewood.

Hatchets were some quality goods. I'd heard that they'd been
used since around the year 600 BCE and that their shape had
hardly changed through the ages. Practically the same thing had

been invented at the same time all around the world, and it'd stayed in circulation ever since. In other words, it was kind of a perfect tool.

It was sturdy, reliable, and could be used for work and battle. You didn't need to train to know how to use it either, like you did with swords, spears, and bows. You just lift it up and then swing it down—boom, done.

"And thanks to that, it's done! I made this for tomorrow's exploration."

"A hatchet? Nice." Sylphy swung it around.

Hey, stop that. It's scary.

"You'd better make one for me too with the firewood and iron ores we find tomorrow. Got it?" She showed no sign of wanting it for herself right away. What a generous mistress she was.

"Aye aye, ma'am." I noticed that the time to craft items that used wood had decreased now that I had acquired this steel hatchet. "Oh?"

Huh, I never would've guessed the hatchet had that kind of benefit. Maybe I can shorten other crafting times once I acquire other tools? It might be a good idea to create as many tools that look like they'd be used in crafting as soon as I can.

I had used up all of the charcoal, so it was time to collect the small furnace and standing hammock and go back inside. I was glad that I could easily remove the furnace and stick it in my inventory. In some games, you'd have to destroy it with a special tool in order to do that.

In the end, I melted down one set of armor and two helmets

to make two steel knives and one steel hatchet. I was also able to make twenty iron arrowheads and three iron ingots. I set my crafting menu to craft twenty steel arrows using those arrowheads. I figured I was more than ready for tomorrow.

"I think that's all I can make today. I ran out of charcoal too."

"Is that so? Then let's rest. I'm pretty tired myself after everything today." Sylphy had been watching me with her hands crossed in front of her chest, and now she turned on her heel to head back into her home.

How do I explain this? It's like she's brisk with all of her movements. She doesn't leave herself open at all. It's going to be hard to outwit this woman, I thought as I followed after her.

Now that I was done refining iron with the small furnace, Sylphy and I had gone back inside. Based on the position of the sun, it was probably nearly evening now. The sky still hadn't turned red yet, but it felt like it wasn't so bright out anymore.

It seemed a bit dim inside the house, since there weren't many windows, but oddly, it didn't seem silent or eerie. But the space probably felt languid because I was beat.

"By the way, where should I put my bed? Can I just put the hammock in a random spot here in the living room?" I asked as soon as we got inside.

Sylphy immediately sat down on one of the rattan couches and leaned back in a way that flaunted her toned body. Good *lord*, whatever higher powers must be out there went *nuts* endowing this woman.

"I don't mind that, but you *could* just sleep in my bed with me if you want." Sylphy wore an alluring smile and gave me a flirtatious glance.

"I can? That's a tempting offer." I was terrified to accept that invitation at face value. I mean, she looked like she could snap my neck with her bare hands. "I think I'm going to pass for tonight since, frankly, I'm *petrified* of you. I'll take you up on that offer once we've come to understand each other better, though."

"You're scared? What's that supposed to mean?" She pouted.

Oh, you can pout too? You look so much cuter this way.

"Because I still don't know you very well. At first, I assumed you were just violent, but once we started talking, I realized how reasonable you actually are. You've opted to help me, and I *still* can't figure that out. You seem to have a pretty high position in this village, and I can tell you're not afraid to use force, given the, you know, shed full of murder. Yet you've obviously got a more innocent side to you from what I've seen. I dunno, I just don't get you. So *yeah*, I'm scared to just jump into bed with you." I decided to just tell her every single thing that I was feeling without holding anything back. It might've sounded like I was teasing her, but from my perspective, I had chosen to take my own life into my hands.

Sylphy sat in silence after hearing all of that.

She was a very clever person—elf? Dark elf?—so I figured it would be pointless to try to fool her; I wasn't all that good at expressing myself to begin with. I decided that being completely open about my feelings would be most effective.

"But then, since I don't know you very well, I *do* want to. There probably are things we'd learn about each other by sleeping together, but maybe it'd be best if we talked about things first? I mean, I have no complaints about us being an item. In fact, I welcome the idea, and there's part of me that's finding it hard to be patient," I continued.

"First you go on this long diatribe about how you're scared, but in the end, you still want sex anyway?"

"They say that 'not eating the meal set before him is a man's shame,' so that's part of it, y'know?"

"Huh? What's that supposed to mean?" Sylphy cocked her head.

Yeah, yeah. That's the kind of gestures and expression I like to see. Now that I'm taking a good look at her, she's more than just pretty—she's cute.

"It's a saying from where I come from. It means that it's shameful for a man to reject the advances of a woman."

"Oh, like how we say, 'when the stove comes to where the dough is, it's time to make bread.'"

"I guess countries in every world have an idiom for this." I laughed; in the end, people were the same no matter where they lived—what they did and talked about didn't vary all that much.

"Hmm, well, let's talk. Luckily, the only things left to do today are dinner and sleep. We can take it nice and slow."

"Sounds good. Since we're on the topic anyway, how about I acquaint you with my Earthling romantic philosophies and virtues?"

Sylphy put on that smirk again. It seemed that she was interested in hearing about life in another world, no matter the topic. I was bringing up a relatively delicate topic, yet she showed no signs of bashfulness at all. "Sounds good to me. I get the virtue part, but what do you mean by romantic *philosophies*?"

"Huh? You know, like the whole set of rules around having a crush, falling in love, and courting and such. Don't elves have that sort of thing?"

But Sylphy only gave me a puzzled look. *Wait, what? Do they not have the concept of romantic love in this world? That can't be, right?*

"I know the word 'love,' and I guess I'd say that I understand it as a general concept. But I've never loved someone before, and I don't know what you mean by 'crush' at all."

"Uhhh... That's a toughie. It's like...one of first steps to falling in love with someone? It's where you can't stop thinking about someone of the opposite sex—or, I mean, they could be someone of the same sex too—and you're unable to concentrate on anything else at all?"

"Isn't that simply the desire to bed them?"

"I can't believe you're putting it so bluntly! That sounds like something some militant platonic-love zealot would say before they clock you upside the skull! Fine, then; it seems like it'll be too much of a bother to explain any more than I have, so why don't you tell me about love and virtue in this world instead? I might be able to explain more about my world after hearing your explanation."

"All right. Very well." Sylphy then began to tell me about relations between men and women in this world.

In summary, they practiced polygyny. Since many men had dangerous jobs, they had a high mortality rate and would leave their wives behind. In other words, there were many widows, and they would be accepted into families as second or third wives. Furthermore, since there wasn't much in the way of entertainment in this world beyond the horizontal tango, they had large families.

A woman was expected to be virtuous during her first marriage, but widows were not held to that same standard. Most women did not remain faithful to their husbands once they were lost, and it was typical for them to remarry. Apparently, men who provided for many widows were respected by society.

"Huh. That's rather... Nope, that is completely different from how things work in my world," I said.

"You mentioned how it was virtuous to remain married to the same partner for life in your world. Not even royalty and titled nobility do that here anymore."

All I could do was groan in response. They said when in Rome, do as the Romans do, but that was gonna be awfully hard to accept after the way I'd been raised.

"You say that, so now I have to ask...aren't you a *maiden* still? Don't you have to be virtuous?" I didn't know if by "maiden" I meant whether she was unmarried or a virgin, but that seemed the best word to go with.

"Do men and women need a reason to want each other?"

"Yeah, because we're not animals."

"I'd say there isn't that big of a difference between people and animals." Sylphy donned her smirk.

"There is one on a philosophical level! But never mind, forget I asked! Let's change the subject!"

For some reason, I had the feeling she was slowly cornering me. I was in danger, and I needed to escape! But I had nowhere to run. She had me trapped. I decided to change the subject to something more appropriate. That was my only means of resistance.

"If we must. Then how about we talk about the other country? I'd say that that's a topic that directly impacts you, wouldn't you agree?"

"Th-that's true. You explained a little, but I would like to hear more."

"Okay, then. I mentioned how the Holy Kingdom and the Empire are at war, right?"

"Yeah. You said that the Holy Kingdom was ruled by humans and the Empire consisted of other kinds of people. And you mentioned how they're fighting over fertile land at the border and how both are dealing with rebellions and whatnot while dragging on the war."

"Mm-hmm, you're generally right. First, I'll tell you about the Holy Kingdom." She gave me a basic summary.

In short, they were a theocracy. They believed in the one true god, Adol, and that Adol had granted the Holy King his right to rule. In their eyes, demi-humans had been created by Adol to serve humans, so it was only natural that they treated them as slaves. By their beliefs, it sounded like humans reigned supreme.

"According to them, those of us who aren't pure-blooded humans are servants created by God to serve humans," Sylphy said.

"That's crazy talk. What gave them that idea?"

"Humans can make children with any kind of demi-human. However, aside from humans, demi-humans can only make children with those of their same race. Therefore, humans are the progenitors of all demi-humans. Or looking at it from the opposite angle, the gods made demi-humans after humans. And because of that, humans insist that demi-humans were meant to serve humans."

"Hmm? It makes sense and yet it doesn't..."

From her explanation, I got the feeling it should be the other way around. You could almost say that demi-humans were the evolved form of humans.

There was a somewhat sci-fi feel to the creation myth of humans and demi-humans. Almost like they had used humans as a base to make demi-humans with improved genes. If what humans asserted was true, then it sounded like this Adol guy must have fancy gene altering technology.

"So, what kind of place is the Empire?" I asked.

"The Empire? Well, there's not much I can say. It's really far away. It would probably take about three months of walking to reach the contested zone between the Holy Kingdom and the Empire."

"That is far."

I had heard that a human could walk approximately 30 kilometers comfortably in a day. If you walked every day for three whole months, that would be 900 kilometers a month, which would make it 2,700 kilometers away... It was hard to imagine, but that seemed like a great distance.

"This might just be hearsay, but the nation is ruled by an emperor who leaves the ruling of the many provinces to his subordinates. The slave trade is prosperous there, and they frequently trade with citizens of the eastern and northern reaches of Pence. They deal in both humans and demi-humans—race doesn't matter."

"I guess they're not so gung-ho about one race being the best, then."

"Mm-hmm. Based on what I've heard, they don't differentiate between humans and demi-humans. However, you need money and power if you want to do anything. The rumors suggest they don't treat their slaves very well and that the enslaved people rebel pretty frequently."

"You'd think they'd treat them better; it'd be more economical to be hospitable."

"Mm-hmm. You've got a good point."

"I would say so." It'd be best if it were a win-win situation for both sides.

"All this talking has made me thirsty," Sylphy said as she went over to the cupboard by the stove and took out two porcelain bottles. She handed one to me.

I shook it a bit and heard some kind of liquid sloshing around inside.

"It's mead. Go ahead and have some," Sylphy said as she drank it straight from the bottle.

I popped the cork-like lid and followed her lead. "This is alcohol? Doesn't smell all that strong."

It was sweet! I had imagined it would taste like honey, but it didn't have the thick, rich sweetness of honey—it was something altogether different. It wasn't fruity either. It had a refreshing smell, like the sweetness of nectar from flowers. As I swallowed, I could feel the alcohol pretty strongly. There had to be more alcohol in this than beer.

"This drink's actually pretty potent. I bet I'd get dead drunk just from one bottle," I said.

"Sheesh, you're a lightweight. This stuff's practically water."

"What're you, some kind of uwabami?"

Time for an explanation! Uwabami were creatures with strong livers who didn't worry about their alcohol intake at all! Watch out if you ever met someone who pushes more booze on you because they're doing fine!

"Well, this stuff is really sweet and strong to me. I'm gonna dilute it with water."

"Seriously?"

At this rate, it was gonna be tough for me to keep drinking. I poured the alcohol into the wooden tumbler I had crafted and then diluted it using water from the plastic bottle. I made it two parts water to one part mead, and that seemed just the right amount for me.

"Is that a canteen?" Sylphy asked.

"Yeah, made of a material we use a lot in my world. It's not very strong, but it's pretty durable."

You could destroy it immediately with a knife, but it wouldn't break if you dropped it. From that perspective, plastic bottles were incredibly handy tools. However, I'd have to think a bit about how to dispose of it when I was done.

"Hmm, what a strange material. It's soft yet tough and transparent. How do you make this?"

"I don't really know myself, but I think it's originally made using petroleum. That's oil that wells out of the ground."

"Oil can be used to make this kind of container? I just can't imagine how that would work." Sylphy smiled as she fiddled with the bottle. She was certainly full of curiosity.

"I've got lots of 'em. Want me to put some somewhere? They should keep for a long time provided we store them in the shade and don't open them."

"Really? Water ladled into bottles usually goes bad in three days."

"I made sure to sterilize them first, so I bet they'd keep for up to a year. However, they won't last long after they've been opened."

"They'll be safe to drink for that long? What incredible technology." For some reason, she was really impressed.

But she did say it took ten days to cross the badlands on foot. When I thought about it, water that could keep for that long in a place without many sources of water really was pretty valuable.

"Now, where were we again? Oh yeah, the Empire. Are those the only two nations on this continent?" I asked.

"No, actually. They're the ones that hold the most power, but there are countless smaller countries. Some small and mid-sized countries even have enough power that the two we've already mentioned have to stay on their guard. It'd actually be more accurate to say that the land on the other side of the badlands isn't the Holy Kingdom's but a vassal state of the Kingdom of Merinard."

"What kind of country is that?"

"A kingdom that had been built by a family of elves who left the Black Forest. They weren't satisfied living off of what the forest had to offer, so they left, crossed the badlands, found a place to settle down, mingled with the humans and beastfolk there, and then the kingdom itself took form."

"So, it was originally a country of elves?"

"Before the Holy Kingdom grew in might and turned them into a vassal state, it was home to diverse races, just like the Empire. While the kingdom itself was small, it had fertile fields and mines that produced superior rock salt and iron. Trade flourished. Even more so once good relations had been established with the elves of the Black Forest," Sylphy told me with this sad look in her eyes. I had to wonder if Sylphy had once lived in the Kingdom of Merinard herself. "It's probably been about twenty years since it was made a vassal state of the Holy Kingdom. There was a rebellion about three years ago, but the Holy Kingdom dispatched their armies to suppress them. All of the non-elven citizens in this village are survivors of the purge of Merinard."

"Really? That explains why they're so...hostile toward humans."

"Yup. I should be clear: it wasn't like the Kingdom of Merinard didn't have any humans living there. Many humans fought for their side during that rebellion."

"Really? But I'm the only human here, right?"

"That's right. I heard that the humans and demi-humans divided when they fled. The demi-humans fled to other countries, while the human sympathizers hid themselves in the Kingdom of Merinard or slipped into the Holy Kingdom's realm of influence. It's not that hard for humans to disappear into the fold there, you see."

Could that be true? Was it actually likely that they would've completely split like that—that not a single one would've come to the forest for that reason alone?

"Your doubts are understandable, but what I said was the truth. They were burned out of their homes or fled without any preparation at all to cross the Great Omitt Badlands, which is pretty much suicide. Many men lost their lives in the badlands. They had practically no food or water, and the gizmas attacked them regardless of the time of day."

Now that she mentioned it, I had a feeling that most of the refugees were women and children. It made sense.

"I'm guessing that gizma is the name of those monsters lurking out in the badlands?"

"That's right. They hide in packs beneath the ground and attack things that pass by. At night, they crawl out and prowl about for prey. They're quick, tough, and powerful. Dangerous too. The Holy Kingdom afforded the demi-humans behind the rebellion no mercy, which was why they had no other means of survival than to flee to the Great Omitt Badlands."

That would be a significant factor in the humans' split with them. I could understand why they wouldn't want to flee to such a dangerous place.

"I understand now," I told Sylphy.

"Good. Well, I think it's about time you start making us dinner."

"Huh? You want me to make it?"

"You don't expect your mistress to cook, do you? Hmm?"

"Damn it... Well, don't complain if it turns out bad."

For dinner, I made a soup made of vegetables and salted lizaf meat, lizaf steak that I had de-salted and sprinkled with spices, naan-like bread made of the mysterious flour, and salad.

"Well, this is pretty ordinary. Are you getting a bit lazy on me now?" Sylphy complained.

"Hey, I'm no cook! I can make a few things on my own, but don't expect anything fancy from the likes of me. Besides, all of these ingredients are still unfamiliar to me, so I don't know how to make better meals with them." I glared at her as I ate my fruit and veggie salad.

Okay, this green, unripe-looking tomato actually does taste like a regular ripe tomato. I might be able to make some kind of sauce with these.

"Very well, then. You may take your time getting accustomed to everything," she said.

"So you're gonna keep making me cook?"

"Do you even have to ask? You're my slave and I'm your mistress, after all. I had no choice but to make things that way, so deal with it. You'll have to work if you want things to change, okay?" Sylphy smirked as she held up a green tomato with her two-pronged fork.

"Grrgh..."

That reminded me: I still had yet to find out why Sylphy was trying to sleep with me. Gah, I should have asked her when I had the chance! But I was sure to have more chances later. I could ask her any moment now if I were so inclined.

Okay... I'm gonna do it.

"By the way, why did you...make that proposition to me earlier?"

"Hmm, good question. Maybe you should think that one over yourself." She responded to my serious question with an infuriating smirk.

I was being serious. Based on how things are done here, I'm pretty sure that it'd cause a serious problem for Sylphy. So why is she smirking now?

"I'm asking because I don't know," I told her.

"You're greatly mistaken if you think I'll answer every single question you ask me."

"Nobody but you knows the inner workings of your mind. I was being serious when I asked." I couldn't help but furrow my brows at her.

Sylphy showed no sign of flinching—she merely took a sip of her mead, her expression unchanged. I supposed she had no intention of telling me.

"I did it out of a bit of self-interest and curiosity. Also, instinct. There wasn't much thought put behind it," Sylphy said at last.

"Instinct?"

"Don't you feel some sort of craving when you see a woman who's your type? That's what I'm talking about. There's no reason behind it."

I didn't understand her at all. I wasn't attractive or anything, but I wouldn't say I was *ugly*. I was probably average. I wasn't overweight, but I wasn't muscular either. I was a bit taller than average, but I didn't have any standout features.

"I don't get it. Are you saying that I'm your type based on my looks?"

"It's not just that."

"Now I really don't get it."

Our relationship had pinballed from predator and prey to guardian and ward, collar aside. It was a big jump from her attacking me in my sleep and the tense discussion that followed to our tour of the village and my little show and tell with the iron ingots. Everything we'd done for and to each other up to this point blurred together, and now that events had left us alone in her house, I *still* couldn't tell if she was serious.

Is it okay? Am I actually allowed?! But this is Sylphy we're talking about here. My mistress, who could kill me with her fingertip should the whim strike her. Is it really okay for me to come on to her? She's not gonna break me in half, right? I was uncertain. Incredibly uncertain. Sylphy was my type too, which left me even more at a loss for what to do. She was a beautiful dark-skinned elf with dynamite knockers. How could I be expected to keep my hands off of her?

I kept thinking and thinking but couldn't come up with an answer. *It's better to stop thinking in circles. Anguishing over this is just going to be a waste of time and mental resources.*

I'd probably be satisfied even if she snapped me in two. Nothing ventured, nothing gained. Abandoning all rational thought? That was fine with me!

"I still don't get it, but I'd be ashamed of myself if I backed down now." When I thought about it simply, there was no reason for me to be so worried. My ideal woman was hitting on me. She was the one who decided whether I lived or died, both physically and from the position she was in. Which meant I should just do whatever it took to make her like me, all while enjoying myself as much as possible.

"That's precisely right. Here I was beginning to think you were some kinda limp-dick too," Sylphy said.

"That's the last thing I want a girl to say about me." I drank straight from the bottle of mead and wiped my mouth. The strong smell of the alcohol intertwined with the refreshing scent overwhelmed my nose. It sure was sweet. "What's common etiquette among you elves for this sort of thing?"

"How am I supposed to know? I'm a maiden."

"Gotcha. I'll just do things like we do back where I come from." I wrapped my arms around Sylphy's back and under her knees and lifted her up. In other words, I was doing the ol' bridal carry.

"Hee hee. What comes after this?"

"I'm taking you straight to your bed, of course. As the experienced one here, I'll take the lead."

"I look forward to that. But do be gentle with me. I may be used to getting hurt, but I am a maiden."

"I shall try my best." It wasn't like I had *that* much experience. However, I would make use of what little I had.

CHARACTERS

シルフィエル
Sylphyel

CHAPTER 3
The Sudden Beginning of My Survival Life

DAY
4

109

I WOKE UP from a slight doze. Sylphy was already gone. Judging from the weak light coming from outside, it wasn't too long after dawn.

Last night...was *good*. Oh, yeah. Sylphy pretended to be unaffected at first, but it wasn't too long before she got just as into it as I was. The fact that she could magic the pain away immediately made it much easier on me. That magic stuff sure did come in handy. I wasn't trying to be rough with her, but the experience seemed to stir up all kinds of sensations in her. The extremely erotic way she looked might have been due to her innocence or something. I was obliged to give her a great time.

However, my body was all sticky from sweat and whatnot now. I slipped out of her bedroom, intent on getting myself cleaned up.

"Oh." When I entered the living room, I found Sylphy drying her hair with a towel. It looked like she had beaten me to the punch.

She was completely naked, as if it were the most natural thing in the world, and didn't make any move to cover up at all. I supposed I was equally guilty.

"Good morning. You mind if I wash up?" I said.

Sylphy stared absentmindedly at my face for several seconds before suddenly raising her hand and pointing at the hallway that led to the bathroom. "I already prepared the water jug for you. Cloths are on that shelf over there."

"Great, thanks." I grabbed a cloth and took the hallway down to the backyard, where I found a jug of water filled to the brim. There was a bucket nearby, so I scooped up water with it and poured it over my head. It was freezing, but it felt good. I gave myself a thorough rinse and then rubbed myself down with the cloth. It was only good manners to keep myself looking neat.

After thoroughly purifying my body, I headed back to the living room to see Sylphy sitting on the rattan couch staring out into space, still in the buff. Her usual daring smile wasn't to be found—in fact, it seemed like her mind was completely elsewhere.

I wasn't sure if she was deep in thought about something or just reeling from last night. I sat down quietly next to her on the couch and hugged her.

"Ah! Mm..." I kinda took her by surprise with a kiss, which she accepted with no resistance. She was like a completely different person from the one who attacked me in my sleep and beat me up.

"Are you all right?" I asked.

"Like hell I'm okay. My dignity is in tatters."

"That's just a matter of difference in experience. There's no helping it."

Sylphy had been quite ignorant about how it all worked. She had a general understanding of the deed itself, but that was all.

She hadn't realized how much more there was to the act than "insert tab A into slot B."

I, on the other hand, did have experience and knew how things worked. She was so sensitive, and she'd done away with the initial pain of the deed with her magic. After that, I couldn't help myself. I wound up having all kinds of fun with Sylphy.

"You beast... How could you do such a thing to a maiden?" She started noisily slapping me.

"Ow, ow, ow, ow! That really hurts!"

"Hmph. We're going hunting and gathering after we eat. I want to get back while the sun is still high in the sky."

"Aye aye, ma'am."

Sylphy seemed to have recovered a bit. I followed her and got dressed. Hmm, was I going to be wandering around the forest wearing this sweatshirt and sweatpants? I had a feeling my clothes weren't going to last me very long.

"I suppose we should do something about those clothes of yours," Sylphy said.

"Yeah. I want you to be able to depend on me, Mistress."

"Good. You'd better work hard."

For breakfast, I cooked up something like pancakes with sweet honey drizzled on top and a side of grilled meat. It was a heavy meal for first thing in the morning, but it seemed reasonable considering how much we exerted ourselves last night—and were about to today.

I also took the opportunity to make lunch and stow it in my inventory. I used the flour to whip up a crude batch of bread and made grilled salted lizaf meat and potherb sandwiches of sorts. Sylphy helped, which I thought would make it taste even better. I was looking forward to lunch.

After breakfast, it was time to go hunting outside.

"Like this."

"Like that. Got it." The chain around my neck jingled. Since we were going to be in public, she had to keep me leashed like some kind of dog out on a walk.

The accusing gazes of the elves all around were hard to bear. Although, when I took a good look, there actually were a few people who looked at me with sympathy. They might have been elves with a human parent or something, so I tried to memorize their faces.

Nevertheless, I saw people staring but didn't hear anyone whispering. Maybe they were (rightfully, by my estimation) afraid of Sylphy's long, sensitive ears picking up anything damning they might have to say.

We passed through the elven residential and industrial areas without incident, and then I caught sight of their marvelous protective walls and gate. Even this early in the morning, they had sentries stationed there.

"Ugh, it's him." I groaned.

"Huh? Oh, you mean Nate? Don't worry about him. He's a weakling."

"Maybe to you, but he's plenty dangerous to me."

I wasn't about to forget how he had thrown me out into the middle of the public square. If Sylphy hadn't shown up in time, I probably would've been beaten to death.

To my surprise, Nate and the other sentries didn't say anything to us at all. They gave us annoyed looks but let us pass on through.

"Everyone in the village knows that speaking up against me means trouble," Sylphy said.

"I got a feeling as much. I guess that means I have to do whatever I can to keep you happy, Mistress."

"Heh heh. You do that." Sylphy's daring smile was back. I was coming around to thinking that the expression suited her. In fact, after the many different sides of her I got to see last night, I actually found it kinda cute. She smiled so boldly now, but in bed she—

She jabbed me in the side with her elbow.

"Hey?! Are you trying to kill me?!" I was worried for a second that she'd cracked a couple of my ribs.

"For some reason, I felt an unpleasant aura coming from you."

Still haven't come around on the whole "merciless violence" part. I mean, I guess the contrast *is cute now that I've seen her range, so to speak. Yeah.*

"Let's go," she ordered.

"Okay."

Sylphy continued to pull me by the chain. Our relationship was one where she held the reins...literally. I didn't find this whole arrangement bittersweet; not one bit, no *sir*. Still, I had nothing to do but accept it. I was her slave, after all.

Past the gate, we arrived at the outer ring of the village. There were few people around. I supposed it was still early enough in the morning that they weren't awake yet.

"Say, what are you guys building out here, anyway?" I asked.

She answered readily enough. "Row houses. Nice, solid work that'll pull their weight in siege conditions—more walls and choke points. They're supposed to replace the shantytown that's sprung up around the perimeter."

"I see. That seems logical, I guess?"

If they were made of stone or brick, I could see hoping that would be reasonably protective, but for those living in them, it would mean their home was always exposed to danger; I doubted it would be very comforting to live in.

"I'm sure it is logical from the villagers' point of view. They figure that the refugees should be grateful for what we give them since we're housing and feeding them. However, the refugees came to us with naught but the clothes on their back. They're mostly beastfolk, and we elves use magic for our farming, so we can't necessarily employ them for that. Although most of them are women, elven men aren't particularly attracted to them, and there are hardly many men in circulation to begin with. Without leverage or some way to contribute, the refugees have no choice but to do as we say."

"It's a tough world out there."

So, this was what it was like after you lost and got a bad

ending. I felt bad for them, but I was a slave now too. I wasn't all that useful... No, wait. Maybe she *did* think I was useful?

I was sure that some of them must have been unhappy being treated like that. Maybe there were even some who wanted to fight the Holy Kingdom and reclaim the Kingdom of Merinard.

My power was more suited for the mass production of weapons. So long as I had the materials, I could outfit an army in record time. If I could mass-produce one of *those* or, in the worst case, one of *those*, then maybe I had a chance?

I'd need information, but it might be possible. Sylphy seemed to have her reservations about the Holy Kingdom and, from what I could tell, had some kind of attachment to the Kingdom of Merinard.

"What are you thinking about?" Sylphy asked.

"A bunch of stuff. Maybe we should talk tonight."

"All right. But right now, we're hunting. You need to focus."

"Will do."

After we passed through the area that was under construction, it wasn't too long before we reached the dense forest. At a glance, it looked difficult to traverse, but as I walked behind Sylphy, the branches didn't catch on me and I didn't once lose my footing. Curiously, I didn't feel hindered at all.

"We're about to enter the hunting ground. You can take off the chain."

"Okay." Sylphy let go of the chain, so I immediately put it into my inventory. I kept the collar on, but I felt much lighter.

"Follow behind me and don't make a sound," Sylphy instructed.

"You can count on me." I imagined pressing the C key and crouched down, going into stealth mode. I started sliding around, imagining pressing the WASD keys—but then I noticed that Sylphy was giving me a strange look.

"Why are you moving so strangely?" she asked.

"This is one of my powers. It's really hard to explain, though." I showed her how I could slide in all directions while crouching. It was good and all that I was able to move in total silence, but I was sure it must have looked really off-putting.

"Watching you move like that is giving me anxiety..."

"Don't worry, it doesn't hurt me. Which reminds me, I can do this too." While I was crouching, I imagined pressing the space bar and jumped on the spot. I also tried moving a bit in the air.

"That's just too bizarre."

"I know, right?" I totally agreed, but I had no choice but to use this power.

After showing a bit of concern, Sylphy gave up dwelling on it and continued walking, keeping me out of her line of sight. *I'm sorry that I'm decreasing your sanity meter just by the way I move. However, I'm going to keep using this power of mine no matter what!*

I proactively picked up everything that had been dropped on the ground along the way. Fallen trees would be good for firewood. I still had lots of uses for all kinds of stones. I started collecting all of the wild plants and herbs we came across after asking Sylphy about them. The key was to not uproot them so that they could grow back.

As for the herbs, I figured there must be something I could craft them into. Maybe some kind of recovery item? In games, they could be used to cure injuries, broken bones, and illnesses, so I had a feeling I could make something really useful.

"Sorry for making you stop so much," I said.

"It's okay. Our main focus this time is gathering rather than hunting. With the amount of effort you're putting into this, you'd better produce good results, got it?"

"That means you're not giving me a quota to make, so I guess you can put faith in me that I'll meet your expectations." I swung my hatchet and turned a good-looking fallen tree into firewood. I didn't have the skill to do that myself, obviously; by accessing the menu for the tree while holding my hatchet, I could select firewood, and my body moved on its own to turn it into firewood.

"What kind of magic is that?" Sylphy asked.

"If only I knew." By chopping five times with my hatchet, I could turn a tree into scattered firewood, no matter how big it was. This power was outrageous beyond reckoning.

"Say, there's something I'd like you to try out."

"Yeah?"

"Can you cut down that tree over there?"

"Sure? I don't mind, and I'm sure you already know this, but you have to wait for green wood to dry for half a year before I can use it for wood or firewood."

"Yeah, I know. But I just get a feeling it might work anyway."

Hatchet in hand, I accessed the moderately sized tree and selected to cut it down. Automatically, my body started whacking away at its trunk. It took a lot of swings to get the job done. It'd only taken me five whacks to turn a fallen tree into firewood, yet here I was, already at twenty and—

"I chopped it down."

"So, you did... What's this?"

"A log?" The tree fell with a heavy sound, and there really was no other way to describe what was left. The branches had been cleared off, and rather than green wood, it looked like a dried log of uniform thickness from end to end.

"What the heck did you do?" Sylphy asked.

"That's just what happened when I cut it down. Maybe this is another one of my abilities?"

"I feel like I'm going crazy." Sylphy knit her eyebrows while touching her temple.

I gave her a sidelong glance as I examined the log. It was 15 meters long. I put it as is into my inventory and found its name was "Wood: Black Cedar."

My inventory was now filled with lots of leaves, twigs, and supple branches since I had just been automatically picking up everything in sight. I was amazed at how many I had picked up.

I accessed the menu for the wood to see what I could do with it.

- Cut in half
- Turn into firewood

Interesting. So I can cut it in half. I went ahead and tried doing this. It took a little bit of time, but I managed to split it in about half the time it took to bring the tree down. The new item's name was "Log: Black Cedar." It couldn't be split into smaller pieces, but "Wood" and "Wood Spikes" had been added to my crafting menu, so I queued them both up to be crafted.

"Can I chop down all of the trees in this area?" I asked.

"I won't be having you despoiling my forest. Only cut down the ones I tell you to."

"Aye aye, ma'am." Between fuel, construction, and crafting, I could never have too much wood. And so, I chopped down all of the trees Sylphy pointed out one after the other. I wound up with fifty pieces of wood. "This should be enough to last me a while!"

"I would certainly hope so." Sylphy eyed me with mild exasperation, but I was happy as a clam.

I could make fibers with the plants, and the twigs and branches could be used for fires or for making bows and arrows. Cutting down trees was awesome.

"I've got plenty of firewood and wood now. We should look for ores next."

"All right. Let's head to the stream, then."

I followed Sylphy deeper into the forest—while doing my stealth crouch, of course. I slid-stalked behind Sylphy as we went along. I was sure an outside observer would seize up at the sight of me, unsure whether to call the cops or a priest.

After leading me along for a little while, she suddenly raised her arm and froze. I followed suit. I surmised from her gestures that there must be something up ahead. I nodded and selected my composite bow, which I had registered to my shortcuts, and took out my arrows with iron arrowheads. Sylphy seemed quite interested in my bow for a moment before looking ahead of us again.

Moving a few more steps, I heard some strange noises—damp, drawn-out crunching, tearing, and popping. Was there some kind of life-or-death struggle ahead of us?

As I was wondering what we would do, Sylphy leaned toward me and whispered, "I'll handle this. Don't be reckless and jump into the fight." She began her silent approach toward the source.

I decided to follow after her at a short distance. I was eager for a chance to test my bow's strength. Plus, I wanted to watch Sylphy fight. However, I didn't want to get in her way, so I very, *very* carefully made my way there.

Oh dear...

It was a gruesome scene to behold. This corner of the forest was spattered with blood. A creature noisily dismantled its prey.

What the heck was it? It looked like a giant camel cricket. I couldn't help but stare at its long, tough-looking bent back legs. It was an ocher color, and in addition to the great arching hind limbs, its body bristled with smaller legs. It was facing away from us, so I didn't know what its face looked like, but even its butt was slick with blood, so I had a feeling it had a stinger there. The tips of its antennae, which stretched behind it, were similarly bedecked in vital fluids. Did it use those for attacking too? Would I have wound up dead if this were the first monster I had encountered? It looked ten times more ferocious than the lizaf did.

As I was covertly checking it out, Sylphy leaped at the bug's flank. She was holding a large knife—really more of a machete. It looked like it'd be strong enough to cut deep, but would it really be enough to defeat it? The thing was as big as a minivan.

"GRAAAAAAAH!" Sylphy had stabbed the right side of its unprotected torso deeply, making it shriek in pain.

The cricket moved to fight back, but she immediately leaped back and disappeared into the forest. She must have realized that she wouldn't be able to kill it in one hit. What an admirable get-away. *Okay, I get it. We've gotta whittle it down.*

The giant camel cricket turned in the direction Sylphy ran, exposing its flank to me. Miraculously, it was the same side that Sylphy had stabbed.

I imagined myself left-clicking and drew my bow. The bow's sight appeared. I pointed the arrowhead at the bug and took aim at the wound; something green and foul oozed from it.

I let the arrow fly straight in. It pierced deep enough that I couldn't see the shaft any longer.

"GISHAAAAA?!" Based on its screams, that arrow had hurt.

I nocked my next arrow and aimed again.

"Haaaaaah!" Right as I was about to shoot, Sylphy suddenly reappeared, driving her machete into a spot close to the bug's head.

I shifted my focus to the base of its right hind leg and shot my arrow. Despite the giant camel cricket's solid-looking exoskeleton, the arrow sank deep.

Its leg was paralyzed, just as I expected. The bug tried to

retreat using just its left hind leg, but then that leg was suddenly absent. After striking near its head, Sylphy had gone around and severed it.

Within the span of less than ten seconds, we had gravely injured it. Having lost its mobility, the bug had no chance against us as Sylphy continued her onslaught.

"It's dead?" I asked.

"Yes."

Sylphy had stopped attacking, so I walked over to her to get a closer look at the two of them. Sylphy was unharmed; no visible wounds or limping on her part. Meanwhile, the giant bug was in a tragic state. Sylphy had cut off the majority of its legs and its antennae, which were probably its strongest weapon. Its head, which was much smaller than I would have expected, sat a fair ways off from the rest of the corpse. *Rest in pieces.*

"So, what the heck was this thing? Can we eat it?"

"We can, but the most valuable parts of it are its carapace and the venom glands in its behind. The legs are fairly tasty if we chop them up and boil them with salt, though."

"What about its hind legs?"

"We can't eat those; the meat's too tough. They do make for great bowstrings, though."

"Huh, nice." I started putting all of the severed legs and its antennae into my inventory. "What should I do about the body? Stick it in my inventory? I bet I can dismember it too."

"Nah, just take it as is. We need to bring it back to the village and give a report about it."

"Got it. Wait, huh?" I glanced at my inventory and opened my eyes wide in shock.

Gizma Antenna × 2
Gizma Left Hind Leg × 1
Gizma Leg × 7
Gizma Head × 1
Gizma Right Hind Leg and Body × 1

"Hey, was that one of those monsters from the Great Omitt Badlands?" I asked.

"Yeah, that's right. This is a relatively shallow part of the forest, but gizmas have never come this far in before. Something must be driving them here." Sylphy shrugged as she cleaned her machete with an offhand spell.

"What do you mean?"

"I mentioned how a great number of the refugees lost their lives in the badlands many years ago, right?"

"Yeah. Ooh..." I knew what she was getting at. The fact that so many people had died meant that their corpses had been abandoned in the badlands. The fleeing refugees wouldn't have dragged the corpses of their family members along while escaping from monsters. "So you're saying that their numbers multiplied?"

"I haven't seen it for myself, but it's not hard to imagine, right? Plus, we haven't seen new refugees in the forest for two years, give or take."

"I see..."

In other words, the numerous gizmas were beginning to overflow the badlands in search of food. I was guessing they weren't cannibals. Which meant that I might have been in a lot of danger before. I had gone to the border of the Black Forest and the badlands and smashed rocks and stuff; if one of them had stumbled across me, I would've been done for.

"Let's get out of here. There's all manner of beasts sure to take an interest in this spot," Sylphy said as she started to walk.

"R-right." I followed after her, internally trembling with fear. I was seriously lucky.

About a half hour later, we finally arrived at a stream, though it was probably more like the kind you'd find in the mountains.

"This is a pretty river," I said.

"Yeah. Monsters don't live in the water, so we're safer here. But it's still a watering hole, so they just might *visit*. Don't let your guard down."

"That'd be scary."

I took my stone shovel out of my inventory. I planned to use it to collect the sand at the bottom of the river. I told Sylphy that by putting it into my inventory, I should be able to pick out iron sand from regular sand.

"That makes sense. I think I heard a village craftsman say something once about how the stones that are as round as a fist are iron ore."

"Did they now? Then I'll just go ahead and put everything into my inventory."

Sylphy smiled wryly. "Don't go crazy now. All in moderation."

I supposed she was right that it wouldn't be good to take so many that I destroyed the ecosystem. I would do it in moderation. But I had all kinds of uses for stones too. I stripped down to my underwear, splashed into the river, and started collecting iron ore and iron sand. The river wasn't particularly deep—probably only about a meter or so. The stream flowed at a moderate speed, though, so I had to take care not to trip.

"Daaang, this is cold. But it's a treasure trove of resources." I swung the shovel underwater. It was pretty heavy, but it felt light as a feather when I imagined myself left-clicking and let my power take over. After collecting a bunch of river sand, I opened the crafting menu to see what I could use it for; I could now craft iron sand, just like I thought I'd be able to. Yay.

I crafted iron sand in the background as I continued collecting stones from the riverbed. Most of them were ordinary stones, but once in a while I picked up a kind of stone called "River Magnetite," which must have been the round iron ores Sylphy had mentioned. *All this talk about ores makes me think of the word s'more. I wonder if I'll get to have a s'more ever again.*

Probably not, huh? Now I feel a bit homesick.

"Hey, put this in your inventory or whatever for me." While I was busy collecting from the river, Sylphy had gone and caught a critter that looked like a cross between a rabbit and a mouse, and it was big enough to carry in both arms.

"Sure thing." I did as she asked and saw that its name was "Labbit Carcass." *It's a rabbit! A really huge one too. Y'know, I think there are rabbits that are over a meter long back on Earth; I've seen them on the internet before.*

Still, this was approaching the size of a small dog... No, wait, I forgot how low a bar that was.

And so I continued my gathering—right up until I ran into a bit of a hiccup.

"I'm back. What in the world are you doing now?" Sylphy asked me.

"I'm cold...so cold..." The river was *freezing.* I thought I could hold on for an hour and a half, but I wound up feeling chilled to my core; I'd lit a flame in my simple furnace and was warming myself up. I was cold, okay?!

"You're sitting here getting all cozy while your mistress is out working hard? You've got some nerve."

"I'm sorry."

This time, she'd caught something that looked like a deer. There was a wound along the scruff of its neck. I had to wonder if she actually managed to kill it using the machete alone.

"That bola's a snap to use. Snagged this yakkey with it and barely broke a sweat!"

Ah, so she had used the bola I had given her before. That made sense; she must have ensnared its feet. She was making the best use of what I had given her.

"So that thing's called a yakkey?" I asked.

"Yeah, but don't put it away yet. I'm going to take out its organs and cool it in the river."

"Are you going to drain its blood?"

"My first priority is to cool the meat first. It'll start to stink otherwise. Take out that rope."

"Huh, interesting. Sure." I took out the rope from my inventory and handed it over to her.

Sylphy adeptly hung the yakkey from a tree and began to split open its belly. I took out the large wooden plate from my inventory and started retrieving the entrails as she removed them. Or at least I tried...

"Huuurk!"

"I don't care if you puke, but do it over there."

I was a *long* way from adjusting to work this gross, dude. Since I was on the verge of spilling my *own* guts, I decided to help by drawing and purifying water from the river using the wooden flasks I made instead while I still felt warm. It was always best to be prepared.

Not too long after, Sylphy finished gutting the carcass and threw it into the river with its pelt still intact. I tried not to look at the organs on the plate as I put them into my inventory.

"This should be good."

"I thought that draining blood from animals was important for making them taste good."

"It is, but cooling the meat is more important. If you don't do it immediately, the remaining blood begins to putrefy." Sylphy answered my question without making any faces as she washed her bloody hands in the stream.

"Wow, I had no idea. Guess that's something only a hunter would know."

I wondered how my dismembering of a beast compared. It wasn't like the lizaf meat smelled or anything. I thought that I had managed to handle it pretty well. Probably.

"What about the labbit you caught earlier?"

"I don't know why, but it doesn't start smelling if you don't cool it down right away. We can wait until we're home to drain its blood."

"Huh, I see." I didn't understand why that was, but I respected her knowledge gained from experience. I knew nothing about the animals in this world, after all.

"And how's your haul looking?" Sylphy asked, side-eyeing my still-blazing furnace.

"Looking pretty good, actually." I hadn't been lazing around. I was keeping the furnace going to get the iron from the iron sand and river magnetites and use them for crafting. "I think it's easier to use the iron ores than those decayed weapons and armor for materials. I dunno how to put it, but I guess it's like I can get more out of them."

"I have no idea what you're talking about, but I'm glad it seems to be going well. What have you made?"

"This, this, and this." I whipped out my freshly made steel shovel, steel pickaxe, and steel axe. "The most important thing to do first is make the tools you'll need for gathering more materials."

"So you can gather things more efficiently?"

"That's right. This one in particular is impressive." I readied my steel pickaxe and swung it a few times at a nearby boulder. The boulder immediately smashed into pieces of iron ores, stones, and some kind of stone that glittered like a jewel.

I found quite a few gems after breaking the boulders around here. So far, I'd found garnets, spinels, beryls, topazes, quartz, and amethysts. I still had yet to find a way to use them in crafting, though. I figured I might be able to sell them. I had no idea what the monetary system was like in this world. I'd have to ask Sylphy tonight.

"I can't even do that with earth magic. Are you sure that tool of yours isn't actually enchanted or something?" Sylphy bemoaned as she inspected the raw gemstone I had handed her.

I chuckled as I handed Sylphy the pickaxe. "Nah, nothing like that. All I did was use it like normal and that's what happened."

She tried striking a boulder a few times, but it didn't work like it did for me. However, she did manage to smash it. I'd have to make sure to never, ever anger her.

"Hmm. I guess this means you're special," Sylphy said.

"Heh. That's right. I'm totally special. And that's why you need to do your utmost to take care of me."

"I'll certainly try," she said with a straight face as she handed back the pickaxe.

Her serious reaction embarrassed me a little. I really wasn't expecting her to respond like that. Shouldn't she have put on that smirk of hers while making some snide remark?

"Uh, um... Yeah. Thanks. By the way, are you hungry?" I asked.

"Yeah, I suppose it is around noon. Let's have lunch."

"Coming right up." I took out two logs from my inventory to use as chairs and placed them on the ground, then took out the lizaf sandwiches I had made this morning and some drinking water. Now we were ready to eat.

"I'm surprised it's still warm," Sylphy said.

"I'm not sure why exactly, but either time stops for things I put into my inventory or the passage of time is just extremely slow. I actually put the tinder I lit into my inventory last night, and when I took it out again earlier, it was still lit."

"That's...amazing. Does this power of yours just ignore the natural way of things in our world or something?"

"It certainly seems that way."

It was amazing that I could cheat time like that. However, I had no idea how it worked. Was my inventory a dimension where time flowed differently?

"You made an axe and shovel too, right? Have you tried using those yet?" Sylphy asked as she munched on her sandwich.

Hey, lady, don't just start talking at me like that. You'll make me choke. I chugged some water to wash down the last of my sandwich. Delicious.

After some audible gulps of satisfaction, I replied, "Yeah, I have. I was able to chop stuff twice as fast as before. I think the shovel's easier to use now, but I'm not sure if it's actually any more effective than the other kind."

"I see. How about creating a gouge and chisel next so that you can make things with the stones and metals?"

"Ooh. Now that you mention it, I did see those on the list." I had no idea what those were for, so I had prioritized making the pickaxe, axe, and shovel.

"If you can make them, do it. I'm pretty sure that the boulders around here should be good for making whetstones too. The village craftsmen occasionally come here for them."

"Whetstones? Now those are important." I was very much in the market for something to keep my tools sharp.

Also, now that I had a steady amount of iron, I wanted to make not only a gouge and chisel but other kinds of tools as well.

"Say, is it okay if I make other kinds of tools besides the gouge and chisel?" I asked.

"Yeah, go ahead. Do whatever you must to increase your power."

"Aye aye, ma'am." Since I had my mistress's permission, I decided to start crafting all kinds of tools out of metal. I crafted a gouge, chisel, saw, gimlet, hard plane, adze, and a file, one after the other.

"Well? How's it going?" Sylphy asked.

"After I completed the gouge and chisel, the list of things I can make increased so much that I feel kinda overwhelmed." Just by being able to work metal and create blades, I'd reached the point where I could do genuine metalworking.

How in the world did I make the blade of a knife, for example, without a whetstone? I supposed it was a bit late to be wondering about the logistics of it all.

"My iron smelting can't seem to go fast enough. I'll look for whetstones while I wait for it to finish."

"Okay. I'll go look for more prey. I don't think I'll find anything, though." Sylphy glanced at the burning furnace before disappearing into the forest.

Ah, I get it. Any prey must have fled because of the smell of the smoke. Sorry about that. She must not have complained because, like she said, today's main goal was gathering. In other words, she wanted to get a better grasp of my power. What a kind, generous mistress I have. I'm going to do everything I can to meet her expectations.

"How the heck do you use these things?" I tilted my head to the side in puzzlement at the gouge and chisel in my hands. I mean, I had *seen* them before, but had I used them? I had some real-life practice with the hammer, saw, file, and gimlet, but I had no memory of ever using a gouge and chisel.

I was pretty sure I could use both in conjunction with a hammer.

"There's no point in thinking so hard about it—best to just try it out."

Chisel and hammer in hand, I imagined left-clicking on a boulder. No reaction. Maybe I was wrong?

"Okay, let's try this instead."

I swapped out the chisel for the gouge and noticed there were holes on the surface of the boulder. *And? What am I supposed to do with this? Can I please get some kind of tutorial?* However, the crafting menu didn't give me anything, and nothing happened when I imagined pressing F1. Bummer.

"Hmmm? Ah, I get it now." After several minutes of tiring effort on my part, I finally figured out how to use the two tools. Using the gouge, I made several holes. Then I stuck the chisel inside those holes and hit it with the hammer. The boulder split at the point where all of the holes lined up. I could freely quarry boulders this way, at least to some extent.

"I'm really not sure what the point of that was." To tell the truth, I had no idea of the merits of this process. It felt like I hadn't acquired all that much compared to how much time I spent doing it... Oh, I could use the shaped rocks as building stones when I put them into my inventory. In other words, these were also tools for gathering materials.

It seemed like it would be a pain to collect lots of building stones from this mountain stream. I would have to ask Sylphy later if there was a better place for procuring them.

After breaking several boulders and collecting what they dropped, I also managed to obtain a whetstone, so I returned to my furnace.

"I seriously can't believe how much more I can make now."

Hmm, based on the number of tools at my disposal now...the time to make *that* would soon be upon me.

What did I mean by "that"? Only a staple of the whole survival-sim genre. *That.*

It had actually appeared in my crafting menu a while ago, but I had ignored it, since I didn't have all of the required components and tools for making it yet. Now that I had plenty of both, it was well within my reach.

"I guess it's finally time...to make a workbench!"

Once made, it was truly time to craft. *Time to get fired up!*

Now it was time to make a workbench. So, I checked all of the materials I needed again.

Basic Workbench—Materials: Wood × 10, Nail × 40, Vise × 1, Basic
Toolbox × 1

I had enough wood and nails. I was able to make those right away. The problem was the vise and the basic toolbox.

Vise—Materials: Iron × 20, Mechanical Parts × 10

Yeah, I should be able to manage that. It took a really long time to craft, though. I was able to make the mechanical parts now that I'd made the gouge, chisel, and file. So long as I had the materials, proper tools, and enough time, I could craft anything, even if I didn't know how it was actually constructed. My crafting powers were amazing. I added what I needed to the queue.

Out of curiosity, I made a unit of ambiguously named "Mechanical Parts" and tried pulling it out of my inventory. It wound up being bolts, nuts, gears, springs, thin metallic sticks, and rings whose purpose was alien to me.

I see. These really would take some time to make by hand. It takes over thirty seconds to make each one of these at the moment. I guess I'll craft those while I look into how to make the toolbox.

Basic Toolbox—Materials: Sturdy Wooden Box × 1, Metal Tools × 8, Mechanical Parts × 2

Apparently, it'll be fine so long as I have eight different metal tools—I should be set with the saw, hammer, chisel, gouge, file, gimlet, hard plane, and whatnot. I can make the sturdy wooden box out of wood and nails, so no issues there. I'm a bit surprised to find that a knife's the prerequisite tool. Though, after thinking about it a bit, I can see how it would be required. And ugh, two more mechanical parts? Well, whatever.

Some time later, I had completed my vise and basic toolbox, so now it was finally time to craft a workbench. My long journey was finally at its end... Or maybe it wasn't so long? Thanks to Sylphy, I was able to start making iron right away, and I was doing pretty well, all in all—putting aside the fact that I had faced off against a lizaf, been beaten up by Sylphy, and nearly pummeled to death by a mob.

"All right. Finished." I placed it immediately, although it did feel a bit weird putting a workbench next to a river.

"Mm-hmm, this is a workbench if I ever saw one." The sturdy-looking bench came equipped with a vise and a shelf for holding tools. It was exactly what you'd imagine a workbench to be.

"Uh-huh... I see, I see." I accessed the workbench's menu and took a look at the list of the things that could be crafted.

In general, a lot of it was stuff I had already crafted manually, but all of their crafting times were shorter. Furthermore, I found several new items to craft as well. "At last. It's my time to shine."

Basic Crossbow——Materials: Supple Branch × 2, Wood × 2,
    Mechanical Part × 1, Fiber × 20
Crossbow——Materials: Supple Branch × 2, Animal Bone × 2,
    Wood × 2, Mechanical Part × 2, Fiber × 20
Improved Crossbow——Materials: Steel Plate Spring × 1, Wood × 2,
    Mechanical Part × 3, Tough Bowstring × 1

I found the renowned crossbow in the list—equally handy punching holes in plate mail and putting down zombies. In games, they took a bit more preparation to use compared to regular bows, but they were powerful. Well, their firing speed left something to be desired. I wondered how they'd fare in this world.

"It looks like I can make the basic kind right now."

I couldn't make steel plate springs with my current simple furnace. I probably needed a better one or something I could use for smithing.

For the tough bowstring, I'd need animal tendons or a lot of fibers and glue. I was all out of animal tendons, and while I had fibers, I didn't see glue anywhere in my crafting menu. I probably needed some kind of equipment for distilling chemicals or something.

I could also make crossbow bolts. They probably required iron arrowheads and wood. But maybe they needed bird feathers for fletching too?

I tried making one, and for some reason it came with a feather. What the heck? I probably shouldn't be too surprised, though, since I made plastic water bottles from unboiled water in a wooden flask.

Best not to think about it too much. Yeah. So long as it works, I don't care. But what do I do about a better furnace? I probably need a big one made of fireproof bricks or something. I might even need a stronger kind than the bellows-fed type.

I checked to see if my workbench's crafting menu had bellows. "Nope."

That probably meant there wasn't that much of a difference between a small one and a big one. However, while I was staring at the menu, I noticed there was now a category for upgrades.

Workbench Upgrade——: Mechanical Parts × 10, Steel Plate Spring × 5, Leather Strap × 2

Hmm... So, steel plate springs are holding me back again. My next goal should be making equipment for advanced iron manufacturing, then. For that, I need to upgrade my furnace from a simple one to a regular one, I thought as I looked over the simple furnace.

"Hmm?" Something else had been added to my upgrade menu.

Simple Furnace Upgrade——: Animal Hide × 5, Brick × 50, Whetstone × 3, Mechanical Part × 10

"Hmmmmm?" I was pretty sure that hadn't been there a

minute ago. Why had that suddenly been added? Was it because I had leveled up or something? Or was there some kind of other requirement I had met and therefore unlocked this function? *Hey, come on, now! Couldn't you have notified me about this? At least give me something so I know what to—hey, wait a minute.*

I imagined pressing the Tab key to open my inventory and then stared at the menu.

"There're more tabs here now." Before I only had my inventory and crafting menu, but now there were tabs for Stats, Skills, and Achievements.

"C'mon, why couldn't these have been unlocked from the very beginning?" I groaned as I looked at through the tabs.

I checked Stats first. It was pretty simple. My current health was explicitly stated to a certain extent. Or rather, there was a visualization of it, so I gleaned what I could from the info. Unfortunately, I didn't have numerical metrics for strength or agility or other stats like you did in RPGs. It only showed my hunger, thirst, health, stamina, exhaustion, and whether I had an abnormal status effect. It was worth mentioning that I did have experience points, though.

I didn't know how I was accumulating experience points, but I knew my level. I was level six right now. I wondered if there was any point gaining levels.

Next, I checked Skills, but...

"Hmm... This is a toughie."

This seemed to be where my level served an actual purpose. There were several skills listed in the Skill column, and I could spend skill points to obtain them. The skills I could acquire were broadly categorized into kinds related to crafting and kinds related to strengthening myself physically. There were five options right now for the crafting type.

Skilled Worker——: Crafting time is reduced by 20%.
Mass-Producer——: When you make more than ten of the same item, the number of required materials is reduced by 10%.
Logger——: Number of plant materials obtained is increased by 20%.
Miner——: Number of minerals obtained is increased by 20%.
Anatomist——: Number of materials obtained from bodies is increased by 20%.

Hmm. It was so hard to choose. Mass-Producer looked good at a glance, but having to craft multiple things at once in order to get the bonus wasn't all that appealing. It would be more useful to increase how many materials I obtained instead.

I didn't feel the need to have Skilled Worker at the moment either, but if I had any recipes that took over ten minutes or an hour to make later, then that would be useful. My current recipes took about ten seconds to make, so I didn't think it'd be that big of a difference.

So, under skills that would enhance my physical abilities, I found:

Heart Healthy——: Stamina recovery speed is increased by 20%.
Fleet-Footed——: Movement speed is increased by 10%.

Strong Arm——: Attacks with melee weapons are increased by 20%.

Sharpshooter——: Attacks with ranged weapons are increased by 20%.

Iron Skin——: Damage taken is reduced by 20%.

Survivor——: Health is increased by 10% and Health recovery
   speed is increased by 20%.

Reptilian Stomach——: Hunger reduction speed is reduced by 20%.

Camel Hump——: Thirst reduction speed is reduced by 20%.

Those were the eight skills currently available to me.

I thought it'd be wise to immediately take Heart Healthy, Fleet-Footed, Sharpshooter, Iron Skin, and Survivor.

Increased Stamina recovery rate would be good for both mining and combat. Together with Swift of Foot, I would be good at getting away. I had no skill with using melee weapons, meaning the Excellent Shooter skill would be better for me. It'd also be good to have Iron Skin just in case I did get hit, and the Survivor skill was certainly directly linked to increasing my life expectancy.

I didn't think I needed the skills for Hunger and Thirst, since I took great care in making sure I had plenty of both. I supposed it would be useful if I went to a place like the Great Omitt Badlands, where it was hard to find supplies.

Hmmm. I was having a hard time choosing. I had six points to spend on skills. I didn't know if I could get them back if I changed my mind, so I really had to think this through.

"I think I'll just come back to this later." It wasn't like I had to pick what I wanted right away. Yeah. Next, time to check the Achievements. "Uh, what's with all of these question marks?"

First-Time Crafter——: Craft an item for the first time. *Unlocks a skill.

???——: Hidden achievement.

First-Time Gatherer——: Gather for the first time. *Unlocks a skill.

First-Time Miner——: Mine for the first time. *Unlocks a skill.

First-Time Hunter——: Acquire materials from a living creature for
the first time. *Unlocks a skill.

???——: Hidden achievement.

???——: Hidden achievement.

So many of the achievements were locked that it didn't do me much good at all. On top of that, I had no idea what the requirements were for unlocking them. What a crappy game to be stuck in.

My First Workbench——: Craft a workbench for the first time. *Adds
the ability to upgrade every kind of workbench and items.
Also adds the Stats, Skills, and Achievements tabs to the
menu. *Unlocks a skill.

Ooh, that answers one question I had. I had a feeling that the workbench had something to do with all of this new stuff. Anything else worth noting?

My First Copulation——: Copulated with a member of the opposite
sex for the first time. And you liked it too. *Increases Health
and Stamina by 10 points.

"And you liked it too"? Excuse me? Get over here so I can whoop your ass! And that wasn't my first time either, it was—oh, wait a minute. It must mean since I first got to this world. That makes sense. And what does it mean by 10 points? There are no numbers in my Stats, so I can't really judge.

> Technician—: Satisfied your partner during copulation. Aren't you good in bed? *Attacks against the opposite sex are increased by 10%.

Who the hell wrote this and why is it any of their concern whether I'm good in bed? Who'd be happy about that bonus after reading it?

"What are you making faces at?"

"Whaaa?!" I cried out in surprise. I hadn't even noticed Sylphy's return.

"Didn't I tell you that monsters come here sometimes to drink? If I'd been one, you'd be dead right now."

"Uh, oh, yeah. You're right. I wasn't paying attention at all. Sorry." I tried to calm my pounding heart. She was probably right; I was being too careless. I really would've been in trouble if an agile monster came at me.

"Anyway, what's this?"

"It's called a workbench. I'll be able to move right ahead making all kinds of stuff now."

"Hmm. Well, good thing you spent your time wisely. I'm thinking we should start heading back soon. Is there anything else you need to gather?"

"Er, sorry, but give me a bit more time before we go. I'll grab what I need as fast as I can."

I bought the Miner skill from the Skill page and started breaking boulders with my pickaxe and digging up dirt. I did feel like I was getting more drops now than I was before. Also, the steel shovel was much more efficient at digging than the stone shovel, so that was good.

In about an hour, I managed to build up a hefty stock of mineral resources and clay, and we decided it was time to go. *Since I have a ton of materials now, I should ask her if I can make a work shed in her backyard when we get home. I'll get to finally build something. I can't wait!*

"There it is at last." I had no idea how long it had been since we left the stream since I had no way to check the time. All the same, we managed to arrive back at the elf village before it started getting dark.

Despite the late hour, folks were still hard at work on the row houses. I was keenly aware of the refugees' piercing gazes.

"Are you tired?" Sylphy asked me.

"Physically, I'm fine. But I'm a bit worn out mentally from being on guard the whole time while we were out in the forest."

"That's just something you have to get used to." She shrugged and pressed on.

Although I still had the collar around my neck, she hadn't

attached the chain. I asked about it before we got close to the village, but she told me not to worry about it; she had something planned. I had no choice but to trust her.

We arrived at the gate, where an elf soldier questioned us, to no one's surprise. "Hey, why isn't he leashed?"

"I see no reason to answer to the likes of you. There's something I need to report to the elders right away, so get out of my way."

"Impure filth! You dare to—urk?!"

Sylphy delivered a blindingly fast punch to his throat. *Yikes! She didn't even hesitate.*

"Speak to me like that again and you'll wish you were dead." All was silent except for Sylphy's icy voice.

I was afraid I'd let out a little shriek.

"Let's go."

"Aye aye, ma'am." I saluted and followed after her.

I don't know how many times I've thought it by now, but brain o' mine, just so we're both absolutely *on the same page about this: remind me never to piss Sylphy off.*

"Hey, was it actually okay for you to do that just now?" I asked quietly as I jogged after Sylphy to catch up to her.

"Hmph. Even if it wasn't, it's not like anyone can do anything about it. They'd be in trouble without me, after all," she replied.

"Really?"

Hmm. Does Sylphy have tremendous power in this village? Or is she just really respected? Why is she treated like she's so untouchable? I was curious, but it seemed like the sort of topic best not broached in public.

"I take it we're not going straight home, then?" I asked.

"I have to report to the village elders that we found a gizma in the forest."

"Ah."

We passed by her house and headed farther into the village. We didn't pass that many locals. Did most of the elves stay cooped up all day?

"What's that huge building over there?" I asked.

"The assembly hall. It's where all the elderly people gather to chat and swill tea all day long." Sylphy smiled wryly and barged right inside. There weren't any guards or anything; there was no one to stop her.

"Oho. I was wondering who had come to visit."

"My, my, isn't this a treat, getting to see a whippersnapper like yourself two days in a row."

"Ho ho ho. Perhaps tomorrow the world shall end!"

The whole hall broke into a clamor of voices. "Don't say something so ominous," said Sylphy. "You won't be laughing once you hear what I've got to say."

I poked my head out from behind Sylphy to take a look. What I saw was a room as big as a tennis court. The floor was covered in something that looked like tatami mats, and the ceiling arched high above us.

The voices I heard had come from elves perched on cushions laid out on the floor while they sipped tea. From the way they talked, you'd expect 'em to be a bunch of creaky octogenarians, yet they didn't seem that old. A few looked the same age as Sylphy;

others looked like children. A scant few looked legitimately old and wrinkled.

"Oh? Is that the human you found in the forest?"

"Hmm, I don't sense much magical ability from him at all."

"Much? I don't sense any."

"How unusual to encounter someone with not a grain of magic in them."

"You think that's what he is?"

"He couldn't possibly be a Fabled Visitor, right?"

They sure talked a lot. There were seven people sitting around one spot with four others posted up a little ways away from them. Maybe they were attendants or something? In any case, there were eleven elves in all.

Only one was male; the rest were women.

"Sylphy, child, who is that man? All you told us yesterday was that you had found a human man and were going to make him your slave," one woman said.

"Don't call me that. I'm here because I have something I need to tell you all. Hey, grab an antenna." Sylphy commanded.

"Right-o." I did as she asked and took one from my inventory.

"We found a gizma in the forest. I suspect it's just the first sign of a broader cause for concern," Sylphy told them.

"Hmm. We feared as much."

"Now that one's come into the forest, it won't be long before they start appearing in droves."

"We might be able to repel them if we focus on defending the village."

"But what about the beastfolk? Do we accommodate them here in the village since we have a proper wall?"

"That wouldn't be feasible. We won't be able to tend to or harvest anything from the magical fields while we're defending ourselves either. We won't have enough food for them too."

"Yeah. It would only end in mutual destruction if we forced ourselves to accommodate them without being properly prepared."

"We'll have to ask them to leave or tell them they can stay at their own risk."

"They're just reaping what they've sown, if you ask me."

The elf elders all started giving their opinions about the situation upon seeing the antenna. I just watched in silence from behind Sylphy. What they were saying didn't leave any room for opposing opinions.

Of course, it wasn't like I didn't have any ideas of my own. I had no idea how many refugees there were, but I imagined there were a lot of them—a hundred or two at the least, most likely. But wasn't it inhumane to abandon them to buy the village's survival?

However, the elves had no obligation to let themselves come to ruin together with the refugees. The refugees had fled to the Black Forest with nothing but the clothes on their backs, and the elves provided for them thus far, even though they had nothing of value to pay them back with. It seemed like a fair argument that the problem with the gizmas only started because they'd had so many stragglers to chow down on. I could understand their point of view.

The elders began speaking again. "Hmm. If only the bulwark was finished."

"Indeed. Then the fields would be protected as well."

"We have no choice but to summon the leaders of the refugees and talk with them tonight."

"Indeed. Sylphy, child, tell us more about this man of yours."

"Stop calling me that." Sylphy bristled, but the elders didn't look perturbed in the least. I was impressed.

"You mentioned how you wanted to make him your property since he has skills for steelmaking," one elder said.

"That's right," Sylphy replied.

"Why did you bed him on the very first night of knowing him? You sure didn't waste any time."

"What?!" The abrupt question left Sylphy flustered. Her face went red all the way to her ears.

Oooh... Now this is a rare condition to see my ever fearless and calm mistress in. Go, elders, go! Make her squirm some more!

The elders explained. "Ho ho. I'm sure you're wondering how we can tell. As it so happens, child, when a woman takes a man, the nature of her magic changes slightly."

"It's a very small change, but it's plain as day when you've been around as long as we have."

"To think that our little Sylphy has finally decided to blossom despite her tomboyish nature."

"But that worries us, child. It's not proper to treat a slave as your plaything."

"But humans do it all that time. Isn't that what they're into recently?"

"Little Sylphy's just going with the latest trends."

"I'm not so sure about that."

"It's a good way to keep her family lineage going. After all, she's the only survivor of the Merinard bloodline. There's no problem if you ask me, even if her fetish raises some eyebrows."

My mistress quivered with rage as the elders continued talking about her. It was adorable. It seemed that no one among the elders believed that I had attacked Sylphy. Well, even if I did have macho bulging muscles, Sylphy was more than capable of defending herself, so it might have been a reasonable assessment.

Something one of the elders said piqued my interest: the Merinard bloodline. So Sylphy *did* have some kind of connection to their kingdom—a direct one at that, if she was a descendant of the royal family.

Did that make her a princess? Princess Sylphyel did have a lovely ring to it. Though, while she was indeed beautiful, she was too powerful for her own good.

"Enough with the jokes." After a moment of cheerful laughter, an elder called the attention of the others.

The mood of the room grew strangely heavy, and their expressions turned grave.

"Sylphyel, daughter of Merinard, I ask you: just who is this man?"

I was amused at how Sylphy still had a faint trace of a blush, but she responded without fear and with a resolute expression on her face. "I have no idea. According to him, he found himself transported to the border of the badlands and the forest. While he speaks and understands our tongue, when he tells me about his homeland, it's all things I've never heard before. I can only imagine he's speaking of a completely different world from Leece."

The elders paused before they began speaking their opinions. "I see. A person without magic who appeared in threshold of the forest, come to save our people... It sounds too good to be true, considering our current circumstances."

"Indeed. However, considering the legend's provenance, it stands to reason that he might be the one."

"So that makes him a Fabled Visitor, then?"

"That's the only way to look at it. There's not enough proof to be sure of it yet, but that's the only conclusion we can draw from what we know."

"Then perhaps we ought to take him into our care."

All of the elders looked at me at once. Sylphy drew me into her arms to obstruct their view. *Ahhh, so nice and soft. I don't mind this at all.*

"Nuh-uh. He's mine," she declared. It made my heart skip a beat.

Huh? Does that mean Sylphy started a relationship with me just because she wanted to use me for something? Bah, I don't care. Even if she did all of this because she thinks I'm a Fabled Visitor or wants to use my abilities, I don't mind at all so long as she treats me like this. So please, continue to dote on me, Mistress.

"Tch. You really do take after that tomboy in your stubbornness. Very well; we can hardly rip him away from you after you've gone and offered him your chastity."

Upon hearing that, Sylphy let me go. I clung to her, but she smacked me in the head and peeled me off. How cruel.

The elders continued conversing among themselves. "But what are we going to do? He may be a Fabled Visitor, but he looks no different from any other human. The refugees and young elves won't accept him so easily."

"Then we'll just have to make them accept him. If he does a good job, we'll be able to protect the village and the refugees as well. It'll be like killing two birds with one stone."

"That makes perfect sense. Do you understand as well, child?"

"Yes, I do," Sylphy responded.

"Do understand, child, that we are not happy with the current situation. We shall assist you so long as the Fabled Visitor obeys you, but we require proof of his nature first. Proceed with utmost prudence in this matter."

Sylphy nodded, turned on her heel, and left. I had no idea what was going on, but she must have. Granted, based on the direction of the conversation, I had a feeling I knew a bit about where this was headed.

"Hey, you." Just as I turned to follow after Sylphy, one of the elders spoke out to me. It would be bad to ignore her, so I stopped and looked back. The one who had spoken to me was an elder who looked like a little girl. A loli who spoke like an old person...I dug it. She had nothing on Sylphy, though. "We haven't heard your name yet. You'll at least tell us that, won't you?"

"Sure, I'm Shibata Kousuke. Feel free to call me Kousuke."

"Very well, then, Kousuke. Take good care of Sylphy. She's a pitiful girl."

"I'll do my best," I said before taking my leave. I'd do my best, however much that counted for. I doubted I'd go so far as to put my life on the line for her. Probably.

We arrived home, but Sylphy just sat fuming on her favorite couch. She wasn't even drinking any mead. Just sitting there scowling in silence. It was scary.

"Uhhh, um, *estás bien?*"

"What's that supposed to mean? Is that some kind of incantation?"

"No, it means 'are you okay?'" At least, I was pretty sure that was what meant. Pretty sure I didn't get that wrong. Probably.

"I'm fine. Just thinking about what must be done."

"You mean what those elders were talking about? Can you explain what happened back there? I was definitely getting the vibe that I'm supposed to do something about the gizmas."

"I don't know what you mean by 'vibe,' but your guess is right. Basically, they want you to prove that you're a Fabled Visitor by using your powers to save the refugees."

"Ah. So, if I remember right, they were saying that it's a problem that the bulwark and residential buildings aren't finished yet?"

"That's right. At the pace they're going right now, it'll take another half a year to complete. We have no idea when the gizmas will start crowding into the forest, but I doubt we have that much time."

"Hmm, I see." From what I had seen, the bulwark they were building was made of stone or brick. It looked like it would take a great deal of materials. "I might be able to do something about that."

"What?" Sylphy looked at me with surprise.

"I think I can use my power to finish the bulwark quickly. I haven't tested it out yet, so I can't say for sure, but I'd like to give it a try. Actually, I had been planning to talk to you about building something when we got home."

"Tell me more."

"Aye aye, ma'am. But I think it'd be easier if I just showed you. Let's go to the backyard."

Sylphy nodded and followed me down the hallway that led to the backyard. The ground was even, so it was perfect.

"First I'm going to make some materials," I told her.

I placed the simple furnace, added some fuel, and got it burning. I inserted clay to start crafting. I was making fired brick blocks, of course. I placed the workbench next to the furnace and started crafting cobblestone wall blocks using clay and stones. I was going to make both kinds to show Sylphy and have her help me pick which kind to use.

"And now it's time to start making my favorite material. I'll show you an ability I haven't told you about yet before it's finished."

I had actually been secretly crafting wood blocks for building. It's good practice in survival games to have some kind of building block registered to your shortcuts so you can build a wall at a moment's notice.

I selected the wood blocks from my shortcuts, and a semi-transparent version of it appeared in my vision like some kind of hologram to show where I'd be placing it. I was looking in the air right now, so it looked like the block was floating. When I imagined the ground, the semitransparent block fell and stuck there. It appeared to be a perfect one-meter cube, but I was able to change its shape to some extent just by imagining it. I decided to make a wall that was thirty centimeters thick and one meter square.

"There," I said.

The wall I built out of wood appeared with a satisfying *thunk*. I tried pushing it, and it didn't collapse for some reason. It was securely fixed to the ground.

"What the—?!" Sylphy said in surprise.

"And this, and this, and this."

"Huh?!"

With a *thunk-thunk-thunk*, I continued placing the wall. At two meters tall, two meters wide, and thirty centimeters thick, it was complete. It might not have been very durable, but it seemed like I would be plenty safe if I were surrounded by this kind of wall.

I tried to kick it down, but I couldn't make it budge.

"This is what I meant. Using enough materials, I can easily make a wall. By the way, I made this wall thin on purpose. It can actually be this big." With a *thunk-thunk-thunk-thunk*, I stacked four wood blocks without changing their thickness, making a wall that was two meters tall, two meters wide, and one meter thick. I tried kicking it too, and it didn't budge. I was sure that it'd be incredibly hard to destroy without some kind of tool. "Oh, and I can make a wall that's just about this big using just one log."

The law of conservation of mass must have gone on vacation. Sylphy gaped at the wall, dumbstruck. *Ah, the bricks and cobblestone wall blocks are ready.*

"By the way, for making a bulwark, I recommend using these brick or stone blocks," I said as I quickly erected walls of each kind. I touched my brow and cast my eyes down. *This was the same kind of expression I had been wearing earlier too! I know, I know!* "Mwa ha ha… With my abilities, I shall reign supreme over rebirth and destruction…"

My hard shift into edgelord mode pissed Sylphy off. "Shut up," she said in an incredibly scary voice.

"Yes, Mistress."

Sylphy walked over to my walls with a frightening look on her face. She tested their feel and strength. I watched her out of the corner of my eye as I added a crossbow to my crafting queue.

I was going to make a basic one and a regular one, along with a dozen crossbow bolts. These bolts were much shorter and thicker than the arrows you'd use with a regular bow.

While I waited for my queue to finish, I started placing some logs to use for targets a short distance away. I would've preferred to use the gizma's carcass, but its carapace was apparently valuable, so I had a feeling Sylphy would beat me up if I riddled it with bolts.

After setting up a few logs, I returned to the workbench to find that the crossbows and bolts were done. I went ahead and set another dozen bolts to craft.

"Now what the heck are you up to?" Sylphy asked.

"I just made a new weapon, so I wanted to practice using it."

I decided to test the basic crossbow out first. It looked quite crude, which I supposed was par for the course since it was basically made out of wood. There was a metal ring on the tip for placing your foot so that you could draw the string using your back strength. There were also metal parts where you hung the bowstring and where the trigger was.

"Whoa, this is surprisingly tough to use." I tried to pull the bowstring back; it took a lot more effort than I imagined. Once I'd drawn it into place, I set the bolt.

"What a strange bow. I can't imagine you can fire multiple shots in a row like you can with a regular one. It looks like a pain to operate."

"You're right that this kind doesn't work for rapid fire, but it has its perks. You'll see."

I readied the bow and the reticle appeared in view. I pulled the trigger and the bolt flew with a sharp *twang*. It pierced exactly where I had aimed the reticle. I imagined myself left-clicking and used a command action to reload.

"Wait, seriously?" My body moved all on its own. I pulled the bowstring back using just my right hand and quickly set the bolt. By doing this, it didn't seem all that much slower than using a bow. I shot again and hit the spot I aimed at. This had some firepower to it. "Do you want to give it a try? I think you'll be able to see for yourself how useful it is if you do."

"Hmm..."

I handed over the crossbow to her. Sylphy looked at it closely and then reached for the bowstring. "Nngh, yeah, I was right. It's a pain."

"Right? That's why you need to put your foot in that ring and use your back muscles to draw it."

"I see. And once it's pulled back, you set the arrow and then pull this lump to send the arrow flying?" Sylphy readied the crossbow just as I did, aimed, and then fired. She nailed the shot without breaking a sweat. "Ah, I get it now. Since you don't have to hold the string, you can take your time to aim without getting tired, and you can shoot immediately once you have the string and arrow set."

"That's right. And it's not that hard to learn how to use a crossbow either. So long as you have the strength to draw it, anyone can use it and hit their mark, even those with no training with weapons."

"So you're saying that even the refugees can help fight?"

"If we get the bulwark built and enough crossbows and bolts made, yeah. This one's the most basic kind, so it's the weakest. I think they'll be pretty powerful at a reasonable range, but I'm not sure they'll be that useful against the gizmas or someone in iron armor."

"I can see that. They might be good enough to use on lizafs, but they need a bit more oomph."

They'd easily pierce living flesh, if you asked me. Against humans, you could shoot them through a helmet's visor or somewhere like that.

"*This* kind uses animal bones to reinforce the bow," I said. "Whoa, this one's even harder to draw." The regular crossbow wasn't all that different in its structure. However, since the bow part was like the composite bow, it was even stronger. I somehow managed to muster the draw strength, set a bolt, and shoot.

"This one seems much more powerful," Sylphy observed.

"Yeah. It might even work against gizmas."

"Let's give it a try. Take out the gizma body and try shooting it."

"Are you sure? I thought you said its carapace was valuable."

"Yeah, I'm sure. It's more important that we ascertain how effective these weapons will be against it."

Since I had Sylphy's permission, I put the gizma's torso a short distance away and then shot it with the regular crossbow. The sound of the bolt cut through the air as it flew, piercing through the gizma's carapace so deeply that we couldn't see it anymore.

"It seems quite powerful. Hey, do you still have some of that rusted armor? If you do, try shooting that too."

"Aye aye, ma'am." I still had some regular rusted armor in my inventory, so I mounted it on a log and shot it. It easily pierced through that as well, sinking into the log. I tried shooting it with the basic crossbow too, and while it did pierce it, it was much weaker.

"There's another kind of crossbow that's even stronger than this one, but I can't make it without the right materials. Also, there's something I wanted to talk to you about."

"Yeah?"

"Would it be all right if I made a workshop here in your backyard? I'll probably be able to make bigger facilities and more workbenches too."

I had a feeling that my inventory had some kind of limit to it. No survival game ever let you have an unlimited number of items in your inventory. Most of them had weight restrictions or a cap on the number of different types of things you could carry. I had a few items I could craft that looked like they'd be good for storing materials, so I also wanted to build a place where I could put those.

"Hmm. Very well, then. You may use the backyard however you see fit. I'll be sure to let you know if there's something I don't like," Sylphy said.

"Great. I'll get started right away."

First, I tore down the wooden, brick, and cobblestone walls with my axe and pickaxe. While the blocks didn't return as is into my inventory, I was still able to recover about 80 percent of their original materials.

I also cleaned up the logs, armor, and gizma carcass that we had been using for target practice, along with the crossbow bolts we had fired.

"Should I do anything with your storeroom?" I asked.

"Just leave it there."

"Will do." Had she given her permission, I would've torn that down as well, but I did as my mistress commanded. The ground was plenty wide and flat, like a sports field, so I could start building right away. "It'd be best if I could put the entrance to the workshop as close as possible to the passage. But I should probably leave enough space for exercise, right? We might want that space for testing out weapons like we did just now."

"Yeah. Don't turn my whole backyard into this workshop of yours."

"Okay."

There was also the fact that we had used this space earlier for bathing. That all in mind, I'd make sure to leave a wide enough space near the entrance to the passage. Now I just needed to think about what kind of model of workshop I wanted.

"I'm a fan of five-by-five survival houses myself." There were quite a lot of people out there who liked to get very creative and build huge houses in survival games. Those types were hardcore about building; the houses they came up with were certainly impressive. I considered them a kind of work of art.

However, those people usually used the game's creative mode, where you got unlimited access to materials. Of course, there were people who built those houses in regular game mode, but that was more like a self-imposed challenge kind of thing. If I had to say, I was more the strategic type than creative, so I prioritized functionality. It wasn't like I hadn't even bothered to begin with since I had no artistic sense whatsoever or something. I just didn't like things going to waste.

First, I made a floor out of wood blocks. I used that to visualize the whole size of the workshop.

"There, there, there, there, there." As I backpedaled, I put down blocks in a straight line. Moving backward was the trick to laying down floors and walls. I laid down the floor row by row, like planting rice. I decided to make the floor 25 centimeters thick. In other words, I was quickly laying down wood blocks that were a quarter of their normal height.

I worked on the walls next. I didn't think there was much call for thick walls, so I quickly made a 30-centimeter-thick wall. The walls were 3 meters tall along the entrance and 2.5 meters in the back to make an incline. This way, once I was done making the roof, water wouldn't overflow over the entrance when it rained.

Even though I was more the five-by-five survival house type, I wasn't about to make the roof flat. Things would just get overly wet if it rained, and I had a feeling the roof would collapse if it snowed a lot.

Finally, I added the door, and that was when I noticed something.

"Crap, it's dark in here."

I needed to add dormer windows. I broke a portion of the wall and added a hole for letting in light near the ceiling. There, that brought in light. I looked around inside.

"There's something about this that really weirds me out." Luckily, it was sturdy enough without any pillars or beams, but there was something about the way the place looked that put me on edge. I used my wood blocks to add some beams across the ceiling, then molded some more of them to look like pillars and placed them in eight spots.

There. They were only there for decoration, but for some reason I felt more at ease. *I suppose appearances really are important.*

I had intended this to be a simple five-by-five building, but now it probably looked like a regular cabin.

I looked around to tell Sylphy I was done, but she had disappeared on me. I assumed she had gone inside, so I went looking for her and found her prepping dinner. Was she going to be cooking it for us tonight?

"I'm done building my workshop," I told her.

She was at a loss for a moment. "I don't think it's even been a half hour yet."

"So long as I've got the materials ready, building is a breeze."

I took an astonished Sylphy with me back outside. *Oops, almost forgot to grab the workbench.*

"You actually did finish it," she said.

"It took quite a bit of my wood, though. I need to replenish." I had used about half of the wood materials I had picked up today, so it wasn't like I was completely out of materials yet.

"We'll go later," Sylphy said as she took a look inside. "There's something off about this place, but it looks like a regular cabin."

"It's probably because I didn't build it like you normally would, so you'll have to just ignore that."

"That could be it." However, it didn't seem that easy for her to get over the feeling since she started knocking and pushing the walls and floor, testing their strength. "Seems sturdy enough."

"Yeah." Truthfully, I had no idea how much damage my cabin could take before it was utterly destroyed, but I doubted it'd just suddenly collapse on me just from normal usage. "Now all that's left is for me to put my workbench and stuff in here."

"Sure, do as you will. This place is your castle."

"Thank you. My mistress brings me such joy. So, about the bulwark—" Sylphy suddenly silenced me by pressing her index finger to my lips. I wondered why she was telling me not to say anything.

"We can discuss that at length after dinner. I'll do the cooking tonight."

"Great, I can't wait to find out how good of a cook you are. But why this change?" I was befuddled, especially after she got so high and mighty about the prospect of a slave making their mistress cook.

Sylphy ignored my question and chuckled, a daring ear-to-ear grin spreading across her face.

"You may still be my slave, but I *am* your wife now since I gave you my chastity. It's a wife's job to show her appreciation for her hardworking husband by cooking, yes?" she whispered into my ear.

"Whoa?!" I cried out in surprise, making Sylphy smirk with satisfaction as she left the cabin. My ear felt strangely hot. "What just happened? Oh man, oh man, oh man." Her sudden fawning had left me at a loss for words.

I need to get a hold of myself before I go back inside, or else I'm likely to make a move on her while she's cooking. The last thing I want is to get a swift kick in the nuts because I let myself get carried away.

"Thanks for the meal." I put my hands together in gratitude before I started eating Sylphy's home-cooked meal.

"You're welcome."

Today we were having... Let's see. Various kinds of finely chopped and shredded vegetables fried with minced meat and then stewed with beans, mead, and spices. It reminded me of Indian cuisine.

Accompanying this was bread made from that same flour I had used. Hers was much fluffier than mine, though. Perhaps the difference was that I hadn't let the dough rise properly. However, I felt like she hadn't taken that much longer to cook it than I had.

"How is it?" Sylphy asked.

"It's really good. I like how spicy it is."

"Oh, that's good."

Oh, Mistress. You mustn't. You mustn't, Mistress! Ahhh! Seeing you smile like that will be the end of me! Ahhh! Don't! Stop, please, Mistress!

"What are you writhing around for?" Sylphy asked.

"You're just so cute it hurts."

"What the hell are you on about?" she snapped with a slight blush.

Frankly speaking, it wound up backfiring.

Calm down, Kousuke. Keep it together. We're about to have a serious conversation, so calm yourself, I thought, reaching for whatever scrap of Buddha nature I had in me in an effort to regain my composure. *What I should be focusing on right now is the food.*

"Did you have this kind of food in the world you came from?"

"It's not quite the same, but we had something similar enough. Sorta reminds me of a kind of cuisine found in a country that's pretty far from where I lived."

"Hmm, so this must taste pretty different from what you're used to."

"Yeah, it does, but I still think it's really delicious." I had no idea if I'd ever be able to return to Earth, but if I was stuck here for the rest of my life, then this was going to become the taste of home. *I'll have to ask Sylphy to teach me how to make this later.*

"I want you to teach me how to make food from where you come from," Sylphy said.

"Okay. I'll do my best to figure out how to recreate it." We wouldn't be able to accurately recreate Japanese food without miso and soy sauce, or kombu and bonito flakes either, if we were going to do anything substantial with soup. *Maybe I could craft them? Hmm, I'll have to add that to my to-do list.*

Dinner conversation came to rest on the topic of the food and seasonings found in our worlds. Once we were finished, we moved to the rattan couch to relax. Or so I said, but it was more like serious conversation time.

"What should we talk about first?" Sylphy asked.

"Hmm, I suppose we need to pin down the details about this siege plan of ours."

Sylphy had changed into casual clothes; she handed me mead in a porcelain cup, then took a cup for herself and held it up to me.

"You guys do toasts here too?" I asked.

"I suppose people have the same kind of customs no matter where they live when it comes to things like alcohol."

We clinked our glasses and drank. It was sweet. Once again, I had to be careful not to go overboard.

"So, the bulwark," Sylphy began. "I think it'll work if we make it out of brick or stone like you showed me earlier. We might be able to muster the materials with time to spare if we ask the refugees for help."

"Thinking long-term, bricks would probably be best. The stone wall looks like it's simply made, but it's actually comprised of rocks meshed together. I think it'd take a while to learn how to repair and reproduce it."

Sylphy told me that there were people among the elves and the people from Merinard who knew how to lay bricks before she took another drink of her mead. She wasn't drinking it straight from the bottle today.

"We'll need lots of clay and fuel," I said. "I can mine for those, or we can use the refugees to help make things go along faster."

"Okay. What do we do about the gizmas?"

"I think we'll be able to fend them off if we get the bulwark built and I make lots of crossbows."

"You're right that those bows performed well against its carapace. Do you think you'll be able to make enough?"

"If you want enough for everyone, then what I'm really short on is animal bones. The other materials are easier to come by; we'll just need to cut down trees and gather more iron ores." By cutting down trees, I'd get all of the materials I'd need besides the iron and the animal bones. I didn't need that much iron for the arrowheads. If things didn't go well, I could probably make do with what I collected today. "How many refugees are there in total?"

"312, last I heard. A little over 80 percent of them can work—the rest are elderly, children, and the wounded."

"Even children can pitch in by carrying arrows. Do you think 300 crossbows would be enough, including some for reserves?"

I did some mental math to figure out how many materials we'd need. *Uh, so from one tree, I can get one log, six supple branches, 18 branches, and 100 fibers, and then from one log I can get 24 wood blocks, and then if I get four supple branches from one wood block... Mental math is hard! But I think I can make 300 crossbows if we cut down 50 trees. With a steel axe, I can cut down 30 trees in 30 minutes, so I should be able to gather enough in under an hour.*

"Yeah, I'm pretty sure the animal bones will be the problem. We'll need to get them from monsters as big as the lizafs, at the very least. They're needed to strengthen the bow."

"Hmm, animal bones... You can't use the gizma carapace instead?"

"Huh?" I hadn't even considered the possibility.

"It's similar enough, isn't it?"

"I...guess? Does that mean I'm allowed to use it however I want?"

"We're the ones who felled it, so we can use it however we want, right?"

"But you said it's valuable."

"Well, that's true. Didn't you get a bunch of raw gemstones from those boulders? Those are worth much more than the carapace." Sylphy grinned. The look she wore told me she was up to something.

"Oh? Okay, then I'll dismember it."

"Go ahead."

Since she had given me her permission, I began dismembering the gizma's legs and torso in my inventory. I wound up with a lot of stuff: gizma carapaces, tough tendons, bug meat, gizma venom glands, and so on and so forth. I checked the crafting menu, and the gizma carapaces did indeed count as animal bones.

"Looks like you're right," I told her.

The tough tendons could also be used in place of the tough bowstring for the improved crossbow. I began to have a much better appreciation for gizmas. They were actually a treasure trove of hard-to-get resources.

"By the way, there's something I've been curious about: how is trade conducted in this village?" I asked.

"Not in a very complex way since we distribute food to everyone as necessary. However, we do barter for luxury food or drink, jewels, weapons, armor, and the like. Meat counts as a luxury in this case."

"I see. And the gizma's strong carapace can be used for a lot of stuff."

"That's right. The right person can turn it into armor, weapons, decorations—there're all kinds of uses for things we use every day as well. Gizma meat is also a luxury food, and its venom glands are valuable ingredients for medicine. The antennae and tendons in its legs can be used to make bowstrings for bows and instruments. We're able to make use of practically every part of it, really. However, we rarely hunt them down on purpose because they're so dangerous."

"Makes sense. By the way, I wound up with a ton of bug meat."

"It's actually pretty tasty."

"Where I come from, we didn't really eat bugs." I had heard that bee larvae and boiled rice grasshoppers in soy sauce and sugar were popular in some regions of Japan, but I had never eaten them myself. Still, depending on how you thought about it, crabs, shrimp, and clams were kinda like bugs? "What does it taste like?"

"It depends on what cut of it you're eating, but it's generally tender and has a light flavor. You can boil it with salt or cook it in oil with galik or pepal with salt."

Galik was pretty obviously just garlic, and pepal was some kind of spice like red pepper seasoning. Based on her description, it sounded more like crab or some kind of crayfish. *I guess I'll try not to immediately hate it without having tried it.*

"However, it doesn't keep for very long. Leave it in your inventory or whatever for the time being," Sylphy warned.

"Will do." I'd wait until tomorrow to try it. "By the way, there's a lot of other things I want to ask you about, but..."

"My family line and such?"

"Wha—!" I really wished she'd stop suddenly leaning in to whisper in my ear. It made me jump every time.

"Are you *sure* you want to ask me that? You might wish you never knew."

"But you're my mistress, whom I care about so dearly. I want to know everything there is to know about you." My eyes darted around the room. She felt so soft, and I smelled something sweet. Maybe it was just the scent of the mead, but I had practically no experience with women coming on to me like this. I was at a loss.

"What an admirable thing to say. However, I have no intentions of telling you. If you really want to know, then you'll have to make me." Sylphy giggled as she started sucking on my neck. Ah, is that what she meant by make her?

Very well. I, Kousuke, am up for the challenge.

"As you may have guessed, I'm related to the Merinard royal family. Actually, let me just spell it out: I'm a direct descendant," Sylphy suddenly said out of the blue after some sparring. She was finally ready to talk after my ardent pampering.

"So you're a princess, then. What's a princess doing here in the Black Forest by herself?"

"It's tradition for members of the royal family to go to the Black Forest once they turn ten years old to be educated by the elves there for the next decade."

"I see."

So she wasn't a hostage. She had mentioned there was trade between the Black Forest and the Kingdom of Merinard; I guessed they must have had that custom so they wouldn't forget they were elves at heart, even if they weren't living in the forest anymore.

"Back then, I had paler skin. My chest was flat as a board, and I was much daintier. I'm sure you'd never be able to imagine it, having only known me as I am now," Sylphy said.

"You're right about that, but I love your body the way it is."

"Mm. Hey, we're having a serious conversation right now, so hands off." She pinched the back of my hand. *Ouch.*

"This is kinda unrelated, but how long do elves live, anyway?"

"We live much longer than humans. I heard we usually live to be about 500 years old on average, though the eldest of the elders is over 700 now."

"Whoa, that's pretty long."

Sylphy had mentioned that the Kingdom of Merinard had become a vassal state of the Holy Kingdom about twenty years ago. Assuming that Sylphy had already been living in the Black Forest at that time, she would have been somewhere between ten and twenty years old. Based on what she just told me, this would mean that Sylphy was somewhere between thirty to forty years old right now. If elves lived to be 500 on average and 700 if they were lucky, that would mean they could live about ten times as long as humans.

So, to calculate Sylphy's age in human years, that would mean she was three to four years old...? Huh? Now I felt like some kind of criminal all of a sudden.

"Why did you get so quiet?" Sylphy demanded.

"Uh, I was just thinking about how elves live such a long time and how old you would be in human years."

Sylphy stared at me in puzzlement and then burst out laughing.

"Aha ha ha ha ha! I suppose if you calculated my age in human years, I'd be a baby! We elves reach maturity around the age of twenty. After that, we stop aging and don't change very much until around the age of 500. From a human's perspective, I guess you could say we stay young for a very long time. You've got no cause for concern there."

"That's a relief." It would be no laughing matter if she really was considered a three- or four-year-old. That went *well* beyond the threshold of what I was cool with.

"However, I am still considered a youngling among elves. Ohw wood Kousuke pwefuh if I wuz eben youngah?"

I burst out laughing at her faux baby talk. There was no way an actual four-year-old could be that stacked.

"I didn't realize you have this kind of playful side," I said.

"I'll have you know an elf's youth is precious. At my age, we're usually still quite playful. We like to go out to the countryside and pick flowers and wild strawberries, and we have fun helping our parents with their work."

"Is that so?"

"It is. But my homeland and my family were taken from me by the Holy Kingdom. I've got to reclaim it and protect my people who fled here. I had to grow up fast, unfortunately."

"And that's why you were hoping to use me, the Fabled Visitor." Sylphy's expression froze at my words. "The Fabled Visitor is supposed to save the elves of the Black Forest during their time of need. You're hoping to use that power to reclaim the Kingdom of Merinard. And that's why you gave me your chastity before telling the elders it was highly possible I was this Fabled Visitor, just in case they decided to take me away."

Sylphy's expression darkened, but she nodded in resignation. "That's right."

"It's okay; I don't mind. I understand where you're coming from." There wasn't much point in me caring—or, more accurately, there weren't any downsides to this situation for me. Sylphy had it harder than me here. Even though she was older than me, she was still at an age where she was considered a child, and she had all of these burdens to bear. "Don't feel like you're indebted to me or anything. If you hadn't found me, I'd most likely be dead right about now. I'm a lucky guy; I get to have this kind of relationship with someone as beautiful as you."

She looked at me with all sorts of emotions playing across her face, so I lightly kissed the tip of her nose and patted her on the head. "I'll do my best so my mistress won't want to get rid of me. I have no idea how I got here, and I have no way to get home. Not that I particularly want to return to my old world, but you took me in when I had nowhere else to go and saved my life. You're stuck with me until I've repaid you. So long as you want me around, at least."

Besides, this was a man's ideal romance: the noble princess of a ruined country was asking me to fight by her side to reclaim her motherland. I would become the leading star in that story by helping her. That was everyone's dream.

Although I was in no way trained to go marching onto the field of battle, I did have unusual special powers. I was just a regular old nobody back in Japan, but here, I might be able to become a hero. *Who doesn't wanna be a hero? That's always been a dream of mine. Whose isn't it, really?*

"Are you sure?" Sylphy asked.

"Yup. I dunno how useful I'll be, but you can still count on me."

"I'd hardly call you useless. That makes me happy to hear, though." Sylphy hugged me tightly, burying her face in my chest as she started sobbing.

Ooooohhhhhh! How adorable are you?! I can't take it! I'm gonna die of cuteness overload!

Ignoring my writhing over how adorable she was, Sylphy continued crying in my chest for a little while before she fell asleep, exhausted. I kept squirming in a most manly way; the sensual feel of her flesh pressed up against me gave rise to evil passions, but at the same time, the desire to protect her and paternal somethings swelled up from the bottom of my heart, so I did not surrender to my carnal desire. I hardly slept a wink that night.

CHARACTERS

アイラ
Ira

CHAPTER 4

The Sudden Beginning of My Survival Life

DAY 5

179

"**G**OOD MORNING," I said to Sylphy the second she opened her eyes.

She gazed sleepily at me for a moment before her face suddenly flushed red. "Forget that."

"Forget what?"

"Never mind, just forget that ever happened." Sylphy hid her face in my chest.

Now, if you asked me, I'd tell you that had the opposite effect, but I decided to leave her be since it was cute. "There's nothing to be ashamed of. We're already like husband and wi—ow, ow, ow!"

Don't bite me! That's not allowed! Not that that part of me has any use, but you're gonna tear it off!

"Then forget what happened," Sylphy commanded.

"Okay, okay. Already forgotten. However, might I offer a suggestion?"

"What?"

"I'll forget during the day, but after the sun sets, I'll remember again. Then, I want you to fawn—ow, ow, ow, ow!"

Stoooop! You're gonna tear it off! Like, seriously, stop already!

"I'll give it some consideration," she said.

"Please do."

She released me.

We cleansed ourselves like we had the previous morning and then discussed our plans for the day over leftovers from dinner (apparently the name for the dish was "keema"), which we wrapped with some chopped vegetables in something like a tortilla. The dish itself didn't have a name; I just thought of it as a clean-the-fridge breakfast burrito.

"So, what are our plans for today?" I asked.

"We're running low on vegetables, so I want to head over to the storehouse and get some more rationed out to us. I'd also like some more mead, so I'll go trade the yakkey for that. If there's anything else we want, let's use those raw gemstones you got yesterday," Sylphy said after swallowing a bite of her burrito. She was back to her usual mood.

"Is there a particular demand for those?"

It wasn't like I had taken a really close look at everyone in the village, but from what I could tell, no one went around wearing flashy accessories. While the elders wore some ornaments, I wouldn't call them flashy.

"Of course there is. Gemstones are catalysts for magic and can be used to make magical tools or spirit gems."

"Ooh, sounds like some fantasy novel nonsense. Can you explain what those things are?"

I had only ever seen Sylphy use that life spirit to heal me and wind magic to blow away the mob and me. It would pay to know the ins and outs of this place's magic system.

"Gems are vessels for magic; you can tell which kind by their color. Red gemstones preside over fire, blue are water and ice, green have the power of wind, and yellow corresponds to earth. Clear gems contain the power of light, while dark ones have the power of shadow. We can use these as catalysts to increase our magical powers," Sylphy told me as she showed me the bangle she wore. It was inlaid with blue, green, and glittery clear stones. "My bangle works as a catalyst for wind, water, and light magic. I can still cast spells without it, but so long as I have it on, I can cast more powerful spells without using as much magic as I would normally."

"Hmm. So it's like an amplifier." I felt a pang of envy; it had to be pretty fun to sling spells around.

"Their power as catalysts can be used in magical tools as well. I'm no artisan, so I don't really know much, but gemstones are necessary for making them."

"I see. And what are spirit gems?"

"A gemstone can also be used to contain spirits. It becomes the spirit's temporary home, so to speak. Spirits are found everywhere in nature, but depending on the location, their specific power may be weaker, or you might not find that specific type at all. For example, you won't find wind or light spirits in a dark cavern with no wind circulation. You also won't find any water spirits in the badlands. You won't be able to use those spirits' magic in those kinds of places. I've got spirits in the gems in my bangle as well."

"As long as you have wind and light spirit gems, you can still use their magic even in a cavern, right?"

"That's right. And it's also possible to use powerful spirit magic in exchange for the spirit gem."

"How epic."

Having to sacrifice something in exchange for a more powerful attack absolutely stoked a man's spirit for adventure. Like the Final Strike skill in a certain famous RPG saga series, for example. Forfeiting all of your skill points for a round in exchange for making a single powerful attack always made fights feel more epic.

"So what you're telling me is that gemstones are strategic materials for elves."

"That's right. An army of a hundred humans is chaff in the wind to an elf with five spirit gems to burn."

"Whoa, that's impressive."

That was nothing to sneeze at. They must've been valuable if they were that powerful. It was a difficult thing to picture. No personal weapon on Earth could do that kind of damage. I doubted even a tank could take out a hundred people in five shots. Naval shelling or aerial bombardment, maybe, but nothing short of that.

"By the way, what actually happens when you use them?" I asked.

"With a fire spirit gem, an arch-fire spirit appears and goes berserk on the enemy lines. The whole area turns into a sea of flame. With a wind spirit gem, an arch-wind spirit summons a tornado or bolt of lightning. Do you want to know what the other kinds of spirits do too?"

"Nah, I get the picture." I had a pretty clear idea of the catastrophic things using them could incur. The other spirit gems were surely no different in terms of strength. "The place outside the Black Forest is the Great Omitt Badlands, right?"

"Yeah, what about it?" Sylphy tilted her head in puzzlement at my sudden question.

"I'm guessing it used to be known as the Omitt Kingdom a long time ago, yeah? Did some spirit gem superweapon do 'em in, or was there some kind of weird spirit uprising that left it the way it is now?"

"I've never heard of such a thing before."

How many days did it take to cross the Omitt Badlands again? How many spirit gems must they have used to turn such a vast region to blasted desert? These elves might actually have been much more powerful than I had even imagined.

"Uh, sorry, I got off-topic. What are we gonna do after we're done getting food and trading?" I asked.

"Let's go introduce you to the refugees. Since I've already told the elders about you, there's no need to hide it anymore. Let's tell them everything about the situation and how you can use your power to build the bulwark."

"All right."

I thought the idea over a bit. I had only told Sylphy about my power thus far because I didn't know why she'd been trying to get closer to me. I might have been raised in a peaceful nation, but I still felt cautious about people who tried to get overly close without revealing why.

But now Sylphy had revealed her goals to me. It all made sense why she suddenly started getting intimate with me. And I was more than willing to help her achieve those goals. It moved me that she was so driven, she'd even offered her chastity to me. Though it was probably more accurate to say that I was starting to fall for her.

Not that I could actually control anything about that. She was beautiful and totally my type. She could be really cute at times too, and I wanted to support her in whatever way I could. Plus, having some kind of big goal made life all the more fulfilling.

"For now, I don't think it's a great idea for my own safety to tell them about my abilities," I said as we took our after-meal tea.

"Hm? What do you mean?" Sylphy looked dumbfounded, as if she thought I expected them to attack me once they knew.

"I doubt they'd do anything to me directly, but you're hoping to reclaim your homeland, right? That would mean you're not just up against monsters; you have human enemies too. I'm sure that from now on, I'll be doing a whole lot of things to help you—often in ways that nobody else possibly could, not to toot my own horn."

"So what you're saying is that you're going to become my weakness?" Sylphy said in a grave tone as she hung her head and rubbed her slender chin. After a moment of thought, she raised her head again and looked straight into my eyes. "I don't care. It just means that we have to stick together all the time. By my side is the safest place you can be."

"Well don't you sound like the hero in some dating sim." Being her biggest weakness made me sound incredibly weak. I was so embarrassed at the thought, I wished I could just disappear.

"I have no idea what that means, but I understand you're complimenting me. C'mon, let's get a move on. We've got a busy day ahead."

"Aye aye, ma'am."

We finished our tea and left her house. We didn't make anything for lunch to bring along. According to Sylphy, we would be eating out today.

"This is the village storehouse," Sylphy told me.

"It's *huge.*"

It stood in a corner of the craftwork sector. I had no idea how many people lived in this village, but it felt like a much bigger storehouse than was actually necessary.

"Apparently it was built back when we first clashed with humans, though I don't really know much about it."

"I see."

If my theory about the Great Omitt Badlands holds, it might've left a hell of a mark on this village, I thought as I followed after Sylphy.

There were a few armed elven guards stationed at the storehouse. Were they there to keep the refugees in check?

"Good morning, Sylphyel. Is that the slave I've heard so much about?" An expressionless man greeted us as we approached. He glanced briefly at me; I didn't feel the same hostility from him as I had from the guard who'd thrown me into the public square.

"That's right. We're here for some rations and to do some trading. We're low on vegetables, so I'd like all of the usual besides dicons," Sylphy said.

"All right, we'll get those prepared for you. What would you like to trade for?"

"I'd like eight casks of mead and eight bags of grainmeal. Also, salt."

"That's quite a big order."

"It's for the refugees." She flicked her gaze toward me. "Take out the yakkey and gems."

"Coming right up!"

I took out the yakkey carcass that we'd gutted and cooled in the river and laid it out on the floor of the storehouse. The fur was still wet, so it made a squelching sound. I also took out a wooden plate and scattered the gems I had mined on it.

The man's eyes widened in surprise at the sight of the raw gemstones.

"I can't believe you've brought so many...and not just that, but a yakkey too... What sorcery did you use to acquire all of this?"

"Hee hee. He's more useful than he looks. So will all this be enough in exchange for what I've asked for?" Sylphy grinned smugly and puffed up her chest with pride. Goodness, my mistress was so cute when she boasted about her slave.

"More than enough. We haven't been getting that many good-quality gems in recently; all of the artisans have been baying at our doorstep."

"Is that so? Then I'd also like to add a good helping of oneel, galik, and pepal to my order."

"Got it." The guards went inside and came back with the bags of grainmeal and big casks. I diligently put them all into my inventory. She was probably planning to treat the refugees.

"All right, let's get going, Kousuke."

"Okay."

The guards saw us off as we made our way to the refugee camp. I was less than thrilled about the prospect; my memory of that morning in the square with them gnawed at me.

The storehouse was fairly close to where the refugees lived. We had to pass through the magic fields, but those took up more height than width, like some kinda multistory parking garage. As we passed by, I kept glancing out of the corner of my eye at them and the bright light they cast. Less than ten minutes later, we arrived at the disorderly camp.

The refugees' homes were built from whatever was at hand. Some looked like they were built out of adobe bricks, others from clapboard, rotting fallen trees, tall thatch, durable cloths—anything and everything that could give shelter from the rain. The fact stood that each and every one was crudely made. It was clear that these houses were only good for sleeping, and just barely at that.

"Yikes," I said.

"We're already at our limits trying to keep them fed. We don't have the materials or tools, so we haven't made any progress at all on building them homes. They were hoping to get their homes built at the same time as the bulwark, but it's been too hard to procure enough materials," Sylphy explained.

The refugees all focused their gazes on Sylphy and me. A lot of them were giving me harsh looks, which was expected. I wasn't sure how to describe how they looked at Sylphy. Was that fear in their eyes? Awe?

"Where are we going?"

"I need to ask their leaders how the discussion with the elders went so I can get an idea of the situation."

We walked past the staring crowd and headed over to a stretch of the camp that stood fairly close to the construction site. I spotted a largish house made of adobe. As we got closer, I started hearing the laughter of children.

"Is this a nursery?" I asked Sylphy.

"It seems so."

All kinds of demi-human children were gathered there: beyond the kids with cat ears, dog ears, and rabbit ears, there was a lizardfolk, a harpy, a lamia, a kid with horns, a kid who looked like an angel, another who looked like a devil, and even a cyclops.

"Aww, kids are so cute," I said.

"Oh? You into them or something?" Sylphy asked dryly.

"No, I was just stating a common opinion."

Kids were unconditionally cute, what with their innocent smiles. *Please don't make such awful assumptions about me.*

The moment the kids spotted me, they began screaming obscenities as they fled into the building as fast as they could.

"It's a human!"

"He's gonna kidnap us!"

"Ruuuuun!"

"Screw humans!"

"Death to humans!"

You can probably gather on your own that it wasn't great for my mood.

"They sure hate you," Sylphy commented.

"It's not my fault! It's everyone else's in this world!" I yelled out, sounding like some kind of pathetic man-child as we approached the building.

As we did, a group of people who had heard the children's shouts approached us. A man covered in scars broke from the group to meet us. He was built like a truck; he walked with a bit of a limp in his right leg, but he still had that old-school "king of the beach" macho vibe. A pair of bull's horns jutted from the sides of his head—maybe he was a minotaur?

"Your Highness," the man said.

"Danan, how many times do I have to tell you to drop the formalities? I don't have the right to be called that anymore."

"I disagree. No matter what you say, you will always be our princess. All those who were there to bear witness to you shrouding yourself in darkness for our sakes feel the same." He kneeled before Sylphy and bowed his head. This must have been the way subjects bowed to royalty here.

Shrouded herself in darkness? What an edgelord thing to say. I had a feeling it had something to do with why Sylphy had darker skin than the other elves, though.

"You're so stubborn. But fine. Anyway, I'm here to talk about what we're going to do about the gizmas. Gather everyone in charge and prepare a place for us to talk."

"It shall be done." The man named Danan stood up and glanced my way for just a moment before walking away. It was such a piercing gaze that I nearly wet myself.

"Mistress, that man scares the bejeezus out of me," I said.

"Before Danan fled to the Black Forest, his wife was assaulted and murdered by a human. He lost his two children crossing the badlands."

"Oh. That's depressing."

That would definitely explain his beef with me. But so long as I had Sylphy backing me up, I would be okay, right? Or would I wind up cut down from behind when called to fight off the gizmas?

"Are you sure it's okay to bring me along? What about your position?" I asked her.

"Good question. I think you'll be fine so long as I can persuade them, but you should probably do as best you can to stay on their good side anyway. I promise that I'll never abandon you; don't you dare forget that."

"I won't. Keep in mind that I'll never abandon you either."

"Hee hee. That makes me happy to hear." An incredibly gentle smile spread across Sylphy's face.

The others who were still here looked astonished. A cyclops woman's eye had opened so wide, it looked like it might pop out; she wasn't alone on that front. It might not have been such a big deal to me, but it looked to be a huge deal to Sylphy's entourage.

"Come, everyone! I've brought firewood and food! I don't know if it'll be enough to bring your bellies to near bursting, but there should be enough to fill everyone's up all the same." Sylphy looked at me and added, "Lend me a hand!" Coming right up, Mistress.

I did as prompted and took the bags of grainmeal and pots of salt out. I placed the pots on the ground, but the grainmeal I dealt with differently.

"Here." I handed one bag after the other to a nearby person.

"Huh?" The person gaped.

"Take this." I also started handing out baskets full of potherbs and other bags to other nearby people too.

"O-okay."

"And this too."

"Wha—?!"

"And this." I turned to Sylphy to ask, "Should I take out the firewood here too?"

"Yeah, go ahead. And the gizma meat as well."

"I can't just put that on the ground, Mistress."

"True. What if you got a kitchen table ready?"

"My mistress has such a fine head on her shoulders." I had nails and wood in my inventory already, so I could craft a table right away. I quickly started making several large wooden tables. "How's this?"

There were several different table designs, but I went with the kind that had a flat tabletop. We'd be able to knead the flour with this. They clattered as I set them out.

"Not bad if you ask me," Sylphy responded.

"Should I put the gizma meat directly on top? Won't it get dirty out here if the wind blows?"

"That's a good point. Think you can make a wall to ward off the wind?"

"I think that'd be a bit too much. Oh, how about I make a wooden box?"

"Aren't we the clever one? Do it."

"Aye aye, ma'am."

I started making several boxes that could be carried in a person's arms. Each individual box didn't require too many components, but making a bunch was a different story. We'd need to cut down some more trees later.

"How's this?" I asked as I took out one of the boxes.

"Looks good to me."

I felt around inside to make sure there were no splinters. It seemed safe to me, so next it was time to stick the meat inside. What in the world did I just pull out of my inventory? Raw crab meat? Shrimp? It was white, semi-translucent, and soft. It reminded me of a huge shrimp.

Sylphy looked into the box as well. "I guess we can't tell what cut of the body it is. It's definitely gizma meat, though."

"Who cares as long as it's edible?"

"True."

I took out the other boxes and started filling them with gizma meat. I wound up with thirteen boxes in all. It probably wasn't all that much if it was to be shared among 300 people, but the grainmeal would have to do to fill their stomachs.

"Now for the firewood," I said as I started laying it out. *How much should I put out? Should I take out most of it but leave some for myself? I guess I'll just see if there's any left over and then use that.*

"How's this?" I asked.

"Hmm, good. What are you all doing? Start cooking. Let the children eat as much as they want," Sylphy commanded, and the people who had just been watching dumbstruck started hurrying around.

They carried the tables and boxes of gizma meat, then brought stones and made an impromptu stove. They cast a water spell on the grainmeal they had taken out of the bags and started kneading it on the tables. People brought out pots and other cooking utensils from their homes. *Ah, pots. It probably would be pretty useful right about now if we had a huge pot or one made of iron. I'll have to make one later if I have enough materials.*

"Your Highness, what is all this?" Danan had returned with what I guessed were the local bigwigs. He was at a loss for words upon seeing how the place had transformed in such a short span. I would've been confused as well to find so much had happened in just ten minutes.

"It'll be a little while before the food is ready. We should talk while we wait," Sylphy said.

"B-but what *is* all this?" he stammered.

"I just wanted to help out. All of this is relevant to the matter at hand. I think we can talk over there. Kousuke, can you make us some chairs?"

"Hmm, I don't have many materials left, but hold on."

Dang it! I should have left some wood for myself. I can make something like stools; they don't take that much. That'd be better than sitting on the ground or standing around, right? As we walked, I quickly whipped them up and placed them slightly apart. I made five of them; I didn't bother making one for myself—I was just Sylphy's slave, after all. It wouldn't make sense if I acted as their equal and sat too.

Danan and the other three gawked at the chairs that appeared out of nowhere.

"Kousuke, there aren't enough chairs," Sylphy said.

"But, Mistress, it wouldn't do for your faithful servant to sit."

"Hmm. Then this is an order: put down a chair for yourself and sit."

"Huh? Well, your wish is my command." I made a stool for myself and sat behind Sylphy at her right hand, far back enough to show I had no intentions of intruding on this conversation.

Danan and the others seemed baffled by our exchange, like they couldn't make heads or tails of our relationship.

"Anyway, I wanted to talk about the gizmas. The elders summoned you to discuss it yesterday, did they not? I'd like to hear what they had to say," Sylphy said.

"Yes, Your Highness. The elders presented us with two options: take refuge deeper in the forest or remain here in the village and help fight. If we choose to stay, they would only be able to accommodate the children behind the walls," Danan answered.

"Tch, those cunning old foxes. I guess that means they have no intention of using the spirit gems, then," Sylphy grumbled.

If they used these powerful spirit gems freely, then they'd easily be able to repel the gizmas. However, Sylphy seemed to think they'd do no such thing.

It was probably more out of logistical concerns than malice. The guy at the storehouse had said it was rare to find so many raw gemstones. I had no idea what an elf's definition of "recently" was; he very well could have meant that they'd been hard up for gems for decades, if not centuries.

Most likely, the elders were more concerned with attacks beyond the gizmas'. They were probably being cautious in case the Holy Kingdom invaded.

Considering the Holy Kingdom was a major nation that split the continent in two, I couldn't imagine what its military forces might be like if they set their sights on the Black Forest. There would be no such thing as being too prepared in that scenario.

It was pretty obvious that Sylphy resented the elders for their decision, but Danan and the others didn't seem too bothered. They knew much more about the warring kingdoms than I did, so that probably had something to do with their passive response. On the contrary, it was more surprising that Sylphy would be so indignant about it.

But I was just an observer. As a slave, it was not my place to question my mistress in public.

"Well, that aside, did they say anything else?" Sylphy asked.

"They mentioned that things might be different if they can get the bulwark built in time."

"Ah. That's what they told us as well. As it turns out, Kousuke here will be the key to getting it built." Sylphy turned to look at me, and everyone else's gazes followed.

Urgh. I didn't feel the same animosity as I had before, but everyone staring at me like that made my skin crawl.

"Allow me to introduce you. This is Kousuke. While he may be my slave, I gave my chastity to him. Therefore, I am this man's mistress and his wife." Sylphy dropped a bomb on them without warning. It seemed she was a big fan of causing confusion and then bending it to her advantage.

"What?!"

"Your Highness?!"

"Calm yourselves. Kousuke is no ordinary human," Sylphy told them.

"It does seem like he has some kind of unusual power," Danan admitted.

"But he is indeed a human, is he not?" asked the taller woman of the two who'd spoken up.

"Yes, he is a human. However, he does not hail from Leece. Kousuke is a Fabled Visitor." Sylphy's declaration was met with silence. I could faintly hear the sounds of the women cooking in the background.

Every single one of their gazes took on a shade of distrust.

Yeah, that's about what I expected! I'd be doing the same thing right about now, were I one of you!

"I understand that that's hard to believe. I didn't believe him either until after I talked a while with him and he showed me the strange powers he possesses."

And then came the barrage of insults from Danan and the others.

"Your Highness, please forgive my insolence, but can you truly be sure that this man is not trying to deceive you?" Danan insisted.

"He looks like a regular human," said the taller woman.

"I don't even sense any magic within him," said the shorter woman.

"Frankly, he doesn't look like he's got much else going for him," said the other man.

I couldn't say any of them were wrong. Especially since I actually was pretty weak! The most I could do was move my body in weird ways!

"I understand why you don't trust Kousuke. However, I ask that you trust in me as I trust him. After you've talked with him and seen his powers for yourselves, I'm certain you'll forget your doubts." Sylphy entreated them earnestly, putting the others in a position where they couldn't protest any longer.

The group began to look me over again; there was a hint of curiosity to their distrust now.

"Let's start with some introductions then. Kousuke?" Sylphy instructed.

"Uh, how much about me should I explain?" I asked.

"Everything," Sylphy said, looking me straight in the eye.

Truthfully, I didn't think it was a good idea, but disobeying her would mean I didn't have faith that she would protect me. Even if I was skeptical, I wouldn't dare betray her.

"Allow me to introduce myself. My name's Kousuke. I doubt you'll believe this, but I'm not from this world. A few days ago, I found myself at the border between the wastelands and the forest. After that, I spent a while trying to eke out a living in the woods; that's where my mistress—Sylphy—found me. It's hard to sum up my abilities, but as long as I have enough of the right materials, I can create lots of things in a short amount of time. I can also carry around a large quantity of items and still have my hands free, and I can move my body in ways that are kinda unnatural. However, I'm a man from a peaceful world. I'm probably weaker physically than your average Joe. And..." I trailed off.

They were looking at me with even more skepticism now, but I didn't let that stop me.

"Sylphy saved my life. She's my guardian, so I am in her debt. In order to repay her, I plan to do whatever I can to help her. That's about all I can say."

I felt like it would've started sounding like a lie if I began repeating myself, so that was about the limit of what I could say. Now it was just a matter of my audience's reaction.

The refugees' mediators stared at me in silence for a time. Were they trying to guess my real motives? That wouldn't be unusual. From their point of view, I was a vile human.

Indeed, I was human through and through. No matter how much I wished to repay Sylphy, I doubted I could happily continue helping out people who looked at me with revulsion every time they saw me. It would probably be difficult for me to stay motivated if the only thing I had to keep me going was my debt to Sylphy. From their side of things, they *had* to accept me to some extent. The reason I begrudged them was because they had surrounded me and nearly tortured me to death on my very first day here. However, I hadn't actually gotten injured, so I could let bygones be bygones if they were willing.

Moreover, my motivation wasn't the only issue. Depending on how things played out, I would end up having to trust them on the field of battle. It would be lethal if they didn't have my back in a moment of desperation. I couldn't hand someone I didn't even trust a crossbow.

The last thing I wanted was to catch a bolt of my own design in the back.

"Very well; we shall trust you for the time being. If the princess says she believes you, then we shall too. However, there shall be swift retribution to be paid if you betray that trust. I, for one, will take my time pulping your carcass long after your head's been parted from your shoulders," Danan said.

I nodded. "I understand." Danan also nodded, wearing a grave expression.

"Now, allow us to introduce ourselves as well. I am Danan. I once served as the commander of the royal guards of the Kingdom of Merinard." Danan clenched his right fist and clapped it to his chest. If I had to guess, it was probably the traditional salute of the Merinard knights.

Danan was a very tall and muscular man. Two thick, sharp horns like a water buffalo's peeked out of his blazing red hair. He was dressed in shabby clothes now, but I was sure he would cut an intimidating figure decked out in full plate. He looked like the kind of person who'd be suited to swinging around a halberd, or some other huge, two-handed instrument of death.

"I guess I'm next, then. My name is Melty. I was a domestic affairs officer. I am pleased to make your acquaintance," said the woman with curly horns like a sheep's as she slightly bowed her head. She seemed young, but she carried herself with an intellectual air. I thought her looks made her quite beautiful, despite her untidy hair and attire. She seemed the type who'd think no one liked her but actually had lots of secret admirers.

She also had a chest that rivaled Sylphy's. It was hard not to notice. I had only glanced at it the once, but it earned me a cold glare from her.

I have heard that women are quite sensitive to such furtive glances. I apologize. It's just my nature as a man. Please forgive me.

"Then I'm next. I'm Ira. I was a member of the Merinard Order of Mages," the woman named Ira said quietly as she looked down. She was wearing a cowl, probably to hide her face—or rather, her eye. She had it pulled down low, so I couldn't really tell what color her hair was, but she was rather unique. She was a cyclops girl, of sorts.

Ira's eye was so big, it took up about half her face. Her mannerisms were cute, so I kinda wanted to take a peek beneath the hood, but I kept myself in check.

The last to introduce himself was a beastfolk with the face of a fox. Like, his whole face looked like a fox's. He looked much more like a beast than the others. "I'm Cuvi. I don't have fancy titles like the others, but I'm nimble. I guess I'm about as strong as your average beastfolk. I think it's better to be quick-witted anyway."

He was lanky and didn't look like he'd be a strong fighter, but I bought the whole "nimble" thing. He wasn't a lean, mean machine exactly, but he looked toned. I had a feeling I'd get along with him.

"Now that introductions are over with, let's move on. As mentioned before, our fates are in your hands, Kousuke," Sylphy said.

"You said that you can create lots of things? What kind of things, exactly?" Melty asked.

"It'd be easier to just show you rather than try to explain. Follow me." Sylphy immediately stood up and started walking away.

The leaders exchanged glances and then looked at me.

"I agree with Sylphy. It's easier for you to take a look and judge for yourselves," I said.

"What are you all dilly-dallying for?! C'mon!" Sylphy yelled up ahead.

I exchanged a look with the four again and stood up. Ira was the only one who wouldn't look at me. Too bad.

"This place good enough?" Sylphy asked.

"Hmm, yeah. I think so," I answered.

There was hardly anyone around in the construction site. They had probably all gone for food. I was feeling a bit hungry myself, but we had a job to do.

"Your Highness, does his power to make things have something to do with this area?" Danan asked.

"Just watch." Sylphy grinned. Now that I knew her a bit better, I could tell she was imagining the look of shock on all of their faces.

"Is it okay if I demolish some of this?" I asked Sylphy.

"Sure, do whatever you want."

"Aye aye, ma'am." I took my pickaxe out of my inventory.

I was planning to level the ground where there was an unfinished wall already. My building blocks were a cubic meter each. I placed my blocks on a flat surface to make sure there weren't any holes in the wall I built.

"You're supposed to dig down about a meter to make a foundation," I grumbled as I swung my pickaxe, destroying part of the bulwark that had already been built.

Nice, adobe got added to my item tab when I destroyed these. I might be able to reuse them.

"Wh-what on Leece?!" Danan exclaimed.

"The bulwark is disappearing whenever he hits it with his pickaxe?" Melty was bewildered.

"It doesn't look like he's using magic," Ira noted.

"I've got no clue what the heck is goin' on, but this is awesome!" Cuvi said.

Once I was done leveling the ground, it was time to start placing brick blocks. The current bulwark appeared to be about two meters thick and 2.5 meters tall, but it had an intricate shape at the top. I figured I'd start by making a wall that was two meters thick and two meters tall.

I made a ton of brick blocks while I was working on my cabin yesterday, so I probably had enough.

"There, there, there, there, there."

With a rhythmic *thunk*-ing sound, I piled the brick blocks into a wall. The building was simple enough work; in less than five minutes, I made a wall that was thirty meters long, two meters thick, and two meters tall.

"I still have some materials left, so I can still build more, but do you see what I'm capable of now?" I asked.

"I'm sure they do, but it's not tall enough," Sylphy said.

"I know, but I'd have to make half blocks for the topmost line, and it doesn't have an even shape. I was planning to do that all at once after I took a look at how the others were made."

"I see. That sounds reasonable enough. But I'm guessing they won't be convinced just by looking at it. Why don't you all go ahead and try touching it?" At Sylphy's urging, the beastfolk with us walked up to the brick wall and started rubbing and pushing it.

"Highness, would it be okay if I kick it?" Cuvi asked.

"This is supposed to be able to withstand the gizmas. It'd be a huge problem if it came apart from a kick. Kick it as hard as you can. Try to break it," Sylphy said.

"Will do!" Cuvi started roughly kicking at the wall. Danan followed his lead and pushed it very hard, like some kind of sumo wrestler's thrust. Melty didn't do anything, while Ira just stared at the wall with her big eye.

"In mere minutes, he was able to make a wall that would normally take two weeks to construct... He does indeed appear to possess some kind of power, just like Her Highness said." Melty folded her arms and nodded in admiration.

"You can't make something from nothing. It's not logical." Ira shook her head and focused her eye on me. I felt like I might be sucked in by it. "What trickery is this? You didn't use magic to achieve this. It's almost like the wall had always been there to begin with; it goes against the natural ways of this world. If this isn't some kind of trickery, then it must be a miracle of the gods or the work of some demon."

"I have no idea what the laws behind this power are myself. I completely agree that it seems like some kind of trick. This power completely ignores the law of conservation of mass and other similar rules of the world," I replied.

"It's illogical." Ira took a step toward me.

"I know."

"I demand that you explain this to me. Thoroughly." She came even closer, and I felt like a scarecrow pinned under a crow's gaze.

I leaned away from her under the pressure of her glare. Up until now, she had seemed so shy, yet here she was getting all up in my grill.

"Sylphy?" I squeaked.

"Hee hee. Explain as best as you can. Trust me, Ira will keep hounding you until she's satisfied. Maybe I'll test the durability of this wall too."

"What?"

"Hurry up and start talking." Ira was already as close as she could get. She was looking straight up at me now. Her small hands seized my collar. She clearly had no intention of letting me wriggle out of this.

"Okay, fine, take it easy. Let's sit down and talk." I took out some logs I had yet to start crafting with and put those on the ground in place of chairs. I also put one down for Melty. "Where to begin...?"

With that, I started telling her how my crafting powers worked.

"That's outrageous, not to mention illogical! Your input simply does not equal the weight of your output. And I don't understand how you manage to produce these perplexing *containers*..." Ira complained when I showed her the plastic water bottle with 1.5 liters of drinking water that I had crafted from one liter of water inside of a wooden flask.

I nodded deeply. "I totally get where you're coming from."

"So you're breaking the rules of the world with this inventory of yours?"

"No, I'm not. I actually made this using a bonfire."

"But you can't just turn water in a wooden flask into water that's safe to drink using a bonfire. You need a vessel for boiling the water first. If you put a wooden flask into a fire, the wood would just burn and the contents would spill out."

"Yeah, you're right. But that's what I did."

"That's simply ridiculous, to say nothing of this so-called inventory of yours. Freezing time for things you put in there just doesn't make sense. In order to make that happen with magic, you'd need a spell powerful enough to wipe half of the Kingdom of Merinard off the map."

"It's fine if you ask me, Ira. There's no need to make a big fuss of the fact that he's able to increase quantities of things. Through him, we can turn regular water into drinking water that'll keep for a long time, and we get 50 percent more of it. I think that's wonderful." Unlike Ira, Melty was incredibly receptive to all of this. As the person who had to manage what little supplies they had day in and day out, she embraced my illogical crafting powers. When she turned her glittering eyes on me, I felt my stomach drop with dismay. "You can make food using this crafting power of yours, right?"

"Uh, yeah, though I haven't tested it too much."

"Oh, but we must—we *must* test this out at once. It would be a godsend if you could increase the amount of food like you do with water. Come, we have to get to the bottom of this right away!"

"I suppose it might help me figure out the logic to this," Ira added.

And so the two of them took an arm each and started dragging me away.

"Help! Heeelp! Mistress, help meee! I'm being kidnapped!" I cried.

Sylphy laughed as she watched. "Ha ha ha! Looks like you've made some new friends."

"Wow, look at you, buddy. So popular with the ladies. Gotta say, I'm veeery jealous," Cuvi said in a monotone as he laughed right along with her.

Meanwhile, Danan was too busy inspecting the wall to notice what was happening.

Sylphy, you liar! So much for promising that you'd protect me!

"You can increase the kinds of things you can do if you get more tools, yes? Then let's put every single kind of cookware and utensil into your inventory," Melty said.

"Based on what he's told us, it's more efficient the closer we get to the raw ingredients. If we have him mill the grain, there's the possibility that he'll wind up with 50 percent more grainmeal than usual," Ira pointed out.

"That would be splendid. Let's have him try it out at once."

It turned out that Ira's hypothesis was right. They kept me hostage as their machine for milling grainmeal for nearly a whole hour. Of course, I didn't get lunch. I was starving...

"This is gizma meat?" It had a tender texture and was slightly sweet. The smell of galik it had been fried with beckoned my appetite. It was moderately salted, which really brought out the flavor, and the thin bread went well with it. It tasted like garlic shrimp. I guessed they'd call it galik gizma here, though.

I sunk my teeth into the sauteed oneel—the purple onion-like vegetables—and galik gizma sandwich. It was delicious.

"What do you think? Pretty good, right?" Sylphy asked.

"Yeah, this is great. Kinda wish I didn't know where the meat came from, though."

Now that I had been released from my milling duties, I was having a late lunch with Sylphy, Cuvi, and Ira.

Danan had already eaten and had gone out on patrol. Melty had decided to skip lunch, saying she needed to come up with a plan for how to distribute all of the extra grainmeal they now had. *Don't come crying to me if you work yourself to starvation.*

"What? You don't like gizmas? Not that there's anything to like about 'em." Cuvi had finished eating a while ago; he only stuck around because he wanted to chat with us. I liked his friendly demeanor.

"Where I come from, we don't really eat bugs," I said. "Never mind that we don't have giant bugs like gizmas either. I mean, we don't have monsters, period."

"No monsters?" Ira balked. "Impossible. So long as magic exists in the world, there are monsters."

"We don't actually have magic there either."

"That's hard to believe. Creatures with no magic whatsoever simply do not exist."

"I'm sitting here with you."

"Then your very existence flies in the face of reason."

"Ouch."

Ira stared at me reproachfully as she munched on her sandwich with her tiny mouth. She seemed so shy at first, yet now I didn't sense any reservations from her. Why the heck had she acted so demure at first, then? I figured I should ask so I could put my curiosity to rest.

"I don't mean this in a weird way or anything, but why did you warm up to me so suddenly? At first you wouldn't even look me in the eye," I said to Ira.

Her expression froze, and she pulled her hat down over her face. Whoops, the shy version of her was back. Maybe I shouldn't have asked after all.

"Humans hate one-eyed folk like me. We're ugly."

"Is that so? Well, it doesn't bother me or anything. I never thought you were ugly."

Ira peered up at me, as if she was trying to parse what I really meant. I looked straight back at her. She was right that she looked quite different from humans, but in Japan, she'd be considered a monster girl and probably turned into a cute mascot character of some sort. I actually liked those kinds of characters quite a lot, so her appearance didn't bother me in the least.

"If you say so." Ira stopped acting shy again, and I was glad for it.

"Aren't you two getting *chummy*," Sylphy commented.

"Huh? I wouldn't say that. Besides, it only makes sense that we become friends, since we're going to be working together to support you," I said.

"Oh, yeah?" I'd tried to smooth things over, but there was an icy touch to Sylphy's gaze. Was she jealous?

Could it truly be? My mistress was just so adorable sometimes.

"No worries, Mistress, I only have eyes for yooourgh?!" I went to hug her, but she got me right in the stomach. I couldn't breathe.

"No getting handsy while the sun's still up, you mongrel."

Cuvi grinned as he watched my suffering. "Heh heh heh. What a cute couple you are."

Can't you see how much pain I'm in, you bastard?! I can't breathe!

"Your Highness, what shall our next move be?" Ira asked.

"Hmm. First we need to make the most use we can of Kousuke's power and get the bulwark finished. For that, we need clay," Sylphy told her.

"Clay? Getting enough should be no problem—it's what we use for the adobe bricks," Cuvi said.

"Also, I believe adobe bricks can be reused as clay to some extent if we add water," Ira chimed in.

"Right. I think the only other thing we needed was fuel, right, Kousuke?" Sylphy asked me.

Coughing, I tried as hard as I could to respond between gasps for breath. "Y-yes, ma'am." I wished she'd be a bit gentler with me.

"Then we'll go collect some."

"But, Princess, we've collected most of the firewood around the village already," Cuvi pointed out.

"Don't worry. Kousuke's got that handled too."

Ira glared at me, uncomprehending. "This doesn't make any sense."

"Look, I thought the same at first too. I mean, how in the world? It's not fair, is it?" I admitted.

"What are we even supposed to say to that?" Wearing an astonished look on his face, Cuvi poked at the log that had fallen on the ground with the tip of his toe.

"All you do is whittle the trunk down a little, and then trees fall. Even the bent ones become straight, and it's not green wood—somehow, it becomes dried wood. This is even more nonsensical than you creating more water out of nothing," Ira insisted.

"This means you can make as much firewood and wood as you want. You could make a ton of money with this," Cuvi said.

"Like I said before: our fates are in Kousuke's hands." Sylphy grinned triumphantly. I was glad to see she was back in a good mood. "I can already imagine the show Melty's going to make of it once she gets a load of this."

"Me too," Cuvi agreed. "Next, she's gonna make you chop down a billion trees. I bet she'll make him cut down the whole forest."

"Ha ha! I'm sure she wouldn't make me go *that* far. Right?" I asked.

Hey, why won't anyone look at me? Hello?

"Keep this a secret from Melty. Do whatever you must to hide it. Got it?" I pleaded.

"She shall be dealt with appropriately," Ira said.

"I shall give it serious consideration," Cuvi told me.

"Ugh, thanks but no thanks for your vague answers!" I could tell my fate was sealed. I supposed at this point I was better off getting ahead of my inevitable quota. "Sylphy, I'm going to chop down a bunch of trees now. You keep marking the ones to cut down."

"Got it. Ira, Cuvi, you two go procure the clay. We've got things handled here."

"True, I'm sure you'll be able to take care of whatever might show up," Cuvi said.

"Your Highness, I want to figure out his power. Cuvi should be enough for procuring the clay," Ira insisted.

"Hmm, I suppose you're right. I'm curious about Kousuke's power too. Cuvi?"

"All right, I'm on it. Try not to strain yourself as much as possible, Kousuke," Cuvi said before dashing off like the wind. He had said that he was pretty average as far as strength goes, but given how fast he could run, he seemed pretty capable to me.

It was nearly sunset, and very little had happened that was worth mentioning. I was pretty darn sick of trees, though. I asked Sylphy if I had cut down too many.

"If the gizmas make it this far, then they're just going to knock down all of the trees in their path anyway. I think it's better for us to thin them out and decrease the number that'll get knocked down. They'd just leave a big mess for us to clean up otherwise." Her logic made sense. It sounded like backbreaking labor to clean up a forest full of fallen trees both figuratively and physically.

Sylphy turned to Ira. "Hey, it's time to make our way back to the village."

"Mm, okay." Ira was straddling a log I'd chopped down while she watched me closely. She stood up and dusted herself off.

"Did you figure anything out?"

"Only that I have no idea how he made this log."

"What's that supposed to mean?"

"This log is abnormal. No matter what part of it I cut to investigate, the grain and moisture are bewilderingly uniform."

"That does indeed sound abnormal. However, it's perfect for our purposes."

While Ira was telling the truth, even an amateur like me could tell that it was an ideal raw material.

"It's almost like the work of a god. I simply cannot comprehend it. There isn't any trace of magic within this hatchet—yet strange things happen when Kousuke uses it. It defies explanation." Ira held out my hatchet; I took it back without comment.

Today I had actually been using my steel axe instead of that hatchet, but Ira had insisted I use it as part of her study. So, after showing her that using the hatchet resulted in the same results as the steel axe, I handed it over to her. Not that it helped her solve anything.

"In conclusion, I've got some special power that nobody understands but only I can use," I said.

"It's so far afield from basic principles of cause and effect that I feel like I'm going to lose my mind," Ira muttered.

"Mistress, this lady frightens me."

"Ira is...a dyed-in-the-wool natural philosopher. She can't stand it when there's something she can't understand. Whip-smart and magically devastating too," Sylphy said as she averted her eyes.

Ah. I got what she was getting at. What she meant was that Ira was one of those people obsessed with research, and I was her next target. Surely Ira wouldn't demand to dissect me, right? Right?! Of course not. Right?

"I suppose I'll have to dissect—"

"What?! Don't say such an alarming thing in such a low voice like that! Mistress! This lady scares me! Help!" I cried.

"Ha ha ha. That's just her way of breaking the tension," Sylphy assured me.

"Yes, I was just kidding. Not even I'm that barbaric. I'd never dissect a *living* human," Ira said.

"What I'm hearing is that when I die, you won't even hesitate to dissect me. Meaning you're not gonna kill me. That work for you?"

There was a slight pause. "Yes."

Why did you hesitate? Hey, don't look away. Look me in the eye so I know you're being honest.

I kept as much distance from Ira as possible as we made our way back to the village. When we arrived, there was a hill of heaped-up dirt waiting for me.

No, it's time to stop trying to ignore reality. This is actually a mountain of clay.

I was so exhausted that I was barely standing when I heard Cuvi's voice. "Yo, looks like you managed to wear yourself out," he said, astonished.

"Say it ain't so, Bernie!"

"Who the heck is Bernie? I'm Cuvi, remember?"

Life in a world where no one appreciates your mecha anime deep cuts was a grim fate indeed.

But more deserving of my attention was this mountain of clay. If I started digging it up with my shovel now to put it all in my inventory, I was certain to end up eating dinner pretty late. I was already pretty hungry from cutting down trees all afternoon, so I really wanted to avoid that.

"Sylphy, I'm not going to be able to work very well after it gets dark. Let's leave this for tomorrow," I pleaded, trembling.

"Of course. While getting all of this ready may be urgent, and I may be your mistress, I'm no tyrant." Sylphy smirked at the sight of me. "I ordered Danan to go scouting. If the gizmas are going to close in on us tomorrow, then I'd have to make you work all night, but luckily, the situation doesn't seem so dire at the moment. Though I *do* think we should try to get things ready as fast as we can."

"You're such a kind and understanding mistress."

"I'll have you collect clay tomorrow too. Today, you need only focus on making fuel in my backyard."

"Got it." If all I was going to do was make charcoal in the

furnace, then I just had to throw in the wood and leave it overnight to craft on its own. Easy-peasy.

Sylphy went over to speak to the people near the hill of clay, took a bundle of something from a woman who was passing by, and then came back over to me.

"What's that?" I asked her.

"Something for dinner, apparently. They even made some for you too."

"Huh? Does this mean they're starting to accept me a little?"

"I guess it's a good thing we made you mill the grain earlier."

"Please don't remind me."

That whole affair had been grueling. I'd had to mill the corn-like grains for an eternity. Huh? You wanna know why that was necessary when I could've just crafted it? Well, I'd considered doing as much myself. However, Ira commanded me to do so, and it turned out that using the quern myself rapidly reduced the amount of time it took to craft. I wished I hadn't accidentally let that fact slip.

Melty's desire for me to make as much grainmeal as possible combined with Ira's desire to discover the secrets behind my powers wound up making a machine of me—a set of arms to turn the quern, driven by a hollow heart. All of the refugees looked at me like some kind of pitiful slave. *Hey, they're not wrong! Ha ha ha ha ha!*

"Anyway, let's go rest at home. We've got some things to talk about too, don't we?" Sylphy said.

"Yeah."

Now that we had a clear idea of what we were going to do about the bulwark, we had to discuss what we were going to do about our vital counterattack. How many of the refugees could carry weapons? How many arrows would we need? Food? Water? Would the elves give us their support? There were just so many things we had to discuss. We had no time for rest.

"I'm exhausted!" I sat down on the rattan couch the second we arrived home.

"Now, now, don't be so lazy. Though I suppose you *did* work pretty hard today." What a great mistress Sylphy was to recognize my hard work even while she chided me.

"I'm hungry too."

"Yeah, yeah." Sylphy sat down next to me and handed me the bundle she was carrying.

The bundle was heavy and wrapped in a giant leaf. I unfolded the leaf and found the thin bread I had gotten accustomed to seeing. It was still slightly warm to the touch.

"Bread, I see."

"So it seems, but there might be something inside of it, considering the heft."

"I think you're right, now that you mention it."

Sylphy quickly took a bite out of one, and I did the same.

"Mmm, it's sweet and sour," I said.

"Yeah. I think this is made from boiled fruit and honey. I believe this one is forest apple."

"Ah, so it's got apple jam filling." Some might consider this an odd choice for dinner, but the bread itself was heavy and filling. Personally, I would have preferred meat, but meat was considered a luxury here by default. The refugees probably had even less access to it.

"What should we discuss first?" I asked.

We had some tea Sylphy brewed before I decided to broach the topic. It was becoming routine for us to chat after dinner.

"Hmm. Well, do you think you'll be able to get along with the four of them?"

"I'm sure that Melty has grasped just how useful my powers are, and Ira... Well, we'll be okay as long as she doesn't lose interest in my powers. I dunno about Cuvi. He seems like a friendly enough guy, but I can't tell what he's thinking at all. Danan, it's hard to say. I think we'll be able to get along provided he's faithful to you."

"That was what I was thinking too. As for Cuvi, that's just his nature. I'm not really sure where he's from, but I heard that he got along pretty well with humans back when he lived in Merinard. He probably holds the least animosity toward humans out of everyone."

"I hope you're right about that. This is a tangent, but I've been wondering—should we give crossbows to everyone? They're really powerful. It would be bad if someone with a bone to pick with either of us decided to use us as target practice. It might be better to only give them to those you trust."

"I'm not saying you're wrong, but do you mean to say that you don't trust them?"

"Those guys planned on stringing me up in public once already. They don't look at me with the same hostility as before, but they've shown their true faces before. There's no way they're suddenly okay with me after the little I've done in the brief time I've been here. I guess the only thing I can do is keep talking to them so that they come to accept me."

"You mean by acting like a fool in front of them like you did today?"

I shrugged. I had indeed played the pitiful yet comical slave today, but I had to wonder how much that actually helped. "For now, all we can do is let them push me around and work me hard, or I'll have to keep impressing them with my powers. I'll keep making more crossbows, but I'll leave it up to you how many to hand out."

"That's a serious responsibility." Sylphy wore one of her rare rueful smiles. She was the one in a position to lead the citizens of Merinard, and she was my mistress. I felt bad for pushing this responsibility on her, but I had to do it.

"I'll do everything I can. I'll try to get at least one of them on my side."

"Please do. I'll handle everything else to the best of my ability."

After our discussion, I headed out to the backyard to start mass-producing charcoal in my simple furnace. At the same time, I queued lots of mechanical parts and iron arrowheads to craft in my workbench.

I was going to use up most of the iron ingots I had on hand, but it was probably best if I made all of the materials for the crossbows and bolts as soon as possible, especially since it could all be crafted while I slept. However, I was a bit wary about the possibility of leaving the simple furnace running and causing a fire.

"All things considered, your power is awfully convenient. It works all on its own so long as you tell it what to do ahead of time."

"Yeah, that's for sure. And I'm glad for it, but... Oh yeah." I suddenly remembered something as I looked at the furnace.

Simple Furnace Upgrade––: Animal Hide × 5, Brick × 50, Whetstone × 3, Mechanical Parts × 10

"I totally forgot—I can upgrade the furnace. Sylphy, is it okay if I use some of my materials to try upgrading it?"

"What do you mean by 'upgrade'?"

"Hmm. Like, tinkering with it so it's better than before. I *assume* it'll shorten the time it takes to make an item, let me make more than one thing at a time, and probably open up some new options in terms of what I can make."

"Oho. Yeah, go for it."

"'Kay."

I canceled all of the stuff I had queued to craft for now and disassembled some of my brick blocks into their component bricks. The workbench was busy crafting the mechanical parts, and I already had the whetstones in my inventory. I could upgrade it right away.

"Okay, here we go." I had all of the materials, so I selected upgrade. The simple furnace took on an unnatural glow. "Whoa! Why's it so bright?!"

"What's going on?!"

After the light faded, my shabby simple furnace had been upgraded to an impressive facility for smithing. The furnace for smelting metals itself was now two sizes bigger than before, and there was also a separate furnace for heating and treating metals. The anvil was also a size bigger now, and it had a sturdy-looking bench for treating sheet metals, along with a pedal-driven grinder.

"This is much fancier than before," Sylphy commented.

"Color me surprised. I wonder what kind of functions it has now." I took a look and, unsurprisingly, it could make all of the things the simple furnace could. I could also make steel plate springs now, though they took a long time to craft. I could even craft things like larger blades and armor.

"What does 'larger blades and armor' entail?" Sylphy asked.

"With the simple furnace, I could only make small things like knives and axes, but now there're all sorts of swords and spears, along with armor made of leather and metal. Should I try making something?"

"No, iron is too precious. It'd be best if we picked an item we know we'll use instead of something at random. Danan's proficient with poleaxes and such. Can you make something like that?"

"I'll look through my options." I picked over the list of weapons, and a halberd was the only thing that matched that description. There was a weapon called a battle axe, but it was a bit different from what Sylphy had described. Something like a bardiche better suited a guy his size.

Bardiches are big axes specialized for slashing attacks, but they can also pierce. Their shape typically resembles a crescent moon or half-moon. Some people say that they're so powerful that they can slice a person in two.

As I thought that, bardiche was added to the list of things I could craft.

"Huh?!"

"What's wrong, Kousuke?"

"I just thought about a weapon that wasn't on the list, and then it popped up in there."

"You increased the list of things you can make just by thinking about it?"

"That's what it seems like?"

"Even for you, that defies belief."

"Right there with ya. How curious."

My power makes even less sense than before, although it's a bit late to question the logic of it all. Maybe I unlocked an achievement that gave me a new feature? I'll have to take a look later.

Anyway, I decided to go ahead and craft the bardiche since it had been added and all.

As for new features... I can repair now? A Repair tab had been added to my smithing station. Curious, I selected it; a list of repairable equipment was displayed.

Rusted Sword → Iron Sword

Rusted Spear → Iron Spear

Rusted Dagger → Iron Dagger

Rusted Hatchet → Iron Hatchet

Rusted Shield → Iron Shield

Rusted Armor → Iron Armor

Rusted Leggings → Iron Leggings

Rusted Gauntlets → Iron Gauntlets

Cursed Rusted Sword → Cursed Iron Sword *You shall be cursed!

Cursed Rusted Spear → Cursed Iron Spear *You shall be cursed!

Cursed Rusted Helmet → Cursed Iron Helmet *You shall be cursed!

Cursed Rusted Armor → Cursed Iron Helmet *You shall be cursed!

I can make all of the rotted, rusty weapons usable again? Whoa, how rad!

"Yeah, right! What does it mean by I'll be cursed?!" I suddenly cried out.

"Wh-why are you shouting?" Sylphy flinched in surprise. *Sorry about that.*

"You remember all the spoils of war you had in your shed? Well, I can use my new smithing station to repair them all—but there's a warning saying I'll be cursed if I touch up the cursed stuff."

"Ah... Well, don't bother with those. You know what they say—the sleeping spirit you do not approach shall not curse you, and all that. Nothing good can come of it."

"Will do. I'll try repairing one of the regular ones."

Repairs took fuel and a small quantity of iron, so I went ahead and queued them all to be repaired after the bardiche was done. I'd be cursed? Thanks, but no thanks. I wouldn't go anywhere near those.

"If we're not going to be giving everyone crossbows, then they'll need some other kind of weapon, right? Should I make spears?" I asked.

"When the time comes. Although, if you're going to be making a lot of stuff, will we need to collect more iron?"

"Yeah." Since I'd made a pickaxe, I was pretty certain I'd be able to collect more now. However, I didn't feel very motivated about the prospect when I thought about having to wade in that icy river again. "To be honest, I'm pretty much out of animal hides too." Now that I was out, I'd need her to get some more wild game for me.

"Then we'll just have to go hunting again. Do you need them immediately?"

"Nah, no rush." I wasn't planning to use them right away, but we'd need them to make armor. Oh, but I did need them to upgrade my workbench. I needed leather straps too; maybe Sylphy had some. "Do you have any leather straps? I need two of them."

"I do, in fact."

"Could you spare 'em? I need them to upgrade the workbench."

"Hmm. Very well."

I watched Sylphy head back into the house while I added charcoal to the smithing station's crafting queue again. Looking closer at my crafting recipes, I could even make glass now.

Glass... I bet I'll need glass containers for more chemical-related crafting. Looks like I just need sand. I got lots of that from when I sifted out the iron sand I collected at the river. I'll go ahead and make some glass.

"I'm back," Sylphy said.

"Thanks a bunch." I went into my work cabin and rechecked the upgrade materials for the workbench.

Workbench Upgrade——: Mechanical Parts × 10, Steel Plate Spring × 5,
    Leather Strap × 2

I had the mechanical parts and leather straps covered, so now I just had to make the steel plate springs. I went back outside to check the progress of my queue. *Oh, the bardiche is ready. I'll go ahead and queue the steel plate springs to craft after the weapons.*

"Danan's weapon is finished," I announced.

"Oh? Let me see."

I took it out of my inventory. *Whoa, this thing's heavy.*

"This has an unusual shape, but it seems quite sharp," Sylphy remarked.

"It's called a bardiche. You're supposed to use the blade's

weight to help drive that edge. I've heard these can bisect a guy in the right hands, but I don't know if that's true."

"Wielded by a master like Danan, it's possible," Sylphy said as she gave it a few test swings in an open spot in the yard. She seemed rather proficient with it herself. "This is a bit too heavy for me, though. I could handle it for short bursts, but it would just wear me out if I had to swing it for a long time."

"I see. I bet something like a scimitar would be good for you."

"Oh? What kind of weapon is that?"

"It's a curved saber." I took a wooden stick out of my inventory to draw a rough sketch of a scimitar. I was pretty proud of it. "It has an arch around this part of the blade. It's for slashing."

"Hmm, it seems like a graceful weapon, but it doesn't sound like it would be suitable for soldiers going up against a gizma or someone wearing iron armor."

"Ah, you're probably right. Against enemies like that, you need a weapon that's more specialized for piercing and striking rather than slashing. If you had a scimitar in that sort of matchup, you'd probably have to aim for vulnerable gaps, like the neck or a joint."

"Hmm. Regardless, it's one you think would be suited for me. I'd like to try it out, so please make one for me when you get the chance."

"Will do."

And so we spent our remaining daylight discussing weaponry in this fashion while I kept an eye on how things were progressing in the smithing station. I learned that Sylphy preferred shorter blades like knives, machetes, and shortswords. Maybe I would make a kukri for her later. She was sure to like it.

CHARACTERS

メルティ
Melty

CHAPTER 5
The Sudden Beginning of My Survival Life

DAY 6

AFTER A LONG NIGHT, a new day dawned. Since I was so tired, Sylphy and I had traded off on offense and defense that evening. Three nights in a row was a bit much. It was a treat to see her so eager!

Sylphy's stamina couldn't be beat. I was thoroughly impressed. Now that she had the hang of things, it was all but impossible to resist her. It was truly a delightful experience.

"Let's work hard to get things done today," Sylphy said. Her skin glistened.

"Yes, ma'am."

For breakfast, we had a heavy meal of roast labbit, stir-fried labbit giblets, and thin bread. She must have been famished from all the exercise.

Everything I queued to craft last night was finished, so I put the smithing station and workbench back into my inventory. I was going to use the smithing station for making bricks, and I might need the workbench for something.

Just as we had yesterday, we passed through the craftsmen's quarter and the refugee camp to the construction site. Our destination was the hill of clay from yesterday.

"Is it just me, or did it get bigger?" I asked.

"It's probably because they added water to turn the dry adobe back into clay," Sylphy answered.

"I see."

I had no idea how adobe was made, but if it wasn't made by firing clay, then it made sense for it to break back down into clay with enough moisture. I was pretty sure I had seen how it was made once on TV—it was made of horse dung or cow manure mixed with straw.

Danan greeted us as we arrived. "Good morning, Your Highness."

"Good morning," echoed other voices.

The refugee mediators and some other people—who I gathered were workers—had already assembled along with them and gotten started.

"Mm-hmm. Let's work hard today to get things done," Sylphy told them.

"Good morning!" I gave my own cheerful greeting after Sylphy's. Positive first impressions are essential, after all. Even the *Kojiki*, Japan's oldest surviving historical record, said so.

"Kousuke, you repaired some weapons yesterday, yes? Take them out," Sylphy commanded.

"Yes, ma'am."

I took out the repaired weapons one after the other. There were four iron swords, three iron spears, six iron daggers, two iron hatchets, and two iron shields. I took the shields out first, laid them on the ground, and stacked the rest on top.

"Danan, these are all my spoils of war that I've had in storage. I asked Kousuke to repair them. Pass them out to those who can fight and use them for defense and hunting."

"Yes, Your Highness!"

"Also, I had him make a weapon for you." Sylphy signaled to me. "Kousuke?"

"Coming right up." I took the steel bardiche out of my inventory and handed it over to Sylphy.

"I took a look at it already; it's of fine quality. Protect everyone with this." Sylphy passed the bardiche to Danan.

Bardiche in hand, Danan examined the blade closely and then swung it a couple of times to check its balance. He then gave a big nod. "This is an incredible weapon. With this, I should be able to cut through gizmas like butter."

"I bet. Kousuke has some other tricks up his sleeve that are sure to surprise you."

"I shall be looking forward to seeing them." Danan gave a slight smile.

With his physique and sternness, he reminded me of a bandit chief or something like that. However, I had a feeling that if I voiced that comparison, he'd split me down the middle, so I kept quiet.

"May I ask how this man came to acquire such a fine weapon?" Danan looked at Sylphy with a questioning gaze.

Of course he would ask that, considering how fast these weapons had turned up. Sylphy and I had only known each other for four days now, and I had only met Danan just yesterday.

Normally, a bardiche should've taken much longer than a night to make—maybe even longer than three days. I'd assume as much in his position.

"Ira's right—Kousuke's power really does defy all logic. I understand if you don't believe it, but it's true. Today, you're going to witness just *how* illogical his power really is." Sylphy smirked. Because of course she would.

Since we first met, I had thought that it'd be nice if she smiled like a regular person, but now I felt much more relaxed when I saw her with that expression on her face. After all, when she smiled normally, it was just so cute—okay, I'll be honest, so *beautiful*—that it made my heart skip a beat.

"All right, Kousuke, get to work."

"Aye aye, ma'am. I'm going to set down my smithing station, so make a little room, please. You there, please move a bit. Pardon me, sorry!" I made the refugees standing near the hill move away and then put my blacksmith station down.

The moment I placed it, there was a murmur among the crowd. I totally understood why; I mean, I'd have been surprised too if such an impressive furnace and whatnot just materialized out of nowhere.

"Sylphy, I think I might be able to repair other kinds of rusted tools, so could you collect some and bring them to me so I can work on them?"

"Hmm, that's a good idea. I'll prepare them."

"Great. Meanwhile, I'll collect the clay and turn it into bricks."

"All right. Work hard for me now."

"Aye aye, ma'am." I gave Sylphy a bow as she walked off with Danan and took my shovel out of my inventory, then I took a moment to set the charcoal in the blacksmith station so it'd be ready to start making bricks—

"Um, you're in my way," I told Ira.

"How in the world did you move such a facility here? It doesn't make sense."

"It's not safe to be near now that it's lit. Don't touch it, okay? If you want to look, stand back a bit."

"Nngh."

It was hard to tear Ira away from the blacksmith station, as she was busy staring at it.

I focused solely on digging. I thrust the shovel in the mountain of clay and put the materials into my inventory one after the other. All the while, the refugees kept hauling over fresh loads of clay atop a wooden board with a pair of rope handles fastened to the sides.

"How are you making the clay disappear?" Ira asked as she watched me work.

"I'm just putting it all into my inventory."

"Grrr... There isn't even a trace of magic at work here. Are you using some other power, then?" She was grumbling to herself, as she was wont to do. I thought she'd have some kind of work to attend to, but she kept clinging to me.

Maybe she was here to keep anyone still hostile toward me at bay, but I wasn't exactly *secure* in the assumption. Her actions spoke more of being devoted to her desires—er, her *intellectual curiosity*.

"Is this enough clay?" Melty asked. She wound up sticking around once she came back with tools in need of repair.

I was making sure not to look at the quern that she had ostentatiously laid next to my feet. I refused. What I was doing right now was more important.

"Mm, maybe. I guess I could stop for the time being; I've collected a fair bit already," I said.

My smithing station had been firing bricks while I dug. Next, I had to turn the bricks into brick blocks; it'd be faster to do that with the workbench than by hand, so I put down the workbench.

"Now there's another new thing here," Melty commented.

"This is my workbench. While the smithing station is good for making iron, firing bricks, and repairing ironware, the workbench can be used for other things. It strengthens my crafting powers, so to speak." That reminded me that I could upgrade it now that I had crafted some steel plate springs. I had Sylphy's permission yesterday, so I figured I'd go ahead and do it. "I think it's going to start shining really brightly, so stop looking at the workbench."

"I refuse to take my eye off of it for even a moment." Ira seemed to welcome the prospect.

"Don't blame me if you go blind." I figured there was no convincing her, so I went ahead and started the upgrade.

As I predicted, the workbench starting glowing.

"Wh-what just happened?" Melty asked.

"I upgraded the workbench. Now I can do more things with it, and it's more efficient," I answered as I looked at Ira, who was rubbing her eye and groaning. Naturally, she'd stared directly into the light. *I tried to warn you.*

"Oww."

"Yeah, yeah. Maybe you should take a seat so you don't hurt yourself." I quickly made a wooden stool and put it down for her. She sure could be troublesome.

Turning my attention back to my newly upgraded workbench, I saw that the display now identified it as an improved workbench. It was now in the shape of an L and entirely made of sturdy iron. The surface area was the same amount of space I had to work with before, but now it had what looked like a sewing machine with a foot pedal.

Oh, I think I might know what this is. It's gotta be a foot-powered lathe. You rotate the object you want to work on while pressing it against the secured blade to shave it down or cut it or punch holes into it.

"What's this device?" Ira asked.

"I think it's a lathe. It's for changing the shapes of metals. Granted, it's basically decoration, since I won't actually use it." I'd be doing all that in the crafting menu, after all, so it didn't really matter what kind of fancy equipment was actually on it. I *could* use the workbench like normal if I wanted; I just didn't want to.

I could scope out the new things later. I needed to start making lots of brick blocks. I moved the finished bricks from the blacksmith station over to the improved workbench and had my workbench pump out brick blocks. I was going to make as many as possible.

"I-I saw it!" Ira sputtered.

"Saw what?"

"A clue to discovering the truth."

That sounded like something a drunk person would say, so I touched her forehead. "Hmm, you seem a bit warm." I wasn't sure if she actually had a fever or if she was just hot from clinging to the smithing station. I wanted to offer to make her some medicine, but that was unfortunately beyond the workbench's abilities at the moment.

I turned to Melty. "Melty, can you take care of Ira? I'm pretty busy at the moment."

"Sure thing. Come, Ira, you should get some rest over there." Melty offered Ira her hand.

"I'm fine. Let me go."

"Drunks never admit when they're drunk," Melty replied.

"I'm not drunk. Besides, one of us has to stand guard for Kousuke. You should order them to stop digging up clay." Ira angrily slapped Melty's hand away and glared at her.

"Hrm, all right. However, you mustn't bother Kousuke."

"I won't. I'm not a kid, so stop treating me like one."

Really? I thought, but I held my tongue since I would probably just make her mad. Speech is silver and silence is golden, after all. Well, maybe the saying about how words can lead to disaster was more applicable in this situation.

Melty left, leaving me, Ira, and the accumulated audience watching me with curiosity.

"So what exactly was it that you saw?" I asked Ira.

"That light shone like the holy magic that priests can use. I bet your power is similar to some god granting a miracle."

"Oh, uh-huh. Yeah, most likely." I suspected as much already. It was just a vague hunch based on the way my abilities were evolving, or perhaps because I'd felt something else's will acting *through* my powers. The snide comments in the achievements also hinted at the existence of someone else behind it.

Also, the power to bring me here and grant me these abilities had to belong to something divine. Ira's remark only reinforced that hunch.

Ira hesitated a moment. "You knew already?"

"Well, you know how I came from another world? I mean, when you think about it, there's only one kind of being out there in the universe that could summon me to this world from the one I came from. Y'know?"

After another pause, she said, "How careless of me."

She looked greatly perplexed as she hung her head, almost as if she was really depressed about this turn of events. Ira had been so focused on trying to comprehend the unusual thing before her that she couldn't see the bigger picture. I totally understood how she felt.

Not long after, I finished crafting the clay into bricks, then finished crafting all of the brick blocks, and all the while, Ira remained in low spirits—in other words, she was in a bad mood from morning to lunch. Bless her.

"Are you going to work on the wall after lunch?" Sylphy asked.

I swallowed a big bite of my food. "Yeah, I think I have enough brick blocks now. If I don't, then we'll just have to get more materials and make more."

Today, Sylphy and I were eating the same thing the refugees were eating: a salty-sweet sandwich made of bread that reminded me of hamburger buns with some animal's giblets fried with a vegetable medley. Sylphy had taken some volunteers hunting with her, and this was the fruit of their labor. The meat tasted better after being left to marinate for a while, so we were going to have that for dinner or eat it tomorrow.

"Your Highness, I have something to say," Ira said suddenly.

"Yeah? What is it?" Sylphy tilted her head inquisitively at her.

Ira had been gloomily munching away at the sandwich up until now, so her speaking up took us both by surprise.

"I've thought up a plain and simple way to prove to everyone that Kousuke is not from this world."

Sylphy raised an eyebrow with interest. "Oh?"

My mind was just full of question marks. However, it would take a while to get *everyone* to believe me the old-fashioned way, so if there actually was a plain and simple method to prove it, then that would be best. I suspected it would go a long way toward toning down folks' hostility.

"If he can remove the slave collar with his own hands, then that should be enough," Ira said.

"Oh." My mistress was at a loss for words.

Danan and Melty both looked equally surprised. Cuvi too—no, he looked more amazed? It felt a bit different from the expression on the other three's faces.

"But if he tried to do that, not only would he not be able to move anymore, but it'd wring his neck and he'd die," Sylphy protested.

"That shouldn't be a problem for him. Kousuke has no magical power to speak of. Not even a little. Zero. I don't think that slave collar actually works on him," Ira explained.

"What do you mean? It's right around his neck right now." Cuvi pointed at my neck.

The collar was indeed stuck there. It looked *stupidly* sturdy.

"That may be so, but I doubt it works as intended. A slave's collar absorbs the wearer's magic, creating a kind of magical circuit. When it's working properly, it blocks orders from the mind to the body and prevents you from moving. At the same time, it squeezes a person's neck using the magic it absorbed from them. However, Kousuke has no magic to absorb. From the moment it was placed on him, that slave collar has functioned as nothing more than an accessory."

"Is that true, Kousuke?" Sylphy asked me.

"How am I supposed to know?" I had no idea how magic or magical circuits worked.

"Try giving him an order, Princess," Ira suggested.

"Hmm... Okay, Kousuke, I command you as your mistress. Strip. Take off every single piece of clothing you're wearing."

"Why *that*, of all things?! I mean, if you really want me to strip, I'll do it, but I wish you'd command it a bit more amicably!" I shouted. If I stripped here, every single refugee would get to see me nude! I was no exhibitionist!

Ira looked smug. "See?"

"Holy crap!" Cuvi blurted.

"My, this is quite the surprise," said Melty.

Meanwhile, Danan and Sylphy couldn't say a word.

What's wrong? Oh, wait, based on what they just said, the moment I started to refuse, I should've frozen and the collar should've started to strangle me, right? That must be what's weird, I thought—and then I realized that Sylphy had never given me a command as clearly as she just did. I had no memory of ever refusing to do something Sylphy had told me to do, for that matter. That was probably why she hadn't noticed either.

"I can't believe it. The collar really doesn't work on you, Kousuke?" Sylphy asked.

"Seems like it. At the very least, it didn't feel like anything happened to my neck."

Up until now, Sylphy hadn't asked me to do anything outrageous, so I had just indulged her requests. I couldn't recall her giving me that many orders to begin with.

"Does this mean you really could take the collar off yourself?" Melty asked.

"Huh? Well, probably." I looked at Sylphy. She nodded, so I tried fiddling with it to try to take it off. *I don't really get how this thing's made... Oh, so the belt goes through here.*

With a little effort, I managed to remove it. Ahh, it had been so long since my neck had been exposed to the air; it felt a bit refreshing. The collar itself wasn't actually too uncomfortable to wear. If it were itchy or something like that, we would have discovered this truth sooner than later.

"If the collar doesn't work, then why haven't you done anything to Her Highness?" It was unusual for Danan to address me directly like this. The fact was, I *had* already done something to her, but I guess that either didn't concern him or hadn't registered for him yet.

"You mean why haven't I hurt her? Because I never had any reason to. Sylphy saved my life, and I'm indebted to her. I'd never return a favor with spite. What do you think would happen to me if I tried to kill her in her sleep anyway?" Obviously, killing your guardian was an invitation for your own destruction. More likely, Sylphy would snap my neck before I even got the chance.

Danan sank into silence as he pondered what I said. I didn't really understand him, but he seemed to have his own way of viewing things.

"I believe we will be able to convince people that he's not from the Holy Kingdom. Kousuke, when do you think you can have the wall finished?" Melty asked.

"Huh? I won't know until I get started, but if I have enough brick blocks, I believe I'll be done before sunset. I'll probably need two or three hours—maybe even an hour to an hour and a half if things pan out well." Since I had all of the materials now, all I had to do was start stacking the blocks to make walls. I had a wide area to cover, but it shouldn't take that long to finish.

"Is that so? When you're done, we'll take the opportunity to announce that you're a Fabled Visitor on whom the slave collar doesn't work. We'll be able to emphasize how you've helped us out of your own free will."

"Hmm. She's right. Let's gather everyone by the time he's done with the wall; I'll give a speech," Sylphy suggested.

"That is a fantastic idea. I shall go ahead and make the preparations."

It sounded like they were making decisions quickly enough. I had no complaints since they were making plans to guarantee my safety. I welcomed it, in fact.

"Okey dokey. Now that I'm done eating, I'll get working on the wall. I'd like to confirm where I should be building first, so could you send someone with me?" I asked as I stood up.

"I shall accompany you," Danan volunteered.

I glanced at Sylphy and she nodded, so I nodded back.

"Pleased to be working with you, er... What should I call you? Mr. Danan?"

"Just Danan is fine. And I'll call you Kousuke. No need to be formal with me."

"Are you sure? All right, then." I wasn't sure why, but Danan's attitude toward me had suddenly softened. Not that I had any complaints about that. He was the most influential among the four, and I much preferred this to him threatening to gore me.

Danan and I left the others and headed to the spot where I stacked the brick blocks yesterday.

"Doo doo doo-doo-doo-doo-doo! Dong! Doo-doo-doo-doo!" I sung to the tune of Prince Neidhart's theme song from *Romancing SaGa*.

"Why are you singing like a buffoon?" Danan asked.

"What, like you don't prefer to have background music while you work?"

"I have no idea what you mean."

I understood his confusion. Once again, my meme game (however strong) was wasted on this audience. Be that as it may, the song kept me going at a pretty stellar pace. Monotonous work like this demanded tunes.

"Anyway, you've made good progress," Danan commented.

"It's because my ability was made for this kinda thing. It's probably not all that suited for battle, though." Not that I knew for sure since I'd only been in honest-to-god combat once. Using my natural movements along with command actions, I could do some tricky maneuvers, but perhaps with some training, I might be able to kill things on sight.

If I slide forward while firing my bow, it would be more like a "stretched out" attack. However, if I slide around without moving my feet, it would probably be hard to gauge the distance for my attacks, right? Well, that's not important right now, so moving on.

"That about does it, huh? As for the gate...maybe this'll be good?"

Metal Gate——Materials: Wood × 40, Mechanical Parts × 6,
Iron Ingot × 8

I made it right away with my smithing station, since it looked like a good fit. When I went into placement mode, I could adjust the size of the gate to some extent. It came with an iron bar, so it seemed like good value for the cost.

"That's incredible. With this power of yours, I bet you could build a fortress overnight."

"I probably could as long as I had materials ready in advance. You can't make something from nothing, after all; it all comes down to availability of supplies."

"Even so, you're able to carry a large volume with your power, right?"

"Yeah, pretty much. I'm useful from both a tactical and strategic point of view. You'd better do whatever it takes to protect me."

"Hmph... I can't say you're wrong."

Ooh, has Danan finally awakened to my charm? It feels pointless to have such a muscular guy doting on me, but it is a pretty big win to have him recognize how useful I am. It definitely increases my survivability.

Before long, the bulwark for protecting the magical fields and refugee camp was finally complete. Well, kinda complete. I still had to put the finishing touches on it. Right now, the wall was only two meters high and two meters thick. I still had to make the defensive equipment to put on top.

"I'd like to hear your opinion about that," I said.

"My opinion? But I don't know what exactly you can do," Danan replied.

"Oh, right. I was thinking of putting up something like a rampart," I said as I used a stick to draw castle walls. You know, like how every other section of it sticks up higher and you can hide behind it and shoot arrows? That kinda thing.

"Ah, you mean crenellated parapets. We'll definitely need such battlements if we're going to be using archers and the like."

"So these are called crenellated parapets?"

"The low wall for hiding behind is called a parapet, and the gaps for shooting arrows are the crenels. Hence, crenellated parapet."

"Huh, I see." It was a simple enough explanation. It seemed like he had brains to go along with all that brawn. Hadn't he said that he was a member of the royal guard? It made sense that he'd be educated if he served directly under royalty. "This is okay with you, then?"

"Indeed. You only need to make the crenels on the outer part of the wall. If you make them on the inner part, then we won't be able to use the wall if it gets occupied."

"Right-o. We also need some stairs for getting up there, huh?" I made some stairs and started on the crenels.

What he said about it being occupied stuck with me, though. I doubted the gizmas would do that, so he must have been thinking about if the soldiers from the Holy Kingdom descended on the village.

I continued getting advice from Danan as I made the finishing touches on the walls. I especially valued his advice regarding the gate. The gate was structurally the weakest part of the wall, so I built turrets on both sides of it for defense. These turrets could station more people than the bulwark, so enemies that tried to storm the gate would be in for a tempestuous onslaught.

I was mostly finished with the walls when the refugees and elves who'd left in the afternoon to go hunting or whatever else came back. Upon seeing my construction, they were stunned.

I'd built all of this in the span of about two hours. It had been a breeze for me since all I had to do was stack the blocks up without much thought. Before I realized it, there was quite a crowd of spectators from all the refugees and kids who'd started following Danan and me. We must've been quality entertainment.

"All done!" I proclaimed.

"So it seems. We need to inspect each part, but it looks mostly finished," Danan said.

As it was supposed to be a bulwark, it'd be meaningless if there were any holes in it. I was pretty sure that the parts of it I built were flawless, but we couldn't be sure about the parts that had already been built. At worst, I might have to replace the whole thing with my brick blocks.

Danan then ordered his men to conduct a thorough inspection of the walls. It was best to have other people do that kind of work; there was no need for Danan and I to do it ourselves. We could just wait for someone to report that there was a gap and then head out to that spot.

As we were waiting, Sylphy and Melty arrived. Ira was missing, which reminded me—she hadn't been around to tell me how illogical my actions were since lunch. Did she get bored of it?

I kind of missed it.

"Looks like you're done," Sylphy said.

"Yup. I think I did a pretty good job." The wall was thick; by all estimations, it could withstand gizma assaults.

"I guess it's time for me to give my speech." Sylphy laughed. That bold laughter was exactly what I expected from her.

All of the refugees were gathered, and I spotted some elves among them too. They were blatantly rubbernecking. Not that that was a big deal. Anyway, it seemed like just about everyone we'd expected was here.

Sylphy stood on top of the freshly built wall and surveyed the crowd. I stood at her side and back a ways. I told her it might be weird for me to stand where I'd be looking down on them, but Sylphy said it would be fine and ordered me to stand here. I hoped she was right.

As I was busy fretting, Melty—who was standing behind the crowd—gave the signal to start. Sylphy muttered something and called upon the power of her bangle adorned with spirit gems before she began to speak.

"Thanks to everyone's cooperation, the walls are finished. These walls are thick and strong. I'm certain that we shall have nothing to worry about should the gizmas descend upon us."

Sylphy was speaking in a normal tone, yet her voice sounded strangely clearer than usual. Surely it was the work of spirit magic. Some kind of spell to better carry your voice, maybe? "As many of you were here to bear witness, Kousuke built these walls within this short span today by himself. I am sure you must all be wondering who he is."

All of the refugees looked at me. Yeesh. If I were at the same level as them right now, I'd probably be having flashbacks to my terrifying brush with death in the square. However, it wasn't so bad at the moment, given the angle.

"This man is not a human from this world. Some of you may know the tales of Fabled Visitors—for those of you who have not, they are extremely rare. They're residents of other worlds who, guided by the gods or the spirits, wander into Leece. This man—Kousuke—is one of those Fabled Visitors. He may look like an ordinary human, but he actually comes from a vastly different reality."

Murmurs rose from the crowd at Sylphy's proclamation. I sympathized. You'd think it would've been in the realm of possibility for them, but people had probably assumed that such tales were merely comforting folklore.

"I understand if you don't believe me. He looks like any other human, after all. However, Kousuke doesn't have a trace of magic within him. Not even the smallest spark. Every single living thing in our world has magic, if only just a little. That goes not only for us demi-humans but also animals, monsters, plants—even the smallest of insects. But as a Fabled Visitor,

Kousuke has none. Ira's arcane eye has confirmed it—Ira, who, as you may know, was a member of the Order of Mages." Sylphy glanced at Ira, who nodded dramatically enough for the crowd to see. "Nevertheless, I am sure that words will not be enough to convince you all. Thus, I would like you all to take a good look at Kousuke's neck. As you can see, he wears a slave collar. Once it's been put on, that's that. As you all know, no one but the slave's master can ever remove it."

At a look from Sylphy, I nodded and removed the collar with my own hands. Whispers once again rippled through the crowd.

"Behold! Not only does Kousuke lack magical powers, but the slave collar has no effect on him. Only a Fabled Visitor could do such a thing. You may also know that Fabled Visitors are endowed with extraordinary powers. I don't think any additional explanation is required as to what Kousuke's is."

Most of the refugees nodded. The walls I had built were right before their very eyes, so they had no choice but to accept that.

"Are there any among you who'd be willing to test whether this collar is genuine? Worry not; I won't punish any who doubt my words. In fact, please *do* voice your dissent so that I may have the chance to persuade you all. Those who would question me, step forward." Three people moved at Sylphy's urging: a person who looked like a lizard walking on two legs, a woman whose lower half looked like a serpent's, and a large woman with cat ears and a tail.

"Hmm. So you three shall test the collar, then." Sylphy took the collar from me to prove that it worked on each of them.

It seemed to be the real deal because none of them could resist Sylphy's orders, and when they tried to remove the collar, they became paralyzed and the collar nearly strangled them.

"Now you try putting the collar on, Kousuke," Sylphy said.

"Are you sure?" asked the feline woman, who had been the last to try the collar.

"Yes, of course. It doesn't work on him."

The catlike woman placed the collar around my neck. Hrm, she had a smaller chest than Sylphy. She also had this wild scent to her. Was that the smell of spices?

"Give him an order," Sylphy told her.

"All right. As your mistress, I order you to kneel," the woman commanded.

"I refuse." I crossed my arms and shook my head. I then took off the collar and handed it to Sylphy. "Sylphy's my only mistress, as I owe her my life."

"Hee hee. You're so admirable. C'mon, I'll put this collar back on you." Sylphy smiled and hugged me before she collared me again.

Mm-hmm, Sylphy has the best boobs. She smells amazing too.

"As you can see, the collar is genuine. I believe that should be enough to prove that Kousuke has no relation to the loathsome Holy Kingdom whatsoever and that he is here to help us. I would like you all to treat Kousuke as our ally from now on."

There was some more bewildered chattering from the crowd, but before long, people started clapping. Among them was Melty, wearing a strangely pleasant smile on her face. From her expression, and the fact that she was the one who started clapping first, I had to wonder if she had been hired to applaud. Was she trying to rile them up? How scary!

"I'm glad you've all come to accept my words. Beginning tomorrow, we're going to start defensive drills to prepare ourselves for when the gizmas arrive. I'd like to invite any with the strength for it to join. That concludes our meeting for today!"

The clapping grew louder, and there were cheers at Sylphy's words. For the time being, it seemed much less likely that the refugees were going to try to attack me. Now all we had to do was find out how things were going with the elves and strategize.

After the speech, the four leaders, Sylphy, a number of refugees, and I held a strategy meeting. There were four new people who joined us, one of whom I recognized from earlier.

"I'm Jagheera. I was a scout for the Kingdom of Merinard." Jagheera was the catlike woman who had put the collar on me before. I kept describing her as a cat, but she was more like a leopard or a jaguar.

"I'm Pirna. Like Jagheera, I was also a scout." Pirna was a small and slender young woman with wings for arms. A harpy, most likely. She had a sharp yet calm and collected look in her eyes.

"I'm Gerda. Former heavy armored regiment." Gerda was about as big as Danan. I wasn't sure what kind of ears she had, but they were round and undersized, and she didn't have any sort

of obvious tail. Maybe she was a bear? She had a calm demeanor, but she seemed pretty strong.

"I'm Worg. I was a member of the Tant town guard." This Worg fellow was clearly a dog beastfolk—or maybe a wolf—with his taut ears and bushy tail. He was of smaller build than Danan and Gerda, but solid and still much bigger than me.

So Jagheera was a speedy type and Gerda was a tank, with Worg sitting somewhere in the middle.

"Sounds like you all used to be soldiers. I'm surprised how many of you are women, though," I said.

"Unlike humans, there isn't much of a difference in physical abilities among beastfolk of different genders. In some species, women are more common," Sylphy said.

"I see."

I couldn't help but imagine that the reason they'd made it through the Great Omitt Badlands was, in part, due to the men who'd given up their lives first. The fact that none of them were elves was probably because all of the elves had all been captured. They were much more "in demand" than beastfolk were.

"We should start working out more definite plans for our defenses. But before we do, Kousuke, how about we show them the gift you've made?" Sylphy said.

"Oh? Will do." I took three crossbows and twelve bolts out of my inventory and laid them out on the table we were all sitting around.

"Are these bows?" said Danan. "I've never seen ones that look like these before."

"Apparently, they're called crossbows. Kousuke, show them how to use one," Sylphy commanded.

"Sure thing." I walked a little ways away to put down a log and placed one of the repaired iron helmets and armor on top, then took up a position about twenty meters away. I put my foot through the metal ring on the tip of the crossbow, pulled back the string with the strength of my back, and set the bolt. "Now I'm ready to fire it. All I have to do is aim and pull this trigger to shoot."

I explained each mechanism of the crossbow, aimed it, and shot the bolt. With a sharp twang, the crossbow bolt's aim was true—it hit the armor squarely, piercing deep into the log.

"As you can see, it's quite powerful. The rate of fire's lower than a bow, but they're easy to use. Anyone will be able to hit their mark to some extent with a little practice," I said.

"So he says. Go ahead and try using them for yourselves," Sylphy offered.

Jagheera was the first to pick one up. She was fast. Ira quickly followed suit. As for the final remaining crossbow, it was down to the other five, not including Sylphy and Melty—no, wait, Pirna had no interest in it at all. Not like she could fire one with those hands.

The other four—Danan, Cuvi, Gerda, and Worg—were looking at the last crossbow with much interest. Noticing that, I offered up the crossbow I was holding too.

"We shall try as well." Gerda picked up a crossbow and handed it to Worg. Cuvi motioned for Danan to take the other one, so Danan picked it up and gazed at it closely.

"This is a fine weapon. Is it okay to leave the string nocked?" Jagheera asked me, looking eager to shoot something.

"I think keeping it that way for long stretches at a time would overburden the string and damage the crossbow, but it's probably fine to have them at the ready during battle."

"I see. A bow of this shape would be useful for hiding in the thicket and sniping things. It seems perfect for scouting."

"The mechanisms themselves aren't complicated; it's just quite powerful in spite of its small size. I think we would need several skilled artisans to make a large number of these. Also, it seems like it would be costly to maintain them," Ira murmured as she closely inspected the crossbow before placing it back on the table. She seemed to have lost interest.

Cuvi immediately scooped it up. He sure knew an opportunity when he saw one.

"You're right that it would be hard to achieve mass production without me. And I'm probably the only one who can maintain them too." I took twelve more bolts out and put them at the end of the table. Jagheera snatched up half of them.

Well, repairing is easy enough with the smithing station, so that's no biggie, I thought.

"The fact that we depend on you to produce and maintain these weapons is a definite flaw. It's not a good thing for there to only be one artisan who can make something or fix it," Danan said.

"That would be true for the long-term, but I do not see it as a problem for short-term use. If you could offer some samples, then an artisan could research it and produce something similar. Maintenance would be possible in the future as well," Melty argued.

"This kind of weapon would be a bit difficult for someone like me to wield," Gerda admitted.

"I'll be able to use it just fine. In fact, I think it's much easier to use than a regular bow. I bet that even citizens with no military training could put them to use," Worg said.

Sylphy watched the lively discussion about the crossbows with much satisfaction. I decided to take the opportunity to ask her something: "Hey, is the wall high enough to keep the gizmas at bay?"

"Hmm? What do you mean?"

"Well, back where I come from, we had bugs that looked similar to the gizmas. They were pretty tiny, so they weren't dangerous at all, but they could jump ridiculously high. Even though they were only this big, if you weren't careful, they could leap as high as your face." I showed her roughly how big they were with my thumb and pointer finger as I said that last sentence.

If a gizma's jump was roughly the same, relative to its size, I could imagine them easily being able to hop over the walls since they were only two and a half to three meters tall with all the accoutrements. Even I could jump that high with a command action, after all.

"Ah, I see what you mean. Don't worry, those tough hind legs of theirs aren't meant for jumping but for charging forward."

"Charging? With those big bodies?"

"That's right. They use their weight and their hard carapace as a shield to charge at their prey. Even heavily armored infantry can be blown away after a direct hit. Their style is to lie in ambush and then suddenly tackle their prey from underground, launching them into the air."

"I see. That reminds me, you were careful not to attack it from the front. You kept circling around it."

"That I did; standing in front of it is just asking to get charged at. It's standard practice to circle around to its sides if you have to fight one. However, its flank isn't entirely safe either. Those antennae can stab at you or even drag you into a charge if you get too close, and it stretches out its stinger if you try to approach from its behind."

"That sounds terrifying. I'm never getting close to one, ever."

"That's wise. It's best to fight it from afar, especially if you use potent magic on them. But think of it this way—as heavy as they are, if they could jump that high, they'd be pulverized by their own weight the moment they landed, regardless of their strength."

"I guess I can see that." I wondered if gizmas were really able to withstand ramming into things with that weight, but they were how they were. It might be best to ask a monster expert those kinds of questions.

Everyone must have run out of bolts to test fire because the crossbows had been returned to the table.

"I love these things. They aren't hard to use and pack plenty of punch. Where's the range on them top out?" Jagheera was all excited, acting like a kid with a brand-new toy. I'd thought her stern yet wild while she was putting the slave collar on me, but she had a surprisingly cute side to her too.

"I haven't had a chance to test them out at long distance, so I don't know. I'm guessing about fifty meters. They can probably fly much farther than that, but I'm not sure how much force they'd still have behind them," I answered.

"Hmm. Guess we'll just have to try and find out."

"Your Highness, just how many of these crossbows can we have prepared?" Danan asked.

Sylphy looked at me. "Well, Kousuke?"

"Huh, good question. With the materials I have right now, I think I can make about 300. However, I'm not sure how far my stock of iron will take us if I need to make a lot of ammunition too."

"Then let's go mine some more tomorrow. 300 crossbows should be plenty, right?" Sylphy asked Danan.

"Indeed. We won't know how durable they are until we test them out further, but I doubt they'll break after ten to twenty shots. We have about 100 to 130 people to defend us, so 300 should be plenty."

"All right. Then, Kousuke, make 300 of them. You should make as many arrows as you can too. Let's aim for 5,000."

"You want 5,000? Yeah, I definitely don't have enough iron for that. For now, I'll prioritize making the crossbows themselves. For the bolts, I'll need to mine loads of iron, but I can work on them as soon as I've got the materials."

"Then do so. Also, leave everything you've already got so we can use it for testing."

"Got it. Is it okay if I keep some for myself?" Sylphy nodded, so I kept only thirty bolts for myself and put everything else on the table.

"You've already prepared quite a number of them," Jagheera commented.

"I think there's around 200 or so? Make sure you collect as many of the bolts you used for test shots as you can."

"Yeah, yeah." I had to wonder if she was actually listening to me as she quickly reached out for the bolts. "Commander Danan, I'm going to go ahead and test this out."

"It'll be dark soon," he warned her.

"You know I can handle myself just fine in the dark." Jagheera snatched up some bolts and ran off toward the wall.

Danan watched her go and heaved a small sigh. "Well, I'm sure she'll be all right. Let's use two crossbows and a hundred bolts to test the limits of their durability. Melty, you manage the rest."

"It shall be done," Melty replied.

"Figure out what other weapons, metallic products, and materials we're lacking. Determine our priority and report to me tomorrow. Don't focus so much on things Kousuke might be able to make but instead what you think we need. Got it?" Sylphy said.

Danan nodded. "Certainly."

"Your wish is my command." Melty's eyes had an unnatural gleam to them.

Uh, Mistress? Mistress! Why do I get the feeling that that turn of phrase is a flag that Melty's going to work me to death? Yikes, why is she cackling? That's not the kind of look any lady should wear.

"Kousuke and I are going to go meet with the elders since he built the wall as promised. Now they have to make good on their end." Sylphy stood up with a sadistic smile on her face. She looked like a predator who had just cornered her prey. But she wasn't going to do anything crazy, right? I certainly got the impression that she was planning to.

"As expected from a Fabled Visitor."

"Indeed. None of us could have ever imagined the wall would be finished right on yesterday's heels. Now we don't have to worry so much about you either, little Sylphy."

"It wasn't yesterday but the day before that, remember? You going senile already?"

"It was just a figure of speech. Why do you have to get on my case about everything, old lady?"

"However, while the wall might ward off gizmas at that height, I'm not so sure it'll be useful against humans."

"Right now, the danger of gizmas attacking is more pressing, so it should do for now. Besides, it would spell the end for us if the humans even breached as far as the village."

"This is true. The forest would be no more if we couldn't stop them before they reached it."

We'd headed straight over to the assembly hall, and the elders were chatty as usual. They left no chance for Sylphy or I to get a word in.

"Ah, yes, this means that they've kept their end of the agreement."

"That's right. Sylphy and the Fabled Visitor—what was his name again?"

"You really have gone senile, haven't you? His name's Gonta."

"You've gone senile too, it seems. His name's Kousuke."

"Oh, that's right. Kousuke. Anyway, it's our turn to keep our word."

"Indeed. We shall provide twenty skilled spirit archers to help fend off the gizmas."

I tilted my head, puzzled at what I would consider a low number. I whispered to a sullen yet quiet Sylphy, "Hey, is twenty a good number of these spirit archers or whatever they are?"

"Spirit archers are elven soldiers who specialize in melding spirit magic with the art of the bow. Twenty of those would be as good as two hundred human archers."

"Are you sure that's not an exaggeration?"

"Arrows enchanted with wind magic fly at more than twice the speed of regular arrows. Arrowheads enchanted with spirit magic disperse devastating power at the point of impact. I do not exaggerate, as a rule."

"Wow..."

So in other words, they were like grenadiers who had an effective range of several hundred meters. Ah, yes. These sorts of people would never have existed on Earth and could only be found in a world of magic.

"We shall dispatch them on the morrow to Danan, as he is the leader of the refugees. Use them well," said one of the youthful-looking elders with an old-fashioned manner of speech. The rest of them nodded in unison.

Sylphy took it as a sign that our meeting was at its end and stood up, so I followed suit.

"We are very grateful. Well, we have preparations to attend to, so do excuse us," Sylphy said.

"Do you now? Sorry for keeping you from your marital bed-chamber overlong."

"Ho ho ho. I'm sure that Sylphy will make the most adorable babies. I can't wait to meet them."

"Kousuke, it must be tiring having to attend to her needs night after night. I'll be sure to have some medicine ready for you the next time we meet."

"It helps elven men keep going even after they've shot their load without pulling out, you see. Perhaps a human like you wouldn't be able to suppress the effects very well, though."

"They should be fine. Sylphy's a healthy gal, after all."

"Spirits forfend, I've had enough! Come on, Kousuke!" Sylphy was fuming as the elders began making lewd suggestions.

"Yes, ma'am!" I fearfully followed after her.

Did they have to pick on Sylphy about everything? I'm the one who's stuck calming her down afterward! Give me a break here!

Sylphy squared her shoulders as she stomped along, and no

one dared cross her path. Doing so would have been like throwing yourself in front of a runaway train. No one would be stupid enough to—

"Impure filth! I need to have a word—grbrhuh?!"

I took that back. There actually was someone stupid enough to do so. And he got himself run over. She sunk her fist into his face, and the aftermath looked straight out of a cartoon. Was he even still alive?

"Another word and you're dead," Sylphy warned.

"I think it's already too late for him," I said.

There was blood gushing out of the guy's face. Left alone, he'd probably start to choke.

"Tch. I can't even bear to look at your ugly face," Sylphy grumbled as she waved her hand, and a ball of light flew over to her poor victim to fix his face. My mistress sure was kind to bother healing him instead of just ignoring him and wandering off. "Phew, I feel a bit better after punching that fool. What was he trying to tell me anyway?"

"No idea." She had punched him before he had a chance to finish his sentence. He'd called her something derogatory, so he was just asking for it, in my opinion.

"Whatever. We don't have time to waste on nobodies. Let's move him to the edge of the street so he doesn't block the way."

"Yes, ma'am." I dragged the unconscious elf to the edge of the street.

Oh, I recognize this guy. It's Nate, that guy Sylphy always calls "limp-dick." In other words, the same jerk who pushed me out in front of a mob. Yup, he got his just deserts. I wish he'd just return to the earth and never show himself again.

"What did this guy do to make you hate him so much?" I asked.

Sylphy hesitated a moment before answering, "His parents and I have a standing dispute."

"Oh?"

"It's not something I feel comfortable talking about here, nor is it that interesting of a tale. I'll tell you if you really want to know, though."

"I'd like to hear it if you're willing to share. You and I have very different definitions of interesting," I said, even though I got the feeling that Sylphy really didn't want to talk about it.

"All right, then. Hmm, maybe it would be better if you knew. I'll tell you all about it when we get home."

"Okay."

As I walked side by side with Sylphy, I secretly took a peek at her face. Her expression looked sorrowful yet undeniably beautiful.

"Now, what shall we talk about first?" Sylphy asked.

After we got home, Sylphy brewed us each a cup of tea, and we seated ourselves on the rattan couch.

"What did you mean by a standing dispute?" I said.

"It all started because of the rebellion in Merinard three years ago."

"I remember hearing about something like that. The rebellion happened after it became a vassal nation of the Holy Kingdom, right?"

"That's right. When I heard what was going on, I just had to do something to help. I stole every single spirit gem in the communal storehouse and headed for the Kingdom of Merinard."

"That sounds...aggressive." I had no idea how many gems there must have been, but it was probably quite a haul. A few gems in the right hands could wipe out a hundred soldiers, so I assumed they were well protected.

"Naturally, I got found out right away, and they sent people from the village after me. They were the parents of the current generation of young elves like Nate. In other words, they mainly sent adults who weren't yet considered elders."

"Ah..." I was starting to see where this story was headed.

"They chased me across the Great Omitt Badlands, which was where I ran into Danan and the others, who were ragged from fleeing. We wound up battling the troops of the Holy Kingdom who were giving chase."

"How many soldiers were there?"

"Well, to be honest, my memories of what happened then are hazy. According to Danan, there were about 5,000 of them."

"That's quite a force." I couldn't even imagine what that many soldiers would look like. There were about 300 refugees right now, so that would have been an absurd difference in military force. Even if Sylphy had brought lots of spirit gems, how many she could take out with each would have been like a drop in the bucket.

"They were tormenting Danan and the others, what with how worn down they already were. If they'd gotten serious, they could have wiped them all out instantly, yet they were acting like a cat that had caught a mouse. I completely lost it when I saw that. That's about where my memories start to fray."

"I think I understand how you must have felt. I can imagine how angry you were." I would've been angry too. I remembered hearing how the humans of the Holy Kingdom didn't see demi-humans as people. Whatever they were doing must have been awful.

"I gave myself over to rage and loathing and attacked the Holy Kingdom's army. As a result of that, I shrouded myself in darkness, and it altered me for good."

"Hmm? What do you mean?"

"When elves give in to rage and hatred as we use the power of the spirits, we shroud ourselves in darkness. That's why my skin is darker now and my body is more suitable for battle."

"So you, like, evolved to specialize in combat? That's pretty cool." That was the kinda thing only found in fantasy. It was hard to imagine someone's body evolving depending on the situation and their role. That sounded much more illogical than my power.

"It's because elves are half human and half spirit that our bodies change under the influence of our feelings and our deeds. Elves shrouded in darkness such as myself are feared by those who understand the circumstances. Some detest us and call us impure."

"So that's why Nate hates you? But wait, what makes you an enemy of his parents?"

"There was no way I could take out 5,000 soldiers by myself, no matter how many spirit gems I had. I managed to halve their forces, but my spells grew gradually weaker. That's when Nate's parents and the other elves caught up to me."

"Ah, and it turned into a battle?"

"Yes. Most of my pursuers lost their lives during the battle, but we managed to annihilate the Holy Kingdom's army. Survivors of that day now call me the Witch of the Black Forest." She certainly was something to be feared if she could kill literal thousands on her own. "Because of that, the elves of this village—the younger ones in particular—resent me. My own recklessness led to their parents' deaths, after all. And because I shrouded myself in darkness, they look down on me and call me filth."

"But isn't that because they're scared of you?"

"Yeah. That fool Nate is the only one who still flares up at me in public. Everyone else keeps silent now that I've thrown my weight around them some."

"I-I see." I chuckled awkwardly back at Sylphy's grin. She would make anyone fear her if she silenced everyone who complained with physical force. Was she Gian from *Doraemon*?

"Well, we call it being shrouded in darkness to make it sound all nice, but in the end, my skin is the mark of a murderer: a sign that I should be feared, but not respected. Danan and the others feel indebted to me because I did it for their sake."

"Is that so...? Well, I've only ever known you as you are now. And I love the way you are."

Nevertheless, I could understand why Danan and the others felt indebted to her. If a pretty girl irreversibly changed her body and was forever marked as a murderer just to save me, I'd feel the same.

"Oh, Kousuke..."

"No matter what happened in the past, who cares? You're pretty. At least, that's what I think. I don't care about the color of your skin at all—in fact, I like it."

"Really?" Sylphy looked relieved to hear it.

I don't care what happened in her past. Sylphy will always be my Sylphy.

I gulped down my cold tea and patted my lap. "Thank you for telling me all that. I'm hungry, so let's eat and then fool around in bed!"

Sylphy let out a bashful grunt and said, "F-fine."

"All right! I'm gonna try my hand at cooking something unusual! Look forward to it," I declared in my most cheerful voice to dispel the mood hanging over us.

I wanted to add more recipes to my repertoire, so I was going to do my best experimenting with a new dish.

"Hmm. I'm not used to this texture, but it's not bad."

"Glad to hear it." I had managed to dish up something like spaghetti aglio e olio using pasta I made from scratch. I kneaded the usual grainmeal with water and a little bit of vegetable oil and stretched it. I folded it and then cut it into flat ribbons. It was done boiling in about two minutes. I threw in galik, pepal, and salted meat that I had pan-fried in oil.

"Hmm, there's something lacking in the execution, though."

"You think so? I like the texture."

"The body of these is limp. I think it'd be a bit better if you added eggs."

Or maybe grainmeal just isn't meant to be used to make pasta. Anyway, we had fruit and a vegetable salad as sides. Since she didn't like the execution, I wanted to try making this again sometime.

Once we were done eating, we had a moment of relaxation to ourselves. If there wasn't anything in particular to do, I was hoping we'd drink a little mead or something and then jump into bed, but there was still work to be done, so that all had to wait.

"What are you going to do today?" Sylphy asked.

"I need to get all of those crossbows made, and I wanted to try making an improved crossbow too. Ah, and a weapon for you."

"Oh? I can't wait."

It felt a bit weird to give a woman a blade as a present, but I decided it was fine since she seemed happy about the prospect.

I decided to first craft everything that the improved crossbow needed in one go.

Improved Crossbow—Materials: Steel Plate Spring × 1, Wood × 2, Mechanical Parts × 3, Tough Bowstring × 1

I had already made a decent number of steel plate springs, and I was able to substitute the tough tendon I got from the gizma's hind leg for the tough bowstring. I decided to make three of them, including one for me. After that, I had to make 300 regular crossbows. I'd acquired more than enough wood and fiber-related materials yesterday, and I was able to substitute the gizma's carapace for the animal bones, which I would have been missing otherwise, so no problems there.

I also needed to turn all of the iron arrowheads I had on hand into crossbow bolts. I had a lot of branches to use as the material for the shafts, so they could be made easily enough. However, I didn't have nearly enough arrowheads, so I had to make those too. That was all I'd be making with the improved workbench. *Time to decide what I'll make with the smithing station.*

"Hmm, I don't see the weapon I was hoping to make for you in my list."

"You can't make it?" Her long ears drooped with disappointment. It was so adorable, I could hardly stand it.

"Aw, don't be so disappointed. It'll work out. Probably. I'll just try the same thing I did with that bardiche." At the time, I'd had the smithing station's menu open and it'd simply appeared after I imagined what it looked like. I was pretty sure I could make the same thing happen again.

I want to make a kukri knife. The blade's bent kinda like a boomerang, but not to the same degree as an actual boomerang. It's a very unique-looking knife. The tip is heavy and wider than the base, and it's very good at cutting things. In videos I saw on the internet, you could slice a hanging slab of meat with one stroke and even cut through bone with a kukri. It could also stick really deeply into a tree when thrown.

As I thought about all of this, it got added to the crafted menu. It worked just as I thought it might.

"Looks like I can make it after all," I said.

"Really?" A big grin bloomed across Sylphy's face. Her ears had perked right up. Seeing her so happy made me happy too.

As for the recipe...

Kukri—Materials: Steel Plate Spring × 2, Wood × 1, Animal Hide × 1

Why does it require plate springs? Well, whatever. The bigger problem is the animal hide. I'm all out of those. I glanced at Sylphy. Her eyes were sparkling with excitement, and I felt reluctant telling her as much. Still, I had to tell her the truth. "Sorry, but I can't make it right now; I don't have any animal hides."

"What...?" Her ears started to droop again but then sprang back up. She rushed into the house and came back out at once. "Would this work?"

"It just might." She had brought out some kind of nicely tanned animal hides. I took them and put them into my inventory, and it turned out that I could indeed use them instead. "Yeah, it'll work. I can make it."

"All right!"

I decided to use two of the tanned hides to make two kukris. It wasn't too long before they were done.

"All done. I made a knife called a kukri for you." Each one came in a sheath made of the nice, tanned hide. I wondered if the appearance of things changed based on what materials I used.

"Ooh, this has an unusual shape."

"Yeah, it's odd to see a blade with an arch like that, isn't it? But they're ridiculously sharp. These things are all about cutting."

"I see. It's got some heft to it."

"I made a second one too, so go ahead and try them. I'm pretty sure you can throw them, so feel free to practice. Let me know if the blade starts to go dull so I can fix it."

"Okay. I'll take good care of these." Sylphy unsheathed it and smiled radiantly. She was adorable, but I wished she wouldn't swing them around with such vigor. I felt like my life was in danger.

I tried to pretend that I couldn't hear the whooshing noises of the swinging kukris and set up my remaining iron to craft lots of arrowheads. Even with the number I had set to craft in my workbench, I wouldn't even have a thousand of them. I really had to go mining tomorrow.

I was done with the smithing station, so I returned my attention to the improved workbench. Going back and forth between the two made it actually feel like I was playing a crafting game.

The improved crossbows were done, so I stuck those into my inventory. I was planning to test one of them out now.

"Hm? Is that a new kind of crossbow?" Sylphy asked.

"Yup. It uses metal for the bow part. I think these should be even more powerful. Nngh! It's stiff?! And it's heavy?!" I had the metal plates to thank for that. It wasn't that I couldn't draw back the string, but a weakling like me with no muscles to speak of wouldn't be able to nock an arrow too many times in a row. It could hurt my lower back too.

"Is it that bad?"

"It feels heavy to me, at least. Why don't you give it a try?" I took out the other crossbow and handed it over to Sylphy.

She drew the string back like I had, but it looked much easier for her. "You're right, it is stiffer. I'm sure trained soldiers and brawny braggarts won't have any issues, but it might be difficult for regular citizens to do this over and over."

"For real. Anyway, let's try shooting it."

They each came with a crude circular sight that made them easier to aim. It didn't have any special ornaments or anything, but it seemed of sturdy enough make. When I aimed, another reticle appeared in my vision. From what I could tell, this one lined up perfectly with the one on the actual crossbow. I pulled the trigger.

With a sharp twang, the bolt found its mark in the log I shot at before I could even blink. It had a much faster initial velocity than the regular crossbow. Sylphy shot hers as well and hit the log dead on.

We shot several times in silence. I didn't want to get tired, so I used command actions to reload. The fact that I could use a command action to easily draw this ridiculously stiff crossbow felt like cheating.

"Interesting. This sight is quite useful," Sylphy commented.

"Right? And it's got a lot more punch."

"It does seem to be striking its targets quite deeply. I wonder if we can even pull these out."

"It's hard to pull these out by hand, isn't it?"

Not that that was much of an issue since I could just access the log's menu and stick them in my inventory. Sylphy chuckled dryly as she watched me do so. My abilities really did make it so I was practically cheating at life. Believe me, I understood.

"I guess I won't make too many of them, and we'll treat them as a special resource that should only be handed out to skilled, beefy shooters. They need steel plates to make, so they require a lot of iron."

"You bring up a good point. These improved ones should probably be used by those who are pivotal to our cause, but let's do as you suggest for now."

"Okey dokey."

"By the way, do you still have things to do?"

"Huh? Yeah, I do. I've got a ton of stuff to make, so I was thinking of working on that a bit longer."

"Oh, all right, then." Sylphy's ears drooped a little.

Huh? What's gotten into her? She doesn't seem angry or anything. Concerned as I was, I pulled myself together and checked the list of things I could craft in the smithing station. I was pretty sure that I could make more things with glass now.

Test Tube——Materials: Glass × 1

Beaker——Materials: Glass × 2

Lab Flask——Materials: Glass × 2

Glass Mortar——Materials: Glass × 2

Glass Pestle——Materials: Glass × 1

Distillation Apparatus——Materials: Glass × 8, Iron × 2

There were quite a few new things I could make with the smithing station. It was obviously a sign that I was supposed to start making medicines. I stopped producing iron arrowheads for now and took back the iron. I was sure I'd need it to make some kind of workbench for these medicines.

However, the smithing station's crafting list didn't have anything that looked like that. *Maybe the improved workbench has it?* I wondered as I made my way over to search the workbench's list.

Druggist's Mortar——Materials: Stone × 5, Wood × 1

Brewing Bench——Materials: Distillation Apparatus × 1, Beaker × 2,
   Lab Flask × 2, Test Tube × 4, Glass Mortar × 1, Glass Pestle × 1,
   Druggist's Mortar × 1, Wood × 10, Nail × 20, Iron × 4

I found it, but boy did it require a ton of materials! However, I did have enough glass, so I could make it. I messed with the order for my crafting queue and decided to prioritize making the brewing bench.

That reminds me, I should check my achievements and skills. I have so, so much stuff to do!

First-Time Crafter——: Craft an item for the first time. *Unlocks a
   skill.

First-Time Dismantler——: Disassemble a crafting item for the first time. *Unlocks a skill.

First-Time Gatherer——: Gather for the first time. *Unlocks a skill.

First-Time Miner——: Mine for the first time. *Unlocks a skill.

First-Time Hunter——: Acquire materials from a living creature for the first time. *Unlocks a skill.

First-Time Repairer——: Repair an item for the first time. *Unlocks a skill.

???——: Hidden achievement.

The disassembly and repair achievements hadn't been unlocked before. It seemed like there was one last simple thing I could do.

My First Smithing Station——: Craft a smithing station for the first time. *Unlocks the Item Creation function.

Ooh, maybe that's why I can imagine an item and a recipe for it gets added to my list? My power was the least user-friendly thing in the world still, considering there wasn't any further explanation. I quickly glanced over the list and didn't see any other new achievements.

Skilled Worker——: Crafting time is reduced by 20%.

Dismantler——: Number of materials acquired when disassembling a crafting item is increased by 10%.

Repairman——: The time to repair items is reduced and the cost of materials is reduced by 20%.

Mass-Producer——: When you make more than ten of the same
   item, the number of required materials is reduced by 10%.
Logger——: Number of plant materials obtained is increased by 20%.
Miner——: Number of minerals obtained is increased by 20%.
Anatomist——: Number of materials obtained from bodies is
   increased by 20%.

New skills had been added as well. *Hmm, now that I think
about it, I should've taken the Logger skill back when I was cutting
down all of those trees... That was a stupid mistake. I already took
the Miner one, so I'll grab the Logger and Anatomist skills now.*

Heart Healthy——: Stamina recovery speed is increased by 20%.
Fleet-Footed——: Movement speed is increased by 10%.
Strong Arm——: Attacks with melee weapons are increased by 20%.
Sharpshooter——: Attacks with ranged weapons are increased by 20%.
Iron Skin——: Damage taken is reduced by 20%.
Survivor——: Health is increased by 10% and Health recovery
   speed is increased by 20%.
Reptilian Stomach——: Hunger reduction speed is reduced by 20%.
Camel Hump——: Thirst reduction speed is reduced by 20%.

There weren't any new skills that would improve me physically. I hadn't leveled up yet, so I could take three more skills.
I decided to pick Heart Healthy, Fleet-Footed, and Sharpshooter.
I'd make shooting a crossbow and then withdrawing my fighting
style.

I think the materials for the brewing stand should be about done? I headed over to the smithing station when Sylphy suddenly hugged me from behind. Something soft pressed against my back.

"Whoa! Wh-what are you doing?" I asked.

"...to bed?" She murmured in such a quiet voice that I couldn't make out the first part of the sentence. Her breath tickled my earlobe. Oh God, oh man. My beats were going at a million hearts per minute. "Do I have to say it again? Come to bed already. It's getting late."

Her blunt invitation made me feel like I had died and gone to heaven.

Okay, okay. My work wasn't nearly done, but there was no way a loyal slave like myself would disregard a request from his lovely and adorable mistress.

I, Kousuke, shall rush straight onto the battlefield! Woo-hoo!

CHAPTER 6
The Sudden Beginning of My Survival Life

DAY 7

L AST NIGHT, Sylphy was as needy as a kitten. Just imagine it, dear reader: a normally calm and collected woman whose public persona radiates violence, crying out with mind-numbing sweetness. I was afraid I was going to spontaneously combust.

Morning came as usual.

After we woke up, Sylphy was dazed for a little while before her face turned as red as a lobster and she froze.

"Sylphy? Miss Sylphyyy?" Hearing me call her name, she covered her face with both hands and curled up in the bed. I shooed her and said her name again, but I got no response. She was pretty firmly clammed up for the time being, so I decided to leave her be.

Fortunately, there was still plenty of water in the jug in the backyard, so I was able to cleanse myself of last night's accumulated sleaze. I went ahead and picked up the items I had been making overnight while I was at it. All of the crossbows were finished, which left us just needing the bolts to go with them. The materials for the brewing bench were also finished, so now I just had to assemble them.

I collected the improved workbench and smithing station and went back inside, but Sylphy still hadn't found her way out into the living room yet. Was she *still* all catatonically flustered? I had a feeling there'd be some kind of counterattack if I bugged her too much, so I decided it would be wiser to just make breakfast instead.

Hmm, what to make? I don't know that many recipes that involve flour... Oh, I know! I can make something like okonomiyaki. I can probably approximate it using grainmeal, cabbaj, and some meat. Oh, but the only thing I can make soup stock from is mushrooms—is that still gonna taste all right? Dang it. I don't have nearly enough time to make sauce from the tomatoes either. I guess I'll just fudge it by adding some shredded oneel and adding more salted lizaf meat.

As I was whipping up the batter for the not-okonomiyaki, I heard the sound of hushed footsteps as Sylphy came out of the bedroom. She tried to be sneaky, but I was keeping an eye on the bedroom door out of the corner of my eye.

Our eyes met. She whipped her head to the side to avoid my gaze and retreated to the backyard. As you might suspect, her face was beet red.

"Goodness, she can be so adorable."

Sylphy had really cut loose in bed—she must've been wound *damn* tight all day. She was almost like a completely different person.

From an elvish standpoint, Sylphy was still a child. She said that elves matured both physically and mentally around the age of twenty, but it wasn't as if folks are magically mature straight out of adolescence.

However, she had lived her life up until now knowing her duty—that she had to be strong for her people. But then she met me. She was probably letting all of that go at night. There wasn't a single human alive who could keep themselves on guard constantly. It couldn't be all that different for an elf.

Now it was morning again and her facade was back, and with it a clarity that threw her memories of the night into shameful relief. It was so magnificent; I wished she could be like that all the time!

I preoccupied myself with the thought as I started making the okonomiyaki. Soon, Sylphy came back inside.

"Good morning," I said.

"Morning." Her face was still red, but she seemed to have regained a degree of poise. Well, that might have been because she'd dumped cold water over her head. "Kousuke?"

"Yeah?"

"Don't speak a word about last night."

"Hmm." It would've been simple to reassure her and tell her there was nothing to be embarrassed about so it didn't bother her in the future. I could've eased her fretting if I told her there was nothing wrong with being amorous when we were at home or alone, and that I liked it.

"Okay." That was all I said; I went back to what I was doing. I wanted to enjoy Sylphy getting all flustered for as long as possible. Ha ha ha.

After an okay-tasting breakfast, we immediately set out for the bulwark. Danan and the others were already present, engaged in some deep discussion. On the table, I spied a map of the topography around the village drawn on a wooden board.

Sylphy had completely recovered herself by this point. Before we left the house, she'd balled her hands into fists and flexed with an audible groan of some sort to get herself psyched up. She was just so cute, I could die.

"Good morning, everyone," Sylphy greeted them.

"Good morning, Your Highness. Kousuke."

"Good morning," I said, laying out one of the new crossbows on the table. "So, this is called an improved crossbo—"

Jagheera and Ira immediately reached for it before I could finish my sentence. They both had their hands on it as they locked eyes with each other; I could've sworn I saw sparks flying between them.

"Don't worry, I've got more. Don't start brawling over it." I took out two more and handed them out to the two ladies. The third I left in the center of the table. I started giving a general explanation of the differences in their performance from the standard model—stronger and heavier frame, stiffer bow. I made sure to mention that they'd quickly tire out anyone but the hardiest fighters.

"I see. The greater demand on the wielder is a concern, but its improved strength is appealing," Danan said.

"Even a few of these will be an enormous asset," Melty chimed in.

"Speaking of equipping, all of the regular crossbows are ready. I can hand them over now, but I doubt it's a good idea to just stack up 300 of them here, right?" I asked.

"That's a good point. Could we take fifty of them for now for training?" Melty asked.

"Sure thing." I started taking the crossbows out one after the other. However, since I had only made crossbows, I doubted they had enough bolts for all of these. I went ahead and gave them all of the bolts I had on my person.

"I believe this should do for training," Melty said.

Danan nodded. "Indeed. Let's get started."

"Kousuke and I will be heading out to gather more iron ore," Sylphy cut in.

"I'm coming too," Ira said. She probably believed she'd see something unusual.

"Take Jagheera and Pirna too." Danan turned to the harpy. "Pirna, search for signs of the gizmas from the skies."

"Yes, sir," Jagheera and Pirna said in unison. Considering their backgrounds, they'd both be perfect for scouting duty.

"Ira, don't you have stuff to do here, like giving directions and making other preparations and whatnot?" I asked.

"Nope. There isn't anyone injured or sick at the moment."

I looked at Danan, Melty, and Cuvi, but not one protested. Ira didn't really seem like the type to go around barking orders. She seemed more comfortable passing research results up the chain, if you asked me.

Since we'd decided who was doing what, we all set off right

away. Sylphy, Ira, Jagheera, Pirna, and I left to acquire iron and patrol for gizmas. Of course, we weren't the only ones patrolling—refugees who were light on their feet went out in pairs in every direction. Even Cuvi had a beat to cover.

Danan, Gerda, and Worg were training refugees on how to use the crossbows. With a day's training, they'd likely come out of it able to hit a gizma without issue.

Melty was busy obtaining supplies for our lines of defense and making rations. She reminded me that I'd be helping her out with that tomorrow. I was *not* looking forward to it.

And as we made our way toward the old mountain stream...

"Why do I have to give you a piggyback ride?" I asked Ira.

"Because someone has to. The two scouts have to be on alert."

Ira was petite and didn't weigh that much, so I didn't mind the actual carrying, but the feeling of certain somethings squished against my shoulder blades and her securely affixed hands were making me uncomfortable. However, she didn't seem bothered, so I just needed to grin and bear it.

"I'm not uncomfortable back here, but there's something off about this," I could hear Ira murmuring.

She wasn't wrong. My stride and the distance I was covering didn't match. Walking was so much easier when I combined my steps with the command actions to make me go forward. It was like being on a moving walkway in an airport.

My body also felt curiously lighter after taking the Fleet-Footed and Heart Healthy skills yesterday. I wasn't getting tired at all from all this walking.

Since Jagheera and Pirna were keeping an eye out, I was able to keep traveling at a brisk pace. We had probably covered twice the distance in the same amount of time as our last trip.

"I'm going to go scout around," Jagheera told us.

"Okay. If you see any prey, go ahead and hunt it for us," Sylphy said. "With Kousuke, we can bring anything and everything home. We'll be heading upstream as he mines, so be careful."

"It shall be done, Your Highness. I shall test out this new crossbow's power!" Jagheera grinned wide before disappearing into the forest, improved crossbow in hand. What in the world was it about crossbows that got that woman so excited? It was beyond me.

"Jagheera's a scout, but her archery skills...leave something to be desired," Pirna explained, having noticed me giving Jagheera a strange look behind her back. "These crossbows of yours shoot straight and true regardless of the user's, er, *shortcomings*. It's no wonder she's taken to it."

That makes sense. I know not all scouts would use a bow, but you'd certainly assume that they could.

"Do you have something as innovative as a crossbow that I could use?" Pirna said, staring at me.

Hmm, something revolutionary that even a harpy could use... Like a bomb or gas shells? Or maybe a Molotov cocktail?

"I have a few ideas, but I don't think I'll be able to make them just yet," I said.

"How unfortunate... Your Highness, I shall go scout as well."

"Take care up there," Sylphy replied.

"I shall." With that, Pirna took to the skies.

The wind buffeted my cheeks; I doubted those wings would be enough to stir up that much of a breeze. She must have been using magic of some sort.

"I guess I'll get digging," I said.

"Dig to your heart's content," Sylphy replied.

Ira watched me in silence. Her big eye looked half-closed, making me feel like she was glaring at me. Was she tired or something?

I took out the steel pickaxe and started breaking moderately sized boulders. Whenever I destroyed one, I'd get stones and iron. If I was lucky, I'd get some kind of gem too. Once I ran out of boulders of that size, I started digging up the river sand. I added the stones from the riverbed to my inventory while I was at it. I was afraid of destroying the ecosystem if I went hog wild, so I tried to act in moderation. Plus, the water was freezing.

As I proceeded upstream, the landscape became more like a gorge.

"All right, I'm gonna dig this up like mad." Seeing the landscape made me want to level it. It'd be okay if I made it completely barren, right?

"That'll probably be okay, but safety first. I'm not gonna be able to save you if there's a cave-in and you get buried alive."

"Good point." No way I'd ever survive getting crushed by falling rocks. If I died, I might respawn somewhere, but I didn't feel attached to testing the idea.

I dug up the wall of rock while being careful not to cause a cave-in. This rock face had small amount of silver and copper in addition to the usual stones, iron ores, and gems. I'd found a good spot for mining; I'd make this my mining hub from now on.

Hmm, what could I use copper and silver for? If I remember correctly, you can make copper into alloys, and those can make bronze and brass. I think they might be used in making bullets too. And some kind of coating? I don't really remember. But brass is used in bullet cartridges as well, I think. I don't remember ever seeing bronze in everyday life. Copper's used in electric cables and other kinds of wires, as well as for water heaters, pipes, and cookware, I think?

Aside from ornaments, the only things I can remember silver being used for is tableware and stuff like circuit board conductors, like copper wire is. Y'know, maybe Ira and the elves can use it for something magical.

As I mined, I crafted the brewing bench. I looked forward to finding out what I could make with it.

Ira got bored of watching me mine and started picking grass, flowers, and roots and then brought them over to me. "Store these."

"Sure thing." In return, I gave her a shovel and rattan basket, and she gleefully went back to picking. After a little while, I asked Sylphy, "What's she been picking?"

"Probably herbs and poisonous plants. She's a master alchemist, you know. She's been essential to healing the sick and wounded among the refugees."

"I see." I checked my inventory and found herbs and poisonous plants in there, as expected. Maybe I'd ask her to give me some later.

Thus, I continued my mindless mining. The cavern along the riverbank seemed to stretch on forever, but I felt uneasy. I wondered aloud if it would be best to climb up and mine from above instead.

"Perhaps, but how do you propose to get up there?" Sylphy asked.

"I've got a good idea," I said, checking how many wood blocks I had. Yup, I still had plenty left. "I'll just stack these up, up, up."

With the command jump, I could pull off a vertical leap about two meters high. And I could place the wood blocks about six to seven meters away. *You know where this is going, right?*

I jumped and placed a wood block underneath me.

I jumped and placed a block on top of that block.

I jumped and placed a block on top of that second block.

Sylphy was completely speechless.

"That's absurd." It had been a while since Ira called me out like that. I wished she wouldn't be so quick to cast judgment. I mean, this was a basic strat.

"That's all well and good that you can get up that way, but how on Leece are you going to get back down?" Sylphy demanded.

"I'll set up a ladder...or do this." I took out my axe and destroyed the wood block under my feet. And then I broke that one and the one under that. "See? Easy, right?"

"I feel like I'm going insane," Sylphy groaned as she rubbed her temples.

All the light had gone out of Ira's big eye. "My mind refuses to comprehend what I've just witnessed." Was it really that crazy to them?

"Doesn't this mean then that you can easily climb castle walls?" Sylphy asked.

"Yeah, pretty much." To tell the truth, I had a much more lethal and effective way of dealing with those sorts of defenses, but I didn't see the need to mention that here. I'd astonish them all when the time came.

And so I continued building my scaffolding of wood blocks as I mined the gorge. My pickaxe whittled down the rock face and the gorge became wider and wider.

"Kousuke, do you think you've gathered enough yet?" Sylphy asked.

"Hm? Oh, yeah, now that you mention it." I had accidentally gotten absorbed in my new goal of leveling out the area. *You know how it can be.*

I realized then that my inventory was full of iron ore, copper ore, silver ore, stones, unpolished gemstones, and mithril ore. *Hmm? Mithril ore?*

"Sylphy, there's something called mithril ore in my inventory."

Sylphy mutely put a hand to her brow and looked up at the sky in response.

"Show us. Now. Take it out." Ira was the one who cracked the whip.

She kinda scared me, so I took one out and handed it over to her. "Uh, here."

Ira was silent a moment before saying, "This is undeniably mithril ore. High purity too."

"Kousuke, how many of these did you get?" Sylphy asked.

"Thirteen, including that one."

In all, I had gotten roughly 1,500 iron ores, 500 copper ores, 200 silver ores, and only 13 mithril ores. I hadn't mined all that much of it.

"Depending on how it's smelted, thirteen of those could make at least two swords," Ira said.

Sylphy hesitated a moment before saying, "Kousuke, don't tell anyone at all about this. Understand?"

"Uh, sure." It seemed I had mined up something pretty re-markable. Mithril was a common magical metal in fantasy games and stories, so I had to wonder if it fetched an astronomical price here. I couldn't help imagining what I would be able to craft with it. "I'll just put that back into my inventory, then."

I held out my hand and Ira laid the ore in my palm, but to my surprise, she didn't let go of it. I gently tried to pull it away from her grasp, but she still clutched it tightly.

"Do you want it?" I asked.

Ira looked at me silently, her eye sparkling. I almost felt like I had to avert my eyes! Not that her eye was actually sparkling or anything, but it certainly felt that way. I glanced at Sylphy, who sighed with a nod.

"You can have it," I told Ira.

Ira gave a strangled cheer of joy and began to spin around with the ore held above her head.

"She looks overjoyed," I said to Sylphy.

Sylphy chuckled dryly. "As a wizard and an alchemist, I'm sure she has lots of uses for it. She's a hard worker; she deserves it."

I doubted Sylphy had a way to pay Ira wages as things stood now, so she must have felt obliged to make these kinds of allowances to cheer people up now and then. At least, that was my assumption.

Around the time I stopped mining and demolished my scaffolding, Jagheera and Pirna reconvened with us. Pirna was empty-handed. but Jagheera had shot an animal that looked like a deer. *I think that's a yakkey? That's a big catch.*

"Heh heh! These new crossbows are amazing! I shot this from more than thirty paces away."

There was a puncture wound and a long cut along the side of its neck. She must've shot it through the neck and then rushed over to it to finish it off with a dagger. Amazing. If it were me, I would've shot the body.

I built a pillar of wood blocks to hang the yakkey from with a rope, and then Sylphy and Jagheera gutted it. They submerged the carcass in the river.

"Let's have the organs here. Kousuke, get a fire ready for us," Sylphy commanded as she and Jagheera started preparing them for cooking.

"Aye-aye, ma'am." I watched them out of the corner of my eye and wondered if there was a fireplace in my crafting menu, so I took a look.

Simple Stove——: Stone × 20

And it seemed I had just the thing. I crafted it right away and put it down.

"Ooh, this is pretty nice," I said.

"Where in the world did this thing come from?" Pirna couldn't believe a quaint little stove had popped up out of nowhere.

"You'll get exhausted if you let yourself be surprised by everything Kousuke does," Ira told the harpy. But even I was positively surprised—as if!

"Come, let's cook." Sylphy and Jagheera were back from getting the entrails ready to cook, so I lit the simple stove and cooked them. While I called them entrails, they only brought what we could cook and eat immediately—the heart, liver, and tongue.

I added some salt I had in my inventory and galik paste for flavor. It was delicious. I also divided out the leftover not-okonomiyaki among us.

By the way, Pirna and Jagheera had brought bread and jerky along, but Ira hadn't brought anything.

"I completely forgot," she admitted.

"You need to be more careful. It's no fun feeling hungry," I warned her.

"I had a feeling you'd have it handled."

"Look, I'm no miracle worker. I can't just conjure food out of thin air."

"Really?" She didn't seem to believe me, but it was the truth.

"I get the feeling you could if you tried," Sylphy said.

"He does have a habit of making unusual things appear out of thin air," Jagheera agreed.

Pirna nodded silently in agreement as she ate a bite of yakkey liver. That seemed to be her favorite part of the animal.

"Look, lemme just make this clear since I don't want you to get the wrong idea about my abilities: I absolutely cannot do something like that. My power is to turn something into a different thing. I do *not* have the power to make something from nothing," I desperately explained, but everyone just gave me a halfhearted "yeah, yeah." It was going in one ear and out the other.

After we finished lunch, I retrieved the chilled yakkey and we headed back to the village.

By the time we made it to the village, the sun was still high in the sky. I didn't know exactly what time it was, but it felt like we had a few hours left until sunset.

"Welcome back, Your Highness," Melty said to Sylphy.

"Thanks. Anything happen while we were gone?"

"We have confirmation that gizmas have invaded the forest. They've only breached the fringes, but I believe it is only a matter of time until they reach the village."

"I see. Perhaps we should assemble a squad of our fastest and try to whittle down their numbers."

"Danan is of a similar opinion, Your Highness."

As the two ladies chatted, I put down my smithing station and started smelting iron.

Basically, they were planning guerrilla warfare against the gizmas. The trees would restrict their movement, creating ideal staging grounds for hit-and-runs to thin them out before they reached the village. Which meant that they would be using projectiles. Which meant we needed those arrowheads and bolts pronto.

However, there wasn't anything I could do while the iron was being smelted. I decided to see what I could do with my shiny new workbench.

"What's that?" Ira asked the second I took my brewing bench out. No surprise there!

"A brewing bench."

"Brewing? Like medicine?"

"Yeah, I'm going to see if I can do that now. Can I use those herbs and poisonous plants you picked earlier?"

"I'll allow it." Ira nodded readily enough, so I opened the brewing bench's crafting menu to take a look.

Distilled Water——Materials: Drinking Water × 2

Small Life Potion——Materials: Herb × 1, Drinking Water × 1

Life Potion——Materials: Herb × 3, Distilled Water × 1

High Life Potion——Materials: Herb × 5, Distilled Water × 1, Ethanol × 1

Poison Potion——Materials: Poisonous Plant × 1, Distilled Water × 1

High Poison Potion——Materials: Poisonous Plant × 3, Distilled
    Water × 1, Ethanol × 1

Antidote——Materials: Herb × 1, Poisonous Plant × 1, Ethanol × 1

Panacea——Materials: Herb × 5, Poisonous Plant × 2, Distilled
    Water × 1, Alcohol × 2

Ethanol——Materials: Alcoholic Drink × 1

Saltpeter——Materials: Manure × 1, Ash × 1

Powder——Materials: Saltpeter × 1, Sulfur × 1, Charcoal × 1

Powder——Materials: Saltpeter × 1, Alcohol × 1, Fiber × 1

"Oh, snap."

"Huh? What's wrong?" Ira asked.

"Nothing," I lied.

I'm sure this requires no explanation, but hoo boy, the last three in that list. I'm not sure what it means by manure, but soil from around the bathroom or a barn should cut it. I watched some show once where they used just that to get the saltpeter to make gunpowder.

That first powder recipe was definitely for making gunpowder. I wasn't sure what the second one was for, but I was sure to find out soon enough. My powers never let me down, no matter what the process was or whatever difficult things I'd have to speed through.

However, there were all kinds of explosive powders out there, so it was kind of scary that the list was just calling them all "powder." I had a feeling that even with the straightforward first type, I'd wind up making a highly efficient, smokeless gunpowder or something like that.

"Irrational," Ira said flatly.

"How I'm acting, you mean?"

"Yes."

For now, I'll make what I can. I have some mead left in my inventory, so I can even make ethanol. I'll also make five small life potions, three regular life potions, and two of all of the rest.

After a short while, all of the potions were ready. The life potions were red, poison potions were purple, antidotes were green, and panaceas were golden. They all came out in glass bottles, but I had no idea where those came from, given what was in the recipe.

As the name would imply, the small life potions were about the size of those tiny glass bottles of seasonings they sell in stores, the life potions in bottles a little over half the size of a bottle of water, the high life potions' were about as big as a mini can of soda, and the bottles for the antidotes and panaceas pretty much matched the life potions'. The poison and high poison potions came in vessels roughly the same size and shape as a ball from a capsule-toy vending machine. The glass looked very easy to break. I had a feeling they might be for throwing.

"These are the medicines you made?" Ira asked.

"Yeah. The red kinds are life potions, the green one's an antidote, and the golden one's a panacea. The purple one just kills you, I'm pretty sure."

"What do life potions do?"

"Heal wounds, I'm guessing."

"Do you drink it? Or apply it externally?"

"I don't know, but I get the feeling that either way might work."

"What do the antidotes do?"

"They cure poisons, judging by the name."

"Which poisons?"

"Probably any?"

"And panaceas?"

"Remedy illnesses, I'd wager."

"Which illnesses?"

"Uh, whichever?"

Every time I gave an answer, Ira's big eye grew duller. *I understand, believe me. I know that what I'm saying sounds nuts. But those are the only answers I can give! And from what I've accomplished thus far with my abilities, I completely understand how wildly ridiculous it is that I can make stuff that cures all that too! I'm pretty sure the answers I gave weren't wrong.*

"Take them all out," Ira demanded.

"Huh?"

"Take out everything you made."

"Um, sure." I couldn't withstand Ira's gaze; she'd gone from a merely *dark* expression to an outright pessimistic one, so I readily offered her all of the potions.

"Make as many potions as you can and give them to me. Got it?"

"But I'd like to keep some for myself, y'know."

The quote "when you gaze long into an abyss, the abyss also gazes into you" ran through my mind. *I can't disobey Ira. I'd be putting my life on the line.* "Gladly, ma'am!"

Well, it wasn't like I told her which recipes used what, so I could still pocket some of them for myself. However, I resolved to tell her that I couldn't make any of the medicines that required ethanol. I had used one of casks we bought without permission, so I would have to tell Sylphy about that later. That one cask made eight units of ethanol, and I wasn't sure if that was a lot or not.

While bowing to Ira's unprecedented intimidation, I made as many medicines as I could with all of the materials I had on hand and gave them to her. I secretly kept two of each kind for myself. I might need to use them, after all. *She won't find out. Totally.*

I filled the same basket she had used for collecting the herbs with the potions. I watched her walk off with the basket and turned my attention to my smithing station.

"Not that I've got anything to do right now."

It was still smelting iron, so I couldn't make arrowheads until it was done. After some deliberation, I decided to peruse the contents of my inventory.

I'm pretty damn flush since I dug up everything. There're a bunch of ores that I don't know how to use too. What do you do with zinc and nickel? I assume they're for making alloys, but I know diddly-squat about that sort of thing. I'll have to rely on the crafting menu's sagacious guidance. I do have a use for this lead off the top of my head, though. I know exactly what gunpowder plus lead plus iron equals.

Eh, I'll just leave that aside for now. I need some kind of manure for making the powder in the first place. They don't raise livestock here, so I guess I'll have to gather the soil from the bathroom. How in the world will I ever explain to Sylphy?

But wait a second. The refugees are alive, so they must make it too. If I just make up some reason, maybe they'll let me collect it all? It'll stink, but...I'll just have to deal with it. I don't wanna do it, but I've gotta.

I looked at my improved workbench's crafting menu next to see if there was anything useful in there.

Spinning Wheel—Materials: Wood × 20, Mechanical Parts × 3,
   Iron × 1, Nail × 20
Loom—Materials: Wood × 20, Mechanical Parts × 2, Iron × 1, Nail × 20

Yeah, I can make these. The question is, can I use cloth for anything right now? But wait, I'll need that to make bandages and splints, won't I? Those are staples in survival games. Bandages can stop any kind of bad bleeding, and you need a splint to heal yourself if you get a sprain or broken bone. They defy all logic even in most survival games, same as painkillers and energy drinks. That's for sure.

I quickly made the spinning wheel and loom and set them out. I could turn the fibers I had collected from plants into thread using the spinning wheel. And with the loom, I could turn that thread into cloth.

Sylphy came over, and upon seeing the spinning wheel noisily rotating, she asked, "What are you doing?"

"Spinning thread?" I understood her confusion. Right now, it looked like I was just spinning the wheel for no reason since there wasn't any thread physically set in it. However, doing this reduced how long it took to craft things, so I wanted her to ignore it.

"Why are you spinning thread?"

"Because I want cloth. There're lots of things I can use it for."

"That's true. You can't have too much cloth."

It went without saying that you can make clothes with cloth, but cloth was also a military resource, as you could use it for making bandages and protective armor. Sylphy was right on the money. Frankly, I also desperately wanted to wear something other than this swiftly decaying sweatshirt and sweatpants.

"Oh yeah, we need to get you something new to wear too."

"Thank you for remembering. It wasn't like I started making cloth to make clothes for myself or anything."

Sylphy had looked me over and said that we needed to do something about it not too long ago.

Just so we're clear, my clothes were washed every day, underwear included. In case you were wondering how, Sylphy would use water spirit magic after dinner to wash them for me. It was kinda fun watching the giant ball of water spin the laundry around and around.

"Are you free right now?"

"Yeah, I'm just smelting the iron. This isn't all that important," I said as I pointed at the spinning wheel.

"Then let's go to the storehouse. I'll pick out some clothes for you."

"Sounds good." I quickly stowed the spinning wheel, loom, and improved workbench in my inventory and headed to the storehouse with her. We wouldn't have to worry too much about paying up, given the fat stack of raw gems I was lugging around.

We arrived without incident, but there was a bit of a scene waiting for us.

"I'll be taking those gems."

"Don't be stupid. You owe me. *I'll* be taking them."

"I'll take this. I'll pay using this bow and these arrows."

There were three people who I could only assume were artisans in a wild uproar in front of the storehouse. The storekeeper looked at a loss for what to do when he noticed Sylphy and me. His face immediately brightened.

"Everyone, the one who mined the gems has arrived!" he announced.

"What?!" the three exclaimed in unison as they whipped around to look at us.

The group of beautiful artisans looked at us with bloodthirsty eyes; they scared the living hell out of me. I quietly hid behind Sylphy.

"Hmph, Sylphyel was the one?"

"Is that guy behind her the Fabled Visitor the elders were speaking of?"

"He looks like any other human, but it's true that I don't sense any magic within him at all."

"Wait, don't come any closer. You're frightening Kousuke," Sylphy warned, and they stopped advancing on us. Despite the crazed look in their eyes, they seemed to have retained their sanity. "Am I right in assuming that you're all fighting over who gets the raw gemstones?"

"Indeed. We haven't seen such high-quality gems in a while," an artisan said.

"Not since Elder Gaston passed away. He was such a master with earth magic." The other artisans nodded to one another.

I see. They've lost all their local talent, and now the market's dried up at the source.

"Kousuke, take out what you got today," Sylphy commanded.

"How many should I take out?"

"The same as last time."

I did as I was told. The raw gemstones clattered onto the wooden plate I set out ahead of time. The lineup was pretty much the same as before.

"Oooh!"

"With this many, we could make this and that and one of those..."

The artisans' eyes glittered brighter than the gems.

Sylphy ignored them, grabbed the plate from me, and headed over to the storekeeper. "Here's what I'm offering today. I'd like to pick out several different things."

"Do as you please. I'll take care of these, so go inside and tell Lisa," the storekeeper responded.

Sylphy passed by him and went on inside, so I followed. I got the feeling that some of the artisans had their eyes glued to me as I left, and that terrified me, so I decided to stick close to Sylphy. *Yeah, that's best for me.*

As soon as we got inside the storehouse, we saw an elf woman minding the shelves. Sylphy was making her way over to her, so I assumed she must be Lisa.

"Back so soon? What do you need today?" Lisa asked.

"I offered as many raw gemstones as last time, and I'd like to pick out some clothes for Kousuke."

"The same amount as last time? Just how many outfits are you planning to get him? I don't think we have that much that will fit his physique."

"Then just bring me everything you have left. Kousuke, if you see anything you want, feel free to take it. You're the one who labored to get those gems, after all."

"Sounds good to me."

"I'll bring what we have in his size," Lisa said, disappearing further inside the storehouse.

Since she'd left us alone, Sylphy and I browsed in the meantime.

"Is there anything you'd like?"

"I'd like some things made of animal hides and glue. Also, booze."

"What kind?"

"I need the strongest stuff they've got. The taste doesn't matter for what I'll use it for."

"Hmm. I know where that kinda stuff is, so follow me." I followed Sylphy, and as I was picking out hides and stiff drinks, we heard Lisa calling for us, so we returned to where we started, the items we picked out in hand.

"This is about all we have in his size. Please go try them on behind that over there," Lisa said.

"Okay." I took the clothes and changed in private.

The clothes Lisa brought were durable, comfortable, and easy to move in. They had a slightly "native dress" feeling to their design.

"How do I look?" I walked back over to where Sylphy was dressed in my new clothes.

The two ladies looked me up and down. *Ugh, this is so awkward!*

"The color doesn't pair well with your hair," Lisa said.

"Well, that's fine. We can just dye it," Sylphy said.

They wanted my hair to match? I felt that the metric they were using was odd, but I wasn't gonna complain; the clothes were comfortable enough. I picked out an extra outfit, grateful not to have to worry about clothes anymore.

After that, we picked up the hard liquor, hides, and such and left the storehouse.

The gazes of the artisans frightened me as we stepped outside. They eyed me like wild beasts with prey in their sights. I was never leaving Sylphy's side ever again.

We went back to the place where I left my smithing station and found Ira there waiting for us. For some reason, she was holding the potions I'd given her before. I was wondered what was up.

"Finally." She looked somehow exhausted. Was she okay? "In brief, I used what reagents and live test subjects I have on hand to test these."

"Oh?"

"To get straight to the point, I was able to confirm that these medicines all have the effects you described. I won't be able to say for certain without a longitudinal study, but I have yet to discover any side effects. These are so immediately effective that I don't know how to assess them." It sounded like the results were beyond description with her favorite phrases.

"Uh, why do you say that?"

"You said these are medicines for healing wounds, removing poisons, and remedying illnesses."

"Yeah, that's right."

"But the usage of these is a matter of life or death. It wouldn't do for us to dispense these irresponsibly."

"You think so?"

"Yes, and yet that's not entirely right." Ira looked down languidly, or perhaps out of sadness? "I...I'm sorry, Kousuke."

"Uh, you don't need to apologize or anything. Wait, are you crying?! Sylphy?! Miss Sylphy, help!"

An alarming volume of tears started trickling down Ira's face. Did she have a lot more tears to shed, since her eye was so big? I was so baffled that I didn't know how to handle the situation. *Why is she crying?! I'm so confused!*

"Leave Ira to me. You go look after your furnace. Put those away."

I had no other recourse but to do as Sylphy said. I obediently collected the medicines that Ira had brought back and turned toward the smithing station. The iron would take a little bit longer. However, I was still at a loss about what had just happened. Why did Ira apologize? The flow of the conversation just made no sense; I couldn't understand what had made her cry.

It went without saying that Ira was a brainiac. Despite how busy it must have been inside that skull of hers, she wasn't very good with her words. You know, the kind of person who would get into conflicts with others because they couldn't explain their erratic behavior to other people's satisfaction and liked to maintain a distance from others. In a nutshell, a poor communicator.

Hmm, let's think back on our recent conversations... She had me make all that medicine and took them all to verify their effects. I know that much for certain. It wasn't out of malice or anything— she just wanted to be doubly sure she could give them to people since whether they worked could be the difference between life and death. Yeah, that part I get.

But then she had said that was not entirely right, apologized, and started crying.

"Nope, can't compute." My brain simply couldn't comprehend it. *Surely Sylphy will be able to coax the reason out of her. Maybe something I said came off as insensitive? I can't begin to figure out where I would've left that impression.*

After a little while, the iron was all finished smelting; just as I had begun mass-producing arrowheads, Sylphy and Ira came back. For some reason, Melty was with them.

"Welcome back," I said.

"Thanks. How're things going here?" Sylphy asked.

"The arrowheads are coming along. I'm going to try to make about 10,000." I had more than enough materials, so now all I needed was the time to actually make them.

I glanced at Sylphy and noticed Ira was hiding behind her.

For some reason, Melty had an uncomfortable look on her face. What was that all about?

"Uh, so, if you have some time right now, could we talk a bit?" Sylphy asked.

"Sure."

There was something distant about the way Sylphy was acting. What in the world? That only made me anxious!

I took out a table and chairs from my inventory and set those down. I also took out four water bottles and placed those in front of everyone. I was the first to reach for mine and drink it. I was pretty thirsty after standing near that fire for so long.

"Uh, so, um. Let me tell you what's going on with Ira," Sylphy said.

"Okay."

Sylphy began her uncharacteristically halting, inarticulate explanation. In short, Ira was jealous of my powers. She was a brilliant wizard and an outstanding alchemist. To put it frankly, my potions incensed her.

By all rights, in order to do alchemy properly, you needed to do a lot of studying and undergo relentless training. And here I had gone and made these medicines with amazing effects in my free time on a whim, which made it seem like I had thrown her life's work in her face.

She had me make all of the medicines and give them to her to verify their effects because the alchemist's code dictated that medicines couldn't enter public use until they'd been through extensive, rigorous testing. But once she was done talking to me and verifying the medicines I had made, she'd realized what her real motive was. That was why she had apologized.

"I realized that you hadn't just gotten your powers for free—the fact is that you had to give up *everything* in order to get them. I'm sorry, Kousuke," Ira apologized.

"Uh, oh? It's okay, don't worry about it? I'm not mad or anything. Yeah." Why was she being so serious? I was so confused. I mean, it was true that my life had been pretty severely derailed, but I'd come to enjoy living here since I discovered my crafting ability. "So what's with you two, then? Why are you being so quiet?"

"Er, well, I just started thinking about some things after hearing what Ira had to say," Sylphy said.

"It's because you came here as a Fabled Visitor that you obtained your powers, yes?" Melty asked.

"Yeah, I guess so." I nodded. Seemed right to me.

"In other words, the price you paid for your powers was your family, friends, assets, and everything in the world you came from," Melty said.

"Yeah, I guess so, when you put it that way." I hadn't been viewing it that way before, but I couldn't say that she was wrong. I had no idea if I could ever return to the world I came from, but I guessed not. If they did know of a way, they would've told me.

"So I was thinking maybe we've been taking advantage of you too much, given all you've been through. I know we're a bit late in recognizing it," Sylphy admitted.

"Ha ha ha. I can't disagree with you. But, y'know, I am

indebted to you, and I don't feel like I've repaid you at all yet. So, don't worry, I don't hold it against you or anything."

Hearing that, Sylphy and Ira exchanged a look and then chuckled dryly.

"You're too good-natured for your own good," Sylphy said.

"I disagree. It's just that it so happens that what I want to do aligns with what you folks want to accomplish. I'm human, after all; I've got my own reasons for doing things," I replied.

"You have goals of your own?" Melty asked.

"I want to discover all the things I can do with my abilities in an environment where I won't starve and I'll be out of the rain and wind. That's all I want, and Sylphy is giving that to me. And since I'm getting what I want, and you're getting what you want while I'm at it, it's a win-win situation, if you ask me."

"It is?"

"Yup. Besides, I owe Sylphy my life. I'd say helping you out counts toward repaying her. It's killing two birds with one stone. That's why I don't mind if you make use of my power for your own convenience. We're going to have a problem if you work me to death, though. I'm only human, and I get tired if I work too long. Please keep that in mind. But don't worry, I don't have any complaints about the way things are now. And I'll be sure to let you know if I do."

"I see. Okay, then." Sylphy's expression brightened.

Melty looked a bit guilty still; she certainly had something to feel guilty about, what with her previous offenses! *You'd better watch out from now on!*

"And Ira, I'm not mad at you or anything, so please don't feel like you have to act any differently from before. I'd love to learn about magic and alchemy; neither of those things exist where I come from."

That wasn't entirely accurate, though—back on Earth, alchemy had been the basis for modern-day natural sciences, after all. Still, alchemy here was most likely a lot different from alchemy back home.

Ira hesitated for a moment before looking up at me. "Okay." Her eye was all red from crying. I bet she was going to drink a ton of water and sleep soundly tonight. I had a feeling that cyclopes must dehydrate themselves quite a bit when they bawl like that.

"That's that on that, if you ask me. I'm glad you were honest with me about this," I said as I held out a hand to Ira.

Ira tilted her head at me, as if she couldn't comprehend why I was reaching out to her. I guessed that this world didn't have the custom of handshakes.

"Back where I come from, we usually shake hands when we make up with each other to show that we're friends again. We call it a handshake."

"A handshake? Okay." Ira timidly took my hand and gave it a little shake. Her hand was so *tiny*. Soft too. It felt different from Sylphy's.

"Now we're friends again. It's a good custom, right?" I asked.

"Yeah." Ira smiled a little. *Good, good.*

For some reason, Sylphy and Melty seemed like they wanted me to shake their hands as well. I didn't have anything in particular to say about how Melty's hand felt. Only that she seemed to work a lot. Sylphy's? Well, I got to hold hands with her every night, ha ha.

I was glad things were all patched up with Ira now. We lived happily ever after.

Not that this was some fairy tale. I was just lucky to be able to fix things so easily. I had let my guard down.

I didn't have to think too hard about what the cause of this kerfuffle had been—it was plain as day that it was my crafting ability. In other words, it threatened those who crafted things the honest way.

With a few swings of my hatchet, I could create the finest quality of lumber from any random tree; with a few swings of my pickaxe, I could mine an abundance of ores and gems. Using the things I acquired, I could mass-produce fully assembled, ready-to-use items in a short span.

I was a walking death sentence for the livelihood of every skilled tradesperson within the same community.

This time, I'd carelessly encroached on Ira's territory. I only avoided the worst possible outcome because I'd been transparent with her from the get-go and she had a naturally good heart. From here on out, I'd work with Ira when using the brewing bench, so all my future forays into medicine were sure to go just fine.

I was also lucky that the things we had sold to the village happened to be things that they were desperately lacking, so it didn't ruffle anyone's feathers. If we'd sold swords or bows and arrows, cloth, clothing, or processed foods, that might have earned me someone's ire.

In other words, I'd been letting myself get carried away.

"You're quiet tonight."

"I'm just reflecting." I sighed as I took a cup full of mead from Sylphy. It was sweet.

"If it weren't for your power, we would be facing the end. Don't let it worry you so much."

"I hear you, but I can't help it."

"If anything, I'll be in big trouble if you don't use the full extent of your powers for me. I have all kinds of problems to deal with, so I need you to." Sylphy gazed into my eyes.

"Is that really what you want? No matter how people might think of me as a result?" I gazed back at her.

"Yes. And I will protect you."

"No matter what?"

"As much as I possibly can. Even I have limits. But I promise that I would never abandon or forsake you. I won't leave your side, even if someone comes after you because of your power."

"Then I have no choice but to fulfill that wish. Heh, I can't help but feel like our roles are reversed here."

I admired how Sylphy sounded like my knight in shining armor. *Well, with love comes pain, or so the saying goes.*

"I'll finish the last of the crossbow bolts tonight. You're planning to head out tomorrow to whittle down the gizmas' numbers, right? I'll go with you."

"All right. Shall we head to bed early tonight?"

"Yeah, after I get some stuff done. I'd like for us to be as prepared as possible."

I wanted to work the spinning wheel and loom anyway.

I headed out to my workshop in the backyard, then put down the improved workbench, spinning wheel, and loom, and got them up and running. I set crossbow bolts and improved crossbows to craft in the improved workbench, more thread to be spun in the spinning wheel, and the loom to weave cloth using what thread I already had on hand.

With that done, all I had to do was prepare for tomorrow and then go to sleep.

"H-hey, Kousuke, we're supposed to relax tonight—mm!"

We fooled around a bit before going to bed. Just a bit. Boobs had wondrous powers, after all.

CHAPTER 7
The Sudden Beginning of My Survival Life

DAY 8

321

HELLO, THIS IS KOUSUKE from yesterday. I fooled around with Sylphy too much last night, and she wound up launching her own counterattack. It wasn't too long ago that Sylphy had been completely inexperienced, so where did she learn a move like that? I could only assume Melty was the culprit since they'd been spending a lot of time together.

At any rate, we were planning to go gizma hunting today. We needed to be ready for anything. While Sylphy was making breakfast, I collected all of the things I made and crafted a splint in the improved workbench. You know, the kind used for healing broken bones and sprains.

If you're wondering why I crafted such a thing, it was because it's an essential item in survival games where broken bones and sprains are a thing. Sprains and fractures tend to be awful debuffs. Your speed and jumping power are significantly reduced, and depending on the game, you can even take damage from slipping. Not being able to move as fast makes escaping from hostile creatures that much harder; it was a surefire way to get your ticket punched.

Generally, you got that sort of debuff by falling from a high place, but in some games, hostile creatures could cause it too. Better safe than sorry.

"Kousuke, breakfast is ready."

"Coming!"

We had thinly baked bread—essentially naan—and spicy chopped vegetables and mushrooms boiled with beans. It was kinda like chili? I didn't remember chili containing mushrooms, but it was pretty tasty all the same.

I put the bread and pot of chili into my inventory for lunch, grabbed my crafting equipment, and then we were off to the wall.

When we arrived, we saw the refugees training so that they'd be prepared against attacks. They all carried a motley spread of equipment; The only uniform part of their kit was the crossbows.

"Good morning, everyone," Sylphy said.

"Good morning!" the refugees replied in unison. They didn't come off as a grim bunch at all. In fact, morale seemed surprisingly high.

Danan greeted her in his usual, polite manner. "Good morning, Your Highness."

"Morning. Kousuke?" Sylphy glanced at me.

"Aye aye, ma'am." I had already placed a table and was dumping all of the crossbow bolts onto it. "I won't be able to lay all of these out here. Though I suppose that goes without saying."

"Wait a minute. We need to do this in an orderly fashion, so could you put them out in bundles of 500?" Melty said.

"Oh, sure thing." I followed her orders and handed over the

amount. After counting them, she went off to distribute them among the refugees. *Must be tough being in charge.*

The refugees put their individual share of the bolts into quivers or wrapped them up with a string and bagged them. *Oh, right. They need something for carrying these around. That was stupid of me to forget.*

"I made some more of the improved crossbows too," I added.

"I'll take those along with the rest of the normal ones you have."

I had 250 crossbows left and 15 improved ones, which I also handed off to Melty. That was the last of what I had to give her.

"If any of the crossbows or bolts get damaged or bent, make sure to get back as many of them as you can so I can get 'em fixed up."

"I shall. I know how valuable the arrowheads are in particular." Melty nodded and then walked over to Danan.

She left the management of the other items I had brought to her helpers, which meant that my work here was done, so I made my way back to Sylphy.

Cuvi was with her, crossbow in hand. "Yo, I'll be stickin' with you today."

"We'll be deploying in teams of three. You, Cuvi, and I will be a team," Sylphy explained.

"I see. What's our marching order?" I asked.

"Cuvi will be the vanguard, I'll be in the middle, and you'll be the rear guard."

"Why's that?"

"Cuvi's quick and he has sharp senses. Even if the gizmas get the jump on us, he won't be done in with one blow."

"You're not wrong. I wouldn't have made it all the way here otherwise," Cuvi said with a shrug.

It made sense. He was the most likely one among us three to survive a fight with the gizmas, seeing as he'd made it all the way to the Black Forest in perfect health.

"Once Cuvi engages a gizma, I'll cover him. I'm the strongest when it comes to melee," Sylphy said.

"I can believe that." Especially considering how she had managed to lead that one gizma around by the nose before dismembering it.

"And since you have the least experience with close-range combat, I'm putting you in the back. That crossbow of yours is suited for someone in the rear guard, where you can take quick shots."

"I'll try my best not to miss my mark."

Shooting the wrong thing with the improved crossbow would be no laughing matter. Sylphy's skintight attire was durable, but it'd be no match for that thing's piercing power.

After confirming our roles within the squad, Danan gave us a short briefing about how we should prioritize our own lives over taking down any gizmas. He said to get back as many bolts as we can and bring the crossbows back if they broke, but that losing our lives over them was pointless, so we shouldn't take huge risks to retrieve everything.

The harpies were already up in the air scouting ahead, but there was a chance that the gizmas might be making their way toward the village borders.

"That's really fast, isn't it?" I asked.

"Yes," Danan said. "They've invaded much faster than we anticipated. At the pace they're going, they'll reach us tonight in the worst-case scenario, but most likely tomorrow. I shudder to think of what we'd do if you weren't here."

"I agree. Without you, we would be dropping everything to flee to the depths of the forest right about now," Melty agreed.

"I'm glad I could help," I said.

Many people came to see us off, including the children, elderly, and those who had incurable injuries. Knowing that these people viewed me as their savior from a fate of cruel and relentless flight made me feel proud.

"It looks like Danan's done with his briefing. Let's go," Sylphy said.

"Okay," I replied with a nod.

"Right-o. Whaddya say, fellow survivors? Let's make tracks." Cuvi nodded back and led us into the forest.

Just how well would the crossbows fare in battle? They were sure to give us some kind of advantage, but I was still a bit worried.

After traveling through the forest for about an hour, Cuvi raised a hand and stopped. He glanced back at us and pointed ahead. I didn't see anything at first, but as I peered closely at the ground, I noticed some dead leaves had been unnaturally parted to the side, leaving the ground bare.

Confirming that we had detected the presence of a gizma, he

let go of his crossbow with one hand and picked up a rock, winging it at the bare patch.

At the moment of impact, the gigantic body of the gizma burst out of the ground, heaving up a shower of dirt with it. So that was the gizma's signature ambush Sylphy told me about! Yeah, there was no way you'd be able to get away from that scot-free if you got caught up in it. It would've been like getting broadsided by a small truck.

"I'll get around it. You attack it while you fall back," Sylphy commanded.

"Aye aye, ma'am," I replied as I set a bolt into the crossbow and aimed.

"SKREEEEE?!" Before I could take a shot, a bolt from Cuvi's crossbow pierced deeply into the base of its neck. *So, they feel pain too, huh?* It flinched and stopped moving.

"Nice shot!" I exclaimed as Cuvi fell back. I took my place right in front of the gizma and fired off a bolt. It flew and stuck right into the center of its face. The bolt sank so deep that I couldn't see the fletching anymore. The gizma shuddered. It must have hurt like hell.

"Hey, Kousuke! Don't hang around in front of it! Too dangerous!" Cuvi called.

"I know." It wasn't like I'd taken this position without a plan; I was well aware of its forward charge.

"GRAAAAAAAAAAH!" In a futile final attempt at stopping us, the gizma rushed at me with incredible speed. Ha ha ha. It truly was a stupid bug, acting on instinct alone.

"Hup." I laid down a cubic-meter wall of brick blocks right in front of me.

Then there was a loud *ker-thunk*!

"That's dirty," Cuvi said.

"Aw, I didn't get to do anything," Sylphy complained.

I couldn't see anything, but I could hear their comments about the dead gizma.

To be honest, I didn't think that this would work so well, I thought as I stuck the gizma's carcass into my inventory.

"Well, normally I'd leave this kinda thing to Mr. Wood Spikes, but I wasn't sure if that'd work on something so big," I said.

"Mr. Wood Spikes? Who's that?" Sylphy asked.

"This." I placed down the wood spike trap I had crafted previously.

Each individual trap had sharp pointy pieces of wood sticking out of it, so you were supposed to line them up on the ground. It was an incredibly reliable tool in this one zombie survival game where you had a week to survive, so back in the day, we called our good buddy "Mr. Wood Spikes" on the internet. The spikes rivaled caltrops in their prickly power.

"You're right, I don't think this would've been enough to stop it," Sylphy agreed.

"I'm not sure it would have been able to pierce the gizma's carapace either," Cuvi said.

They both had a point. "Yeah, it'd probably have to be made of metal or something."

I took out my pickaxe and collected my brick blocks. I planned to set these wood spikes outside the bulwark. I could make them without using a crafting station, so I'd been making a lot of them.

After that, I brought down gizmas one after the other using my brick block strategy. Cuvi would flush them out, and the two of us would make the first strike. Then I'd intercept its charge with the blocks, and if that wasn't enough to finish it off, Sylphy swooped in to make the killing blow.

About half of the gizmas met their end ramming themselves into the bricks; even if it wasn't enough to kill them, it certainly hurt enough to stop them, so it was an easy kill for Sylphy.

"This has never been so easy before," Sylphy marveled after we killed our eighth.

"I doubt we have any chance of losing so long as they don't take us by surprise," Cuvi said.

From the gizmas' point of view, I bet our tactics were straight out of a nightmare—after being painfully assaulted, they'd come at us with their deadly ramming attack in a rage only to smack into a stupidly solid wall from out of nowhere. I supposed Cuvi was right about our tactics being dirty.

"Ha ha ha! I've still got more dirty tricks up my sleeve."

If only we had the time, I could set up sites chock-full of traps a little distance from the village. At present, the best I could do was add thorns to the walls and dig a dry moat with Mr. Wood Spikes and all his friends lining the bottom of it. Naturally, lots of soldiers wielding crossbows would be deployed there. The troops would definitely need an underground passage, or perhaps a passage in the air for retreating through once those defenses were breached. *Hm? Wait a minute, does gravity affect my blocks? I should probably check.*

"Why are you making a wall without warning?" Sylphy asked.

"I'm doing an experiment." I stacked two wood blocks vertically and then broke the one that was on the bottom. "Ahh, I see. So that's how it works here."

The block that was on the top was frozen in midair. It didn't budge even after pushing or pulling.

"Cuvi, am I just overly tired or am I seeing something weird right now?" Sylphy asked.

"I see it too, so I think you're okay," Cuvi reported.

"Ha ha ha. We'll be able to make a base in the sky." The question was, would this block continue to remain floating? If my power had some kind of upper limit to its range, then the base might just suddenly drop and break apart.

I decided to test for a weight limit, so I put another wood block next to the one that was already in the air, and a brick block as well.

"Okay, it's not falling," I said to myself as I tried getting on top of the block and jumping up on and down on it. It felt as stable as solid ground. It didn't move at all. My brief flirtation with the idea of building a castle in the sky returned, all the more tempting now. *But even if I did, we'd need an easy way to get there and back, like teleportation or some kind of aircraft.*

"Sorry for taking so long. What's with you two? Why do you look so tired?" I asked.

"Nothing, just...now I feel like I know why Ira's always crying out 'absurd' and 'illogical' around you," Cuvi replied.

"I understand."

"Don't agree with him. And here I had my heart set on not letting myself be bewildered by the things you do," Sylphy muttered.

After my experiment, we resumed gizma hunting. We had managed to take three more with the brick blocks when something unexpected happened.

"Hm?" Cuvi's ears suddenly perked up, and he looked in a different direction.

I followed his gaze but didn't notice anything out of the ordinary. "What's wrong?"

"Gizma howls. And not just one or two of them."

"Maybe there's a squad taking on a group of them. Let's go check it out," Sylphy said.

"Got it. I'll lead the way." Cuvi took off running.

I wondered if we'd be okay just charging recklessly in like that, but Sylphy didn't say anything, so I kept my mouth shut and followed.

After about ten minutes of running, we came upon a spot where several old-growth trees had been smashed to splinters. The gizmas' work, to be sure.

"It's close," Sylphy said.

Cuvi pointed. "That way."

This close to the action, even I could hear the sound of splintering trees and gizma howls. *Speaking of which, how in the world do those things howl? They don't seem like they have vocal cords.*

"There! Take care with your aim and try to draw the enemy's attention!" Sylphy commanded.

"Understood," Cuvi said.

"I'm on it!"

We kept running and came upon a crowd of three gizmas. There were several refugee soldiers I didn't recognize fighting with them. One looked like a squirrel beastfolk, another a lamia carrying what looked like a lizardfolk on her tail, all running full tilt from their gizma pursuers.

My best guess was that the lizardfolk had been injured, and they accidentally ran into these other gizmas when they were trying to retreat—an all too familiar scene from any survival sim, as a persistent mob links up with others while their prey kites them around the map. The squirrel beastfolk appeared to be trying to buy time by drawing their attention toward the trees.

"I'll cover them," I announced, intercepting the gizma chasing the lamia and the injured.

"What are you doing?!" the lamia exclaimed in surprise.

"Don't worry about me, fall back!"

The gizma immediately charged, so I placed bricks and then started moving back, building a horizontal wall between us and the gizma. I used the command jump to leap to the top of the wall. The gizma had already stopped moving as I aimed and fired.

"SKREEEEEE?!" I must have hit a critical spot, because the gizma stiffened with a jump.

I loosed another bolt, finishing it off. It was easy to tell that it was dead, as its body was suddenly flagged as something I could stick in my inventory.

I spotted Sylphy driving her kukri into the second gizma's neck. Cuvi and the squirrel beastfolk were firing at the last one, which looked considerably weakened by now. I fired at it from the top of the wall to provide backup.

"SKREEEE!" After three bolts, the final gizma breathed its last.

Yup, these crossbows seem plenty effective against them.

I decided to collect the gizmas' carcasses later and instead hurried over to the lamia. She was looking over the lizardfolk's wounds a little ways away. From what I could tell, the lizardfolk's right leg had been injured—it was bent in an unnatural direction and covered in blood. I could even see bone sticking out.

"An open fracture," I said.

Luckily, I had the splint and life potions on hand. Ira had given her stamp of approval for the potions, so I wanted to test and see—err, I mean, aid the poor thing.

"I'll heal you. It might hurt, but try to fight through," I said.

The lizardfolk nodded quietly. "Okay."

Hmm, no facial microexpressions or sweat going on here, so this might be hard to handle. I took out some drinking water from my inventory and washed out the wounds first. The lizardfolk didn't even groan as I did—must've been a hardy one.

"And now I'll just take the splint and...there!" As I held the splint with one eye on the broken leg, I saw a pop-up that said "Use." I selected the pop-up, and my body automatically moved to expertly to place the splint and wrap the bandage around it.

"W-wait! We need to heal the broken bone first!" the lamia protested as I was wrapping the bandage.

"I know, I know." I agreed with her, but I figured this would work just fine.

"Gwuh?! Whoa?!" The lizardfolk cried out in pain; the second I was done wrapping the bandage, the broken bone began to mend itself, like it was going back to normal all on its own. Frankly, it was disgusting to watch. It must have been an absolute bastard of a recovery from the sound of it, but that wasn't much of an issue here. Ha ha ha.

Once the leg was back to normal, the splint glowed and then disappeared, as if it had broken or something. *Huh, that was weird.*

"I-It just healed on its own," the lamia blurted in disbelief.

"It must have been something like a special kind of holy magic. I don't quite understand it myself," I said.

"You don't know how that just worked?!"

I brushed off the lamia's complaints and took out a life potion. After taking injuries that bad, the lizardfolk probably needed the more potent variety.

"This medicine has Ira's stamp of approval. Drink up." I popped the cork and handed it over.

"All right." The lizardfolk drank down the contents without any hesitation.

"How does it taste?"

"A little bitter... Hmm?!"

"Wh-what's wrong?"

"The pain's completely gone." The lizardfolk stood straight up, stepped a few times to test the healed leg, and then put all their weight on it. "It's healed!"

The lamia was reeling. "Huh?! But your leg was mangled!"

"Mm-hmm, but now it's healed." The lizardfolk tried jumping. It really did seem a-okay.

Was it just me, or did the splint and life potion seem a bit too overpowered?

Sylphy and everyone else came over as the lamia shuddered.

"Your injuries...seem okay now?" Sylphy said.

"What?! But you were a mess! What kind of magic did you use?" the squirrel beastfolk asked.

"He treated me and gave me a potion. Thank you so much. I was afraid they were going to have to amputate it." The lizard-folk, who had a killer poker face, offered me a head-bow of appreciation.

"No problem. I'm glad I could help."

"Was it that bad?" Sylphy asked.

"Worse than you can imagine! The bone was sticking straight out!" the squirrel beastfolk insisted.

"Really?" Both Sylphy and Cuvi looked doubtful.

Yeah, I wouldn't have believed it either if I hadn't seen it for myself. Here the lizardfolk was now, jumping around like a fool.

"We don't know if you got back all of the blood you lost, so I think it would be best if we headed back to the village just in case," I suggested.

"Yeah. How many gizmas did you manage to take down?" Sylphy asked the squad.

"Two."

"Counting the three we just bagged and the ones from earlier, that makes thirteen total. I'd call today a success. Let's head back to the village."

"Okay, I'll get us ready to withdraw," I said.

I stuck the brick blocks and gizma carcasses into my inventory, and the six of us carefully made our way back to the village. We killed two more gizmas along the way, making fifteen in total between us.

"I am glad to see you all back safely," Danan said upon our arrival.

"We thought we'd swing by to drop off an injured fighter, although they've already been healed," Sylphy explained.

It didn't seem like any gizmas had arrived at the village yet.

"We've learned some things while we were out there," Sylphy said.

"What is it?" Danan asked.

The rest of us followed the two of them to our typical meeting spot. It was the only place that had a table and chairs; we didn't really have a lot of other options.

"Are we the only ones who have returned?" she asked.

"As of this moment, yes."

"I see. I think it'd be best if you deliver this as an order when they return."

"Why is that?"

"Well..."

Our squad had managed to work up a nice pace, but that was solely due to my tactics with the blocks and Sylphy's prowess in melee combat. According to Zarda—the lizardfolk—and the other two in that group, the crossbows hurt the gizmas, but they just didn't have enough firepower between the three of them.

They had been using regular crossbows; in the team's own words: "It pierces their armor, all right, but it takes more than ten bolts apiece to bring one down—give or take a few depending on how lucky a shot you are."

"With three people, you can get about two shots in first."

"After that, it turns into a running battle, which might draw other gizmas."

Sylphy summarized their findings to Danan.

"I see," Danan said.

"I think it'll be safer if people travel in groups of six instead of three."

"I believe you are right. Very well, I shall give the order."

"Please do."

Danan stood from his chair to give the order when I noticed he was dragging his right foot as he walked. And that was when inspiration struck me.

"Wait a minute," I cut in.

"What is it? I need to give the order as soon as possible."

"Just give me a couple of minutes. I'd like you to sit down again so I can look at your foot."

Danan gave me a puzzled look but sat down anyway. I walked over to him and took the splint out of my inventory.

"You can't fix that with a splint. Are you trying to make a fool of me?" Danan said, full of indignation.

"Now, now, just lemme do my thing," I soothed him as I gazed at his foot. There it was: the "Use" pop-up. Without a moment's delay, I selected "Use" to place the splint and started wrapping his leg with the bandage automatically.

"This is pointless—hmm?!" All kinds of popping and cracking sounds came from his bandaged leg. Danan scowled for a moment, but then the sound stopped, the splint broke, and it disappeared. Danan's expression returned to its usual stern look. "What the hell did you do?"

"I treated you. Here, drink this medicine too." I took out a small life potion and handed it over to him.

Danan hesitated for a moment before bracing himself and slugging it back in one go. "Not as bad as I thought it'd be."

"Great. So, how does your leg feel?"

"The pain's gone." Danan stood up, bent his bad leg, and started flexing and extending it again. It seemed okay. "I feel like a fairy's gone and played tricks on me."

"Just be happy it's all better now. Go ahead, get to work."

"Hmph. I suppose you're right. I'll thank you later." Danan turned and ran off. He seemed sprightlier than before.

"You healed Danan's leg? With that thing alone?" Sylphy was in awe.

"It might even work on feet and arms too," I said.

I had just done it on a whim since it could heal sprains and broken bones. I didn't know it would work for sure at the time—I just figured that if we could heal the injured, then we should. It'd only give us more fighting power and improve my relationship with the community here. *I, Kousuke, shall do everything in my power to suck up to everyone, so long as it guarantees that no one will try to kill me!*

"Hmm. Cuvi?" Sylphy said.

"Yes'm. I'll go gather them all."

"Thanks. Kousuke, what to do...?"

"About what?" I asked.

"I'm not sure if it's a good idea to bring you with us hunting gizmas. If there's an accident and we lose you, then everyone who could be saved will be lost."

"To be honest, I actually do want to fight. I think I have another ability that'll grow stronger by defeating monsters."

"Really?"

Oh, right, I haven't told Sylphy about the levels, skills, and achievements at all. I glanced at my stats and found I was at level nine now. *Nice, I gained three levels while we were out there!*

"Not an ability for making stuff, but it makes me physically stronger," I explained.

"Oh? Cuvi, how long do you think it'll take to retrieve everyone?" Sylphy shifted her attention back to Cuvi.

"I don't think it will take too long. I know where they all should be."

"Got it. Then we'll go hunting again after lunch. Everyone who's out already should be back by then. There might be more people who were injured, so we'll treat them as best as we can, and then they can go back out after we reorganize the groups."

"Understood."

While we waited for Cuvi, I asked Sylphy what I should do about the gizmas we killed with Zarda's team. It probably wouldn't take that much effort if I was the one to dismember it, but I would only be able to acquire its carapace, meat, venom glands, and tough tendons. If we did it by hand, we could acquire stuff like its internal organs and the ends of its claws, so while it took extra time and effort to do, it was still worth doing.

"We don't care so long as we get our share," Lianess, the lamia, said.

Zarda nodded in agreement. "Yeah."

"That's true. Oh, but we don't need the meat, right? There's gotta be a ton of it, since our share is two gizmas' worth. Most of it'll probably go to waste if we split it only among ourselves," Nakul the squirrel beastfolk pointed out.

She had a point—that one gizma Sylphy and I had killed had been enough to feed all of the refugees. The majority of it was sure to rot if they split it between the three of them. Apparently, gizma meat was quick to spoil.

"Good point. Should we give it to Melty so everyone can have it?" I suggested.

"Sure," Nakul said.

I decided that I would dismember one of the gizmas in my inventory and hand over the acquired meat, venom glands, and materials to them. However, I had way more gizmas in my inventory—including the eight we'd killed during our hunting trip and two more we'd nabbed on the way home. Naturally, we couldn't collect the two Zarda and her (I hadn't been able to tell, but it turned out that Zarda was a woman) team had defeated before we met them, so their share was two gizmas' worth out of the five we were all together for.

"Okay, I'll take out two gizmas' worth of carapaces, venom glands, strong tendons, and antennae," I said.

I dismembered two of them and started laying the materials out on the ground. The glands I set on top of two wooden plates.

"I can't believe how much there is. I'll go get us a cart," Nakul said.

"I'll go with you," Zarda offered.

"I'll stay here and keep watch," Lianess said.

They started figuring out how they would deal with the materials, so Sylphy and I decided to go hand the meat over to Melty. It was proper to leave managing these resources to her.

"What about Cuvi's share?" I asked Sylphy.

"There's eleven left, I think? So four for Cuvi, seven for us."

"Okay."

I dismembered our share's worth of gizmas. Now I wouldn't have to worry about not having enough tough tendons and carapaces. We also had a ridiculous amount of gizma meat.

We asked around about Melty; after a few minutes, we finally found her carrying a heavy-looking box. She was stronger than I thought.

"Oh, Your Highness! Back already?"

"Yeah, we were helping an injured friend back. We procured a large quantity of gizma meat, so I'd like you to distribute it," Sylphy said.

"And just how much is a large quantity?"

"Nine gizmas' worth for now."

"That is quite a lot. Gizma meat doesn't keep very long, even cured. This is quite the conundrum."

"It won't spoil as long as it's in Kousuke's inventory, so we should be okay on that front. Would two gizmas' worth do for today?"

"Is that so? Very well then, I shall take two gizmas' worth of meat from you." She gave me quite the look as she spoke. It frightened me. I was so glad that Sylphy was my mistress. In Melty's hands, my powers were sure to be exploited in all sorts of ways.

I put the box that Melty was carrying—which contained yams—into my inventory, and we wound up going to the refugees' communal cooking space. This was where they'd cooked the gizma meat yesterday too.

I handed over a mountain of meat to the ladies in the kitchen, who decided that they would use it in lunch and dinner. Nobody was gonna be short on protein today. I also dropped off Melty's box, which she'd been on her way to deliver.

Sylphy, Melty, and I were watching the ladies cook as we discussed what to do with the materials we had acquired when we heard Cuvi say, "There you are. I've gathered everyone together."

"All right. I'll see you later, Melty."

"Take care of yourself out there, Your Highness."

We made our way to the plaza near the walls, which was where Cuvi had gathered all our wounded hunters.

"Finally." Ira was there waiting for us. "If you're going to be treating people, then I have to be here as well. Everyone in this village is under my care, after all."

"I see," I said with a nod. It made sense that she would feel some sense of responsibility over everyone. Ira sure took her role seriously. "Who wants to be first?"

However, no one stepped forward. I couldn't say I was too surprised. While Sylphy had given that speech to convince them that I wasn't their enemy, nobody wanted to volunteer to show a complete stranger their injuries—their weaknesses—without prior notice, especially not a *human* stranger.

"Don't worry, I'm here. I won't let him do anything weird to you," Ira reassured them.

"They don't trust me," I said.

"Of course not."

One patient finally came over to us—a young beastfolk girl dragging one foot behind her. She had droopy ears like a lop rabbit.

"Is it your knee?" I asked her.

"Yes. A gizma got me with its antenna three years ago."

"Okay. I'll get you fixed up in a jiffy." I took out a splint from my inventory. The girl and Ira shared an inquisitive look as they tilted their heads.

"There's no point in putting her knee in a splint at this point—her bone was broken and healed in a crooked position, which is why it hurts," Ira said.

"Just lemme do my thing." I placated her as I used the splint on the girl's leg. My body moved automatically to set the splint, and then I wrapped it up with a bandage. "There we go."

"I told you, there's no point in—"

"Hmm?!" The beastfolk girl's body suddenly quivered. We heard a now-familiar chorus of pops and crackles as bones and tissues shifted into place. Once they stopped, the splint glimmered and disappeared.

"How does it feel?" I asked.

"Uh... What?! It doesn't hurt! It doesn't hurt anymore!" She stood up, flexed her knee a couple of times, and then hopped up and down as a joyful smile spread across her face. It was hard to believe she was badly hurt just a few minutes ago.

Ira was silent. I glanced her way to find her eye wide open and staring ahead. The expression on her face seemed familiar... Oh, right. Like those images of a dumbfounded cat with a galaxy in the background I had seen on the internet.

"Who wants to be next?" I asked.

The next patient was a lizardfolk with an injured right arm. After what happened with Zarda, I wasn't going to leap to any conclusions about their gender this time. In any case, I went to go apply the splint when a hand blocked me.

"Wait, let me do it," Ira entreated me with a serious look on her face, having recovered from space-cat mode.

Hmm, I doubt it's gonna work, y'know. Sylphy couldn't get the results I did when she tried using the pickaxe I made on a boulder. I had a feeling the same thing would happen this time as well.

Reluctantly, I indulged her. "Okay."

It's not like there's any harm in letting her try. It'd be a godsend if someone other than me could use this thing with the same effect, I thought as I handed the splint over to her. With incredible speed and precision, she placed the splint and then wrapped up the bandage.

"How does it feel?" Ira asked.

"I don't feel anything," the lizardfolk answered in confusion.

Uh-huh, so it doesn't work if someone other than me uses the splints I made. I figured as much.

"Then lemme do it over." I unwound the bandage from their arm and reused the splint from the pop-up screen. *Hmm. I'm starting to get used to the feeling of my body moving on its own like this.*

"Huh? Whaaa?!" Just as before, their arm made a bunch of ugly gristly noises and then completely healed. The lizardfolk thanked me profusely as they left.

"Buh...?" Ira had gone back into space-cat mode. This time, her mouth hung half-open.

I continued healing people one after the other with the splints. Unfortunately, they didn't work to regrow lost limbs.

"Too bad," a large bear beastfolk said, chuckling with resignation. She was missing her right hand from the wrist down.

Dang, it'd be nice if I did come across an item that could heal something like that.

Meanwhile, Ira was still agog after witnessing such an illogical scene. It seemed like she had failed a sanity check but passed her idea roll... Bless her.

"Absurd. Illogical."

"There you go again," I muttered.

Sylphy chimed in, "Actually, I have to agree with Ira on this one."

"I totally agree." It was more than absurd that all I did was apply a splint and wrap it up with a bandage and I could cure all kinds of injuries—regular sprains, broken bones, even severed tendons. Ira wasn't *wrong*.

"But, like, how do I put it? Your power is...all over the place," Sylphy added.

"That describes it to a T," Ira said.

"I think I'd describe it more as sloppy," I replied. It kinda felt like all kinds of settings from different games had just been tossed together and thrown into me. All of my desires were met, but its execution was haphazard at best. I imagined some kind of system engineer struggling to keep up with their client's unreasonable requests on time. Ha ha ha. That'd be funny if it were true. "Well, the World of Gods probably has its own problems to deal with, right? I'll just be grateful there's no bugs."

Sylphy gave a firm nod. "It's been very useful, so I have no complaints."

Yeah, let's just leave it at that. Ahh, this cooked gizma sure is tasty. It's so tender. If I didn't know what gizmas actually looked like, I'd just write it off as like, a jumbo prawn.

"It looks like the soldiers are back from the forest."

"Yeah. It doesn't seem like anyone's been injured for now."

The people who had come back were carrying gizma hind legs and carapaces on their backs. I wasn't surprised they had decided to bring something back for their troubles. They replenished their supply of bolts, ate, and then reformed their groups. I saw Lianess the lamia and Nakul the squirrel beastfolk among them. I didn't see Zarda, so she must have been resting.

"Are we going to go hunting again?" I asked.

"We can. What do you think we should do?" Sylphy asked.

"Hmm, good question."

Visuals are imperative for firing on the enemy. In other words, it's important to maintain our field of vision around the bulwark. It'd be good to have traps to buy us time before they actually reach us too. Barbed wire and wood spikes work fine against humans, but gizmas are a completely different beast. In fact, they're more like tanks. I have a feeling they'd just trample what I can put up without being affected in the least.

Maybe there's a chance they'd get their legs tangled in barbed wire? I don't know if I have the materials for that. I do have barbed wire listed in my crafting menu, but it takes a hell of a lot of iron to make. Is it okay to use up so much right now? I have a feeling that there must be an easier way that wouldn't cost so much.

"I have some ideas," I said.

"Oh yeah? Go on, tell me."

"There's a good chance we'll be fighting them at night, so we'll need lights to see them."

"True. Do you have any ideas?"

"I'll prepare some torches."

"Uh, well, torches would certainly allow us to see, I guess?" Sylphy was cocking her head at me with a jumble of thoughts written on her face.

"I doubt they'll be normal torches," Ira said sharply with a glare.

Ira was starting to get an idea of what my power was all about. She was smart.

"I can also set up brick blocks to interrupt their charges," I added.

"Ah, that might just work." Sylphy nodded, seemingly recalling how much damage the gizmas took ramming themselves into my impromptu walls.

If we put torches on top of the brick blocks, that would get us the expanded field of view we needed. After we were done eating, we decided to visit Danan and tell him that I would be doing some construction to strengthen our defenses.

"Hmm. It would be best if I gave my opinion after. Go ahead and try building something." Danan readily gave us his blessing. It was starting to feel like he was getting used to dealing with me.

Since I had his permission, I decided to cut down all of the trees immediately surrounding the village so we'd have visibility on the gizmas as they approached.

"Maybe cutting them *all* down is a bit much," Sylphy protested.

"But they're all gonna wind up being knocked down when the gizmas attack. And the spirit archers are probably going to blow them away with their attacks too, right? It's best if we cut them down now and make good use of them while we still can."

Sylphy frowned and gave a little grunt, but she couldn't say I was wrong, so I carried on unimpeded. The materials from the trees could be used for making torches and laying out wood spikes. I was forever impressed with how many different applications I'd found for timber.

"I think that about does it," I said at last.

"Urgh, the forest..." Sylphy's ears drooped as she looked at the bare earth around the village.

I'm sorry, Sylphy, but I had to harden my heart for this endeavor... Secretly, seeing all the space I'd cleared was oddly satisfying.

"I'm going to start placing the bricks. What kind of shape should I make?"

"Squares aren't good enough?"

"Yeah, they're fine. I guess I'll have them be a whole block big." Taking the size of the gizmas into consideration, I left a certain amount of space in between blocks. If they were too close together, they'd be able to walk on top of them, and that'd defeat the purpose. I also made small walls here and there by lining two blocks next to each other, which were sure to soak up the force behind the gizmas' charges.

Once I'd finished setting the blocks, we gazed down at of the scattered blocks from atop the bulwark.

"What do you think?" I asked.

"Yeah, I think this'll make the approaching the bulwark pretty difficult."

If our foes were human-sized, they'd be able to use the blocks for cover, but for a critter the size of a luxury SUV, there was nowhere to hide. Also, we still held the high ground.

"I'll move on to the torches." I approached the bonfire that had been lit inside the bulwark, opened the crafting menu, and moved all of the torches I had crafted into my inventory.

Torch——Materials: Wood × 1
Torch——Materials: Wood × 1, Charcoal × 1
Torch——Materials: Wood × 1, Cloth × 1

The first recipe was made using the bonfire. The other two were recipes that could be crafted by hand and with the improved workbench. Obviously, crafting it with a bonfire used the least materials.

I wondered if one kind was better than the other, but they all stacked as the same item after I tried crafting the individual recipes. In other words, they were all exactly the same no matter what recipe I used. Making them with the bonfire was the most economical method.

I started placing the torches on top of the brick blocks. Seeing them stick straight up on top of the blocks all on their own made Ira's eye go dull, but I decided not to let that bother me.

Before long, all of the blocks had torches, and the sun set as I placed wood spikes around the outside of the bulwark. Thanks to the torches, the whole area was lit up like it was still daytime.

"Hey, Kousuke?" Sylphy said.

"Yes, Mistress?"

"Those torches seem like they're not going to ever burn out."

"Well, they're torches. They do what they do."

"Uh-huh." Sylphy sighed in resignation, pressing her temples.

It had been well over two hours since I placed the first torches, and they weren't burning out, let alone getting any smaller. But, I mean, they were torches. It was only common knowledge that once set, they'd keep burning until they were destroyed. Ha ha.

"Fire that won't ever stop burning..." Ira looked dead inside. Her cutest feature, her big eye, had completely lost its shine. From a magical point of view, I wouldn't be surprised if those torches were an abomination. Not that they were okay by normal laws of physics either—it was like they were flipping thermodynamics the double bird, cackling and asking for a fight.

I was standing on top of the bulwark, gazing at the blocks I'd set in the kill zone and wondering what to do next, when I spotted everyone who went out gizma hunting trickling back into the village from the forest.

They were surprised to see how the village had changed, but after spotting me on top of the bulwark, they seemed to grasp the situation. I got the feeling that the refugees were starting to recognize my absurdity. By absurdity, I didn't mean me personally, but my abilities. Well, maybe we weren't mutually exclusive...

"By the way, are we going to stay here keeping watch for the gizmas today?" I asked Sylphy.

"No, there'll be guards. Danan said those who aren't keeping lookout were to rest, so we'll be heading home too. It's pointless for everyone to exhaust their stamina."

"I see."

Makes sense. We wouldn't want everyone be worn out by the time the gizmas arrive. I looked up at the sky and was disturbed by what I saw. "Hey, does the moon look red to you, or is it just me?"

"Hmm? No, it looks the same as it always does to me."

"Really?" The name of this world's moon was Lanicle. The sun and a huge planet also hung in the sky, but they seemed fine at the moment. The thing was, the moon actually did look red to me. Like the blood moon had risen once again. Please be careful, Kousuke. "Ira, what about you? Does the moon look red to you?"

"If I had to say what color Lanicle usually is, it'd be yellow. And it looks yellow now too," Ira said while gazing up at the moon.

Yet it looked red to my eyes. Could there be a more ominous sign in a survival game than a blood moon? Nope.

"What's wrong, Kousuke?" Sylphy asked.

"I don't know why the moon only looks red to me, but from what I know, a blood moon is an omen that enemies are going to start charging *en masse*," I explained.

"Really?"

"Do you think I'd make up something like this?"

Sylphy looked at Ira, who thought this over for a moment before nodding. "I think that everyone, including me, has come to realize that Kousuke's abnormal by now. I believe it would be wise to listen to him and strengthen the guard."

"Yeah, you're right. I'll go talk to the elders," Sylphy said.

"And I'll tell Danan."

"What about me?" I asked.

"You stay here, okay?"

"Okay, Mistress."

I thought things over as I watched Sylphy and Ira rush off. *I should probably leave watching the perimeter to the beastfolk on guard duty. I'm sure they've got better eyesight than me anyway. What should I do, then?*

"I could make more weapons, I suppose." However, I doubted I could make anything stronger than crossbows for now. I could make the composite bow, but I wasn't sure how it compared to crossbows in terms of power. If only there was a weapon that was definitely stronger per hit. "Hmm, I doubt I've got enough time to make gunpowder."

I guess I could dig up some soil from the bathroom? But if I'm not careful, I'll have to contend with that awful outhouse smell. But I should do it anyway, shouldn't I? I looked fruitlessly at the smithing station's menu. *If I had lots of oil, I could probably make something like a Molotov cocktail, though.*

My thoughts whirled as I heard the howls of countless gizmas rising from the forest depths—or maybe they were coming from close to the badlands. In any case, it was still far off. But it sounded like they had begun their march.

"No point in wishing for something I don't have now." I took out the improved crossbow from my inventory and aimed it. I had a mountain of crossbow bolts at my disposal. In fact, I had made 10,000 of them just in case, and I still had over 5,000 of them in my inventory. "Righty then. Come at me, bugs!"

I had a massive wall they couldn't jump over, obstacles to slow them down, wood spikes spread out outside, and all the crossbows and archers to use them I could ask for.

Heh, victory was all but decided!

"Aim! Fire!"

I heard the sound of countless snaps of bowstrings. I couldn't really hear the fletching of the bolts themselves cutting through the air; I wasn't sure if that was because they were small or because bolts were actually quiet flyers. *Maybe the sound of a bolt in flight is a private whisper to the person it's meant for.*

"SKREEEEE?!"

"SKROEEEEE?!"

All I could hear were the gizmas screaming in agony as they died. *So, lemme tell you what happened.*

"Our army's sure something," I said.

"Ha ha ha. With enough of these weapons, we are undeniably overwhelming." Jagheera laughed as she drew back the string on her improved crossbow.

She wasn't wrong. Each volley chewed through rank after rank of gizmas; the kit I'd supplied everyone had proven quite effective. *Too* effective, thanks to how many crossbow wielders we had.

"What's our headcount?" I asked.

"I heard we numbered a little under 200."

"Wow, 200 people firing at 20 gizmas per volley... Yeah, they never stood a chance against us."

The gizmas crawled out of the forest in a ceaseless stream, but the vast obstacle course I assembled slowed them down; carcasses choked the narrow paths between the blocks, forcing the next wave of gizmas to crowd together at the edge of the kill zone, where we promptly shot them to pieces with our next volley.

The survivors found the going that much slower as they waded through bodies. Some started trying to circle around, but they wound up being shot in the flanks and paralyzed. Others tried climbing over the carcasses to break through the lines, but they stood out like sore thumbs from up here on the rampart.

"Don't let them get any closer! Shoot!"

And just like that, they'd be riddled with bolts.

"Everyone's so quick at reloading," I mused.

"It's because we beastfolk have such strong bodies. I doubt our reload time would be much slower if we were all equipped with improved crossbows," Jagheera said.

"I see. Maybe I should've made more."

Jagheera had taken up her position next to me, firing one shot after the other. She told me she had picked this spot next to me because she figured she wouldn't be wanting for bolts, no matter how many she used. She certainly possessed keen insight, which I supposed you'd need as a scout.

"It looks like we won't need those spirit archers after all, huh?" I said.

"You're right about that."

Countless bodies filled the kill zone. Our pace had slowed from a volley every ten seconds at the start of battle to every fifteen seconds. If we kept going at our starting pace, we would've used up about 5,000 bolts within four minutes.

Melty approached. "Kousuke, we are running low on bolts."

"Take as many as you'd like." I kept 200 for myself and Jagheera but took out the rest of my remaining bolts and handed them over. I was sure glad I had made 10,000 of them.

Not even an hour had gone by, and the rate at which the gizmas charged had slowed down, so Danan ceased our volleys and ordered that we wait to shoot until we drew them out, probably to conserve bolts. Letting them get closer to the wall would make it easier to retrieve the bolts later anyway.

"How long is gizma meat good for before it starts going bad?" I asked.

"Hmm? Probably about half a day," Jagheera replied.

"I see. Should I go collect them then?"

"Huh? You wanna go out there?"

"It should be fine if I bring people who are good at melee, right? Gizma meat is pretty tasty. I wouldn't want it to go to waste."

I left the dumbfounded Jagheera and headed over to Danan, who was giving orders. He had taken up a position above the gate at a spot I'd made to his specifications. It was pretty spacious, so it made for a good command post and a solid choke point where you could intercept and hold off the enemy.

"Oh, Kousuke. What's the matter?"

"The gizmas aren't coming so frequently now, right? I'd like to go collect their carcasses. I should be able to do it quickly enough with my ability, and the meat won't spoil that way either."

"Ah. Very well, let's organize a squad to send into the fray with you. Worg, I'm leaving you in charge here."

"Yes, sir," Worg responded, saluting. It seemed as though he was something like Danan's adjutant.

"If it's someone for close-range combat you require, I shall go with you," Gerda the bear beastfolk volunteered.

Gerda was quite big and looked pretty powerful. She seemed like a carefree gal, though, which made me wonder if she could actually fight. She had one of the swords I had repaired and given to Danan hanging off her hip, but an iron sword meant for human hands looked out of place on a big bear beastfolk like her.

Ahhh, crud. Since I wasn't planning on any of us fighting the things up close and personal, I didn't make any weapons at all. Do I have anything I could give her? Oh, maybe this'll do.

"Miss Gerda?"

"Yes? What is it? And feel free to call me just Gerda."

"Oh, okay. Sure. Uh, so that sword doesn't seem like it really suits you."

"Ah, yeah, you're right. I honestly wouldn't be surprised if I snapped it right in half." Gerda touched a hand to her cheek and chuckled awkwardly.

To put into perspective how big of a person she was, the thing was nearly half as long as I was tall, and it looked like a shortsword on her.

"Can you tell Danan that I'll be on standby around the gate? I'm gonna try to make a weapon that'll suit you better. What kind do you favor?"

"Wow, are you sure? Back when I was heavy armored infantry for the Kingdom of Merinard, I used a custom-made tower shield and long mace."

"A tower shield and a long mace, eh? Got it." I left a smiling Gerda and picked out a spot close to the gate that had some space.

I had spent far more time crafting stuff here than at my workshop at Sylphy's. The refugees were coming to recognize it as my workspace.

Well, that's fine. Anyway, I should get crafting while Danan's pulling the team together. I put down my smithing station, inserted some fuel, and looked over the list of weapons. I didn't see a long mace.

I imagined a mace, with its long and durable handle and sturdy head. Then I imagined a much bigger mace.

Long Mace—Materials: Steel Plate Spring × 3, Iron × 3

Yeesh, expensive materials. Then again, it is *practically made of solid metal. Now let's see if there's a tower shield. Tower shield, tower shield... Not on the list. There's a scutum, though. Maybe that's good enough?*

Scutum—Materials: Animal Hide × 3, Cloth × 3, Iron × 1

It looks like this is a shield made of iron but reinforced with animal hides. Gerda would surely make better use of a shield made of proportionally more metal. I imagined the scutum, subbed in a thin yet solid steel plate reinforced with wood and leather. *That glue we got from the storehouse should work to bind them.*

Heavy Tower Shield——Materials: Steel Plate Spring × 3, Wood × 2,
    Animal Hide × 2, Adhesive × 1

Yeah, that should do. Time to start crafting. I should pick out a weapon for myself too. Hmm, I am a complete noob at this, though. I'm probably better off using a crossbow or gun, but I should take into consideration the possibility that I might get involved in up-close-and-personal kinda combat. What would work for me, then? Then again, common soldiers all have the same kinds of weapons, no matter where they're from: spears or clubs.

Steel Spear——Materials: Iron × 3, Wood × 2
Spiked Club——Materials: Iron × 2, Wood × 2
Mace——Materials: Iron × 4, Wood × 2

So, I decided to make those. The spiked club looked like a fiendish version of a nail bat. *I'll see how it feels compared to the mace.*

I was working on crafting those when Danan and the others came walking over. Sylphy was with him; the spirit archers must have been deployed on top of the bulwark. That sure took her a while.

"Welcome back, Sylphy."

"Thanks, Kousuke. Are you really planning to go out there?"

"I can't let anything we can make good use of go to waste. Gerda, I finished your weapons. Try them out." I handed the long mace and tower shield over to Gerda.

"Wow, thank you!" She looked as gleeful as a kid on Christmas day.

Okay, I understand you're happy and all, but I wish you'd give it some test swings somewhere else. The sound of it cutting through the air is scaring me.

"These have a good weight to them. I'll be able to smash the gizmas to bits," Gerda said.

"That's great." I cleaned up the smithing station and tested how my own weapons felt. The spear was heavier than I had imagined. I could probably use it as a blunt weapon too. I found the spiked club felt better in my hand than the mace did. The mace just felt a bit too heavy for me.

"Are those your newest creations?" Sylphy asked.

"Yeah, to test out. I don't like how the mace feels, though."

"That so? Then give it to me."

"Huh? Uh, okay." I handed it over.

Whoa, she's swinging it around as easily as a twig. Her arms weren't that thick and felt soft to the touch, but she was surprisingly strong. Was it magic or something?

"Are we all set to head out?" Danan asked.

"Yes, sir!" the team shouted in response.

The lineup was me, Sylphy, Danan, Gerda, a woman who

looked like a red-skinned oni with a horn on her head (brandishing a huge club made of wood), a lizardfolk wielding an iron spear (I couldn't tell their gender), a man with the face of a lion gripping two iron swords (whose leg I had healed this afternoon), and Ira, who was brandishing a staff.

"Ira? Are you gonna be okay out there?" I asked.

"I'll be fine. They didn't make me court wizard for no reason."

"If you say so."

Was she going to fire beams out of her eye? Just kidding. She was probably going to fight with some kind of magic. I looked forward to it.

"Our objective is retrieval of the gizma carcasses. Kousuke's doing the heavy lifting. Everyone else, protect him. Understood? Open the gate!" Danan ordered.

The bar was removed and the large doors reinforced with iron opened. *All right, time to go nuts and fill my inventory to bursting!*

"Your power is—how should I put it? Odd," the lion-faced man said.

"Sir Leonard, you should already know as much from that business with your leg today," Ira told him.

"You have a point."

His full name was too long for me to remember, but Leonard had once been a knight, so everyone addressed him as "Sir." He was of a different station from Danan, who had been a royal guard.

He must have been the one people were referring to when they mentioned the Kingdom of Merinard had a master swordsman.

"I don't really understand it, but it does seem like a useful kinda power to have. It's different than magic, right?" This came from Shemel, the red oni woman with the club. She was even bigger than Danan and Gerda. She had to be easily over 2.5 meters tall.

"Yes, his power is a bit different from magic. In fact, he doesn't have any trace of magic within him," Ira explained.

"That means he and I are alike! I can't use magic at all either." Shemel grinned viciously.

"Let's get a move on. There could be trouble if the gizmas start advancing," the lizardfolk woman named Madame Zamil said as she vigilantly surveyed the area, iron spear at the ready.

"Right. Though I wouldn't mind getting the chance to try out this weapon," Gerda said.

"Such a nice weapon. I wish I had something like that." Madame Zamil looked at me pleadingly.

It was hard to read lizardfolk, but I could tell from her eyes. The eyes were the window to the soul, after all. She definitely wanted me to make her something.

I'd heard that Madame Zamil had once been a spearmanship instructor back in the Kingdom of Merinard and was a master with the weapon. In fact, everyone with me now was powerful enough to take a gizma down on their own.

Sylphy's power required no explanation at this point. As Danan had once been a royal guard, he was a force to be reckoned with in battle. Apparently, Gerda had used her Herculean strength to defeat a gizma with her bare hands once. Sir Leonard was known as "Leonard the Twin-Fanged" for his skill with dual blades. Shemel had once been a high-ranking adventurer called "The Meat Masher." Madame Zamil didn't have anything like a nickname, but given that she had once been Danan's instructor, I knew she had to be skilled. Word had it that Danan had never once beaten Madame Zamil in a sparring match.

Me? Well, my job was to sneak around picking up corpses, safely hidden in the shadow of all these superbeings.

"Did he make your weapon as well, Danan?" Madame Zamil asked.

"Yes, he did, ma'am," Danan answered.

"I would like some better swords myself," Sir Leonard said.

"If you're asking for a weapon, then I'd like an actual weapon. I mean, this is just a log. Look." Shemel motioned with her club.

The three of them turned to face me, and I looked to Sylphy for help. She nodded at me. *Oh, okay.*

"Sylphy's given me her permission, so I'll make something for you all later. Please think about what kind of weapon you would like," I told them.

"Understood," Madame Zamil said.

"Mm." Sir Leonard grunted his agreement.

"Will doo-hoo!" Shemel said.

The three looked satisfied. Well, whatever. My fighting prowess was of no importance. If I made such powerful people indebted to me, then they were sure to protect me in an emergency.

As Shingen Takeda had once said, "People are my castles, my stone walls, and my moats."

"SKREEEEEEEEE!"

"Hmph, looks like we have company," Sir Leonard said.

We heard more gizma howls coming from the dark forest. *Uh-oh, is this their second wave?*

"That doesn't sound good. Should we run?" I asked.

"What are you worrying about? They won't be able to surround us, let alone charge us here," Sir Leonard said casually. I hadn't even noticed he had already drawn his swords.

"I wish I shared your optimism, Sir Leonard."

"The old man's not wrong. The only thing they can use in a place like this is their antennae," Madame Zamil said.

"Do not refer to me in such a disrespectful way."

"As if titles matter on the battlefield."

"Well...you're not wrong."

Despite the fact that the gizmas were going to show themselves any second now, they were joking. It was odd how relaxed they seemed.

"Kousuke, don't worry about them. You just focus on collecting the bodies," Sylphy said.

"Aye aye, ma'am."

Everyone but Sylphy, who remained behind to protect me, rushed into battle against the gizmas. I kept an eye out for them out of the corner of my eye as I collected one carcass after the other.

"Hah!" Danan attacked! The gizma's head was sliced in two straight down the middle!

"Aye!" Gerda attacked! The long mace smashed the gizma's head in!

The gizma attacked! It snapped its quick antenna at Sir Leonard!

"Hmph." Sir Leonard lopped the gizma's antenna right off! Sir Leonard launched a counterattack! He beheaded the gizma!

"Hah!" Madame Zamil attacked! It was a critical hit! She stabbed the gizma right in the face and killed it!

"Take this!" Shemel attacked! The gizma was mashed into pieces. Huh? Why?! Why did she mash it?!

"Shemel, we won't be able to collect the gizmas if you pound them like that," Sir Leonard admonished her.

"Sorry 'bout that. Sometimes I don't know my own strength." Shemel apologized as she scratched her head with her log club.

"Burst forth, thunder. Lightning!" A bright light flooded the area, followed by a thunderous roar.

I looked to the source to see thunderbolts flying out of Ira's staff, routing several gizmas.

"Holy crap! Magic's incredible! Don't you agree, Sylphy?! Look, she used magic! Magic's amazing!" I babbled excitedly.

"Stop acting like a kid who's seeing magic for the first time... Then again, I suppose this *is* your first time, isn't it?" Sylphy replied.

"Yeah! I've only ever seen you using that healing spell before."

"Ah. Well, Ira's destructive magic is on a different level, her being a mage and all. It's not something you get to see every day."

Hearing Sylphy's praise, Ira looked kinda proud as she threw up a small peace sign.

"Hey, you all make it sound like I'm the oddball human here, but if you ask me, you're the odd ones." I mean, I didn't have the power to chop, smash to pieces, stab to death, or mash a bug the size of a small truck in one blow, let alone electrocute one.

"Anyone can become an expert with magic or weapons if they put their mind to it," Sir Leonard said.

"Oh yeah? Is that what you really think?" Shemel responded.

If that were true, then the humans of this world were far stronger than I could ever be. Without my crafting and command actions, I'd be completely powerless.

"Our worlds just have different ideas of common sense," Sir Leonard explained.

Maybe. I found it a bit hard to agree with that statement; their powers made sense enough, but mine didn't follow any world's understanding of how anything worked, even the one I came from. That must have been why they all eyed me with curiosity.

"If you've got time to ponder life's mysteries, you've got time to move your feet. Get back to it," Sylphy commanded.

"Aye aye, ma'am."

She's right. Now's not the time to be standing around with my head in the clouds. I went around the entire kill zone while my protectors hacked and slashed away, picking up carcasses as I went. Believe it or not, I picked up 216 of them. *Lemme think. So, two of these would be enough to feed all of the refugees for a day, which means that we've got enough food for 108 days.*

"I bet Melty'll be pleased," I said.

"Not just her, but all of the refugees too. Having gizma meat makes a huge impact on their eating habits," Sylphy replied.

"Yeah! Meat really elevates a soup," Gerda chimed in.

"Gizma meat makes great soup stock," Sir Leonard agreed.

I got the feeling that the two might actually be foodies.

"And it's because of you that I can join the hunt once again. I've been eating without doing my part for the people, so I'll be sure to make up for that."

"I quite doubt that, Sir Leonard. All an old man like you cares about is sating your overdeveloped palate," Madame Zamil pointed out.

"Why should I desire to eat anything less than the finest fare the world can offer? Gah, these blades from the Holy Kingdom are dull. They're practically useless at this point."

"They say that master swordsmen should not be picky about their swords... Be that as it may, we all have our limits. Look, this spear is just plain awful."

"These weapons look like they'd shatter into pieces if we use too much magic with them."

Sir Leonard and Madame Zamil looked my way. *I know, I know. You don't have to look at me like that.*

"I'm not picky as long as it can handle me," Shemel said.

Everyone seemed intent on making me whip up weapons for them the second we got back to the village. *Sylphy, save me!*

"It shouldn't take you too long to make, right? Go ahead and make them something to repay them for guarding you today.

By the way, I'd also like a weapon with a bit more reach." How could she betray me like this?!

"Yes, ma'am," I muttered.

Ira tugged on the hem of my shirt. "One for me too."

"You want one too?" I tilted my head as I gave her an inquisitive look. Ira didn't use weapons, right?

"I want a staff made of you-know-what."

"You-know-what? Oh, *that*... Hmm, I'm not sure I can make something like that with what I've got to work with right now. I'm guessing that magical staves require specialized techniques and ornaments and stuff?"

"Hmm, you're right. I'll draw up a design for you, then."

"D-don't make it too complicated, now. I might not be able to make it right if it's too intricate."

I don't know how accurately I can make something based on someone's design, especially one they put a lot of thought into. However, since I can make bolts and nuts, there's a good chance that I can make some designs that require a high level of precision. Right? That's what I'm gonna believe. Yeah.

We heard cheers as we passed through the big gate back into the village. Everyone who couldn't participate in the battle mobbed us the moment we came into view. *Hey, quit that! Who just touched my butt?!*

"Ha ha ha. Aren't we the popular one?" Sylphy, who wasn't being mobbed, laughed cheerfully. *Stop laughing and help me!*

"Now, now, give Kousuke some space. He's still got work to do." Sir Leonard clapped his hands and rescued me from the sea of new fans. I was overcome with gratitude. "It's time for you to make me those swords."

My heart, swelling with thankfulness, deflated like a sad balloon. It was clear that this old man only did things for his own selfish ends.

"And make me a spear," Madame Zamil demanded.

"You can make something for me last," Shemel said.

I had no way out! Not that I really had any reason to squirm.

"You need to tell me more concretely what kind of weapons you'd like. There are all kinds, y'know. Like, for swords, do you want it to be light and sharp? Or heavy and solid? Or do you want one that's particularly sharp, or one that's more focused on impact or piercing power? Do you want it straight or curved? Do you want one or two edges? Do you want one you hold in one hand or both hands? Long or short? I can go on."

"Huh, you know more about swords than I thought. I prefer broadswords that excel at slashing and carry some *weight* behind the blow. If I had to pick, I'd say I prefer single-edged blades more," Sir Leonard told me.

"I'd prefer a spear for piercing. However, I'd like the blade to be a bit long and capable of slicing as well," Madame Zamil said.

"I'm not particularly picky, but I'm no expert in lining up my swings. I'd prefer a blunt weapon, if possible," Shemel said.

"Got it." After hearing their requests, I opened the crafting menu in the smithing station and looked to see if I had any weapons that fit their criteria. Nope, none. I decided to first take the steel spear I had in my inventory out and show it to Madame Zamil. "This is the standard steel spear I can make, but you'd prefer one with a blade that's a bit longer, right?"

"Hmm, this is a nice spear... If the blade were about *this* long, that'd be ideal."

"When I take durability into account, I think the blade will have to be broader and heavier."

"I don't mind. In fact, I'd say this one is far too light."

"Okay."

It sounds like she wants something more like a shortsword with an unusual hilt, I thought to myself but I decided to try to make it as ordered. *Hmm, I feel like I've seen a spear like that in a manga before... Oh yeah, that one. That manga called* Ushio and Tora *with the yokai-killing spear. I'll go ahead and make it in that one's likeness.*

Sir Leonard would probably like falchions. They're broad and solid with some heft to them, so they're good at cutting. They're what you'd expect a barbarian to carry, but they tick off all of the boxes, so they should be good enough.

Shemel's weapon is a no-brainer. When you think of a red oni's weapon, you think of greatclubs—kanabo, the long metallic kind with the spikes.

By imagining what all of these weapons looked like, listings for the beast spear, falchion, and kanabo appeared in my inventory.

Uh, that name for the spear is almost lifted straight from the source material! Is this allowed? No one will get mad, right? Well, I suppose there're no copyright lawyers in this world to worry about!

I went ahead and selected the new weapons from the menu and started crafting them. I made sure not to look at how many materials the kanabo was going to cost me. *Ha ha ha. I'm gonna have to go mining again soon.*

"All done." I took out the two falchions, beast spear, and kanabo and went to hand it to each—holy smokes! The kanabo was really heavy! I couldn't even hold it!

"Huh, these swords have a somewhat crude feel to them, but they're practical," Sir Leonard said with a satisfied smile.

"Marvelous," Madame Zamil said with a similar expression.

"Ha ha ha! I like this!" Shemel was beaming.

How in the world is she able to swing the kanabo around one-handed so easily? That thing has to weigh over thirty kilograms. I guess she was wielding a huge log up until now...

"I wonder if more gizmas are going to come," I said.

"That's a good question. There seems to be a lull for now, but who knows if they'll come out in swarms again," Sylphy replied.

"Then I should probably make some more bolts."

"Yeah, go ahead and do that. That's the best way you can contribute, after all."

Our retrieval team had broken up, and everyone but Sylphy and I headed over to the bulwark again. Sylphy and I stayed in my workspace to make more bolts. Granted, Sylphy was only here for moral support.

I queued up the arrowheads in my smithing station while I dismembered the gizmas in my inventory. I was also able to recover shot bolts that way too. Some of the bolts' arrowheads broke, but I could mend them using the smithing station.

Sylphy watched me at work without saying anything in particular. *I wonder what's going through her head right now? Women's hearts sure are complex.*

"Sylphy?"

"Yeah?"

"What kind of weapon do you want?"

"Hmm... Anything's fine, so long as you're the one who makes it."

"At least pick a type of weapon." I chuckled awkwardly, which made her laugh too.

"If you insist. Some kind of blade, then. How about a sword?"

"A sword?"

"Yeah, something that you think would suit me. Oh yeah, how about one of those scimitars you mentioned before?"

"A scimitar?" I had indeed recommended that to her once. An elegantly decorated scimitar would suit someone as beautiful as Sylphy. Perhaps you'd understand what I mean if I called it a shamshir instead?

Well, the name wasn't that important. However, I doubted that scimitars, what with them being so thin and more specialized for slashing attacks, would be that effective against the gizmas or someone wearing armor, even if I made it out of iron or steel.

I considered making it out of mithril instead. Ira had asked for a mithril staff, after all. It'd probably be a good way to test the material.

"Okay, I'll give it a try."

I'll make a scimitar out of mithril. I want it to be decorated with gems too. It has to be sharp, strong, unbending—an exceptional sword that fully utilizes the special qualities of mithril. The blade should be the pale color of moonlight, which would fit Sylphy's image.

Mithril Scimitar—Materials: Mithril Ore × 4, Gem × 5,
Silver Ore × 2, Iron × 2, Steel Plate Spring × 2, Leather × 1

Ooh, there it is. Right in my menu: a mithril scimitar. Now let's queue that up to craft.

"Holy *cow*, that's a tall order!" I exclaimed.

"What's the matter?"

"Well, I'm trying to make you a special weapon, but it's gonna take *forever*."

"Oh? How long?"

"Four hours."

"That...is a long time."

That was the longest crafting time I had ever seen here. As it so happened, the second-longest crafting time I had seen was Shemel's kanabo, which had taken two and a half minutes.

"What on Leece are you making?" Sylphy asked.

"You'll just have to wait and see."

Didn't mithril swords normally take months, maybe even years to make? It only made sense that, even with my power working overtime to compress the task, this sword was gonna be an ordeal.

We were on high alert after that, and I went out to collect the occasional gizma carcass until past midnight. Around the time the date ticked over, the gizmas ceased their attacks. The moon went back to its usual yellowish color as well.

It seemed like we had somehow managed to overcome the gizmas.

The day after the battle, Sylphy and I ate some of my inventoried edibles for breakfast and went to visit the bulwark. The spirit archers and crossbow-wielding refugees who had finished standing guard were sleepily eating breakfast.

Danan had been on guard duty all night, but he didn't look tired at all. What was he, that pink battery-operated bunny?

"Good morning, Your Highness."

"Morning, Danan. What happened after we left?"

"We didn't see a single one. I sent out a patrol at sunrise, so we should hear back from them before long."

"I see. You were in command all night, weren't you? Go get some rest."

"Yes, I was. I'll get in some sack time as soon as I see the chance."

As the two of them talked, I was busy accessing my smithing station, which I had left here overnight. *Yup, it's done.*

"Sylphy."

"Yeah? What is it?"

"Your weapon is ready."

I took the mithril scimitar in its leather scabbard out of my inventory and handed it over to Sylphy. The pommel and guard were decorated with gems; it looked like a treasured sword with all its detailed engravings.

Sylphy looked surprised at how it sat in her grip. For some reason, the blade felt as light as a feather. "Kousuke, you didn't..."

"Go on, draw it."

She nodded and unsheathed the sword. The beautiful curved scimitar shone bluish-white in the morning rays. The blade was thin yet finely sharpened. It looked like moonlight that had been forged into a sword.

"How incredible..." Danan breathed. "Princess, is that made of...?"

"Yes, mithril. Kousuke, does this blade have a name?"

"No, I didn't give it one. Back home, the moon's got this pale, milky color, and I wanted to make something that captured that. If we give it a name, maybe something like Moonbeam or Moonlight? Agh, those are a bit too obvious, huh? Hmm, Blue Moon's not very good either. Oh, how about Pale Moon?"

"Pale Moon? Yeah, I like that. From now on, this blade shall be called Pale Moon." Sylphy raised the newly named Pale Moon, eliciting clapping and cheers from the refugees who had been watching us.

Ooh, widdle ol' me is digging the applause. I think they really like it?

"Finely crafted mithril swords are considered national treasures in every nation in our world. The fact that this was given by a Fabled Visitor brings it even more prestige. I wouldn't be surprised if people see this sword as the symbol of the Kingdom of Merinard's revival," Ira said as she materialized out of nowhere, making me cry out in surprise.

In her hands was a big piece of paper bearing some sort of diagram. *Ah, yes. I got it. Using this mithril ore too, right? Yeah, yeah.*

"Kousuke, take out one of the gizma carcasses. I want to test out my new blade," Sylphy commanded just as I was taking the goods from her.

"Aye aye, ma'am." I laid out one of the carcasses I had yet to dismember. This one had been killed from melee attacks and didn't have any bolts in it. From the hole in its face, I surmised that it was Madame Zamil's kill.

"Hah!" Sylphy swung Pale Moon and cut cleanly through the gizma's carapace.

Whoa. Was that for real? She cut through it so smoothly that "like a hot knife through butter" didn't even begin to describe it.

Sylphy swung Pale Moon again and again, dismantling the gizma in the blink of an eye. It took less than a minute to cut the gizma to bits. *Damn. Maybe this sword's a bit too overpowered.*

"That is a marvelous blade. However, you must take care not to accidentally strike yourself," Danan warned.

"Your Highness, I would gladly train you any time you desired," Leonard offered.

"And feel free to ask me as well," Madame Zamil said.

"I'm sure I'll call upon you," Sylphy told them.

I had a feeling that I'd be making wooden practice swords next.

We wound up staying on alert all day in case the gizmas attacked again. In other words, I spent the day mass-producing more crossbow bolts and doing maintenance on the crossbows that had been used last night.

The gizma that Sylphy sliced apart was thoroughly washed and stewed all the way down to the shell for lunch. The flavor just about knocked me on my ass. Did they make the stock from its carapace?

As it turned out, a gizma's shell was far too valuable as raw material for tools of all stripes to be used in cuisine, except as a delicacy reserved for nobles and royalty. We'd quite literally eaten like kings.

Incidentally, Sir Leonard had been over the moon about the prospect and taken over in the kitchen. He was a man truly driven by his desires; I couldn't begrudge him for it.

Soooo...

Really, all I had to do was set all of the day's business in my crafting queue and then sit around twiddling my thumbs. I had nothing better to do, so I perused my achievements, skills, and level.

I was now level 12. *Nice, I leveled up again.* Now I saw not just a gauge for my health and stamina, but also numbers to go along with it. Right now, I had 120 points for both health and stamina. I also had six more skill points to spend and some new achievements.

My First Brew——: Brew a potion for the first time. *Unlocks a skill.
My First Creation——: Create an item for the first time. *Unlocks a skill.

The "My First" series grew ever longer. The brewing one was easy enough to understand, but the creation one? I hadn't had that one yet when I made the bardiche for Danan.

My First Brewing Bench——: Craft a brewing bench for the first time. *Unlocks the numeric display for health and stamina.

Ooh, that explains it. What else did I get?

Novice Hunter——: Kill 10 monsters. *Raises health and stamina by 10 points.

So this is why my health and stamina are at 120 points. Maybe the next achievement is for killing 100 of them?

Novice Weaponsmith——: Make 100 weapons. *Improves weapon production time and quality by 5%.

5%? How are you supposed to tell the difference? I suppose masters might actually be able to tell. In any case, now I'll be able to get more achievements from crafting weapons, and I'll be able to gradually improve the quality of what I make too.

> **Fantasy Smither——:** Make a weapon using a fantasy metal.
> *Decreases the time it takes to craft items using fantasy metals by 10%.

Oh, this must come from crafting a weapon out of mithril. 10% is actually a good boost.

> **Heartthrob——:** On good terms with over five members of the opposite sex. Don't come crying to me if you get stabbed. ☆
> *Attacks against the opposite sex are increased by 5%.

Screw off with that sassy bit at the end. But more importantly, I have no idea what or whom this achievement is referring to. Aside from Sylphy, the only women I know are Ira, Melty, Jagheera, Pirna, Gerda, Madame Zamil, and Shemel. Oh yeah, and those three who had been cornered by gizmas—Zarda, Lianess, and Nakul... Huh, I actually do know a lot of women! And there's also all of those ladies I healed too. But surely this doesn't include any of the elven elders, right?

Wh-who's to say, though? Better not to think about it. I only have eyes for Sylphy anyway, and that's good enough for me.

> **Survivor——:** Survive the night of a Blood Moon for the first time.
> *Unlocks skill level-ups.

And that was the last one on the list. *Skill level-ups? Does that mean I can increase the effects of skills I already acquired? I'd love to test that out. Onward to skills, then.*

Skilled Worker——: Crafting time is reduced by 20%.

Dismantler——: Number of materials acquired when disassembling a crafting item is increased by 10%.

Repairman——: The time to repair items is reduced and the cost of materials is reduced by 20%.

Mass-Producer——: When you make more than ten of the same item, the number of required materials is reduced by 10%.

★ Logger——: Number of plant materials obtained is increased by 20%.

★ Miner——: Number of minerals obtained is increased by 20%.

★ Anatomist——: Number of materials obtained from bodies is increased by 20%.

Creator——: Lowers the difficulty level for item creation.

I wasn't sure what exactly the Creator skill's effect was, but I had a feeling it would be a no-brainer pick. Maybe it would come into play when making weapons with more complicated mechanisms or machines.

★ Heart Healthy——: Stamina recovery speed is increased by 20%.

★ Fleet-Footed——: Movement speed is increased by 10%.

Strong Arm——: Attacks with melee weapons are increased by 20%.

★ Sharpshooter——: Attacks with ranged weapons are increased by 20%.

Iron Skin——: Damage taken is reduced by 20%.

Survivor——: Health is increased by 10% and Health recovery
  speed is increased by 20%.
Medic——: Effects of recovery items are increased by 20%.
Reptilian Stomach——: Hunger reduction speed is reduced by 20%.
Camel Hump——: Thirst reduction speed is reduced by 20%.

*So the new skill added here is Medic, huh? And it increases the
effects of recovery items? This is pretty useless if you have plenty of
them prepared ahead of time. I guess I can see it being a useful skill
if I end up short on resources. Now, what should I use my six skill
points on? First up, Creator. Duh.*

Thinking about what might lie ahead, I got the feeling that
I should take that Mass-Producer one. *If I want to keep helping
Sylphy, then obviously I'll be mass-producing all kinds of things.*

*Since I know how much time mithril weapons take to make now,
it might be best to grab Skilled Worker as well. Dismantler and
Repairman are tempting, but...I'll pass on them for now.*

*And it wouldn't hurt to take some skills that directly improve my
life expectancy.* I considered taking Iron Skin and Survivor, but I
decided I wanted to try leveling up a skill first. *Which one should
I level up? Hmm, Miner, I guess. I'll have plenty of uses for mineral
resources from now on, after all.*

★ Miner II——: Number of minerals obtained is increased by 40%.

I spent two skill points to level up Miner. *I'm glad I decided to
try doing this first; if I took Iron Skin and Survivor, I would've only*

had one point left and felt pretty down that I couldn't try this. I guess I'll take Iron Skin. 20% less damage is a pretty big boost.

★ Skilled Worker——: Crafting time is reduced by 20%.

★ Mass-Producer——: When you make more than ten of the same item, the number of required materials is reduced by 10%.

★ Miner——: Number of minerals obtained is increased by 20%.

★ Miner II——: Number of minerals obtained is increased by 40%.

★ Anatomist——: Number of materials obtained from bodies is increased by 20%.

★ Creator——: Lowers the difficulty level for item creation.

★ Heart Healthy——: Stamina recovery speed is increased by 20%.

★ Fleet-Footed——: Movement speed is increased by 10%.

★ Sharpshooter——: Attacks with ranged weapons are increased by 20%.

★ Iron Skin——: Damage taken is reduced by 20%.

That was what my current skills looked like. I'd made some good choices, if I might say so myself. If I knew I was going to have to be on my own, I'd take different skills, but there wasn't really any call for me to participate in combat. I was comfortable as a craftsman with some basic self-defense fundamentals.

There was only one thing that worried me.

"Were these attacks coincidental or not? That's the question."

The night of the gizmas' raid happened precisely eight days since I got here.

It reminded me of what happened in a well-known zombie survival game. There was a blood moon every seven days that spawned hordes of zombies that attacked you. If we applied that game's rules here, then that would mean there might possibly be another huge attack at night in seven or eight days, which would make it my fifteenth or sixteenth day here. I really hoped it was just a coincidence, though.

If there're going to be large-scale attacks against us by some creature or another every week, then I need to fortify our defenses. I should probably tell Sylphy about this, right? But there were proper warnings and omens that the gizmas were going to attack... I'm probably just overthinking this. I'll talk to Sylphy tonight about it just in case.

"Hmm, attacks every week?"

"I might be seeing patterns where there aren't any. But I can't entirely deny it either, considering how my power also follows nearly incomprehensible patterns."

I'd told Sylphy about the potential of a weekly blood moon over after-dinner drinks. Sylphy liked Pale Moon so much that she had taken to wearing it at all times. In fact, she liked it so much that she wasn't even drinking that much of her mead—she was more focused on polishing and oiling the sword.

"I doubt there'll be any more attacks as large-scale as last night's, but it might be best to stay alert for the next week just in case. The current bulwark might be good for fending off gizmas, but it's too low for humans. There aren't that many monsters that could easily jump over it either, but it would be a good idea to reinforce the walls for the future," Sylphy said.

"So...?"

"Yeah, I'll suggest we fortify the bulwark to Danan and the elders. While you're the one who'll probably be doing most of the work, I'm sure that the citizens of Merinard and the elves will be willing to help procure materials."

"Great, thanks."

"You don't need to thank me. It's only natural that I do whatever I can to alleviate your worries, especially since that will benefit everyone." Sylphy was done taking care of Pale Moon, so she sheathed it and smiled softly at me.

Ahhh, what an angel to behold. Lately, she had been starting to smile more naturally around me. I felt proud to be the man she smiled for.

"So you'll be back at it all over again starting tomorrow?" Sylphy asked.

"Yeah. I'd like everyone to gather clay, and I want to go mining."

"Again? You sure like hacking away with a pickaxe."

"You can never have enough ore."

I needed a ton of iron just for turning all of the crossbows into improved crossbows. I still had enough wood for now, at least. I had a mountain of materials from the gizmas, so I had plenty of tough tendons.

"Then I suppose we should turn in early tonight."

"Hmm, yeah. But before I get to bed, I should start on Ira's request—" I rose from my chair, but then Sylphy suddenly grabbed me by the hand, pulling me in for a kiss. The sweet smell of mead combined with Sylphy's natural scent were enough to melt my brain.

"You dare bring up another woman's name when we're finally alone?"

"Wha? Oh, right. Sorry." I hadn't meant for this to happen, but it seemed I had put Sylphy in a bad mood. No, wait, she was just pretending. I could see the laughter in her eyes.

"It seems to me that a slave who doesn't put the needs of his mistress first needs to be punished, don't you agree?"

"Uhhh, yes. I think?"

"Hee hee. Time for your punishment, then," Sylphy said, lifting me up in her arms and carrying me into her bedroom like a newly wedded bride.

Huh? Whoa, she's strong. Wait a minute, shouldn't our roles be reversed? Sylphy? Miss Sylphy? Whoa, uh, whaaa?!

"I'll never be able to get married after that," I cried as I recalled my utter defeat the night before.

"Hee hee. Luckily, you already belong to me," Sylphy cooed with a smile.

Well, I was only faking the crying part.

I'm beginning to think that Sylphy is a sadist and just hasn't realized it yet. I'm a vanilla kinda guy, y'know? I swear, you gotta believe me!

We cleansed ourselves of the previous night's sins together and flirted all morning. Sylphy was in an incredibly good mood today. I wasn't sure if that was thanks to her persistent excitement about Pale Moon or because she had managed to seize the initiative and maintain dominance during our wrestling match in bed last night. I was really hoping it was the former...

Today I was being a devoted slave and making breakfast. I was all out of things I knew how to make. Maybe it was time to try something new?

"What's taking so long with breakfast?" Sylphy asked.

"Don't worry, I'm on it!" I took out the simple stove that I had used the other day to make roast giblets from my inventory. I also placed the smithing station.

Simple Stove Upgrade——: Wood × 10, Stone × 30, Iron × 10, Cutting Board × 1, Knife × 1, Cooking Utensil × 4

This is the one. I can easily make the cutting board out of wood, so I'll go ahead and set that to craft. Will anything work for a knife? There's a kitchen knife in the smithing station; I'll go with that. For utensils, I've got the pot and frying pan Melty gave me before. Now I just need two more... Maybe a metal bowl and grater will do? I can make those in a jiffy with the smithing station. Annnd upgrade!

"Why does it always have to be so bright?" I complained.

"You've got to warn me when you make these things suddenly light up! It's blinding."

"I'm sorry."

The simple stove became a kitchen counter! I took some ingredients from Sylphy's kitchen. I had experience using grainmeal, cabbaj, oneel, pepal, galik, dicon, and honey, but she had other ingredients and spices I'd never really touched before. Plus, we still had a ton of gizma meat.

Bread——Materials: Grainmeal × 1, Drinking Water × 1, Salt × 1

Dried Pasta——Materials: Grainmeal × 2, Drinking Water × 2, Salt × 1

Stew——Materials: Grainmeal × 2, Drinking Water × 2, Vegetable × 2, Meat × 2, Salt × 2

Steak——Materials: Meat × 2, Black Pepper × 1, Salt × 1

Salad——Materials: Vegetable × 3

Curry——Materials: Grainmeal × 2, Drinking Water × 2, Vegetable × 2, Meat × 2, Salt × 2, Fruit × 2, Spice × 4

Those were all I could make with what I had on hand. I was kind of underwhelmed by the selection. *Maybe this is where item creation will really shine? But why do practically all of these recipes require salt? Ugh.*

"Well, how does it look?" Sylphy asked.

"I'll be able to whip something up. Should I make a big meal for us this morning?"

"Yeah, since we'll be heading out."

"Okay."

I'll make two loaves of bread, a stew, two steaks, and two salads. I'll just stick whatever leftovers we have into my inventory and make lots of curry and bread for lunch.

"All done. We gonna eat out here?" I asked.

"Hmm, yeah, eating outdoors once in a while can be nice."

I set down chairs and a table in the backyard and placed the crafted meal on the table. The stew came out inside of a pot. *Hey, where the heck did this pot come from? Actually, I shouldn't bother to question it at this point.*

The steak and salad came on wooden plates. I wasn't gonna question it at all. Nope, nuh-uh. The bread didn't come with anything extra.

"Ooh, such a feast for breakfast. So, what kind of meat is this?" Sylphy asked, pointing to the steak.

"Probably beef?"

"And what kind of meat did you use to make this?"

"Ha ha ha. Gizma meat, of course."

Sylphy hesitated a moment before saying, "Nope, not going to ask." Such a smart mistress. She was used to my powers!

It was a waste of time to question my abilities or try to rationalize them, so we completely abandoned doing either and enjoyed the stew. I had made all of the spoons, knives, forks, and whatnot at the workbench earlier.

"This is good. The meat tastes like fowl. And this red, carrol-like vegetable is quite sweet and tasty," Sylphy commented.

"I'm just not gonna bother dwelling on how the meat and vegetables I used for this recipe came out as completely different food."

By the way, the carrol Sylphy mentioned was a vegetable that was like a yellow carrot, though these were as long as burdock roots. There was also potato in here, which I definitely did not use to make this recipe, and somehow the stew was made of a white sauce, even though I didn't use any milk. But I didn't let it bother me. To care was to lose. The gizma meat had somehow turned into chicken, but I wasn't gonna let that get under my skin!

"And this bread is surprisingly fluffy and soft," Sylphy said.

"It's good if you dip it into the stew. It's kinda bad manners, but who's gonna complain?" I told her.

The freshly baked bread really was soft. It looked like French bread, but it was round and not nearly as long as a baguette. I didn't know what it was called, but it was bread all the same!

The steak was most definitely beef. It was cooked to medium doneness and tasted as delicious as a normal steak. You wouldn't have guessed this had originally been gizma at all! Well, I bet a gizma cooked with galik would be pretty good in its own right. Like a huge lobster steak.

The salad was your average salad. Though the vegetables it was composed of were quite different from what I had crafted it with! Ha ha ha ha!

And so, after a delightful and fancy breakfast, we headed to our usual spot at bulwark. I had my workspace right next to the gate. We found Ira waiting for us, her big eye sparkling with anticipation.

"Sorry, I haven't had a chance to make the staff yet," I apologized.

"Noooo!" Ira looked aghast, and her shoulders drooped.

I'm sorry, but there's just no beating Sylphy...

"Well, it's unfortunate, but there's no rush... It's too bad, though," Ira said, dismay written all over her face.

"I'll get it done as soon as I can." I felt really guilty seeing her like that, especially since it was all because Sylphy and I had been too busy canoodling.

As I was looking over Ira's drawing, Sylphy brought Danan over. I hadn't noticed her fetch him.

"So, I hear you wish to fortify the walls," he said.

"Mm-hmm. At its current height, it won't help us against humans or other kinds of monsters, right?" Sylphy asked.

"You're quite right about that. Anyone who's strong or magically enhanced could clear them easily."

"How tall should we make it, then?"

"I would like it to be three to four times taller than it already is."

Right now, it was about 2.5 meters tall including the upper passageway with parapets, so that meant he wanted it to be about 8 to 10 meters high. That was gonna require a whole lot of materials.

"It probably needs to be approximately three times higher if we want it to match the height of the village's walls, doesn't it?" Sylphy asked Danan.

"Yes, that's right."

The village's walls were made of wood, but they were curious in that you couldn't see any joining points in the wood at all. I had heard that the elves had cast spells on trees to form them and that they were resistant to fire, magic, and physical blows. They looked to be about eight meters tall, by my reckoning.

I turned to Sylphy. "Should I keep making it out of clay?"

"Hmm, I guess so."

"Okay, then I'm gonna need a whole bunch of clay."

I should probably get another smithing station. I've got enough materials, so I'll get started on that. My work will go much faster if I've got one dedicated to working iron and the other to baking bricks. And if I don't have anything to make with iron, then I can use both to make bricks. I should make another simple furnace for making charcoal too.

Thus began a series of challenging days for me.

"If we may be up against humans, then we need a foundation underground," Sylphy said.

"Since they might dig a tunnel underneath to try to get in?"

"Exactly. Three meters deep would be great, I think."

"I see... Then should I dig one? Two meters wide should be good, right?"

"Yeah."

I broke a block in the wall with my pickaxe and started digging. The steel shovel could easily dig up soft dirt like the kind here in the Black Forest, so it was a cakewalk. First, I figured I'd dig about three meters down.

"Are you okay, Kousuke?" Sylphy called out.

"Yeah, no problems down here."

"You might run into water if you dig that far, so be careful."

"That shouldn't be a problem."

I was naive enough to actually believe that. I did indeed run into water about three meters down, and while it wasn't enough to make me drown or anything, water was starting to pool at my feet; I couldn't make much headway like this.

"You're covered in mud now, aren't you?"

"This sucks."

I could have put a brick block down before the water came seeping out, but if I had, I'd be half trapped underground in the dark. I'd also start running out of oxygen if I completely shut myself in down here. I'd wind up causing my own death if I let myself get carried away digging like mad.

"I'm sorry, Sylphy."

"What? You don't have anything to apologize for."

Sylphy was a big help here. She used the magic of her light and wind spirit gems to brighten the darkness and keep clean air flowing. She used earth spirit magic to dig holes too. She truly was some kind of goddess.

"I'm happy to help out, you know?"

"You are divine. Literally. I shall devote my life to worshipping you."

"Hee hee. I like the sound of that."

While Sylphy and I were busy laying the foundation together, Ira suddenly came down into the hole. "I'll help too."

"You will?" I asked.

"I'm going to show you just how great magic really is." So she claimed, but I didn't really believe her.

"Uh, okay?"

"It's probably because you looked so amazed when you saw her during the battle," Sylphy offered.

"Maybe."

Whatever her reason, our work went at a quick pace. Ira's earth magic helped out enormously, just as she boasted.

"I'm surprised the water's not coming out," I said.

"I'm casting my spells in such a way that water doesn't seep through and the soil won't crumble."

"Wow, magic really is amazing!"

"Hee hee. Of course it is."

I was extremely grateful, since Ira dug out the deepest part and I didn't have to get covered in more mud. Sylphy and I took care of digging out the two higher meters, while Ira did the deepest last meter in practically no time at all.

"I dunno what I would've done without you two. I probably would've gotten really depressed if I had to do that alone," I said.

"That would happen to anyone, slaving all by themselves in the dark like that," Sylphy told me.

"Yeah, it's morbid," Ira agreed.

Thanks to the ladies' assistance, we finished building the foundation in three days. The first day was spent getting the process down through trial and error, so it really only took two days of actual work.

"Now that the foundation's ready, next is working on the wall itself, right?" Sylphy asked.

"Yeah, but I'm still waiting on the bricks." I had made a

considerable number these past three days, but I still didn't have nearly enough of them. Once I got started, I would have to temporarily destroy the top of the current wall, so it was going to get shorter. That would weaken it, so I wanted to wait until I had a healthy stockpile of brick blocks before I got into it.

"I do have a fair number of cobblestone wall blocks. How about I try making houses with them?" I asked Melty, since she was the sole person in charge of matters involving the daily lives of the refugees. She was used to this sort of thing, having once been an officer of domestic affairs.

"That's a good idea. A lot of our houses are quite drafty, so fixing that would help us a lot." Melty's grin in that moment frightened me. She looked harmless enough, but she wasn't to be underestimated, what with her penchant for calmly pushing hard work on others.

"Uh, well, I'll see how well I can do."

"Why do I get the feeling that you are uncomfortable around me?"

"Maybe you should put a hand over your heart and give that a good think-over."

"Hmm?" She looked quite cute as she placed a hand over her well-endowed chest and tilted her head to the side, but I wasn't one to be fooled. Despite her looks, she was strong enough to carry a quern under her arm that I couldn't even lift.

Anyway, since I was gonna build a house, I secured a plot of land.

"There is plenty of space to work with," Melty said.

"Yeah, there's some distance between where everyone lives and the bulwark."

Having picked a spot, I started figuring out the layout of the house and how thick the walls would be.

"Make the layout of the house look like this," Melty told me.

"So, a foyer, a living room with a space for eating connected to the kitchen, two bedrooms, and two storage rooms?" I asked.

"Yes. I would suggest making the walls about this thick."

"About 60 to 80 centimeters, then. Should the walls inside be the same size?"

"Yes."

"Then I should make the house a little bigger to account for how thick the walls will be."

After pinning down how tall to make the ceiling and such, I decided to get started constructing the house. Really all I had to do was adjust the size of the blocks I already had and place them, so it wasn't going to take more than ten minutes.

I used wood blocks for the floors and got the house built in a jiffy.

"That was fast..." Melty was amazed.

"Yep, that's how it is when I've got the materials already."

The interior hadn't been decorated at all, so the house obviously still needed some work.

"But what about windows?"

"Oh yeah." I accidentally forgot to leave holes for the windows. I broke some blocks with my pickaxe and placed them elsewhere. "That should do it."

"Hmm. We still need to make doors and fill these window frames, but this is very good work. What are the walls made of?"

"Stone and clay. I've got a mountain of stones from previous trips, so we should be fine provided we've got enough clay."

"We need clay for these as well, then?"

"Yep." The clay was being used to make bricks at the moment, so I didn't have any extra to work with.

"You can make houses out of wood too, right?" Melty asked while looking down at the flooring.

"Huh? Yeah, I could, I guess." I readily nodded without thinking. That was a mistake.

"Then let's make the other houses out of wood. I'm sure that all you have to do is cut down more trees to get more wood, after all."

"Uh, okay."

After that, she made me cut down a ridiculous number of trees. Naturally, Sylphy came with me to prevent me from going overboard.

"Just grin and bear it, Sylphy."

"Well, I'll be fine. It's not about me; we're doing this for everyone's sake." So she said, but she'd grimaced when she heard how much wood I would need for these houses.

Still, I could never have enough wood. I've sung its praises in detail enough, but it bears repeating.

Days flew by, devoted to mining, logging, making iron, baking bricks, and building. I'd wake up in the morning, get washed, have breakfast, and then head to the wall. I'd spend the morning mining at the gorge and cutting trees in the forest, and then we'd head back to the village, where the citizens of Sylphy's kingdom would give me the clay they gathered, which I would toss into the smithing station for crafting bricks.

"I want swords made of mithril too."

"I'm sure I would be even stronger in battle if only I had a mithril spear."

"I demand a new crossbow, you hear?!"

The old man who let his desires drive his every action, the lizard lady, and the cat lady began to beg me for new weapons.

"Hee hee. Hee hee hee." Ira weirded me out with that creepy grin on her face as she rubbed her cheek against her shiny new mithril staff.

"We cannot live on meat alone. Make more grainmeal!" Melty would force me to mill yet more grain.

"Have you made a new kind of weapon that harpies can use yet?" At first it was just Pirna, but soon other harpies began to beg me for weapons as well.

Other stuff happened too, but that's the gist of it.

"Lately, I get the feeling that people have figured out what my power can do; I think they've started warming up to me more."

"Isn't it nice being so in-demand?" Sylphy asked, averting her eyes.

"Sylphy, I want you to look me in the eye and ask me that again."

Then, on a different day...

"Our grandchildren still aren't on the way yet, huh?" an elder asked us.

"Is that why you invited us here? Not that any of you are my grandparents," Sylphy grumbled.

"Ho ho ho. Now, now, don't be like that. We all think of you as our granddaughter."

"Her children would be our *great*-grandchildren, then. You really are going senile," another elder said.

"It's just a figure of speech. And what makes you think I'm going senile? I'll have you know I'm as fit as a fiddle."

"You're only dressing younger than your age."

"You haven't changed at all in the past 500 years. I pity you."

"Hmph, you're asking for it. Let's take this outside."

We had to watch as the elders got into an argument that was more like a wizard's duel, what with all the spirit magic they were flinging about. Wow, these old people could wreak some real havoc. It was like the end of the world.

Today marked the seventh day since the gizmas' raid on the village. It was my fifteenth night after arriving in this world.

"Does the moon look red tonight, Kousuke?" Sylphy asked.

I looked up at the moon from the top of the newly rebuilt rampart. The moon always looked bigger than I was used to, but it was a yellow-gold color. "Looks normal today. But wow... The moon is beautiful, isn't it?"

"Yeah, it does look beautiful tonight. I'd love to see a moon like yours beyond my hands or on my hip, but I do like the gentle glow of our moon," Sylphy said as she gazed skyward, looking content.

I'd meant to take a page from Natsume Soseki's book and express my love in a romantic way, but it wasn't like that guy had existed in this world. Oh well. My feelings for her wouldn't change just because she didn't understand the nuance of what I was saying.

"What should we aim to do next?" I asked.

"Next? Hmm..."

Sylphy and Danan had used their time this week to send scouts into the Black Forest and the Great Omitt Badlands. The scouts reported that there weren't any more gizmas in the forest—and, as it turned out, there were less gizmas in the badlands than before.

"Shall we go reclaim Merinard?" I asked.

"That certainly is a dream of mine." Sylphy had already told me as much the day she confided in me with her life story. What else would Merinard's princess in exile want?

"I'll do whatever I can to help. I'm your slave, remember? It's a slave's duty to help their mistress any way that they can."

"Kousuke..."

"Ha ha ha. Don't make me say anything more. It's so embarrassing." *Like I'd want to leave Sylphy after all we've been through. We men sure are simple creatures, huh?*

"But it's not realistic. Even if everyone here in the elven village endorses my will, we're a group of 300 people at most. It'd be impossible for us to oust the forces of the Holy Kingdom garrisoned in there."

"Aw, don't be like that. There's gotta be a way."

Numbers were the foundation of all great battles. It was incredibly difficult to win against a group with an overwhelming headcount. But that was only in situations where the groups were composed of the same quality of soldiers and using the exact same tactics.

"If we can't beat them with numbers, we'll dig in and put up fortresses. It'll be even better if we use traps. Plus, we've got crossbows on our side," I pointed out.

You think that's dirty? Cowardly? Mwa ha ha. Those are compliments, if you ask me.

If necessary, I could just use my most precious creation. This past week, I had taken what chances I could find to collect soil from the bathroom. I had started making you-know-whats in secret.

"When you put it that way, it seems so easy," Sylphy said.

"I'm an optimist, y'know."

Now that I had all of the materials and crafting components I needed, we had plenty of options if the goal was just for Sylphy and me to survive. I had a feeling Sylphy would get mad at me for phrasing it like that, though.

Sylphy's gaze hovered on the moon as she thought for a moment. "Okay, I've decided: I shall reclaim the Kingdom of Merinard!"

If that's what she wanted to do, then I would follow her and do everything I could to help her. I was her devoted servant, after all!

"Okay. We've gotta talk to Danan and the others about it."

"Yeah. All right, let's go, Kousuke."

"Aye aye, ma'am."

Sylphy walked away, brimming with determination. I followed. Lanicle, the golden moon, and Omicle, with its blue seas and white clouds, watched over us as we went.

GOSSIP

Ira's Story

"**N**OW WE'RE FRIENDS AGAIN. It's a good custom, right?" Kousuke said as he shook my hand with a smile on his face.

"Yeah." A smile spread across my own face as well.

Even though I had been so mean to Kousuke, he wasn't angry at all. In fact, he tried to meet me halfway.

I wanted to find the words to thank him then, but I had too many gears turning all at once in my head to form a coherent sentence. That was how it always was for me.

People gave cyclopes like me a wide berth to begin with; being terrible at articulating myself didn't help my case.

I was confident in my knowledge of magic and alchemy, and while I prided myself on my abilities, I just sucked at stringing sentences together. But Kousuke didn't seem to mind—he treated me normally. He wasn't like everyone else.

Moreover, he never seemed annoyed when I asked him questions about his mysterious power or followed him around. Sometimes he looked perplexed, but I never got the sense that he was getting truly aggravated. In fact, he was kind to me. He was just a really nice person all around.

Right now, he seemed a bit perplexed because Her Highness and Melty wanted handshakes too. And for some reason, that expression of his warmed my heart. It was a curious feeling, as if I was soothed just by looking at him.

"You wanna shake hands again too?" he asked, looking at me.

I reflexively nodded. "Yeah."

Sigh. That was all I could muster. But Kousuke held my hand again, and in that moment, I got the feeling I knew what was warming my heart so.

However, I decided to postpone that conclusion for a little while longer. It'd be a shameful failure of academic rigor to arbitrarily decide something was true when I didn't know for sure. What kind of natural philosopher would that make me? I thought I should understand my feelings a bit better before deciding.

Yes, I'd hold off just a bit longer.

AFTERWORD

THANK YOU SO MUCH for buying *Survival in Another World with My Mistress!* Volume 1.

My name is Ryuto. It's nice to meet you. I'm something like a bear that inhabits a testing land. And for those who already know me, it's nice to see you again.

Although there are many light novels about other worlds out there, I found that there weren't any about someone with the same powers found in crafting survival games. So, I decided I'd write one myself! And that was how *Survival* was born.

This writer loves third-person exploration games with survival elements. I blended all kinds of games into this book. For example, from that famous game with the world made of blocks, the game where hordes of zombies attack every seven days, the one where you have to explore a snowy mountain, that game where you start off by punching down trees in a world filled with dinosaurs, and that game that takes place in a post-apocalyptic world where you're called a general and have to do what other people say... Though I do play more obscure games too!

Why do I like these kinds of games? Because I enjoy conquering worlds where you're isolated, free to do whatever you want, and devoted to just trying to keep yourself alive. Am I just a lone wolf... N-naaaah. Those games have multiplayer too, y'know...? Not that I've ever done—

You know what? Never mind. This topic is hitting a little too close to home.

Now let's talk about the novel! Yeah! I'll talk about some background stuff that I can't add in the main story here! I'd especially like to talk about the demi-humans—not what they are, but the lives and characteristics of the demi-humans introduced in this volume.

First, let's start with elves. As I'm sure you know, elves are beautiful, have long ears, and excel at magic. In general, elves have spear-shaped ears, and the ones in this world can move theirs. So cute. They live for over 500 years at least, and some can even live to be 1,000 to 2,000 years old. I gotta wonder what's up with their telomeres.

Also, while they have bodies, their spirits have a special quality where they change according to extreme emotions. For example, they could take on a dark-brown skin color and get really ripped. Or they might shrink down and take on a snow-white pallor, while their life span and magic aptitude extend beyond the norm.

Next, let's talk about the beastfolk.

While beastfolk might be the general name for them, they come in many shapes and forms. They also vary in how bestial they are as well. There are some who walk on two legs, some who look like humans with animal ears and a tail, and others with animalistic body parts from the knees or elbows down. However, most have bighearted personalities, so they see anyone who's even a smidge beastfolk as one of their kind. They don't care about differences in bestial characteristics from one person to another.

Beastfolk can be largely divided into herbivores and carnivores. People with elements of herbivorous animals such as cows, sheep, goats, giraffes, elephants, and hippopotamuses usually have gentle dispositions, whereas those with elements of carnivorous animals such as dogs, wolves, lions, tigers, leopards, and bears are often more intense. Bears are omnivorous, but in some worlds, they're categorized as carnivores since they usually charge at players the second they see them. Those are meat-eaters if I've ever seen them.

These are just generalizations, though. There are some herbivorous beastfolk who are more excitable than others and carnivorous beastfolk who are disproportionately calm. Danan and a few others are the more excitable kinds of herbivores.

Next, cyclopes... Oh, crap! I'm almost out of space for the afterword! Aw, that's too bad! I guess I'll have to write about them in the *next volume* (he says, being totally obvious).

That about does it for this afterword.

I would like to give a heartfelt thank you to I from GC Novels for approaching me, Yappen for doing the illustrations, everyone who was involved in the publishing of this novel, and you, the readers, for picking up this book.

I'll see you again in the next volume!